Destruction of a Dream

Destruction of a Dream

Thomas F. Davis

VANTAGE PRESS
New York

This is a work of fiction. Any similarity between
the characters appearing herein and any real persons,
living or dead, is purely coincidental.

Published by Vantage Press, Inc.
516 West 34th Street, New York, New York 10001

Manufactured in the United States of America
ISBN: 0-533-13384-X

Library of Congress Catalog Card No.: 99-97061

0 9 8 7 6 5 4 3 2 1

This book is for my lovely wife, Sue, who stood by me no matter how down I got on myself, and my four wonderful children, who encouraged me to live my dream. This is for you, Tom, John, Nicole, and Pat.

I also want to give special mention to a dear friend who taught me it's better to reach out for your dream and fail than to live wondering if it ever could have happened. Thank you, Jean.

Acknowledgments

Special thanks to Chris and Karin Elias.

1

The silence of the night was broken by the blaring of the sirens. Lights illuminated the darkened grounds, searching out any movement at all in the wooded area. The smell of death filled the air around the prison walls. The shouts of men rang everywhere, shouts of anger and pain. Two bodies lay in pools of blood.

A booming voice shouted over the confusion, "Lock down all the cells and give me a count on who's missing!" The man shouting out all the orders was a heavy man in about his late forties. His thick mustache covered part of his lower lip. He reached out and stopped one of the men running by him by grabbing his arm. "Lester, get a doctor down here for these two men."

Lester gasped as he looked down at the two bodies lying on the ground and in a squeamish voice replied. "Jeez, sir, they don't need a doctor. My God, they both must have been stabbed a hundred times."

The man with the booming voice snarled as he yanked on Lester's arm, "I know they're dead, damn it. Just get the doctor down here, now!"

Lester pulled his stare away from the two bodies on the ground, regained his composure and shouted out his acknowledgment, "Yes, sir!"

The man with the booming voice then turned as more of his men left the grounds with dogs to search for the man or men responsible for the death of his two guards. He closed his eyes tightly to try to hide the truth from himself, but in vain. For he knew that no one would be safe as long as this murderer remained at large. The man's thoughts were interrupted as Lester came back holding a small piece of paper.

"Sir, Green gave me this for you. He said this is the only prisoner not accounted for."

Lester handed the heavy man the slip of paper. He took it. As he saw the name on the paper he looked back up at Lester and said in a stern voice, "Unless you want to see more lives lost, we better make sure we find this bastard before the day's out."

The May sun was just beginning to rise over the sleepy town of Barnsville, a small rural community in the Upper Peninsula of Michigan, a quiet and peaceful town, a town of the type where people dreamed of raising their families. The town's citizens lived in a world of their own. They felt protected from the crime and violence outside their city limits. The wooded area that surrounded Barnsville displayed the majestic beauty with the start of spring. The town glowed with peace and tranquillity. The picture of white picket fences surrounding homes would have been perfect for the town itself. Those homes inside the town limits still portrayed an earlier America. Still you had your citizens that wanted both the past and the pleasures of the modern world. Those built their homes outside the town limits, spread far apart from each other, the nearest neighbor a good hike by foot or a short drive by car. The town in general was left untouched by modern technology. The flavor of the past lived in Barnsville. In the heart of the town were two gas stations, three restaurants, and a hardware store. During the tourist season in the summer, dozens of small all-around stores would sprout up within the town limits, selling anything and everything that a tourist might want. One of the most popular shops that opened was the one of an old Indian guide. He sold trinkets and told the stories of the wandering souls at Harrison Point, warning any who might want to visit the forbidden area of the dangers of the dead Indian warriors. The tourists would smile, buy the trinkets, then venture to the forbidden place called Harrison Point. They would walk the narrow path searching for any hints of truth about the roaming souls of the dead warriors. Some tourists swore they saw visions of ancient warriors floating above the cliff. All who went through the town admired its quaint beauty and naive innocence. It was unusual for people from the city to see such trust and faith in their fellowman. It was not hard to see that most of the citizens of this town never ventured to the city very often.

Near the center of Barnsville was the office of the town doctor. This was the only modern building in the entire town. It was an all brick-building, with tinted windows around the entire building. The doctor had all the modern equipment and a large staff; he would take care of only minor medical problems. For any true emergencies he would send the folks of Barnsville to the hospital in the city.

The sheriff's department office stood at the end of town. A rugged-looking building, which resembled the sheriff's offices of the old west, but that was where the similarity ended. The mayor made sure that the sheriffs' department was well staffed and had the most sophisticated equipment the town could afford to buy. The mayor ran into a lot of resistance because of his buying sprees, which he would justify by saying, "To keep our town the paradise it is we need to make sure we have the protection to keep out the evil that surrounds us."

Despite the flowery speeches that the mayor would make, the townspeople talked of cutting taxes, and eliminating some of the sheriff's deputies. The community felt six deputies were far too many for a town like Barnsville. The only major crime the town had seen in the last forty years was a shoplifting spree by a gang of ten-year-olds. The residents of this community felt safe and secure from the violence of the big city.

The one item that everyone appeared to agree on was the education of the children of Barnsville. Most felt that building an institute of higher learning in their small town would help keep the young minds within the safe surroundings of the town and help build the economy for Barnsville.

The college was located directly across the street from the high school. Many of the young students would only take a trip across the street to further their education. To fulfill most of their dreams, some would venture on and leave Barnsville to attain their goals. Others would stay, preferring the quiet and beauty the small town had to offer. Sadly, though, there were those who had no choice but to stay. These lonely souls appeared trapped within the tiny town limits of Barnsville, to painfully forget their dreams and hopes forever.

Tina Riley sat at the kitchen table staring at the cup of coffee that sat in front of her. Her short blond hair barely touched the collar of her robe. Her bangs lay neatly above her forehead. Tina's beauty and youthful appearance would fool anyone into guessing her age at thirty-nine. Her deep blue eyes stared aimlessly into the dark brew of her coffee. There was a hint of sadness in her lovely eyes, a sadness she had carried with her for many years. Tina pushed back her chair and rose slowly to her feet. Glancing up at the clock on the wall, she saw 5:00 A.M. Tina walked out of the dining room and straight to her bedroom. Opening the door quietly, she peeked in. Lying in bed, stirring restlessly, was her husband. A faint smile creased Tina's face as she watched him. For he was the only man Tina had ever loved in her entire life. Today would be the day that Tina would tell him their marriage was about to be made complete. Tina had taken the pregnancy test two days ago, then again this morning; each time it proved positive. Finally all their dreams would be fulfilled. Tina was pregnant. She eased the door closed, so as not to wake him. He still had a little while before he had to get up for work.

Tina walked back to the dining room. Picking up her coffee, she took a sip of it, her mind in deep thought as she did. How would she tell her husband that she finally was pregnant? After all these years, their dream of having a child would finally be a reality. Tina had to explain to Zeke how she was able to work around the unjust punishment that God had been putting them through. Tina knew it wouldn't be an easy task to accomplish. For her husband, Zeke, refused to believe that God or anyone else was punishing them. Zeke thought that in time things would work out; all they had to do would be maintain their faith in each other. Tina knew better. She knew she would have to take matters in her own hands.

Tina sat back down at the table and set the cup of coffee down gently. Leaning back in her chair, she continued to try to devise a way to tell Zeke the good news. She debated on whether she should tell him or keep their doctor's appointment in the city and have her doctor tell him the news? She closed her eyes tightly, trying to make up her mind which course to choose. Which way would be the most convincing for her husband to believe? Whispering softly, Tina made up her mind.

"The doctor; it is the only way Zeke will believe that this time I am really pregnant."

Tina appeared satisfied with her decision. She was sure it was the only course to take, especially with how skeptical her husband had become. She couldn't blame him, though. Not with all the disappointments she had put him through. She had told Zeke on a regular basis that she thought she was pregnant, gotten his hopes

4

up, then found out it was a false alarm and painfully watched as he would try to hide his disappointment.

Tina knew that Zeke loved her; she also knew that deep down inside Zeke held a resentment toward her. There was no doubt in Tina's mind that God was punishing her for the mistake she had made when Zeke and she had first married. What hurt her more was that she knew Zeke kept his anger toward her buried deep inside him. Tina's thoughts raced back in time. Tears clouded her eyes as pictures from her past danced in front of her, visions of a day in her life Tina wished she could forget. The memories of the past became clearer. Closing her eyes tightly, Tina stopped fighting and allowed the memories to replay in her mind. Further and further her mind drifted into the past. She drifted to a time she tried to bury in the caverns of her mind.

Zeke Riley stood about five-foot-nine. His hair was jet-black. His hazel eyes danced with excitement as he entered his apartment. He noticed Tina, sitting at the end of the couch. She was staring out the front window. Her mind seemed miles away. Zeke closed the door behind him and stood in the doorway for a moment. Tina didn't turn toward the sound of the closing door. Zeke walked over to his wife and sat next to her. Putting his arm around her, he kissed her cheek. Then in the most cheerful voice he could muster up he spoke.

"Mr. Martin gave me a raise today; it sure will help get us caught up on some of our bills."

Tina didn't reply.

Zeke turned her around gently to face him. Tina's eyes were red and puffy. Before Zeke could question her on why, Tina began crying. Sobbing, she buried her face in Zeke's chest. Confused, Zeke asked, "What's wrong, sweetheart?"

Tina looked up at Zeke. Tears rolled down her cheeks as she replied, "I'm pregnant, Zeke."

Zeke's voice exploded with excitement. "Pregnant! That's great. I'm going to be a father. I can't believe it. How long have you known?"

Tina jumped to her feet, glaring at Zeke. She couldn't believe how naive he was acting. His response should have been the same as hers. Now was not the time for a child. There was too much in both of their lives to complete before they brought a child into this crazy world. Tina's voice trembled with anger and frustration as she snapped at Zeke, "How can you sit there and be so selfish? I'm not ready to have a child; neither of us is. What about my career and your dreams? Do you plan on me quitting school? Are we supposed to put all of our dreams on hold? Zeke, think about it. This is not the time to start a family."

Zeke chose his words carefully; this was a different side of his wife he had never witnessed before. Calmly, in a soft voice, Zeke replied, "Tina, we can make it work, if we try hard enough. After the baby's born you can go back to school. You don't have to give up your dreams, just postpone them for a while."

Tina turned away from her husband, quietly saying, "*Postpone* is the right word, Zeke, but it won't be my career that I postpone."

Zeke stared hard at his wife. His voice became slightly agitated as he asked, "What are you trying to say, Tina?"

Tina turned around. She had no expression in her eyes as she replied, "I am going to have an abortion, Zeke."

Zeke's face turned beet red with anger. He glared at Tina, who stood in front of him defiantly with her arms folded, waiting for him to reply. Zeke couldn't hold back the pain and hurt that Tina's words ripped through him as he shouted back, "Just like that you are going to kill our unborn child? I have no say in the matter? What gives you that right? It is my child, too."

Tina's tone remained calm and emotionless. "We can't afford a child, Zeke. You work as a cook, barely making over minimum wage. Do you really feel you will be able to support a family? Pay for my and your schooling at the same time? Zeke, this decision is killing me. I am choosing a profession where I can help the sick and save lives. You want to be a writer. Think darling; do you really feel we can accomplish all that with a child?"

Tina's words stung Zeke, the coldness in her voice, the logic she used in justifying ending a life. The hurt and anger still echoed in Zeke's voice as he pleaded his case.

"I am willing to try or even sacrifice some of my dreams. Tina, you are talking about killing a child. Our child. I don't care what man's laws say. To God we would be committing murder."

Tina's calm disappeared as she screamed back, "I thought you loved me! How can you be so cruel as to say something like that?

Murderer, that is what I would be? If that is how you feel, then the hell with you. If that is how God feels, then the hell with him."

Tina's rage was now in full bloom as she waved her hands, and her voice grew louder as she continued to scream at Zeke. "What I want is to be able to bring a child into a world where there will be love! Where we could provide and properly take care of it! Read the papers, Zeke, better yet, look around you. The hate and evil in this world are here for a reason. I'm sure mothers of this planet didn't plan on bringing murderers and thieves into this world. Maybe if these mother had forgotten God's laws for a change and used common sense our world would be a better place."

Zeke looked shocked; all the years he had known Tina he had never seen this side of her, a cruel and ruthless side. Zeke's words showed his disbelief.

"Tina, I can't believe how you are talking. Are you trying to tell me that people who are poor shouldn't have children? That all the suffering in the world is their fault?"

Tina squeezed her eyes shut tight as she snapped back, "I don't know what I mean, Zeke." Tears rolled down her face as she added, "All I know for sure is that I wouldn't love this child the way I should. That scares me, Zeke. A child needs total love. Why can't you understand now is not the time to have children? Please don't hate me for what I feel. I need you, Zeke; I need your support, please."

Zeke turned and headed back out the door but he stopped and snapped back at his wife, "I love you, Tina, but what you want to do is wrong. God will help us make it. Think about that and put some faith in me."

The words from the past echoed through Tina's mind. She had fought to forget that day and the weeks after that, the tears, words of anger, and words of reason. She had persisted every waking moment till finally Zeke gave in. That was twenty years ago. Tina had completed her schooling and fulfilled most of her goals in life; everything she had strived for was coming into place. Her dreams had become a reality.

Todd Martin, the owner of the Golden Aces, had promoted Zeke to assistant manager. Zeke quit school and devoted his full attention to his job. He tried a few times to get a few of his writings published without success. Gradually he drifted away from his dream of being a writer, forgetting his desires to write that one unforgettable novel. He poured all his energies into his job. Between his salary and Tina's they were able to buy their dream house, a brick ranch three-bedroom home located near the woods on the outskirts of town. When everything fell into place, Zeke and Tina decided it would be a perfect time to raise a family. The abortion Tina had five years earlier was now only a faint memory. Months, then years passed with no success. Frustration began to smother them. They grasped for reasons why. First they both felt that it was because Tina's body had to get back to normal. All those years on the birth control pill had to make her system crazy, but years slipped by without her becoming pregnant. Doctors examined them both, never finding anything physically wrong with either of them. That was when it began to happen. Tina started becoming obsessed with the idea that God was punishing her. The guilt from her past began to weigh on her. Her personality changed, gradually at first. She would calmly mention to Zeke that maybe God had heard their conversation years back and was punishing her. Zeke thought he had convinced her she was acting silly. Then her father died. He had committed suicide. Tina from that day on became convinced that God had a vendetta against her, despite what Zeke or doctors would tell her. She knew she would either find a way to amend her sins to God or find away around them. Now twenty years had passed and a million tears had flowed. Tina had found a way to fit the final piece to her dreams. She would now be able to say those words she had practiced saying for so long: "Darling, we are going to have a baby."

Tina felt a strange type of pride swell inside her. She, a mere mortal, had found a way to conquer God's anger. It took months of planning and scheming on her part. A plan that if Zeke had ever found out about it would in all reality end their marriage. That was a risk Tina knew she had to take. For Tina knew without a child, their marriage would be just a hollow shell. Today victory was hers and Zeke's. Today she finally could put the ghost of the unborn child from the past to rest. Tina would prove to God that his anger toward her had been wrong. She knew she would be the world's greatest mother. There was no doubt that Zeke would be the greatest father.

Tina's thoughts shifted. She glanced up at the clock on the wall. Five-thirty, it was time to wake Zeke for work. She stood up from the chair and walked to the bedroom door, opened it, and quietly walked inside to where Zeke slept peacefully. Gently she nudged her husband, calling out his name to wake him.

"Zeke, Zeke, time to get up!"

Zeke mumbled something, Tina couldn't understand. Again she called out her husband's name.

"Come on, Zeke! Wake up; you don't want to be late."

Zeke rolled over and opened his eyes slowly. He smiled when he saw Tina leaning over him. Glancing over at the clock, he yawned and in a sleepy voice asked, "Are my clothes ready?"

Tina's mood changed abruptly. For no apparent reason she snapped at Zeke as she stormed out of the room, "Yes, Zeke. your clothes are ready! You know you could help around here. I work, too. All I ask for is some cooperation. Like you getting your own clothes once in a while."

Zeke shook his head in disbelief as Tina slammed the door behind her. He couldn't believe Tina's mood swings anymore. One minute she would be sweet and lovable. The next she would be as mean as a wounded animal. Tina's personality grew worse each year. Zeke knew deep down inside that his wife needed professional help. The guilt she carried with her over the abortion and not being able to become pregnant afterward was becoming dangerous.

Zeke rolled out of bed, reached over, and picked up his robe that was hanging over the chair. Slipping it on, he walked briskly to the bathroom and shut the door behind him. Zeke stared into the mirror and cringed at the reflection staring back at him.

Zeke Riley was forty years old, his black hair sprinkled with gray. His hazel eyes showed the stress from his job. Hidden beneath the bags under his eyes were the effects of that stress. His eyes had become dull and lifeless. Self-pity and anger swelled inside him. He had not accomplished one goal in his entire life. All the dreams from his youth were now behind him. All that he had left to him now were his childish fantasies, dreams of how different his life might have been if he had ever taken the time to write that great novel he had talked about. He wondered if fame and fortune had slipped past him. Quietly he shrugged it off. All they were now were

9

empty dreams. Nothing else really mattered to him anymore, except Tina, whom he truly adored.

Zeke now had become the manager of the Golden Aces restaurant. It was the oldest and most prosperous restaurant in Barnsville. Todd Martin still owned the Golden Aces. He also had become the mayor of Barnsville. Zeke had worked at the Golden Aces since he was a child. Martin was the only employer Zeke had ever had. Though working at one place showed stability, it depressed him that he still worked there. Serving fast food all his life had not been his plans for his future. He and Tina had talked about moving to a big city like LA or New York, a place where his talent as a writer would flourish, but they never went further than Barnsville Community College. Money became tight, so Zeke dropped out of school. Tina finished school and received her degree. She landed a job in town with the local doctor, Frank Parker. Though Parker respected Tina's ability as a nurse, there was something about the man Zeke didn't like. The doctor had an air of arrogance about him. Zeke knew that some of his feelings were twinges of jealousy. Parker had been a football hero in high school and was ten years younger than Zeke. The doctor had money, respect in the community, everything Zeke had ever dreamed of. It seemed women would drool over just the mention of Parker's name. Even though Zeke knew Tina would never cheat on him, the thought of her working with that man every day made him sick with jealousy.

Zeke turned away from the mirror and turned on the bathwater, took off his robe, and slid into the tub. The bathroom door opened slightly.

Tina put Zeke's clothes on the counter, saying as she did, "You better hurry; it is getting late." She closed the door behind her.

Zeke ignored his wife's words and enjoyed the pleasure of his bath. The hot water felt great. Gently he rested his head back on the edge of the porcelain tub's ledge. Closing his eyes, he tried to relax, to prepare himself for the stress that he knew his day would bring.

The water did have a soothing calm on him, but he couldn't shake the anxiety ripping him apart inside. Tina's disposition lately had become worse, and his concern was growing deeper. She had become only a faint shadow of the woman he had married twenty years ago. Her temper would flare at any given moment. Minutes later she would smile and act as if nothing had happened. Once Zeke had suggested that they seek out counseling. She became so enraged, she threw a lamp at him. Zeke never suggested it again.

Zeke shook these thoughts out of his mind and quickly lathered himself with soap. Rinsing quickly, submerging himself under the veil of the hot water, he repeatedly plunged into the bathwater, to cleanse his body and, subconsciously, the painful troubles in his mind. Feeling awake, Zeke jumped out of the tub, drained the water, and grabbed a towel from the towel rack. Vigorously he dried himself off and quickly dressed. Grabbing his toothbrush, Zeke quickly brushed his teeth and rinsed his mouth out, grabbed the brush on the counter, and ran it through his graying hair. Walking out of the bathroom, he flicked off the light. He saw his red-striped tie resting on the door handle as he closed the bathroom door. Grabbing the tie, he quickly put it on and walked into the dining room. Making his way to the hall closet, he opened the door and pulled out his maroon sports coat and slipped it on. Closing the door, he checked himself out in the full-length mirror on the closet door. Satisfied with the way he looked, he made his way over to the dining room table. Tina had a cup of coffee waiting for him in his usual spot at the table. Zeke glanced into the kitchen. Tina stood at the sink washing dishes. He knew the only reason Tina would be doing dishes at six in the morning would be to release her anger. Zeke took a couple of sips of his coffee, then carefully questioned his wife.

"So, what have you planned for your day off today?"

Tina ignored her husband's question. She washed the last dish in the sink, drained the water, and joined him in the dining room. Sitting across from Zeke, Tina continued to give her husband the silent treatment. Zeke felt the frustration building up inside him. He forced himself not to show it as he attempted to cheer his wife up and get her out of her current mood.

"Don't make supper tonight. When I get home we will drive into the city, have a quiet dinner, then maybe catch a movie or something. We are both off tomorrow; we can sleep in. What do you say let's have some fun tonight?"

Tina broke her silence, asking in an inquisitive tone, "Zeke did you forget we have a doctor's appointment tonight? You have to be home by five. Our appointment is at six-thirty. If you want, we can have dinner afterward. This appointment is very important to me."

Zeke grimaced; the thought of going back to the doctor's for more tests made him sick to his stomach. All the silly questions they would ask, then the poking and prodding with needles, it all seemed so senseless, especially when Zeke knew they would give him and Tina the same answers they have been receiving for years: "Well, according to all of our tests, you and your wife are perfectly capable of having children. Just relax, it will happen someday."

Zeke knew, though, that the only problem was that "someday" was rapidly passing them both by.

Tina watched Zeke carefully. She knew he desperately wanted to say something but couldn't find the courage to do so. Tina decide to help him out by asking, "What, Zeke? You look as if you want to say something; what?"

Zeke continued to search for the right words to express his feelings about going to the doctor's again. He rubbed his eyes gingerly with the tips of his fingers, trying to compose the right words to use to state his case. Finally he began, attempting to display how he felt about her. Zeke's voice conveyed sweetness as he slowly expressed his emotions.

"Tina . . . you know I love you and there is nothing in this world I wouldn't do for you. It is just that this obsession you have with having a baby is unhealthy."

Zeke paused. Tina's stare was ice-cold. Ignoring her angered look, he continued.

"The doctors have told us every time we go there to relax and it will happen. Why don't we take their advice for a change? I know how it hurts not having a child around the house. Believe me, it hurts me just as bad. Despite the pain, I think it is time we begin to face reality. Maybe we will never be able to have a child."

Tina's blue eyes bore through him; her glare was unsettling. Zeke looked away from her stare. Tina's voice shook with anger as she screamed back, "Why can't you be honest with me, Zeke? Tell me why you don't want any children? You stopped caring, didn't you? You blame me, because I had the abortion. I'm right; tell me, Zeke! Tell me that's why you stopped caring?"

Zeke felt a strange sense of fear swell inside him. Tina's eyes revealed a rage that he had never seen before. Forcing himself to maintain a calm voice, he responded to Tina's accusations.

"Tina, how can you even think that way? You know that I care. I even suggested adopting a child. Do you remember how you responded to that?"

Tina screamed back her reply: "Yes, I remember! I said it then and I'll say it now. I don't want someone else's mistake. I want a child that I bore myself. I want to feel the life grow in my body. Can't you understand that?"

Tina hesitated as she realized the anger that flowed with her words. Quickly she took a deep breath and attempted to calm herself down. Tina knew she had to get Zeke to visit the doctor; this time she knew the results would be different. Staring at her husband, Tina thought to herself, *Maybe I should tell him about the test?* She quickly talked herself out of doing that: *No, he wouldn't believe me; it has to be the doctor that tells him I am pregnant.*

Tina took a deep breath and leaned forward. Her voice changed from anger to pleading.

"Zeke, please indulge me this one last time. I know the doctor will give us the news we want to hear."

Zeke threw his arms in the air. The calmness he had tried to maintain vanished.

"Tina, that is what you have said the last five times we have gone. I'm fed up with all of this. Don't you realize that we are getting to the age where having children is becoming less likely? Look at you; I don't know you anymore. You work late all the time. Lately I have to just about beg you to go out with me. Tina, you are changing, and damn it, it is beginning to scare the hell out of me."

Tina burst into tears. She covered her eyes with her hands, and through her sobs she yelled, "You don't care anymore! I don't ask a lot from you, do I? You keep telling me that you don't hold any resentment from the past. I don't believe you anymore, Zeke. I really think deep inside you hate me for what I did and that's why you fight not to go through with our doctor appointments."

Zeke completely lost his composure. Rising to his feet, he kicked back his chair and pounded his fist on the table. Years of frustration and anger exploded as he screamed out his anger toward his wife.

"Don't care! How dare you say that to me! Who the hell has allowed you to turn our lovemaking into a community circus? 'Doctor said we have to make love tonight. My temperature is perfect;

13

now is the time.' Christ, Tina, where have the warmth and passion gone from our lives? What has happened to the woman I married? You have changed, Tina; you have become a heartless bitch. This obsession with having a child is destroying our marriage.''

Tina wiped the tears from her eyes. She ignored everything Zeke had just said. Looking up at him, her blue eyes shimmered. Despite the redness that surrounded them from her tears, they glowed with beauty. Tina asked softly, "Just this last time, Zeke. I promise I won't make you go through it again. Please.''

Zeke stood upright, turning his head, desperately trying to avoid looking into Tina's eyes. Guilt began to overwhelm him. Tina looked so helpless and fragile. Like a helpless child, reaching out for him to comfort her. Zeke ran his fingers through his hair, glancing up at the clock on the wall. Six-ten. They had been at it for ten minutes, yet it seemed like a lifetime. Zeke turned his attention back to Tina, though he had tried not to look into her lovely eyes, but it was impossible. He found himself gazing deep into them. A chill ran down the back of his neck. Tina's eyes glowed with disarming beauty. Zeke forced himself to glance away as he quietly replied, "OK, Tina, we will go, but this is the last time. Whatever the doctor tells us will be final. Now I have to go, or I'm going to be late.''

Tina jumped to her feet, flung her arms around Zeke's neck, and tried to kiss him. Zeke, still feeling the anger, gently pushed her away. Despite how much he adored his wife and knew how badly she needed his support, he couldn't hide that his pride had been hurt. He had given in to her again. It had to be her eyes. They melted him inside. He would always lose a fight with her as long as he allowed himself to gaze into her eyes. Zeke turned and headed out the front door. He heard Tina call out as he shut the door, "You wait and see, Zeke! This time it will be different!''

Zeke closed the door behind him, not replying to Tina's final words. He walked over to his '84 Mustang that sat proudly in the driveway. It was one of the few possessions Zeke owned that he truly treasured. Despite the few rust spots near the door panel, Zeke was proud of his car. Zeke stopped before unlocking the car door. His eyes moved upward to the sky. He watched as the morning sun began slowly showing its beauty, peeking out over the treetops in the distance, a giant red ball. Zeke whispered an old sailor's expression as he watched the red glow in the sky.

14

"Red sky in morning, sailor take warning."

Smiling, Zeke pictured the beauty of the sun shimmering on the lake, its red glow reflecting a ghostly sky above. He and Tina would sit many summer mornings on the cliff overlooking the lake, watching as the sun rose. Zeke let out a painful sigh as his memories seemed like a lifetime ago. His thoughts raced back in time, back to when he and Tina had carried no burdens or worries in their lives.

Two young teenagers lay next to each other on the cliffs of Harrison Point. Zeke smiled and whispered, "Tina, I think I will write a story about this place. You know about all the Indian warriors who sacrificed their souls to the gods?"

Tina, chuckling, asked, "Why not write about all the love that is sacrificed here instead?"

A serious look came on Zeke's face as he replied, "You call what we did today a sacrifice?"

Tina smiled as she shrugged her shoulders. "Maybe. I don't really know if after tonight you will still love me the same tomorrow."

Zeke grabbed Tina and hugged her tightly, whispering, "I swear to you, Tina, that I will love you till the day I die."

Zeke's thoughts came back to the present as he took a deep breath of the morning air. He hoped to drown out the anger that boiled inside him, but it was futile; the anger would not subside. Zeke knew that it was not anger alone that burned inside him. It was also the painful claws of fear tearing away at him. Fear for his wife. The fear she would eventually do something to hurt herself. The burden of guilt grew with each passing day Tina became more obsessed with the idea that God had chosen to punish her for the abortion years ago, that God's anger prevented her from bearing children. Sundays when they sat in church Tina would kneel, crying as she prayed, begging God to forgive her. Zeke also recalled times late at night hearing Tina sob, talking to God as if he was sitting next to her, asking him, "God, what do I have to do to be cleansed of my sins?"

Deep down inside Zeke knew Tina needed professional help. He never found the courage to force her to obtain that help. There were times he wished he had been more forceful in not allowing her to have the abortion. Then he realized she had every right to choose for herself. Her career was important to her. It had to be her decision to make. Zeke closed his eyes, thinking back to how Tina would laugh and joke with him in the morning before he went to work. The laughter had diminished. Incidents like what had just happened were all too common. Slowly Zeke opened his eyes. Tears caressed the corners. Wiping them away gently, Zeke glanced back at the house. The urge to run back inside, grab Tina, and hug and kiss her burned inside him. His pride would not allow him to do so. Reaching down, Zeke opened the door to his Mustang and slid inside. Sitting there for a moment, he stared at the large picture window of his home, his mind still raging a war to run back inside and tell Tina he loved her. Zeke started up the engine. He then saw the drapes in the window move slightly and sensed Tina's eyes staring out from the other side of them. Zeke's anger disappeared. His heart began to melt as he felt those blue eyes staring at him. Smiling, Zeke whispered the vow he had given to Tina years ago: "I will love you till the day I die."

Zeke put the car in gear and slowly pulled out of the driveway.

2

Tina watched as Zeke's car pulled out of the driveway. Straining her eyes, she attempted to follow the taillights till they vanished down the street. Guilt began seeping inside her. Shame crept inside her soul. Tina moved away from the window and walked slowly back to the dining room table. Her thoughts refused to release the guilt she felt tearing inside her. The guilt squeezed her soul tighter in its frozen grip. Tina's knees began to buckle. She collapsed in the chair. Her body began trembling. Tina cried out; her voice quivered as she tried to free herself from the painful secret she was hiding.

"I did what I had to do for Zeke and me. I ended it with Frank. It is all over now. Everything will return to normal. I had no choice, no choice at all."

Tina's hands shook as she reached over to grab her coffee cup. The sudden blaring of the telephone startled her. When she dropped the cup it fell on the oak table, spilling its dark brew all over the white tablecloth. Again the phone rang, calling out for someone to answer it. Tina glanced up at the clock on the wall. She knew it would be impossible for it to be Zeke; he had just left. The phone chimed, begging for someone to acknowledge it. Tina covered her ears with her hand trying to drown the sound out. The sound remained, as the phone seemed to be ringing louder, refusing to be ignored. Rising cautiously, Tina headed toward the nagging sound. Standing over the phone, Tina stared at it, as if she was trying to will it to stop ringing. It rang again, relentlessly, echoing its sound throughout the room. Reaching down, Tina lifted up the receiver. Quietly she spoke.

"Hello?"

Tina could hear heavy breathing on the other end. Tina's voice became stern as she demanded a reply.

"Hello. Who is there?"

The silence broke as a deep voice replied, "Hello, Tina. Please don't hang up. I need to see you."

Tina recognized the voice right away. It was Frank Parker. An eerie chill seeped through her body, a feeling of despair, which showed in her voice.

"Frank, why are you calling me? I thought I made it clear to you? I don't want to see you anymore."

The deep voice remained friendly, replying, "Tina, you know that you really don't mean that. I miss you; I need to see you."

Tina felt her heart pounding, her anger building inside her. She forced herself to remain calm as she replied, "No, I don't want to see you. It is over, Frank. I mean that."

The voice on the other end persisted, "Why, Tina? What have I done?"

Tina's voice began quivering as she snapped back, "Damn it, Frank, I told you already. I don't want to hurt Zeke. If he found out it would crush him."

The gentleness disappeared from the voice on the other end. "To hell with Zeke. You're hurting me. Doesn't that count for anything? We had something good; why end it?"

The quivering left Tina's voice, replaced with an eruption of anger as she snapped back, "Frank, I don't want to discuss it any further. I said it is over and I meant it."

Frank's voice became more irritable as he became more persistent. "Tina, I'm coming over. I will be there within the hour. We will discuss it then."

Tina quickly tried to convince Frank that she meant what she was saying. "Frank, no. Please, I—"

Tina didn't finish her sentence. A dial tone buzzed in her ear. Slamming the phone back on its cradle, Tina cursed violently.

"Damn him, he can ruin everything."

Tina's thoughts began to flow. *Frank could destroy everything I have worked so hard for. I could even lose Zeke. I couldn't bear that, not Zeke. He is the only man I have ever loved.*

Tina's mind began to race back in time, zooming back to a happier time, when she first had met Zeke.

Standing in front of the high school, Tina stared at the ground, patiently waiting for the bus that would take her home. A voice called out behind her. She glanced behind her. Standing there was a smiling boy.

"Hi. How are you doing?"

The boy was slender, about sixteen years old. He had a broad smile on his face. Reaching out his hand, he introduced himself.

"Zeke Riley is my name. You must be the new girl in school?"

Tina nodded her head yes.

Zeke continued, "Where did you move from?"

Twitching nervously, Tina shyly replied, "Detroit. My dad was a policeman there."

Zeke let out a low whistle. His voice grew lower as he said, "Man, I bet you are glad to get away from that place?"

A frown crossed Tina's face. Her voice showed her disgust with Zeke's comment. "I loved living in Detroit. Why should I have been glad to leave there?"

Zeke appeared surprised by Tina's response. Quickly he tried to explain what he meant. "You know? Detroit, murder capital of the world? Drugs, everything? You know what I mean?"

Tina snapped back quickly, "No, I'm afraid I don't. What I recall about Detroit is museums, theaters. Fancy restaurants, wonderful people who liked me for who I am, not where I was from. Is any of that available here in Barnsville?"

Lowering his head, Zeke whispered his reply: "Hey, I'm sorry. I was just trying to be friendly."

Tina didn't ease up her verbal attack on him. "Insulting someone is a strange way of being friendly."

Zeke lost the friendly tone in his voice as he snapped back, "Hey, I'm sorry; forget I even tried talking to you." Zeke turned to walk away.

Tina called out to him, "Hey, where are you going? You can still ride the bus. Just try not to insult me again."

Zeke rolled his eyes at the arrogance in the voice of the new girl at school. Zeke didn't attempt to hide his rudeness as he replied, "I am really not in the mood to ride. I will see you around in school."

Tina's voice became friendlier as she called out, "Tina, Tina Stark!"

Zeke stopped and turned around, putting his hands on his hips. His face showed his confusion as he said, "I beg your pardon?"

Tina laughed as she replied, "That is my name. Tina Stark."

Zeke regained his smile as he asked, "Can we start over? Maybe this time I can avoid making an ass out of myself."

Smiling, Tina nodded her head yes.

Zeke ran back over to her and extended his hand out. "Nice to meet you, Tina Stark. My name is Zeke Riley."

Tina took his hand. Smiling, she replied, "Nice to meet you, Zeke Riley."

Zeke let go of Tina's hand slowly. Gazing into her haunting blue eyes, he asked, "Would it be rude of me if I asked why you moved here? Especially since you seem to like the big city so much."

Tina shifted her schoolbooks in her arms. Still smiling, she answered Zeke's question: "No, it wouldn't be rude. I told you my dad was a policeman in Detroit. I guess my dad saw a lot of what you talked about earlier. My mother died in a car accident two years ago."

Zeke lowered his voice as he replied, "I'm sorry."

Tina still smiled as she continued, "Thanks. It was rough, but I've learned to live with it. Problem is my dad became very protective of me. All he would do on his day off would be look in the newspaper for property far away from the city and the violence he had become accustomed to." Tina paused as she saw the bewildered look on her new friend's face.

Zeke said barely above a whisper, "Tina, you don't have to talk about this if you don't want to. I didn't mean to bring up any painful memories."

Tina shook her head back and forth, replying, "I have learned to accept my mother's death. I still miss her, but I know she is in heaven watching over me."

Tina smiled, adding, "Really, Zeke, it feels nice to be able to talk about it with you. For some reason, I feel I can talk to you."

Zeke beamed. A strange feeling blanketed him. It felt good standing next to Tina. listening to her, and gazing into her beautiful blue eyes.

Tina went on with her story: "Anyway, my dad got all excited when he heard about this town of Barnsville. I guess a friend of his told him it was like stepping into a time tunnel and going into the past for old-fashioned values. To my dad it was great; to me . . . *boring* is the only word I can really think of."

Zeke nodded his head in agreement, replying, "I guess that would be the right word. Nothing exciting ever happens here, but if you want I can show you some neat places to go."

Still smiling, Tina nodded her head and added, "Sounds good, but I'm afraid you would have to meet my dad first."

Zeke shrugged his shoulders, saying, "Let's do it."

Smiling, Tina assured her new friend, "Zeke, you will like my dad."

"I'm sure I will. I know I like his daughter." Zeke's face turned beet red. He couldn't believe what he had just said.

Tina giggled and continued, "That house my dad found is just down the street. I still can't figure out how a cop from Detroit ever found a town like Barnsville? It's funny; one day he just told me Detroit wasn't a proper place for me to grow up. He took an early retirement, and here we are. Now you know my whole life story."

Tina shrugged her shoulders as she added, "I hope I didn't bore you?"

Smiling, Zeke shook his head as he replied, "Of course not, and I know you are going to see why your dad chose our town. It is a great place to live, Tina."

Zeke paused, then added, "Dull compared to the big city, but I know you are going to love living here."

Tina opened her mouth to reply but stopped as the bus pulled up. She looked away from Zeke as she asked, "Would you like to come home and meet my dad now?"

The bus door opened. Tina climbed the steps. Zeke followed her, quietly replying, "I would love to."

Tina headed for the back of the bus, Zeke following her; they sat in the last seat.

Tina stared out the window as the bus pulled away. Quietly she told Zeke, "You know, you're the first person I have really talked to since I moved here. It feels good to be able to talk to somebody. There is something I didn't mention about my dad."

Tina hesitated, then grudgingly added, "My dad has a drinking problem. After my mom died, Dad had a tough time facing it, but moving here has helped. My dad hasn't touched a drop in nearly six months now."

Tina stared at Zeke, then quietly asked, "Do you still want to meet my dad?"

Zeke smiled broadly as he quickly responded, "Of course I do. I hear drinking is like a sickness and people sometimes just can't help themselves."

Zeke quickly added, "Plus losing someone you really care about makes people do things they normally wouldn't do."

Zeke felt uneasy in the way he was trying to comfort his new friend. Tina smiled as she could see the uneasiness in Zeke's manner and quietly said, "Thank you, Zeke; it's nice to have someone who understands. I'm glad you want to be my friend. I really haven't made many since I moved here. I guess it takes time to gain people's trust in a small town."

Blushing, Zeke meekly replied, "I guess I should be honest with you, Tina. I have been trying to muster up the courage to talk to you for the last two weeks. I think every guy at school has. You being from the city, though . . . it kind of scared us off."

Tina turned and faced Zeke, a puzzled look on her face, as she asked, "Why?"

Zeke looked away from Tina's stare. He felt awkward as he answered, "I guess we all felt you would think we were boring compared to the guys you knew in the city. Face it, Tina: we don't have a lot to offer in the way of excitement here in Barnsville. The way you dress, walk, you just seemed so, I don't know, cool."

Tina started laughing. "Now that you have talked to me, I'm not so cool?"

Zeke felt awkward as he stumbled through his words: "No, that's not what I meant. I think you're the prettiest girl I have ever laid eyes on."

Zeke face burned with embarrassment as he added, "You must think I'm a total ass?"

Tina stopped laughing. She rested her hand on Zeke's knee. In a warm and comforting tone she replied, "No, I think you're very sweet."

Before Zeke could reply, the bus stopped. Tina whispered, "This is my stop; are you sure you want to meet my dad?"

Zeke just nodded his head yes. The young couple both got to their feet and headed off the bus. The bus drove off.

Tina could sense the anxiety in Zeke. Smiling, she took Zeke's hand and quietly reassured him, "Relax, Zeke. I know you're going to like my dad."

Tina let go of Zeke's hand and walked toward an old white house. Zeke followed close behind. Tina climbed up the wooden steps, stopping for a moment, and pointed to the green swing on the porch.

"This is something I never had before. I love sitting on the swing at night with my dad. We just sit out here for hours looking at the stars in the sky. I must admit I could never do that in the city."

Zeke smiled weakly as he said, "I guess living here all my life I never noticed it. Maybe this weekend I will take you to Harrison Point. If you want to see something spectacular, that is the place to go."

Tina motioned for Zeke to follow her replying as she did, "That would be nice. Come on inside; I want you to meet my dad."

Tina opened the screen door, calling out, "Dad, I'm home!"

A raspy voice called back, "I'm in the kitchen, sweetheart!"

Tina motioned to Zeke to follow her as she headed for the kitchen. Zeke hesitated, wondering how he had wound up in this girl's house, meeting her father already. Zeke's thoughts were interrupted by Tina's soft voice.

"Come on, Zeke; my dad won't bite you."

Zeke slowly followed, mumbling under his breath, "I must be nuts."

Standing in the kitchen, over the sink, was a tall, hulking figure. Zeke knew where Tina had inherited her blue eyes. Her father's eyes were an even deeper blue than Tina's.

Tina wrapped her arms around the huge man's neck and kissed him on the cheek. The whole time, the man never took his eyes off Zeke, who stood shyly in the kitchen entranceway. Tina's voice had a strange glee to it as she introduced Zeke.

"Dad, I would like you to meet a new friend of mine, Zeke Riley."

Zeke extended his hand. Tina's father's smile disappeared as he also put his hand out. Zeke felt a twinge of pain as the big man squeezed his hand tightly.

"Nice to meet you, Zeke. My name is James, James Stark."

Zeke stammered his reply: "W-w-welcome to B-b-barnsville, Mr. Stark."

Stark released his firm grip on Zeke's hand. A huge grin spread across the big man's face as he asked, "You been showing my little girl around town?"

Zeke shook his head no as he answered, "No, sir, but I would like to."

Stark let out a grunt. He watched as Zeke's eyes went to the carcass of the deer on the back porch. Stark could see the disgust in Zeke's eyes, so he playfully asked, "Tell me, Zeke, do you like to hunt?"

Zeke, his eyes still glued to the dead animal on the porch, shook his head no as he answered, "No, sir, I don't."

Stark faked a look of surprise as he questioned Zeke further: "Have you ever been hunting, Zeke?"

Zeke forced himself to take his eyes away from the disgusting sight on the porch and found some courage as he sternly replied, "No, sir, but I never wanted to. I think it is cruel to shoot animals."

Stark glanced over at his daughter, who was showing her displeasure at her father's tone of voice. He ignored his daughter's apparent anger and continued his questioning.

"Do you eat meat, young man?"

Zeke shot a glance over at Tina, a helpless look on his face. Tina, apologetic, shrugged her shoulders. Zeke wondered how his first conversation with Tina's father had turned out to be about something he felt so strongly against. Zeke mustered enough to courage to reply, "Yes, sir, but that is different."

Stark snorted as he shot back, "How is that different? Do the animals they turn into steaks commit suicide?" Stark's sarcasm dripped from his words. He folded his arms as he waited for Zeke to reply.

"Sir, I don't even like holding a gun. If that bothers you I'm sorry."

Before Stark could reply or Zeke add anything to his statement, Tina blurted out, "Dad, stop. Who in the hell cares if Zeke hunts or not? You're giving him the third degree as if you were still a cop."

Stark turned and winked at his daughter. Turning back toward Zeke, Stark said, "I'm just trying to make conversation. I was going to invite the young man to go hunting with me."

Tina folded her arms as she said, "Dad, I told Zeke he was going to like you. You're proving me wrong."

Stark smiled as he replied, "I guess my daughter's right. I'm sorry, son; I do get carried away at times."

24

Zeke forced a smile as he replied, "I understand, sir. Most of the people in our town are hunters. I am just not one of them."

Stark put his arm around Tina as he proudly stated, "My little girl here can shoot a gun better than me. She is a true markswoman."

Tina rolled her eyes as she snapped back, "Thanks, Dad. Now Zeke can flee our home in complete terror. He is going to think we are both crazy."

All three of them began laughing. Stark put his free arm around Zeke. Holding both of the children tightly in his arms, Stark said. "I think I'm going to like you, young man."

Tears trickled down Tina's face. Gently she wiped them away from her eyes. Remembering her past caused an unbearable pain. Tina walked toward her bedroom, stopping to glance at the picture on the end table, a picture that reflected a happier time in Tina's life. Wrapped by a golden frame, it was a picture of her father and Zeke, standing side by side, proudly holding up a large bass, they had caught. Tina reached over and gently picked up the picture. Cradling it gently in her arms, she walked into her bedroom. Tina's head began throbbing as she tried to fight back memories she had hidden deep in the caverns of her mind. Sitting down on her bed, she held the picture out in front of her. Tears ran freely from her eyes as the past crashed through the barriers she had blocking memories from her mind. Tina pressed the picture hard up against her chest, crying out, "Daddy, I'm so sorry!"

The painful past unmercifully continued to burn in her mind.

3

Tina cried out as the memories relentlessly flooded her mind. Showing no mercy, they raged through her mind, unlocking painful visions, she tried to keep buried deep inside her.

"Why, God, why must you bring the past back in my mind? Haven't I suffered enough for you? Please bury these thoughts. I can't bear to relive them again. For once, show me that merciful side I hear so much about."

Tina's pleas were not answered. The past crashed through the barriers of her mind.

"Dad, you are acting like an old fool. It's not like Zeke and I don't try to come over here more. We both are so busy right now we don't have the time. It has nothing to do with your drinking. Even though it is senseless. Dad, you are looking for a reason to feel sorry for yourself. Right now I am your best excuse."

Tina stood on the first step of her father's porch. Anger shook inside her. Her father had begun drinking again. This time it was worse than before. Tina couldn't hide her anger as she continued to lecture her father.

"When we do visit all you ever talk about is us not giving you any grandchildren. For God sakes, Dad, we get tired of hearing it. From what I can see, I wouldn't want a child to be exposed to you anyway."

Along with Tina's anger she felt pity for the man standing in front of her. Once a proud man, he had become feeble and ashamed. Booze had become his comfort, his companion. For the only two loves of his life were now gone, and his heart would not accept it.

Stark 's voice trembled as he replied, "Tina, you've changed. You have become cold toward me. Tell me, what have I done to make you so ashamed of me?"

Tina could hear the pain in her father's voice. Her heart wanted to cry out and tell her father that she couldn't bear hearing him talk of children any longer. Tina felt the guilt and shame for not telling her father what she had done. She knew deep down inside if her father ever knew what she had done he would never forgive her.

"Tina, please, why can't we be a family again? I will stop drinking; I promise. All I ask is that you and Zeke visit me like you did before. Maybe we can all go fishing again. Please, Tina, give me another chance to be a good father."

Tina backed off the step to solid ground. Her blue eyes glaring hard at her father, she shot her reply back at him.

"Sober up first, Dad; then maybe we can talk. Right now all you are doing is having a pity party. I am not a little girl anymore. I do have a life of my own to take care of."

The pain poured out of Stark's voice as he asked, "Being a women means you don't need your dad anymore? Is that what you're saying, Tina?"

Tina could feel her father's pain. Her words became gentler as she replied, "I didn't say that, Dad; please don't put words into my mouth."

Stark patted the green wood on the swing on which he was sitting. Forcing a weak smile, he asked, "Why don't you come up here and sit next to me like you used to? We can talk like the old days. You can tell me when you and that son-in-law of mine plan on giving me a grandchild to play with."

Stark's words struck a nerve inside Tina. Shame swelled inside her soul. Tina's eyes burned as she fought back the tears. She snapped back in anger, trying to hide the shame from her dad, "That is the booze talking, Father. You have lost your self-respect, and you're trying to regain it through me. I don't have time for this. Call me when you stop dwelling in all this self-pity."

Tina turned and stomped toward her car, her heart aching to scream out the truth to her dad, to tell him it wasn't him but her and the shame she felt that kept her away. She stopped when she reached her car. She slammed her fist down on the hood and turned toward her father's house. He no longer was sitting on the swing on the porch. He had gone inside the house. Tina stood and stared at her father's house. She began debating whether maybe she should go inside and explain everything to take away the hurt he was feeling, but telling him the truth might cost his love for her. No matter which way she chose, she knew her father would feel betrayed by his daughter.

Tina opened the door to her car and slid inside. Looking at her father's house again, she whispered, "I love you, Dad. When I find the courage I will explain everything."

Tina started up the engine, put the car in gear, and slowly pulled out of the driveway.

Tina drove down the street to the church. The pain in her heart became unbearable. She needed comfort, someone to turn to. She pulled to the curb of the church and got out of her car and walked up the steps to the old white building. She opened the huge white oak doors and stepped inside. Her eyes went to the crucifix of Jesus. Trembling, she walked down the aisle and knelt at the altar at the foot of the crucifix. Tears ran down her eyes as she clasped her hands together and she prayed out loud.

"God, listen to my prayers. My father is falling apart. I know he is lonely, and I want to be there for him. This can happen if you will allow me to have a child. I'm a good person who only made one mistake in my life, but I know you can forgive me for that. Please, a child would help my father face life again. The shame I carry will always be there. All I ask for is your forgiveness and allowing me to have a child."

Tina, sobbing, bowed her head, gripping her hands tighter as she did.

Tears ran freely from Tina's eyes as the memories faded. Anger filled her mind as she remembered how God had answered her prayer. After that day Tina would never see her father alive again. That night James Stark took his own life. Tina glared up at the ceiling and with rage in her words shouted, "Your answer to me that day was clear, God! I knew from that day forward I would be at war with you. You took my father before I could even tell him I loved him. I will never forgive you for that."

Tina leaned over and opened the drawer to the nightstand next to her bed. Inside rested the only two items her father left her. One was a note he had written for her, which only said: "Please forgive me, Tina. I have lost the courage to live." The other was a .38

police special. Tina treasured the gun; she felt as if her father's spirit somehow was inside it, protecting her from any harm that might ever come to her. Tina learned how to shoot when most children were learning how to ride a bike.

Gently Tina held the revolver in her hand, gently stroking the barrel, whispering to it as if it could hear and understand what she was saying, "You are finally going to have a grandchild, Dad. If it is a boy, I am going to name him after you. James Riley, that has a nice ring to it. I hope you have forgiven me, Dad, for all the pain I caused you? I guess, you being in heaven, God has already told you the real reason I stayed away? I know he has had to tell you of the punishment he has handed down on me. Don't tell him, Dad, but I found a way to beat him. I am going to have a baby. Dad, I won."

Tina kissed the barrel of the gun, caressing it gently in her hands.

"I love you, Daddy. I always will."

Tina kissed the barrel again, then eased the revolver back inside the drawer, spreading the note carefully over it, as if it were a blanket to keep the gun warm.

Wiping the tears from her eyes, Tina rose to her feet. She walked over to her closet. Opening the door, she searched for something to wear. Her hands stopped on the sleek bright red dress. A smile eased on to her face. Taking the dress off the rack, she held it up to her. This was Zeke's favorite dress in her entire wardrobe. Backing up, still clutching tightly to the dress, Tina sat down on the edge of her bed. Laying the slinky dress delicately over her lap, she closed her eyes. Her mind again traveled back through time. Like a raging whirlwind, her thoughts pulled her back in time.

"Zeke, are you sure you don't want to go to the Christmas party?"

Zeke glanced up from his paperwork. Smiling, he said warmly. "I'd love to, but I have to get these year-end reports done for Mr. Martin. You go ahead without me. It is your office party, not mine. Anyway I get the distinct feeling your boss doesn't care too much for me."

Tina put her hands on her hips as she scolded her husband, "That is silly. Dr. Parker has never said a cruel word about you."

Zeke continued to smile. He then noticed the dress Tina was wearing. "I see you are wearing my favorite dress."

Tina glanced down at her apparel, then back at Zeke. Her words were soft as she said, "Sweetheart, if you are not going, then I will change into a different dress. I remember the promise I made; this dress is for your eyes only."

Zeke stood up from his chair. Smiling, he motioned for Tina to come over to him. Bowing her head slightly, she made her way to where Zeke was standing. He wrapped his arms around her, kissing her gently on the forehead, whispering, *"I want you to wear the dress darling. Show those snobs how beautiful you are."*

Tina kissed Zeke gently on the lips as she said warmly, "Zeke, I wish you were going. I hate to go to this party alone."

Smiling, Zeke made a silly face as he teased his wife playfully. "Yes, I really hate to miss this wild party with Doctor Conceited Parker."

Tina frowned as she snapped back, "That's it; I'm not going."

Zeke started laughing as he tried to sound sincere: "Hey, I want you to go. You need to have some fun. Now get out of here. I have a lot of work to finish."

Zeke kissed Tina again. Tina eased away from his grip, turned, and walked out the front door.

Tina's mind drew her deeper into the caverns of the past. She fought to keep the images from appearing, but in vain.

Tina walked briskly through the office door. She hung her coat on the rack standing in the corner, smoothed out her dress and glanced around the office. The music was blaring out Christmas tunes. Tina's coworkers were laughing and drinking, enjoying the festivities being offered by their boss on this night. Tina's eyes searched the room. She couldn't spot Frank Parker anywhere in the crowd. Her eyes then scanned over to the glass door that led to Parker's office. Standing in the hall were Frank Parker and his wife, Mary. They were violently arguing about something. Mary was waving her arms wildly as she spoke.

"You bastard, I know you were with that bitch last night. What kind of father are you? You can't keep that thing in your pants even during the holidays?"

Parker spit back his angry reply: "Fuck you, Mary. Maybe if you fixed yourself up instead of looking like some worn-out old hag I wouldn't need to sleep with someone else."

Mary grabbed her stomach as she shouted back, "You don't seem to mind getting me pregnant! What does that make you? Does that make you a man, Frank?"

Tina winced as she watched Frank slap his wife with his open hand.

Mary grabbed her cheek. She fought back the tears and just glared back at her husband.

Tina sensed from Mary's reaction that Frank had hit her before. Mary showed no surprise, no shock, only pure hate. Mary whirled around, stomping down the hall toward the glass door. Tina moved back, hoping that Mary didn't see her spying on them. The glass door flew open. Mary scurried past Tina, who watched as Mary stormed out the main entrance, gruffly slamming the door behind her.

A slight smile crept onto Tina's face. The time would be perfect to begin phase one of her plan; a way to work around God's unjust punishment and to finally have her child and prove God and everyone else wrong.

Frank Parker was an arrogant, conceited fool. He felt every woman in the town of Barnsville wanted to go to bed with him. Despite his good looks, Tina found him repulsive. Parker was the father of three children He and his wife were expecting their fourth. Yet this pig scorned his blessings and screwed around endlessly on his wife. He had no morals. His only passion in life was to jump in bed and prove his manhood. Parker had made many passes at Tina over the years she had worked for him, but Tina had always turned him down. Zeke would be the only man in her life. But times were different now. Tina realized she had to do something or she and Zeke would be condemned to an eternity without children. Tina knew that it was her actions from the past that had caused God's wrath on her and Zeke. She also knew that it would be up to her to battle the immortal, to find a way to place the final piece of the puzzle, to complete her and Zeke's dream: adding the blessing of a child to their marriage. Tina decided Frank Parker would be the perfect pawn to use in her plan.

31

Parker walked through the glass door. Straightening his tie, he acted as if nothing had happened at all. He glanced around the room and smirked as he watched his employees making fools of themselves as they drank and danced.

Tina ran her tongue over her lips to make them moist. She then swayed over to where Parker was standing. She nudged him gently, to get his attention.

"Merry Christmas, Doctor."

Parker turned his head slightly, smiling broadly as he saw Tina standing next to him. Bowing slightly, he gasped, "Merry Christmas, Nurse Riley. You look absolutely gorgeous tonight."

Giggling like a schoolgirl, Tina replied, "Thank you, Doctor."

Tina looked around the room at everyone drinking and laughing, adding, "Your party seems to be a major success."

Parker nodded his head in agreement, then asked, "Why aren't you joining them? I'm sure you could use some fun."

A wicked smile creased Tina's face as she replied in a sensuous voice, "I don't know? Maybe I decided to wait till you showed me that surprise you keep telling me you want to give me."

A sickening grin appeared on Parker's face as he read between the lines of what Tina was trying to tell him. Parker reached down and took Tina's hand in his. His voice rose slightly above a whisper.

"I have your surprise in my office. I guarantee you will just love what you're going to see."

Tina fought back the urge to laugh in the fool's face. His lines wouldn't work on a naive schoolgirl. Looking down at the floor, Tina replied in the sexiest voice she could conjure up, "Is it a large gift? I like surprises that are big."

Frank's palms became sweaty as his grip on Tina's hand grew tighter.

Tina suppressed her laughter, watching the pompous ass get excited with her every word.

Parker struggled not to stutter as he spoke. "If it's big you want, I'm sure you are going to love what I have to give you."

Smiling, Tina replied in a sensuous tone, "I'm sure I will, Doctor. I'm sure I will."

Parker smiled, then led Tina through the glass door to his office. As Parker opened the door to his office, Tina took a deep breath and followed him in.

*　　*　　*

Tina shook with embarrassment from the taunted visions of her past. Clutching the red dress tightly in her hands, she spit on it and hurled it to the floor. Her anger choked her. Guilt began smothering her as she screamed to the heavens to justify her actions.

"God, you forced me to sleep with that pig! You left me no choice. Zeke and I needed a child to complete our dreams."

Tina glared at the ceiling as she aimed her anger towards the heavens.

"You have stripped me of my dignity, but I swear to you, God, you shall not defeat me."

Tina's breathing grew heavier. She couldn't shake the memories of Frank Parker. Her conscience cried out, screaming in her mind.

"Parker was only a tool. A tool needed to provide the final piece of Zeke's and my happiness."

Tina shook her head violently and kept repeating her words.

"A tool, that is all you were, Frank. A tool for completing dreams. Did you hear that, God? I won't allow you to make me feel like a whore. I am pregnant; I defeated you."

Tina buried her face in her hands, repeating, "I defeated you, God."

Her own words did not bring her comfort. She couldn't shake the guilt pitted in the center of her heart. The years were taking their toll on her. She knew she was fighting the battle against God on her own. No one believed her, not even Zeke. She heard the whispers from the townspeople; they thought she was losing her mind. She forced herself to start keeping her war with God a secret, but there were times she just couldn't stay quiet. Her father's death, what more proof did the world need? She asked for help, and God had taken her father away from her with him thinking she hated him. Tina would never forgive God for that. To allow a bastard like Frank Parker children was a travesty. Tina knew she would fight this war alone. No one would ever have the courage to fight at her side, not even Zeke. The war now was close to an end. Tina would have to fight one more battle, the battle of her guilt feelings toward sleeping with a monster like Parker. Tina knew she had to if she was to give the gift of a child to Zeke. She needed to quench the

33

painful feelings that burned inside her. Frank Parker coming to her home was not by any means easing her guilt. She knew she had no choice. She had to deal with Parker. It would be the only way she could complete her plan. For her and Zeke's happiness, she had to face the bastard one last time.

4

The Golden Aces was a fast food restaurant with the reputation for being created for those who didn't care what went into their stomachs. Todd Martin had opened it in Barnsville to capitalize on the growing industry. The Golden Aces stood alone in Barnsville as the only fast-food restaurant. Todd Martin not only was the owner; he had become good friends with Zeke's family. Martin had given Zeke his first job. Zeke knew it would be a great experience for him, but he thought it would only be a stepping-stone for his future, not the foundation for his career. Martin gave Zeke more and more responsibility as the years went by. Zeke climbed to the top of the restaurant employee hierarchy. Todd Martin relinquished most of his power, promoting Zeke to general manager. Zeke, unknowingly, became an important part of Todd Martin's future, Martin spending less time at the Golden Aces and more time seeking votes for public office in Barnsville. Unlike Zeke Riley, Todd Martin's dream became a reality. Martin ran for mayor of Barnsville and won. Martin felt he had shown his loyalty by turning over the full operation of the Golden Aces to Zeke, not realizing he had just written the concluding chapter to Zeke's dreams. Zeke Riley never would taste the victory of being a writer.

Zeke drove through the deserted streets of downtown Barnsville. There was no activity at all in the small town. All the shops in town, still tightly secured, were not ready to open for at least another two hours. Zeke gazed at the small shops lined up on his way to work. Mixed emotions flooded his mind. After forty years trapped in this small town, one part of him wanted to roll down the window and scream at the world for sentencing him to life in such a dull and drab town; a town where nothing exciting ever happened, where life went on from day to day in a normal and calm way. A slight smile crossed Zeke's face as he realized that in reality he was a lucky man. For God had allowed him to taste what heaven must be like.

Zeke slowed down as he reached the driveway of the Golden Aces. Turning, he drove to the back of the restaurant. Pulling into his regular parking place, Zeke noticed something moving by the field. A strange sense of fear ripped through him. Leaving his car lights on, Zeke squinted at the dumpsters by the open field. His heart began to pound as he was sure he saw some type of movement, a shadow of some kind. Zeke remained frozen in his seat, peering into the field, waiting for something to jump out at him. Nothing happened. Calming himself down, Zeke convinced himself that it must have been an animal running through the field. Turning off the engine of his car, Zeke leaned back in his seat, still leaving his car lights on. Staring into the field, he knew he had least another hour before his first employee would arrive.

The darkness began lifting from the skies, allowing the beginning of the new day to arrive. Zeke leaned forward and pushed in his car lights. He knew he had to prepare for his early-morning ritual. Zeke would make a pot of coffee before he started any of his work. His best friend, Bob Hanson, the local sheriff, would arrive by seven, and the two of them would sit and drink coffee as they swapped stories for a half hour. Then Bob would leave. Zeke's first employee would arrive, and the true day of work would start. Predictable, dull, but a part of the life Zeke Riley had chosen to live.

Zeke took the keys out of the ignition and slid out of his car, closing the door. Zeke found himself still peering into the field in front of him. The uneasy feeling would not leave him. Slowly he turned and headed for the back door of the Golden Aces. Fear began gripping Zeke as he quickened his pace toward the back door. His heart pounded like a bass drum. Reaching into his pants pocket, he grabbed hold of his work keys and yanked them out. Panic began smothering him. Suddenly he heard the sound of footsteps behind him. Fear would not allow him to look. Instead he bolted for the back door. The footsteps behind him grew louder. Zeke, trembling, forced the key in the lock and turned it. Before Zeke could open the door, a cold, hard piece of metal jabbed into the back of his neck. A harsh, angry voice bellowed behind him, "Hurry up and open the door, asshole, before I put a bullet into your fucking skull!"

Fear engulfed Zeke's body. He tried to speak but only groaned. The metal object dug deeper into the back of Zeke's skull as the voice snarled, "Now, asshole, or I will splatter your brains all over this parking lot!"

Zeke pushed the door open, falling hard onto the tile floor from the force of his movement. The door slammed hard behind him. The hideous voice echoed through the room.

"Is there an alarm system in this place?"

The temptation to lie crossed Zeke's mind. Instead he nodded his head yes.

The voice behind him bellowed out the next order: "Shut it off now!"

Zeke rose slowly to his feet, avoiding looking at his assailant. Staggering over to the alarm box on the side of the wall, Zeke punched in the alarm sequence. The red light went off, with the green one taking its place. Zeke backed away from the alarm box. The humming of the coolers in the background was the only sound flowing through the kitchen. Zeke welcomed the peaceful song of the machinery. The tranquil sounds only lasted for a brief moment.

"Is it off?"

Zeke nervously nodded his head yes.

The voice then snapped out its next command: "Take me where you keep your money."

The steel barrel pushed hard up against the back of Zeke's neck. The voice snarled, "Move it!"

Zeke turned around, keeping his eyes fixed on the tile floor, not wanting to see the face of the man screaming out the orders, moving quickly through the swinging doors. Zeke was being followed closely by his attacker. Zeke stopped at his office door, his keys still clutched tightly in his hand. Trembling, Zeke inserted the key into the lock, turned it, and opened the door to his office. The man behind Zeke shoved him through the door. He maintained his balance, shielding his eyes, as the man turned on the office lights. Zeke swiftly knelt down by the safe, his palms wet as the sweat poured from his body. Zeke wiped the palms of his hands on the sides of his pants. He then began turning the dial on the safe. Zeke's hands would not stop shaking. He kept passing up the numbers to open the safe. Biting his lower lip, Zeke tried to force himself to calm down and to concentrate on the safe combination.

The clicking noise behind him choked him with even more fear. Zeke knew the sound. It was the hammer of the man's gun, followed by a growling voice.

"I believe your ugly ass is stalling. Asshole, I think you better open the fucking safe now or I'll blow you in half!"

Zeke kept his back to the intruder, throwing his hands in the air, crying out, "Please, I'm trying! I will get it this time."

"Then do it or you will die, motherfucker!"

Before Zeke could lower his arms, the shrilling sound of the back buzzer rang through the air. The gun rammed into the back of Zeke's neck. A large hand grabbed him by his collar, forcing him to his feet. Zeke now was forced to look into the eyes of his tormentor. A large black man stood in front of him. Jagged scars ran vertically across the man's face. The light shining down from the ceiling reflected off his bald head. Zeke attempted to turn away from the man's piercing stare but couldn't. The black man pulled Zeke closer to him, snarling, "Who the hell is that?"

Stammering, Zeke replied, "I d-d-don't know. . . It is prob-b-b-ably one of my emp-p-ployees."

Moving the gun under Zeke's chin and giving it a firm thrust, the intruder spit out his warning: "Get rid of whoever it is. Or both of you will die."

Moving the gun from under Zeke's chin, he pushed Zeke out of the office, sticking the barrel of the gun in the center of Zeke's back to remind him that death was close. Again the buzzer echoed through the restaurant. Zeke hurried his pace to the back door. Leaning forward, Zeke peered out the peephole to see who was beckoning him from the other side. It was Sheriff Bob Hanson. He stood tapping his foot impatiently, waiting for Zeke to open the door.

A harsh whisper came from behind Zeke: "So who is it?"

Zeke closed his eyes, terror now running rampant through him as he replied, "It's the sheriff."

The black man pushed Zeke aside and stared out the tiny peephole himself. He saw the same impatient man standing in front of the door. Turning his attention quickly back to Zeke, he aimed his revolver in the center of Zeke's skull. As the buzzer went off again, the attacker waved his revolver and hoarsely commanded, "Get rid of him now or both you bastards will die. Am I being clear to you, asshole?"

Zeke nodded his head yes but knew that would be difficult. He and the sheriff had been sharing coffee and stories for the last five years. How was Zeke now going to just "get rid of him"? Taking a deep breath, then slowly exhaling, trying to relax himself, Zeke calmly called through the door, "Who is it?"

The answer came back quickly.

"It's me, Zeke, Bob. Who else would it be at this hour?"

Zeke tried to maintain his composure, despite having a gun pointed at the middle of his head.

"Sorry, Bob. I have been so busy trying to play catch-up, I forgot what time it was. I haven't even started the coffee. I am going to have to skip our bull session today. I will make it up to you tomorrow. I have to get back to work or I won't get the restaurant open in time for lunch."

Hanson persisted. "Zeke, at least open the door. Hell, I find it impossible to hold a conversation this way."

Zeke could see anxiety building in the man holding the weapon across from him. Zeke knew it would not be much longer before the man finally cracked and someone was going to wind up dead. Zeke forced himself to be rude to the man he called friend. He was sure Hanson would understand later.

"Damn it, Sheriff, maybe you have time for this idle chitchat, but I don't. So unless you have a purpose for keeping me from my work . . . I suggest you leave and allow me to take care of my restaurant."

An eerie silence lingered in the air. Zeke could hear his own heart beating. Finally the silence shattered as the sheriff replied ruefully, "I'm sorry, Zeke. I didn't mean to interfere with your work. I will talk to you tomorrow. Good-bye."

Releasing a sigh of relief, Zeke whispered, "Good-bye, Sheriff."

Zeke knew by the tone in Hanson's voice he had not been very convincing in the excuses he gave the sheriff. Zeke just hoped that his assailant hadn't noticed it also.

The black man carefully moved to the peephole and looked out. He sneered as he saw the sheriff still standing by the patrol car. Swearing loudly, the thief jumped back and faced Zeke.

"You must have given him some type of fucking code. He is still out there!"

Zeke's entire body became rigid. He did not allow himself to make any moves that might enrage the man any more than he already was. Zeke watched intently as the black man paced back and forth, gazing out each time through the peephole. Snarling, he asked without really wanting Zeke to reply, "Why is he still out there? He must have some type of fucking reason to be just standing there? He knows something is fucking wrong. Damn you, what type of fucking signal did you give him?"

Before Zeke could give a response, a gun barrel came crashing down the side of his face. The impact drove Zeke to the floor. He could feel the trickle of blood oozing down his cheek. Standing over him was his attacker. He had an evil grin on his face. His voice had a harsh and vile tone.

"For your sake, you better hope your friend out there leaves."

Zeke wiped the blood from his cheek. His breathing became irregular. Terror began gripping his entire body. Zeke found himself feeling like a helpless child. He wanted to run, but there was nowhere to run to. Pools of tears began forming in his eyes. Crying out, Zeke pleaded in a panicky voice, "You must believe me! I gave him no signals. I'm not that stupid. Please just take the money and leave. You can go through the front door. I'm sure he doesn't know what is going on in here."

Zeke's attacker glanced over his shoulder at the front entrance. The large picture window revealed an emptied lot. The entire front area clearly visible from the counter, the black man realized what his victim was saying might work and turned his attention back toward Zeke. Aiming his gun at Zeke, he barked out his next command.

"Get your ass off the floor and open that damn safe."

Quickly Zeke rose to his feet. He held his hands high in the air, showing the black man that he was not going to attempt to become a hero. Slowly Zeke eased by the black man, but just as he reached the swinging doors his attacker screamed, "You fucking bastard! You *did* signal him!"

Zeke's eyes darted over to the large windows in front of the building. He watched in disbelief. Two patrol cars pulled into the front lot. Zeke nervously shouted over his shoulder, "I swear to you, I didn't say anything to arouse his suspicion! You heard what I told him—"

Before Zeke could finish his statement, the phone by the back door began to ring loudly. Its piercing sound echoed through the kitchen. Zeke heard his assailant's voice scream over the nagging ringing sound, bellowing out his orders: "Answer it! Move!"

Zeke turned abruptly and moved as fast as possible to the phone. Picking it up, he cautiously spoke in to it.

"Hello?"

Zeke felt the cold steel of the black man's gun press hard up against the back of Zeke's neck; a cruel whisper warning him, "Say the wrong words and your white ass will be spread all over this fucking floor."

Silence filled the other end of the phone. Zeke repeated more firmly the second time, "Hello?"

A very cautious voice replied, "Zeke, it's me, Bob. Can you talk freely? If not, just say no."

A voice that Hanson had never heard before replied instead.

"No, Sheriff, your friend can't talk, but he can die if you don't do exactly what I tell you to do."

Hanson cringed as he listen to the demands of the man inside the building with his friend.

"I want a car, money, and safe passage out of this hick town. It's that simple, Sheriff. I leave and no one gets hurt. Of course if you or any of your men try to become heroes, then this man will die. Please don't try to sneak in on me from the front. From where I stand, I have a perfect view of everything. What do you say, Sheriff? Do we have a deal?"

Hanson hesitated for a moment before replying to the man's demands. rubbing his fingers over his eyes Hanson sternly replied, "Release your hostage, and then we will talk. I promise you that you will be treated fairly."

A cruel laughter came over the other end of the phone, accompanied by a sarcastic reply.

"Right, Sheriff, and I promise you I will only shoot him three or four times before I rip out his fucking heart."

The black man's tone changed quickly as his words became cruel and harsh: "Sheriff, if I don't get what I want this bastard will fucking die. Now if you can't meet my demands tell me now. . . . That way your friend and I both can die quickly."

Hanson felt the panic stab at him as he blurted out his words quickly.

"Wait a minute; don't do anything foolish. I didn't say I couldn't do anything. We can talk. Tell me, how much money do you want?"

Hanson waited for the voice to answer; what was seconds seemed like a lifetime to him. Finally the voice returned.

"Call me back, Sheriff. I will give you the details in a half hour."

Hanson's voice showed his inexperience as he shouted back in a panicked tone, "Why a half hour? Tell me what you want and I can work on getting it done." Hanson heard a dial tone on the other end. The man inside the restaurant had hung up the phone. Hanson slammed the phone down on its receiver, cursing loudly.

"Damn it!"

Then he slammed his fist against the phone, repeating angrily, "Damn it! Damn it! Damn it!"

Hanson knew he had handled the situation wrong and his poor judgment might cause the death of his dear friend. The sheriff stood rigid in front of the pay phone, debating whether to call the man back now. Maybe if he used the right words with him he would convince the man to let Zeke go. Hanson wanted to do something, anything, to free Zeke. The trouble was reality began seeping into Hanson's mind. As he shook his head, he knew all he could do was wait as instructed. Disgusted with the way he had handled his first professional crisis, Hanson walked slowly back to his patrol car.

5

Tina tightened the belt on her robe. Bending over, she picked up the red dress she had tossed on the floor earlier. She sat on the edge of the bed, laying the dress neatly across her lap. Her mind dashed back to a time when the dress gave her good memories. She giggled slightly as the memories flowed through her mind back to the first time she had worn the dress for her Zeke.

Tina could see herself standing at the entrance of her bedroom. Zeke was sitting restlessly on the couch, his back to her, his hands firmly pressed against his eyes.

"Are your eyes really closed, Zeke? You are not trying to peek, are you?"

Zeke let out a heavy sigh as he replied, "Yes, Tina, they are really closed. Now will you show me this great surprise?"

Zeke laughed quietly as he added, "It isn't going to bite me, is it?"

Tina promenaded over to where Zeke was sitting. She positioned herself to be standing right in front of him; running her fingers through her hair. Smacking her lips quietly, she attempted to lower her voice to a sexy throaty tone.

"OK, Zeke, you can open your eyes now."

Zeke removed his hands slowly from his eyes. Still keeping his eyes tightly closed, he playfully asked, "Are you sure, Tina? I am beginning to enjoy all of this suspense."

Tina snapped out of her pose. Putting her hands on her hips, she began scolding Zeke.

"Zeke Matthew Riley. Do you want to see the surprise I have or not?"

Laughing, Zeke opened his eyes gradually. His laughter stopped as he gazed at his wife standing in front of him. The red dress shimmering on Tina's body made her erotically appealing.

Zeke's eyes widened. Quietly he whistled through his teeth, showing Tina his complete approval of what she was wearing. Zeke began exaggerating heavy breathing, as he exclaimed, "You're gorgeous! That dress is hot."

Grabbing his chest, Zeke continued, "My heart. Woman, quick come over here and bite me."

Tina turned away from him, replying in a teasing voice, "Too late. I'll wait for the mailman."

Both of them began laughing. Zeke then reached up and grabbed Tina around the waist, pulling her down toward him, kissing her softly on the lips. He gently moved her away. Staring deep into her blue eyes, he whispered, " I don't know how I would ever exist without you, sweetheart."

Zeke drew her closer to him, adding, "I love you."

Once again he kissed her gently. As their lips parted, Tina rested her head on Zeke's shoulder. Warmly she whispered in his ear, "You will never have to find that out. God, I love you, Zeke."

The flowing tears fell like heavy rain, drowning out the rest of her memories. Tina's hands were now clutching the red dress tightly. Suddenly she began tugging and ripping the dress apart. Piece by piece Tina tugged and ripped till all she was holding in her hands were shreds of what once had been a lovely dress. Tossing the remaining material clutched in her hands to the floor, Tina then grabbed her own hair, yanking on it hard as she screamed, "I did it for Zeke! I did it for Zeke!"

Releasing her hair, Tina buried her face in her hands and began to sob uncontrollably. The guilt over what she had done began stabbing at her heart. Falling to her knees, Tina tried to ease her pain by revealing the good that had come out of what she did.

"We have our baby, Zeke. We beat all the odds and defeated . . . God. That is all that should matter. Not how I did it, just that I did it."

Slowly Tina stopped her crying. Wiping her eyes with the back of her hands, she climbed back to her feet. She straightend out her robe. Desperately she tried to regain her composure. Glancing down at the floor, she saw the tattered rags of her red dress lay scattered everywhere. Her bedroom looked like a war zone. Tina blinked her eyes a few times. The tears were causing a burning sensation. Shaking her head, she began to talk aloud, again attempting to justify what she had done.

"I must stop feeling so guilty. I know my methods were a bit barbaric, but it is the end results that count. Zeke and I are finally going to fulfill our dreams. We will finally have our child. I will learn to live with my guilt. Zeke will never find out, unless I continue to act like a raving lunatic. All I need right now is a hot . . ."

Tina's sentence trailed off as the chimes of her doorbell rang through the house. Her body went tense. She knew it was Frank Parker at the door. The chimes rang again. Indecision crept through Tina's mind. Vibrating through the house, the chimes rang again. Tina tried to ignore the sound, hoping Parker would go away. Again they rang. Tina knew she had no choice. She had to face her problem now, or she and Zeke could never live a normal life again. Feeling comfortable with her decision, Tina left her bedroom. She walked over to the picture window and peeked out from behind the drapes. Standing on her porch was Frank Parker. Tina watched as he paced back and forth, stopping only to push in the doorbell. Reluctantly Tina walked to the front door. Drawing a deep breath, she calmly opened the door.

Frank snarled as he brushed passed her in the doorway, "It is about time! What took you so long? I told you I would be here in an hour."

Tina stood with her back to him, still holding the door open, staring out at the morning sky. Clouds were beginning to hide the sun. Rain scented the air. Tina could sense a storm brewing, both outside and in.

Frank's voice broke Tina's concentration. She could feel the irritation flowing through his words. Slamming the door as hard as she could, Tina whirled around to face him. He stood there with his arms folded. Glaring at her, finally he started his questions.

"Tina, tell me what I have done wrong? Why the sudden change in how you feel about me? I have gone over it in my mind over and over and can't think of one damn thing I have done wrong. So please explain to me what in the hell is going on?"

Before Tina could give a reply, Frank added angrily, "Please don't hand me this crap about not wanting to hurt anyone. I'm not buying it. Just tell me what I have to do and I will do it."

Tina felt the rage swell inside her. Fighting to restrain the anger, she calmly replied, "Frank, you have done nothing wrong. It is me. I realize that I still love my husband. I can't keep taking all these chances. I am afraid he might find out. If that happened, I know I would lose him. I can't allow that, Frank. You should feel the same about your wife and kids. They need you, Frank, much more than you need me."

Tina's eyes gave her away. Frank knew she wasn't telling him everything. Quickly he began to dispute what she had just said.

"Tina, I need you and I know you need me. I'm not going to stand here and listen to all this nonsense about how much you love your husband. I know it is not true. You love me, Tina; admit it. Your husband cannot make you feel the way I do, especially in bed."

Tina continued to fight to restrain her anger. She ignored what Frank had said and calmly replied, "It is over, Frank. Please leave, and don't call me again."

Disregarding her demand, Frank walked over to the couch and sat down. As he patted the cushion next to him, his voice became gentle.

"Please, Tina, sit down. I think we should talk this over rationally."

Tina released a heavy sigh. All she wanted him to do was leave. Frank went on patting the cushion next to him, his eyes pleading for Tina to sit down.

Realizing that if she was going to get Frank out of her home and her life she would have to humor him a while longer, Tina slowly walked over to the couch. Sitting on the far end, she snapped, "I'm sitting, Frank, so talk."

Frank studied Tina closely. He noticed her eyes were red and swollen. Thinking the tears were for him, Frank smiled and spoke slightly above a whisper.

"Have you been crying, Tina?"

Tina didn't answer. Frank continued to pry.

"Why, Tina? Tears are not necessary. We don't have to end it. We can make this all work out. You just have to trust me."

Frank slid over to her side of the couch. He put his arm around her. Tina slapped it off her shoulder. As Tina glared at Frank, her anger finally erupted.

"You arrogant ass! You think I've been crying because of you?"

Tina began to laugh through her anger. Sarcasm dripped from her words as she asked, "What makes you think that I give a damn about you? The sight of you makes me sick. Now get out of my home!"

Frank's face flushed red with anger and embarrassment. Pausing, he tried to maintain his composure as he attempted to reason with her.

"Calm down, Tina. Listen to yourself. You're not making sense."

Frank went to reach for Tina again; she leaped to her feet screaming at him, "Stay away from me! Don't you dare touch me, you lousy bastard!"

Frank held his hands in the air, frustration building inside him. But he continued to maintain his calm as he talked to her.

"OK, Tina. I won't touch you. In God's name, woman, what has gotten into you? I love you, and despite what you tell me, I know you love me, too."

Tina's rage boiled over as she snarled, "Love! You don't know the meaning of the word. You pathetic fool. Can't you see I used you? I never loved you. I despise you. My skin would crawl each time you touched me. Now I can free myself from you. So get out of my home and out of my life!"

Frank couldn't bottle up his rage any longer. Vaulting to his feet, grabbing Tina by the shoulders, he shook her violently as he angrily questioned her.

"What are you talking about? How did you use me? Tina, I demand to know what you are babbling about!"

Tina's face cringed in pain as she pleaded, "Please, Frank, you are hurting me."

Frank pulled her toward him, shoving his face toward her, attempting to kiss her. Tina screamed as she pushed him away. Ignoring Tina's scream, Frank yanked on her arm and pulled her entire body flush with his.

Frank's eyes glazed like those of a mad man as he snarled, "I know what you used me for, bitch. You needed a man to make love to you. Well, here I am!"

Releasing one of her arms, Frank freed his hand. Slowly he began to disrobe her. Frantically Tina pushed away from Frank's grip. She tumbled backward, crashing hard to the floor. Tina pulled her robe back over her bare shoulder. Fear began to smother her as she pleaded with Frank, "Frank, leave please. You don't understand how wrong you are."

Lust and anger flowed through Frank's body. Moving quickly toward her, he spit out his words.

"What don't I understand, Tina?" Reaching down to grab her, he sneered. "That you want me to beg to fuck you?" Frank reached down to grab her again.

Tina crawled backward to avoid him. She screamed as he grabbed her leg, "I'm pregnant, damn you. I am pregnant!"

Tina's words hit Frank hard. Letting go of her leg, he backed away from her. Frank's eyes widened. The shock he felt showed in his face. Frank's voice repeated Tina's words in a hollow echo.

"Pregnant?"

Tina rose to her feet, keeping her distance from him, wrapping her arms around her shoulders for comfort. Anxiety seeped into her soul. Frank's fury may have left, but Tina's fear hadn't. She knew that at any time he might decide to try to rape her again. Tina glared at Frank, repeating to him, "Pregnant, Frank."

Frank had moved back to the couch. He sat down and stared up at Tina. She could see his anger had now shifted to total worry. Frank's words came out like those of a child in trouble as he asked, "Is it mine?"

Hope leaped into Tina's thoughts. She could sense the tension in Frank's voice. Frank was definitely concerned, not for Tina but for himself. This was exactly what Tina needed to finally rid herself of Frank Parker. She moved closer toward him, her confidence growing.

"No, it is Zeke's. I just found out yesterday. Now you know why we have to end this."

Tina paused, waiting to see if Frank would say anything. When he didn't, Tina continued.

"Maybe I should have told you everything from the start. Believe me I wanted to, but I was shocked and confused. I didn't know how you would react."

Frank continued to stare at her, a puzzled look on his face. Tina's actions for the last few days had been strange. This explained that. Other things began to cloud the picture. Finally Frank asked,

"How can you be sure that it is his? Doesn't it seem odd to you after all your years of marriage you haven't been able to have a child till now?"

Tina didn't reply. Stopping directly in front of Frank, she tried to think of the right response to give him, something that would convince him he had no reason to worry, to convince him that the child belonged to Zeke, not him.

Frank's voice grew serious as he continued.

"Tina . . . I know a good doctor, one who knows to keep his mouth shut. I think to be on the safe side . . . you know, your age and everything. I feel it would be to both our benefits for you to see him."

Tina's eyes bore through Frank. She clenched her hands tightly into fists, fighting back the urge to reach out and grab Frank. To shake the life right out of him. Tina knew what type of doctor Frank was referring to. Angrily Tina asked, "What kind of doctor, Frank? What is it you are wanting me to do?"

Frank ran his fingers nervously through his hair. Lowering his head to avoid Tina's eyes, Frank quietly explained, "Tina, I can't take the chance that you may be carrying my baby. I would lose everything. My wife would destroy me. We both know that. I know what I am suggesting is going to be tough, but for both of our welfare I think you should have an abortion."

Frank's words pounded into her soul. "Abortion," she whispered. How could he think that way? Frank was a doctor and a father. Anger and fear raged inside Tina as she snapped back, "I told you the baby I am carrying is Zeke's. You have nothing to worry about. I will never allow anyone to know about us."

Tina paused to catch her breath, then added in a fierce voice, "I will not have an abortion, Frank. This child is mine and Zeke's."

Shaking his head, Frank tried to reason with Tina.

"Listen, Tina, I can understand how tough it is to think straight right at this moment. You may be right; it may be Zeke's baby. The key word here is *may*. You are risking my future on that tiny word. Think about it. You and Zeke have been trying to have a baby for years, with no success. Not until . . ."

Frank's sentence trailed off. He stared strangely at Tina, asking her in a curious tone, "Tina, what did you mean when you said you were using me?"

Tina turned her head away from him. As she tried to think quickly, her words came stammering out.

"N-n-nothing. They were j-j-just words. I w-w-was angry."

Frank sprang to his feet. He grabbed Tina by the arm, jerking her around to face him. A sick sensation seeped through him. He snapped his question again.

"What did you mean! How were you using me? Whose baby is it, Tina?"

Frank's eyes burned with fury. He squeezed her arm tighter. Tina tried to break away from his grip but couldn't.

Tina's voice became hysterical as she screeched her reply.

"Zeke's! You must believe me it is Zeke's baby. Please, you are hurting me."

Frank ignored her pleas. He squeezed harder on her arm as he yanked her closer to him. Again she tried to pull away, but Frank's strength prevented her escape. Pulling her directly in front of him, he growled, "Whose baby is it, Tina?"

Fear choked Tina as she struggled to answer.

"Zeke's, honest. Please. Frank. you're hurting me."

Frank's rage out of control now, he didn't hear a word Tina had said. Clenching his free hand into a fist, he shouted, his fist crashing down on the side of Tina's face, "You lousy whore! You used me to get pregnant, didn't you? This all was some kind of fucking game you came up with. Am I right Tina?"

Tina screamed in agony, "It is Zeke's baby!"

Frank's fist struck her again on the side of the face. the force driving her to the floor. Frank refused to release the grip he had on her arm. Again he hit her. Tina struggled to her knees, her screams ringing through the entire house. Frank continued to hit her. He released her arm, Tina crumpled to the floor. Frank shouted over her cries of pain, his voice filled with disgust, "That's what you meant by 'using' me, isn't it, bitch? You needed me to father you a bastard child. You sick fucking whore!"

Frank kicked Tina hard in the side. Sharp pains riveted through her entire body. Tina cried out, "Frank, please stop!. The baby! You are going to hurt the baby!"

Frank stood over her seething in hate. Spitting on her, he screamed, "Baby! What do I care about your bastard child? I want it to die. Do you hear me, slut? I want it to die! I want you to die!

You used me like some fucking test tube. Your husband wasn't man enough to give you a child. So just use good old Frank! You are one sick bitch!"

Frank backed away from Tina. He began to calm himself down. He stared down at Tina. She had curled into a ball to try to protect herself from Frank's blows, her body completely battered and bruised. Nervously Frank began to run his fingers through his hair, realizing what he had done. Quickly his mind began to race, trying to think he knew he would be in serious trouble if she went to the sheriff. Desperately Frank shouted at Tina, "You wanted me out of your life, bitch? You will get your wish. I don't want to see your fucking face at my office. Do you understand? You are through, finished, but if you mention to anyone that I was the one who beat you I swear to you that I will bring up everything. I may go down, sweetheart but I will take your sweet ass with me. I would love to see the excitement in your husband's eyes then. Keep your mouth shut and you can have your bastard child without interference from me."

Tina's face was bruised and swollen from Frank's blows. Her side still throbbed with pain. Tina glared at the vile and evil man standing across from her. Cringing in pain, she blurted out her response.

"Don't worry, Frank. I won't drag you into this. Please just leave."

As he clutched his fist, Frank's body began quivering. He couldn't let it go. His pride felt stripped from him. Strangely enough, he felt violated. Snapping out his words angrily, he asked, "You planned this whole thing right from the start, didn't you? Coming on to me at the Christmas party, begging me to make love to you every single chance we had. Tell me the truth, Tina. You planned everything didn't you?"

Frank had moved next to her as he spoke. He nudged her with his foot on her sore side as he repeated, "Didn't you, bitch?"

Flinching from his foot touching her sore side, she snarled at him, "Yes, Frank, I planned the entire affair. You were easy, you're so damn conccited. You honestly believe every women in the world wants you."

Tina grabbed her side as the pain stabbed her. Fighting back the tears, she spit out the rest of her anger at Frank.

"You are a total disgrace as a husband and father. A pig like you gets all the breaks in life. What I did may have been wrong in your eyes or God's, but I would do it again. Do you know why, Frank?" Tina paused but didn't wait for Frank to reply. "For love, something you will never know or feel."

Frank shook his head in disgust. Turning to leave, he bellowed out his anger.

"Insane! You are completely insane, Tina. You and that loser you're married to deserve each other."

Tina watched Frank intently as he headed for the front door. She cringed when he stopped and turned around.

Glaring at her on the floor, he demanded, "I want the keys for the office. I don't trust a piece of trash like you. I don't want you to have any excuses to come anywhere near my office."

Struggling to her feet, Tina snapped back angrily at Frank, "They are in my room. Wait here, I will get them for you."

Holding her side carefully with her hand, she limped toward her bedroom. Frank yelled again.

"Tina, I hope you realize you ruined a perfect thing! Whether you admit it or not. No one could have ignited passion the way we did."

Tina paused. Turning around, she glanced over at Frank. He had made his way to the center of the room, that smug look on his face. Tina winced; the pain grew worse. She gave no verbal response to Frank's statement. She just glared at him. Hate began to suffocate her.

Frank began to feel uneasy as he stared back at the woman he had just brutally battered. Quickly he ordered her, "Get the damn keys, Tina."

Tina forced a wicked smile. She could sense Frank's uneasiness and enjoyed watching the bastard squirm.

Frank, trying to hide the tension in his voice, yelled, "What are you grinning at, you crazy bitch? I could walk over there and knock that stupid smile right off your face. Now get my keys before I decide to do it."

Tina smiled as she turned and walked through the bedroom door. She paced over to the nightstand by her bed, her thoughts now on the beating she had received from Frank. He had not only hurt her but might have hurt her unborn child. Tina's anger grew intense. Years she and Zeke had tried to have a child. Finally it happened and this vicious animal tried to take it away from her again. She stared at the nightstand where the keys and her father's .38 police special lay. Her father's words of wisdom echoed in her mind: *"Learn to use the gun, dear. You never know when death might stare you in the face."*

Tina knew her father was a wise man. That was how he had survived so long on the Detroit police force. She missed him so badly. Tina felt the burden of guilt for his death but felt God should share the blame. After only three short years in his self-proclaimed heaven, Tina's father had shot himself. Bending over, Tina opened the nightstand drawer. Lying in the front part of the drawer was her father's revolver. It was wrapped in his good-bye note to Tina. Lying by the gun were her keys for work.

Tina began to shake as she could hear her father's voice softly speak to her from the gun: *Tina . . . sweetheart, don't let anyone hurt you or my grandchild. Use the power I left you to protect my grandchild. I forgave you once, but if you allow any harm to that child I won't be able to forgive you again.*

Tina threw her hands over her ears, trying to drown out the sounds of her father's voice but couldn't as his words continued.

Kill him, Tina! Kill the bastard!

A strange smile creased her face as she whispered her reply.

"Yes, Father, you're right. I must protect my child."

Standing, gazing at the two items that seemed to be taking refuge in the drawer, she grabbed the keys. Frank began screaming insults from the front room again.

"I feel sorry for the bastard child you are carrying! A whore for a mother and a loser for a father. The best advice I can give you is to have the abortion and spare the child the pain and shame it would live through. How many other men have you had fuck you in your quest for this child?"

Tina's hand gripped the handle of the .38. She lifted it out of the drawer and held it high in the air. Her grip grew tighter around the handle of the gun. Frank's insults sent rage dancing through her body. Glaring at the gun in front of her, she whispered, "Dad, please help me find the strength to do this."

The sound of her father's voice echoed with passion and love: *Tina, my soul is with you, I will never leave you.*

Gently she slid the revolver in her robe pocket, closed the nightstand drawer and turned to leave. She stop and stared at the tattered pieces of red rags scattered on the floor.

"How fitting," she thought. Grunting from the pain, she bent over and grabbed a large piece of the tattered dress. Clutching it tightly in her hand, Tina left her bedroom, closing the door behind her.

Frank was still shouting insults as he paced back and forth waiting for Tina's return. Hearing the closing of the bedroom door, Frank stopped pacing and glared at Tina. He held out his hands and complained, "It took you long enough. Give me my damn keys so I can get out of this nuthouse."

Tina's gorgeous deep blue eyes stared right through him.

Frank began to feel uneasy. Fear began running through his veins. Attempting to hide his paranoid feelings, he snapped at her, "Stop staring at me! Give me my keys and I am out of here!"

Tina's voice was cold and even.

"You are a evil man, Frank. God showered you with blessings. That I find cruel and strange. You are a doctor, yet when you thought this baby was yours you wanted to put it to death. You chose to destroy a life to preserve a standard of living you have been accustomed to. This is Zeke's child. You were only a useful tool to allow it to happen. All I wanted from you was to leave and allow Zeke and me to enjoy our child. Your silly pride would not allow that. Instead you beat me in an attempt to harm my baby."

Frank interrupted in a rude voice.

"Tina, just give me my keys. Forget the long-winded speeches."

A wicked smile creased Tina's bruised face. Her voice was cold and emotionless.

"Frank, you're not listening. I can't allow you to go unpunished for the pain you inflicted on my baby and me."

Frank began backing up toward the door. A strange sense of fear choked him. Panic setting in, he shouted, "You're crazy! Keep the fucking keys. I don't want to ever see you again."

Tina jerked the revolver out of her robe. In a demanding voice she cried out, "Stay right where you are, Frank! What is your hurry? All out of insults? Come on. A man like you must have a few more somewhere in that sick mind of yours."

Frank froze in his tracks. His eyes looked directly at the gun aimed at him. Throwing up his hands, he pleaded, "Tina, put that away before someone gets hurt."

Tina ignored his pleas. She held up the tattered red rag and quietly asked him, "Do you recognize this, Frank?"

Frank's eyes glanced at the tattered rag in Tina's hand. Quickly he shouted out, "No! Tina, please put the gun away."

A sly grin on her face, Tina prodded Frank on.

"Look at it, Frank. Look closely. You know, maybe if you can tell me what it is I will let you live."

Frank, trying to humor her, stared at the piece of red rag Tina was waving in front of him. Frustrated and scared, he shouted, "No! Damn it, Tina, I don't know what it is. Put the gun away and we can discuss everything. Including that red rag."

Tina began chuckling. Holding the red rag higher in the air, she mocked a hurt tone in her voice.

"Rag, Frank? I'm hurt. This is part of the dress I was wearing when your slimy hands touched me."

Quickly Frank replied, "Of course, I remember. You looked beautiful. Now please put the gun away. Tina, I promise I won't tell anyone what happened here today."

Tina's voice became hard as she replied, "Frank, that dress I wore was for Zeke's eyes only. Look at it now!"

Tina held the tattered rag high in the air as she added, "You are a true bastard, Frank. The only good thing you have ever done in your life was to help Zeke and me complete our dream. Then you spit out insults about that. God for some reason allows you to go on without being punished. I won't."

Tears choked Frank as he pleaded for his life.

"Tina, I was wrong. Please, I love you, that's why I acted so mean. I was hurt. I need you, and I want to take care of the baby."

Tina burst into a wicked laugh as she yelled out to the heavens, "Did you hear that, Dad? Frank loves me. He wants to take care of the baby. Isn't he wonderful?"

Frank whispered in terror, "Dad? Tina, who are you talking to?"

Tina waved the gun as she replied in a cold voice, "My father is here, Frank. His spirit is here watching over me. He loves me and he knows you tried to hurt me and his grandchild."

Frank's voice became frantic as he shouted, "Tina, you're acting like a lunatic! Put the gun down. I'll just leave and I swear I won't ever bother you again."

Tina's blue eyes danced with hate as she spit out her reply.

"That promise I know you will keep, Frank."

Tina cocked back the hammer of the .38 revolver and aimed it at Frank.

Fear now totally engulfed Frank. He knew Tina was completely out of her mind. Quickly Frank lurched toward Tina in desperation to get the gun. Tina squeezed off two shots, striking Frank both times in the chest. Screaming out in pain, Frank crashed to the floor. Disbelief hovered in his eyes as he felt his soul leaving him. He tried to call out, but the pain choked off his cries.

Tina walked slowly over to where Frank had fallen. Blood oozed out of his chest. He stared up into Tina's deep blue eyes. Coughing up blood, Frank tried to speak. Words wouldn't leave his lips. He reached up and grabbed onto Tina's robe, his eyes pleading for her to help him. Tina dropped the tattered rag she held in her hand on top of Frank's bleeding body. Grabbing a handful of her robe, she jerked it free from Frank's grip. The force of the robe leaving his hands sent his head crashing to the floor. He lay sprawled on the floor, his arms extended, the torn piece of the red dress resting on his body. Tina spit on his wounded body as she cursed softly.

"I'm not a whore, Frank, and my child is not a bastard child."

Calmly Tina put her gun in her robe pocket. She stared down at Parker and watched as he choked away the rest of his miserable life. Tina quietly added, "You should have listened when I told you it was over, Frank. I guess now you finally believe me, don't you?"

Parker's eyes glared up at Tina; death danced in them. Tina slowly turned and walked away, leaving Frank in a pool of blood to pay for the hurt he had done to her and her unborn child. Frank was to die. A causality of war or a tribute to her child, either way, Frank Parker would not inflict harm on anyone ever again.

6

A carnival atmosphere filled the air outside the Golden Aces restaurant, people gathering, pointing, and staring at the events happening in front of them. The town deputies threw up barriers for the crowd to stay behind. A strange excitement electrified the air. Nothing like this had ever happened in Barnsville before. Danger, robbery—these were events that they watched on TV or read about in the newspaper. Not in their wildest dreams could they ever imagine it happening to their small community.

Sheriff Bob Hanson stood in the back of the building, away from the craziness that was occurring out front, totally amazed at how bad news could spread so rapidly. Hanson, a native Barnsville citizen, still found it hard to believe that any crime like this would plague his town, especially one of his closest friends he had in Barnsville. He and Zeke as children would talk of their dreams, Zeke of becoming the great author and writing the great American novel that would bring tears and laughter to all who read it, Hanson of becoming a famous actor in Hollywood, maybe playing a character in Zeke's book. Together they would rise to stardom. Sadly, though, both men's dreams faded; they never left the safe haven of their town.

Hanson found himself running for and winning the office of sheriff, which was ironic, since he deplored violence of any kind.

Hanson's jet-black hair highlighted his hazel eyes. He stood six-two: total muscle. His looks were what you would expect from a Hollywood actor. Those visions Hanson knew were now over. Reality, painfully enough, stood a hundred yards from him, a reality Hanson never dreamed of facing. A cold brick building sheltered a man who held Zeke's and maybe the fate of Barnsville in his hands. As sheriff, Hanson's job now was to free Zeke Riley safely and apprehend the man responsible for bringing Barnsville to the same standards as the rest of the world.

Hanson drew a deep breath and exhaled, in hopes of relaxing himself before talking to the day shift employees of the Golden Aces, who stood nervously watching the building in front of them. Not wanting to appear like he wasn't in control of the situation, he strolled over to where they all huddled. Greeting his deputy Bill Starr with a nod of his head, Handson turned his attention to the four people standing in front of him. Hanson began by questioning the elderly lady, Mary Harper.

"Good morning, Mrs. Harper."

Mary Harper was the prep cook at the Golden Aces. She began working there the day the restaurant opened, thirty years ago. Everyone in town knew and loved her. The years had been kind to her. She looked much younger than her age of sixty-three.

"Not so good of a morning, Sheriff. Not till you get young Mr. Riley out of the clutches of that madman inside there." Mary pointed to the back door of the restaurant.

The others behind her began murmuring the same thoughts.

Mary continued, "How could something so terrible like this happen in our town, Sheriff?"

Hanson shrugged his shoulders as he answered her.

"We are not immune to the world's problems, Mary. I wish we were, but we're not. I have a few questions for you and your fellow workers. Please think hard before any of you answer."

Mary and the three others behind her nodded their heads in unison. Hanson began asking his questions.

"First, did any of you see anyone come into the restaurant who was a stranger in town? Someone who made you feel suspicious in any way?"

Mary turned to the others behind her. They looked at one another with inquisitive looks. Mary turned back to Hanson, replying firmly, "No."

"Did any of you notice any cars parked here late last night that were not yours?"

Again they glanced at one another. Again Mary answered for all of them.

"No."

Hanson took off his hat and ran his fingers through his black hair. Staring at the group of people in front of him, he tried to think of the right way to ask his next question. Hanson fitted his hat carefully back on his head. Glancing back at the building, then back to Mary Harper, he asked, "Mrs. Harper, would you know if Mr. Riley keeps a gun in the restaurant?"

Mary didn't bother to wait to consult with her coworkers. She blurted out instantly, "Of course not. Mr. Riley hated guns. Always has. He would complain because his wife kept one in the house. Sentimental reasons, his wife would tell him. We all know how much he loves his wife. So he allowed her to keep it, but I know he hated the thought of it. Sheriff, what importance would Mr. Riley having a gun have anyway? You wouldn't want him to use it, would you?"

Hanson shook his head no. Moving closer to Mary, he whispered, "People have a tendency to play hero when under too much stress. I just want to be sure that Mr. Riley doesn't have that chance. If he listens and does exactly what his attacker tells him . . . I know we can get him out of this unharmed."

Mary nodded her head in agreement as she replied, "I'm sure Mr. Riley has no gun, Sheriff."

Forcing a smile, Hanson ended his questions: "Thank you, Mrs. Harper."

Looking out at the other three employees, Hanson added. "I want to thank all of you for your cooperation. Please go home. We will contact you when everything is under control. If any of you should remember anything that might be of use, please contact us immediately. Thank you for all your cooperation. My deputy will escort you folks back to your cars."

Hanson turned Bill Starr, adding, "Bill, I need you to do me a favor after you take these kind folks to their cars."

The portly deputy nodded his head yes, then motioned for the group of employees to follow him.

Hanson moved back to his car. He reached in the driver's side window and picked up his mike. Pushing in the button, he called into the station.

"Hanson here. How is my request going for some help here, Marge?"

An elderly female voice came over the other end: "They said they would send some, Sheriff. I could use some help myself. This place has turned into a mad house. The phones have not stopped ringing. Even the mayor has called to inquire how everything is shaping up. He said he would be there to look into the situation personally. I imagine you have your hands full already?"

Hanson replied in a weary tone, "I do, and the mayor coming is not going to help matters any."

"Did Bill bring the cellular phone to you, Sheriff?"

Hanson glanced on the front seat of his car and saw the cellular lying on the seat and smiled as he replied, "Yes. Thanks for responding so quickly to that, Marge."

"You're welcome. Have you heard from the man inside the restaurant yet?"

Hanson glanced over at the building, then replied, "Not yet, but I am going to try and contact him shortly."

Hanson paused, then added, "Marge, I am not afraid to admit this. I have a bad feeling on this. There was something in the tone of the abductor's voice that scared the hell out of me. It also doesn't help, him having a perfect view of the front and back of the lots. I never had to handle anything like this before. For Christ sake, Marge, if I screw up I could get my best friend killed."

With a touch of sympathy in her voice, Marge replied, "Don't get discouraged, Sheriff. I'm sure whatever plan of action you take will be the proper one. Just follow your instincts. You will get Zeke out of this mess without a scratch."

Rubbing his eyes, Hanson quietly replied to Marge's confidence in him, "Thanks, Marge. I hope you are right. Especially since my friend's life is depending on my instincts. I better call our friend in there and start the ball rolling on this. I don't want him to get nervous and do something stupid. Thanks again. I will check back later. Marge, keep bugging the state boys for some backup on this."

"I will nag them to death, Sheriff."

"Hanson out."

Hanson hung up the mike and stood back up. He turned as he heard his deputy call out to him.

"They are all taken care of, Sheriff! Man, it is a zoo up front. Henry from the *Barnsville Gazette* is spouting off the Constitution to me about the freedom of the press. I don't know how much longer we can keep this under control."

Hanson shrugged his shoulders as he replied in a tired voice, "It is all new to them, Bill. They are like children with a new toy.

Trust me; if garbage like this occurred every day, they wouldn't even think twice about it."

Starr nodded his head in agreement, adding, "You are right, Sheriff. When I was in Detroit, a robbery like this might not even hit the paper. Hell, I thought I got away from all this madness when I moved to this town."

Hanson frowned slightly, replying, "Bill, you of all people should know you can't run and hide from crime. Not in the type of society we live in."

Starr regretfully nodded his head in agreement, then asked, "What is the favor you need from me, Sheriff?"

Deputy Bill Starr had a completely different background from that of his boss, Sheriff Hanson. Starr came from the city, a Detroit police officer for ten years. Through the ten years of service, Starr had seen many violent crimes, each one taking a piece of Starr's emotions from him. Keeping everything bottled deep inside him, he grew distant from his family and his friends till one day all his emotions erupted for the world to see. A minister had been gunned down in his church in cold blood. No apparent motive for the crime could be discovered. No money had been taken, nothing of value removed; it was just a brutal and senseless murder of a good and decent man. Starr's breakdown forced him into early retirement. He searched the entire state for a place to raise his family away from all the hatred in the world. He remembered when he was a rookie cop James Stark was the first to treat him like an equal. Despite the difference in age, Bill Starr and James Stark had become good friends. Stark had retired, but he wrote to Starr about Barnsville: "A touch of heaven, Bill." Years later, Starr took his friend's advice and moved his wife and two sons to the paradise in the Upper Peninsula of Michigan. It didn't take him long to find work. The town council recommended to Hanson that he take Starr on as a deputy. Hanson agreed. Starr accepted the position and made it clear to everyone that he had no aspirations of doing anything but staying the deputy, though his experience dictated differently. His physical features fell short of what one might expect from someone who had been a police officer for so many years. He stood only five-nine. IIe was overweight, a round, portly man, with a jovial attitude. One of the first things Starr did when he reached town was try and locate his friend James Stark. Shock and dismay struck Starr when he heard of Stark's suicide. That was when he met Tina. She couldn't hide her excitement about meeting someone who had worked with her dad. After the first meeting between the two, a strong friendship began to form.

Hanson forced a smile, asking, "Do you know if anyone has informed Zeke's wife on what is going on here?"

Replying, Starr's voice couldn't hide his concern.

"I really don't know, Sheriff. I hope not. I would prefer Tina be told by one of us rather than hearing it from a neighbor or on a TV news report."

Hanson put his hand on Starr's shoulder, saying quietly, "I know you are a good friend of Tina's. Maybe she would handle the bad news better if she heard it directly from you?"

Starr nodded his head in agreement. "Thanks, Sheriff. Tina's really been depressed lately. This situation is not going to help any. We have to get her husband out of there in one piece. I don't think she could handle any more sadness in her life."

Hanson knew the tragic story about Tina's father and that Starr, who was ten years older than Tina, had became a brother figure in her eyes, a link to her father's past. She would sit for hours listening to Starr's stories of his days on the force in Detroit. It was a strange friendship in one sense but one Bill Starr cherished.

Hanson knew that Tina's unhappiness stemmed from her failure to have a child. It drew her into a deep state of depression. Zeke felt as if he would lose his mind from worrying. He didn't know what to do. Zeke, not one to burden his friends with his problems, felt he had no other choice in this situation. He confided in Hanson, not for advice but for a sympathetic ear. From what Zeke had told him, Hanson knew Tina was on the edge and this wasn't going to help matters.

Hanson took his hand off Starr's shoulder. Firmly but still in a quiet voice Hanson said, "Bill, make sure she doesn't attempt to come down here. The last thing I'm going to need is a hysterical woman, on top of everything else that is going on here."

"I will do my best, Sheriff."

Starr turned and walked away, heading toward his car.

Hanson watched as Starr slid into his car and drove off. The sheriff didn't envy his deputy for what he had to do. Facing a loved one with this type of news would be a special hell of its own.

Bill Starr started the engine of his patrol car, pulling out of the back parking lot onto the suddenly crowded streets of his town. His memories began bursting in his mind. Faster the thoughts from the past raced through the caverns of his mind, getting stronger as he headed toward Tina's home.

Jane Starr stood with her arms folded as her husband put on his coat. He could see the anger in her eyes as she tried to reason with him.

"Bill, I'm telling you that woman is nothing but trouble. Every time she gets depressed she calls you. Why doesn't she call her own husband? That should be his job, not yours."

Starr paused at the front door and glared at his wife. Shaking his head, he fought back his anger and explained himself.

"Jane, Tina has gone through a lot lately. Her father was there for me when I was on the force. Where has your compassion gone? For Christ sakes, you knew her father; the man committed suicide. I hope to God if anything happened to me someone would be there to comfort you."

Tears rolled down Jane's face as she blurted out, "I want you here to comfort me. It seems that all you do anymore is go over to that woman's house. If I didn't know better, I'd think you had a thing for her."

Starr exploded with anger.

"Damn it, where is your compassion? Can't I care about someone without you thinking I'm fucking them?"

Tears ran down Jane's face as she said in a sobbing voice, "Bill, I love you, but when I see you with that woman it hurts. She's using you and you are blind to that fact."

Starr threw his arms up in the air in disgust as he yelled back, "Jane, stop acting like a jealous fool! I have no romantic feelings for Tina. I'm just a friend, nothing more."

Jane's anger cut through her tears as she screamed back, "I swear, Bill, this bitch is going to end up destroying both of our lives! Call her, tell her to tell her problems to her own husband and leave mine alone."

Starr opened the door and yelled back as he walked out the door, "Grow up, Jane, and learn to give me some credit! I do know what I'm doing. I'll see you tonight." Starr slammed the door behind him.

Starr cringed at the last conversation he and his wife had had. She hadn't talked to him for two days because of their fight. He wondered out loud as he drove to Tina's home, "Why can't my wife understand the hell this girl is going through? Christ, now I have to spring this news on her."

Starr let out a heavy sigh as he whispered, "I'll be there for you, Tina."

Starr turned down the road that led to Tina's home.

7

Hanson sat in his patrol car and stared at the back door of the Golden Aces. Pain filled his heart as he thought about his best friend being held hostage by the bastard inside. What made Hanson feel worst was his helplessness. He knew that he wasn't properly trained to handle this type of situation but it wasn't supposed to happen in this town. The people who lived in this town had never experienced any type of violence except from TV or the out-of-town newspapers. Most tourists who visited Barnsville thought of the citizens as naive dreamers who could never handle the real world. To Hanson's dismay, today would prove those people either right or wrong.

Hanson's thoughts were rudely interrupted. A horn blared behind him. He turned quickly to see who it was. A state trooper car pulled up next to his and stopped. A tall figure stepped out of the car. The man put on a brimmed hat and walked over to where Hanson stood and stopped directly in front of the sheriff, extended his hands, and introduced himself.

"Good morning. I'm Captain David Overstreet. I'm with the state police. Your office requested our assistance on this case. I gather from the persistence of the lady who kept calling our office it's a life-and-death situation?"

Hanson reached out and gripped the trooper's hand. The two men shook hands. Hanson released his grip and replied, "I'm Sheriff Bob Hanson, and yes, Captain, as Marge told your office, it is very serious. We have a hostage situation. It appears to be a lone gunman. I have to assume he is not from this area. From what little I have talked with him I would judge by his accent that he is black."

Overstreet turned away from Hanson and stared at the building where Riley's life hung by a thread. The word *hostage* made Overstreet cringe. Overstreet knew that one small mistake could cost the lives of too many people. He then asked without looking away from the building, "Has he made any demands yet?"

Hanson nodded as he replied, "Yes. He wants a car, money, and safe passage out of our town."

Hanson paused to release a sigh, then added, "He said he wants his answer within the hour. I was just getting ready to call him again."

Overstreet ignored the last statement Hanson made and turned toward him. The trooper's square jaw was a very distinguishing feature about him; his heavy bushy eyebrows rose ever so slightly as he inquired, "Have you checked the area around here for any cars that don't belong?"

Hanson shook his head no.

Overstreet continued with his questions, his voice becoming slightly harsh.

"If you feel he is not from this area, did it cross your mind how he might have gotten here?"

Hanson quickly defended himself as he snapped back, "I asked if any strange cars were spotted in the lot. The employees here said no."

Overstreet's tone became a scolding one as he asked, "I am sure you had your office check to see if there were any stolen cars reported in the immediate area?"

Again all Hanson could do was shake his head no.

The irritation grew in Overstreet's voice.

"Sheriff? How do you suppose this man planned to escape after he robbed this restaurant?"

Overstreet glared at Hanson, waiting for a reply, but got none. Overstreet continued with his tongue-lashing of the young sheriff.

"Did you feel he might decide to go on foot?"

Again Overstreet paused to allow Hanson to defend his actions; again Hanson remained silent. Overstreet went on lecturing.

"He must have a car or a bike, something, stashed in this area. I would advise you to call your station to see if there were any cars reported stolen in the last twenty-four hours. Then I would like you to instruct your deputies to fan out and check a six-block radius for any cars, trucks, anything that doesn't belong here."

Overstreet paused as he glanced into the wooded area behind the restaurant. Pointing to the woods, he added. "My men will search this wooded area. Sheriff, we need an edge. If we find the vehicle he drove we can hopefully lift prints from it, find out who we are dealing with and what chances our hostage might realistically have of surviving."

Overstreet turned his attention back to Hanson, his tone becoming a bit more fatherly as he scolded, "That is proper procedure, Sheriff. Taking the time to cover all possibilities may just save that hostage's life."

Hanson's face turned beet red. His anger boiled inside him. Fighting hard not to show his emotions, Hanson replied calmly to the state trooper, "My first responsibility, Captain, is the safety of the townspeople. I had to seal off the back entrance so no innocent bystander would wander back here. I would love to follow all those fancy police procedures you just spouted off, but I don't have the manpower. Not to do it the proper way. I have only three damn squad cars and six deputies. If you noticed when you pulled in the driveway, half the town here is watching the events that are going on. I need most of my men just to keep them away from this area. I also had to send one of my men to inform the hostage's wife of what is going on here."

Hanson paused to see if Overstreet would give him a response; he gave none. Hanson continued, his anger obvious as he spoke.

"My office requested help because this town has never experienced this type of violent crime. You are here to assist me, not ridicule me."

Hanson stopped to take a breath, then finished, "I do agree with you: he must have some type of transportation stashed around here. You have your men handle crowd control. That will free up my deputies to search the woods and town for the man's car. In the meantime, I have a cellular phone on the front seat of my car. I'm going to get ready to contact him again. To make sure that I don't screw up precious police procedures again, would you prefer to talk to him?"

Overstreet, a true professional, felt all of the sheriff's reasons for not checking the obvious things he had mentioned were nothing more than lame excuses. The trooper hated working with small-town sheriffs. To him, their ignorance was more dangerous than a criminal's gun. You can prepare for a criminal to shoot, but you never know what stupid things ignorance will do. Overstreet realized he needed to keep a harmonious working relationship with this man. He must soothe the sheriff's petty feelings. Overstreet attempted to apologize, even though he knew he had said the proper things to Hanson.

"Sorry, Sheriff, sometimes I do get carried away with certain things. I am sure you are doing the best you can with the limited manpower at your disposal. I also know experience is the best teacher."

Overstreet took off his hat and ran his fingers through his hair as he added, "Sheriff, I've been dealing with this all my life and still make mistakes. I guess at times I can come across pretty strong. I know you did the best you could with your experience in these matters."

Hanson still felt the anger burning inside him but remained silent. Overstreet went on trying hard to win the sheriff over.

"I mean that, Sheriff. Nothing in the world means more than experience."

Hanson rolled his eyes as he snapped back, "Great! Now all I need to do is make sure we have more violence in Barnsville and I will be able to handle these types of incidents more professionally. Is that what you're telling me?"

Overstreet released a heavy sigh, then replied in a low voice, "That's not what I meant. Let's just drop the whole thing. I'm sorry for the tone of my voice earlier."

Hanson didn't reply. Instead he glanced over at the back door of the Golden Aces.

Overstreet's eyes did the same. Overstreet then said in a monotone voice, "Go ahead and call our friend in there and see what type of information you can get on him."

Overstreet turned and pointed to the wooded area as he added, "I have three more cars in front helping your deputies with crowd control. I already have some of my men searching the surrounding area for his vehicle."

Hanson's anger still burned inside him, despite Overstreet's apology. The trooper had a touch of arrogance about him that Hanson didn't like. Overstreet appeared to have a Gestapo attitude about him. Hanson knew that Overstreet saw everything in black and white. He had no gray areas, no compassion in his heart. Overstreet mentally appeared only to be eager to "get the job done," which Hanson knew to be right, unless it might mean a human life was lost in the process. Hanson replied in a callous voice, "Let's head back to my car. That's where the phone is."

Hanson didn't wait for Overstreet to reply but moved past him and walked toward his car. Hanson glanced behind him and saw Overstreet following him. He was matching Hanson step-for-step in a military fashion. Hanson began to get a strange feeling as if he were in a military parade. Left, right, left, right, Overstreet marched in step behind Hanson, who stopped as he reached his car, Overstreet right behind him, standing rigid, waiting for Hanson's next move. Neither man said a word. The friction in the air reached a high intensity. Hanson reached in his front window and picked up the phone lying on his seat. Pausing, he turned around and faced Overstreet who now hovered over him. Hanson could no longer contain his anger. The silence broke as he warned Overstreet, "Before we go any further, captain, we might as well clear the air so we both know where we stand. If you ever talk to me like I'm some kind of idiot again, I will knock you on your pompous ass."

Overstreet gave Hanson a sly grin, not commenting on what the sheriff had said.

Hanson ignored Overstreet's sarcastic grin, adding, "This is my town, Captain, and the safety of the citizens that live here is my first responsibility. I may be ignorant of all the procedures that you have been taught. I may even make a dozen mistakes in your eyes before this is all over, but I swear to you if I think you are endangering Zeke's life in any way I will pull you right off this case. Do I make myself clear?"

Overstreet's grin vanished. His tone of voice grew harsh as he snapped back, "Make your call, Sheriff. Save your threats for the real problem inside that building."

Hanson began to say something back but stopped. Overstreet turned away from the sheriff and stared at the back door of the Golden Aces. Hanson's palms began sweating as he held the phone in his hands. He realized what he was really doing, stalling, stalling so as not to deal with the real problem: a gunman holding his best friend one hundred yards away and him helpless to do anything about it. Hanson continued to stare at the phone, trying to think of the right words to use to a madman. What if he said the wrong words and this bastard just started shooting? How could Hanson live with the guilt? Hanson's troubled thoughts ended as Overstreet's voice rang in his ear in a harsh whisper.

"Damn it, what are you waiting for? Make the call, Sheriff, or would you rather I did it."

Hanson wanted to hand the phone to Overstreet and let the burden ride on his shoulders but knew he couldn't do that. Instead, he shook his head no. Holding up the phone, he reached into his shirt pocket and took out a small piece of paper that had the restaurant's number on it. Slowly he dialed the number. A slight chill ran up Hanson's spine as he heard the ringing on the other end. Reality began to seep through his body. Hanson began to tremble slightly. He knew he was not going to be talking to a ten-year-old boy about swiping a candy bar from a store. He now would be dealing with an element of crime that he only knew existed because of television and the newspapers. He now would be bartering for a friend's life. One mistake and Zeke Riley could wind up dead. Hanson began to realize that his anger at the state trooper was only a facade to cover up his fear building inside him, the fear that grew more with each ring of the phone on the other end. It seemed to ring forever. Each ring made Hanson's heart beat just a bit faster. Taking a deep breath, Hanson prepared to deal with the bastard inside the Golden Aces.

8

Zeke sat on the cold tile floor. He pushed himself as far as he could go into a corner of the room, watching his abductor closely as the man paced back and forth in front of the phone. Like a caged animal the man paced back and forth. Zeke knew the man's patience was growing thin. At any moment the man's temper could explode. Zeke knew his fate was at the mercy of a madman. His fear stabbed painfully at his heart. Closing his eyes, he tried to fight off the terrified feelings inside him, battling with reality, forcing himself to remember happier times in his life before this nightmare began. He searched through his memories for the perfect time to travel to, voiding out the present, allowing his mind to drift back into the past, to forget the madness of the moment. Further and further back he allowed his mind to drift.

"Zeke, what is so important that you had me sneak out of the house at three o'clock in the morning? If my father finds me out here at this hour he will kill me and you."

Tina stood with her arms folded, wearing a dark blue robe that sparkled slightly in the moonlight. She had sneaked out of her home when Zeke called her and told her to meet him in front of her home. Zeke had urged her to hurry and explained to her it was a matter of life or death. Now she stood in front of him, arms folded and a worried look on her face. Zeke felt like a complete idiot for being so melodramatic. Forcing a weak smile, he took Tina's hand and pulled her gently toward him.

"Tina, I have been trying to tell you something all day. I couldn't find the courage till now to talk to you about it."

Tina quickly interrupted him, "Zeke, it is three in the morning. Couldn't you have found the courage for this speech, oh say, around seven P.M. or so?"

Zeke snapped back, his voice losing its shyness, "Tina, please, this is important. Allow me to at least finish a sentence."

71

Zeke stopped to see if Tina would interrupt him again. She smiled and said nothing. Zeke continued.

"Tina, we have been seeing each other for some time now. I think we both have had a lot of good times together. I have a good-paying job, with a secure future."

Tina snapped impatiently, "Zeke, will you please tell me what you are trying to say? Before my father finds out I'm standing outside in a robe in the middle of the night."

Embarrassed, Zeke spoke faster: "OK, Tina, but please give me a break. This isn't easy to just spit out."

Tina's deep blue eyes began showing some concern at the strange way Zeke was acting. She stared hard at him and asked, "Are you trying to break up with me, Zeke? Is that what you are trying to do, end our relationship after all these years?"

Zeke smiled, pulling Tina tightly up against his body. Kissing her gently, he whispered, "Tina, I love you. I want you to marry me."

Tina's eyes widened with excitement as she nervously asked, "Oh, my God Zeke, what did you say?"

Zeke started laughing as he repeated, "I said I love you. I want you to marry me."

Tina let out a shriek that echoed through the night air. Grabbing Zeke, she hugged and kissed him as she repeated her reply.

"Yes. Yes. Yes."

Zeke's happy visions were shattered by the black man's stern voice.

"You, stop your fucking crying and come here!"

Zeke struggled to get to his feet. He felt like weights lay on his shoulders as he dragged his feet to walk to where the black man stood. Finally standing in front of his abductor, Zeke trembled as he kept his eyes glued to the floor.

The black man asked gruffly, "Did your mama give you a name?"

Zeke didn't raise his eyes as he replied, "Zeke, Zeke Riley."

The black man jumped back on the prep table that was behind him. He reached over and grabbed a coffee cup and took a sip from it as he studied the man in front of him. Quietly he said, "Hmm, well, my name is Harlen."

Zeke, still staring at the floor, stood mute.

Harlen chuckled as he repeated Zeke's name, "Zeke, that is a strange name. Why would anyone saddle their kid with a name like that?"

Zeke raised his eyes slowly. He saw the man smiling. Half of his teeth were missing. The man's smile glowed with evil. Zeke tried to remain calm as he replied.

"My parents named me after my great-grandfather. He helped settle this town. But I did get teased quite a bit as a kid. Children can be cruel, but I have learned to become proud of my name and its heritage."

Harlen folded his arms. His smile disappeared. A harsh and cold tone rippled through his words.

"You poor baby. They teased you as a child because of your name? Life must have been a bitch!"

Harlen unfolded his arms. He ran his hand over the scars on his face as he continued.

"They teased you because of your silly ass name? Well, I got tormented because of these lovely scars on my face. Aren't they beautiful? Would you like to know how I got them?"

Zeke didn't dare answer.

Harlen raved on.

"From my father. Good old Dad. Do you know why? Because I spilled his fucking beer. I broke his precious bottle of beer on the floor. It shattered into tiny pieces. My dad went nuts. He began to hit me, over and over again. I fell to the floor and he grabbed the back of my neck and wiped my face in the broken glass and beer. My mom rushed me to the hospital. I spent hours on the operating table. The doctors didn't think I would live. I did, though. Do you know how old I was, Zeke?" Harlen didn't wait for Zeke to guess. "Eight fucking years old. Do you want to know what they did to my old man? Not one damn thing. Not even a warning."

Harlen paused, still rubbing the scars on his face. His voice grew softer as he added, "I took care of it myself Zeke. When I got older I put a bullet in his fucking skull."

Zeke found himself backing away from where Harlen sat. The rage flowed through the black man. Zeke now knew for sure his abductor was insane. Zeke trembled as he said, "I'm sorry, sir. I didn't mean to stir up any painful memories."

Harlen's eyes bore through Zeke. His words burned with anger as he shouted, "Shove your fucking sympathy! I don't want or need it. Especially from you. A sniffling middle-class coward."

Harlen again smiled, then added, "The only reason I'm telling you this, boy, is so you realize I won't think twice about blowing your fucking head off. Do you believe me, Zeke? It's very important to me that you know I won't hesitate to blow your fucking head off."

Zeke wanted to vomit as the fear pounded in the pit of his stomach. Harlen laughed wickedly as he could see the terror ooze from Zeke. Harlen then harshly added to his gruesome story, "When I pulled my gun on my old man, do you know what he did? He spit in my face. He knew he was going to die. The bastard wouldn't give me the satisfaction of showing any fear. They call that having balls. Something you seem to lack, Zeke!"

Harlen waited for Zeke to argue with him. Zeke didn't. He backed up to the corner and sat back down on the tile floor. Once again avoiding eye contact with Harlen, not wanting to feel the man's wrath again, instead Zeke chose a tile to maintain his concentration on. Harlen let out a disgusted grunt and picked up his coffee and gulped the remaining bit down. The kitchen now filled with silence, Zeke was at one end staring at the tile floor, Harlen at the other glaring at the phone, trying to will it to ring. Harlen jumped as the sudden ringing of the phone startled him. He bounced off the table, grabbing his gun, and headed to the phone. Quickly he picked it up and with his eyes fixed on Zeke in the corner he spoke.

"It is about time, Sheriff. I thought maybe you forgot all about me and your friend in here."

Hanson replied quickly, hitting the button for the speaker so Overstreet could hear, "I didn't forget about you. Why not allow your hostage to leave? Then we can discuss all of your needs."

Harlen began cruel laughter.

"Perfect, Sheriff. I will turn over my hostage and you and all your buddies will drop your guns. Then I will walk out and be allowed to leave like nothing ever happened, right? You must think I am fucking stupid, Sheriff! If you want your friend in here to live, you will start listening. Trust me when I tell you I will put a bullet right between his eyes. Now do you want to talk or shall I prove to you I am a man of my word?"

Hanson turned to Overstreet. The trooper remained calm as he quietly instructed Hanson, "Talk to him, Sheriff. We need time; stall for time."

Hanson nodded, then went on with his conversation with Harlen.

"I'm ready to talk. Do you have a name I can call you?"

Laughter came from the other end of the line, followed by a sarcastic reply.

"I'm sure you have many names you would like to call me. Take your pick; I'm not fussy."

Hanson ignored Harlen's sarcasm.

"Very well. What is it that you will need to release your hostage?"

Harlen let out a disgusted grunt and said in an angry voice, "They haven't changed, Sheriff. Except now I know exactly how much money I will need. So get a pencil or crayon and write this down so there is no mistake in what I want."

Harlen paused for a moment. He glanced over at Zeke, who still was staring at the floor. Harlen continued with his demands.

"First, a car that will drive me out of this town. Second, I want a hundred thousand dollars in cash. Third, safe passage out of this town. When these three small demands are made I will release dear old Zeke."

Hanson gasped as he replied, "That is a lot of money. We don't have that kind of money in this town. Demands like that are going to take time. I need to come up with a way to raise that kind of money; it might as well be a million dollars."

Harlen retorted calmly, "Sorry, Sheriff, it seems you really have a problem, but I won't take credit cards. Cash only, and you have two hours to meet my demands."

Overstreet tapped Hanson on the shoulder to get his attention. Hanson turned around in the hope that Overstreet had an answer.

Overstreet quietly said, "Stall; tell him you need more time."

Hanson nodded. He knew that it wouldn't be just a stall tactic; it would be the truth. Barnsville didn't have that much cash in its entire town limits. Hanson's voice showed a trace of panic as he pleaded with Harlen, "I must have more time than two hours. You must believe me when I tell you this town does not have that type of cash. I will have to try and arrange for an outside source to get that amount of money. I will agree with all your terms, but I need more time."

Hanson glanced back at Overstreet to see if he had anything to add. The big state trooper remained mute. Hanson pleaded again.

"Listen to me, if I could end this entire ordeal now I would. I am telling you the truth: unless you will take less money I will need more time."

Harlen hissed through his teeth, then in a sarcastic voice replied, "I won't take a penny less, Sheriff. I figure you and this town has inconvenienced me long enough. I think two hours is more than enough time. You are trying to stall, Sheriff, and that is going to get your friend here fucking dead."

Hanson's voice rose in anger and panic as he shouted back, "Damn it! I am not stalling. We don't have that kind of money in this town. Zeke is a friend of mine. I wouldn't play games with his life. I am telling you the truth when I say I need more time."

Overstreet broke his silence as he leaned over and gruffly whispered in Hanson's ear, "Damn it, Sheriff. Don't let him know how important his hostage is to you. For Christ sake, he might make his demands for less time now."

Hanson ignored Overstreet's comment and waited for Harlen's reply.

The long pause broke as Harlen calmly replied, "Christ, Sheriff, I must be getting soft. Tell you what I'm going to do for you. To show you how much I like this fucking town I'm going to give you six hours, Sheriff. Not one minute more, and if you're fucking with me, my buddy Zeke and me will die."

Harlen hung up the phone. He gave Zeke a toothless smile and walked back over to the prep table, hopped back on, and made himself comfortable. Harlen then reached into his shirt pocket and pulled out a crumpled pack of cigarettes, scrounged the last one in the pack and shoved it in his mouth. Still grinning at Zeke, Harlen reached into his pants pocket and pulled out a pack of matches and lit the cigarette. He took a deep drag on it, inhaling a mouthful of smoke. Slowly he exhaled it in the direction of Zeke.

"It should be over soon. One way or another."

Zeke looked up at Harlen. His curiosity getting the better of him, he asked cautiously, "Why me? Why did you choose this place to rob? How did you know what time I would come into work this morning?"

Harlen took another drag from his cigarette and blew the white smoke in the air, forming small circles of smoke for his amusement. He then crushed the butt on the prep table. Smiling his toothless smile, he asked, "Why should I tell you anything?"

Zeke's voice trailed off as he replied, "You don't have to tell me a thing if you don't want to. I'm sorry; it's not that important anyway. Please forget I even asked. I will just be quiet."

Harlen burst into wicked laughter as he waved his gun at Zeke, who found himself cringing, and throwing up his arms as if he could block any bullets that flew his way.

Harlen's laughter stopped. His voice grew serious as he snapped at Zeke, "Relax! I am not going to shoot you, not yet anyway."

Harlen glanced back at the phone, then turned his attention back to Zeke.

"I needed money. I chose this place because it looks like the only building here which would have any money. You just happened to pull in before I had a chance to break in. Which surprised me. I thought nothing in this shoe box of a town opened till midmorning. My specialty is break-ins, not armed robbery, but as you can see, I am a quick learner."

Harlen paused. He could see from Zeke's facial expression that he didn't believe everything Harlen had said. Harlen smiled, asking in a tone of mock concern, "Is there something I said that disturbs you?"

Zeke looked away, not wanting to look into the man's eyes.

Harlen's voice grew louder.

"I asked you a question, asshole!"

Zeke wished he never had brought up the subject. The anger in his abductor's voice became fierce. Zeke quietly and very deliberately replied, "I had no intention to upset you, sir. I guess I just assumed you knew what time I would reach the restaurant. That you had planned to rob me at gun point."

Chuckling, Harlen said, "I'm glad I shoved a gun in your skull. It sounds like you would have been disappointed if I didn't?"

Zeke shook his head no as he nervously answered, "No, of course not. I don't know what I'm trying to say. Please let's just forget this conversation."

The anger grew in Harlen's voice as he snapped back, "I give the fucking orders here. Not you, asshole."

Harlen sneered and shouted out his words: "Now let's see if I can guess what the little fucker was trying to say!"

Harlen scratched his gun gently on his chin. Smiling, he said in a sarcastic voice, "I think what you are trying to say is that I appear to more of a fucking gun-wielding madman instead of a quiet, peaceful safecracker?"

Zeke didn't reply.

Harlen's rage turned into laughter. He jumped off the prep table and knelt down where Zeke was sitting. Staring into Zeke's terrified eyes, he asked, "I think, asshole, you're paying me a compliment? If not, are you trying to fucking insult me?"

Zeke forced himself to look into his abductors' eyes. Carefully he chose his words as he answered, "I would not insult you, but from the little you have told me about yourself, I would picture you taking what you want by any means available."

Harlen stood straight up. He stared down at Zeke not saying a word. Moving away from him and taking his familiar spot on the prep table, Harlen continued to stare at Zeke coldly. The silence continued for a few more seconds.

Harlen finally broke the quiet hush as he spit out his angry reply, "You don't know shit about me. All you see is a black man and you assumed the rest. I have lived in hell all my life. I have had to fight for everything in my life just to survive. What about you, Mr. Middle-Class White Man? Has your life been a complete struggle? Of course it has. I bet you are tortured with the burden of making house payments on your big home. Hell, you even told me of the cruel children you had to face who teased you unmercifully because of your name. Christ, I'm just a fucking insensitive bastard; your life must be a fucking nightmare."

Harlen chuckled at his own remarks. His voice then dropped to a harsh whisper.

"You and people like you is what created me. This society is trying to force us to live in complete poverty. Being black in this country is a curse. We are a proud people, but you and others like you failed to see that. Instead you treat us like a deadly plague."

Zeke forgot his fears for a moment as he began to argue with Harlen.

"I agree with you that most black people don't receive the same breaks as whites, but we did not create you. It was not a white man who gave you those scars."

Harlen slammed his fist down on the prep table as he screamed, "The hell it wasn't! My dad wanted better for us, but white society would not allow that. Why the fuck am I even bothering talking to you anyway? I don't need to stand here and explain myself to you or any other fucker in this world. Fuck it! Maybe you should know more about me. More than likely we both are going to fucking die today!"

Harlen closed his eyes and slammed his fist hard again as he screamed even louder this time.

"My father gave up! He tried booze and drugs to hide his pain. Believe me when I tell you I feel you and others like you helped my father put these scars on my face. In fact, I blame you assholes more than him every time I look in the fucking mirror."

Harlen held up his gun and coldly added, "Just like I know you might as well have pulled the fucking trigger of the gun that I used to kill the bastard."

Despite the raging anger in his abductor's voice Zeke continued to debate him, not knowing how he found the sudden surge of courage.

"You are doing what you accused me of. You are stereotyping all whites. I feel our two races have came a long way in gaining peace and harmony among us."

Harlen spit on the floor as he answered in a angry tone, "Fuck your peace and harmony. Give us the damn right to have equality. We are not children you try to appease with meaningless words. Talking like that make you sleep better at night, asshole?"

Harlen waved his gun in the air as he ranted on.

"You fucking bleeding hearts make me sick. You offer laws to tell us we even exist. What kind of insanity is that? You may not have put these scars on my face, but the ones I bear in my soul are from you and people like you."

Zeke knew this conversation was getting out of control. No matter what he said, Harlen would twist it to fit his anger. Harlen raged on, his words came out as if this argument had been spoken many times in his life.

"Tell me, Zeke, how many black families live in this precious little town of yours?"

Zeke hesitated before he replied, "None."

Zeke quickly added, trying to sound convincing as he did, "They would be welcomed if they did want to move here. I can honestly say that we believe in equal rights in the town of Barnsville."

Harlen chuckled as he shook his head.

"Your generosity is amazing. If I were you, though, I would stick to what suits you best. Being a coward, you sure in the hell are not a spokesman."

Zeke snapped back quickly, not realizing the anger that had seeped in his voice, "Listen, just because I don't want to die does not make me a coward. I have a wife I love, dreams that I desperately want to fulfill. Just because you look at death as a badge of honor doesn't mean everyone should. From what I can see, you are more afraid of living than I am of dying."

Harlen vaulted off the table, rage burning in his eyes.

Zeke realized now he had made a mistake in saying what he felt.

Harlen grabbed Zeke by the collar of his shirt and shoved his gun into Zeke's ear, growling fiercely, "You are good at making speeches. Why don't we find out how good you are at dying?"

Harlen cocked the hammer of the gun back. The sound vibrated through Zeke's entire body.

Zeke swallowed hard, trying to keep back the fear that mounted furiously inside him.

Harlen eased the hammer back into a safe position, removing the gun slowly, saying as he did, "Keep your fucking observations to yourself. You might live a hell of a lot longer that way."

Harlen moved away from Zeke and hopped back on the prep table.

Zeke let out a sigh of relief. He glanced over at Harlen sitting on the table. Harlen's cold eyes just stared at Zeke. It appeared Harlen wanted to see through Zeke's soul to steal that from him, too. Zeke looked away from Harlen and, still trembling, he gazed down at the tile that had become a safe haven from Harlen's evil glare.

Harlen's rage began to subside. Though he hated to admit it, some of what Zeke had said was true. Harlen Jones feared life more than death. Harlen's thoughts began to run wildly. Like a roller

80

coaster times of his highs and lows in life raced in his mind, not showing any mercy as to what events appeared. Suddenly a memory that Harlen reserved only for his sleepless nights danced before him, a nightmare Harlen fought hard to keep from surfacing, but he failed. Traces of tears ran slowly down the black mans face as his mind forced him to relive his past.

9

Young Harlen Jones leaned up against the wire fencing in front of his father's home. Next to Harlen was his friend Jimmy Washington. Both boys stared intensely at the red-brick home in front of them. Jimmy began biting his lower lip, fighting hard not to show how scared he really was. Harlen with a blank stare on his face never took his eyes off the home in front of him.

Jimmy, still looking around, asked nervously, "Harlen, are you sure you really want to do this, man? Maybe we should put a hit on the fucker? Don't you think that would be the way to do it? Shit, then you could go somewhere and have an alibi. What do you think, man?"

Harlen turned and stared at his friend. Jimmy Washington stood about five feet, four inches, tall. His bony body had a nervous twitch to it. Jimmy always appeared to be trying to start some new type of dance step. He glanced back at the house, then at Harlen.

"Man, I think you should think this over. You're talking about smoking your old man, you know. Come on; I know some brothers who will do this for hardly any money, man. Talk to me, man."

Harlen glared at Jimmy. His voice had a cruelty about it as he replied, "If you don't have the stomach for this then take off. The last thing I need right now is a fucking pussy with me."

Jimmy started moving his feet as if he were dancing as he snapped back, "Hey, man, I'm no pussy. I'll blow the motherfucker away myself. I just want to make sure you aren't having second thoughts. The man is your blood."

Harlen slowly moved his hand across the rigid scars on his face, wincing each time he felt the jagged edges touch his fingers. Glaring down at Jimmy, Harlen quietly and coldly replied, "The bastard is going to die for what he did to me. So either you are with me or you're not. I don't need no fucking sermon from you."

Jimmy held up his hands, his voice turning high-pitched. He shook his head violently back and fourth as he shouted back at

Harlen, "Chill, man! I'm with you. You're the man. Let's blow this motherfucker away."

A slight smile crossed young Harlen's face. He glanced up and down the street. No one was in sight. Reaching down, he pulled a .45 revolver from his belt.

Jimmy whistled through his teeth, "Man, where did you get the cannon from?"

Harlen checked to make sure the gun was loaded, then snapped back at Jimmy, "Don't worry about it. The gun is clean; there is no way it can be traced back to us."

Jimmy shook his head as he tried to sound confident as he spoke, "I'm not worried; I'm cool. So how are you going to do it? Are you going to wait till the son of a bitch is asleep to snuff him out?"

Harlen smiled again. A chill ran down Jimmy as Harlen calmly replied, "Hell, no. I want the bastard to see who is ending his miserable life. I want him to go on his knees and beg me to let him live. The motherfucker is going to suffer before he dies. Suffer like I have all these years."

Jimmy glanced down the street. Panic overwhelmed him as he saw a Detroit police car slowly heading their way.

"Hide the cannon, man. Cops, Christ, someone must have seen you pull that damn thing out."

Harlen kept his back to the street and calmly shoved the gun back in his belt. He pulled his sweatshirt down to cover it up. Hissing through his teeth, he snapped at his friend, "Relax, Jimmy, or you are going to make them suspicious."

Jimmy's voice couldn't hide his anxiety as the patrol car stopped at the curb.

"They know. Damn it, we are going to fucking jail."

Harlen shot a fierce look at Jimmy as he whispered angrily, "Shut the fuck up, Jimmy, and let me do the talking."

The patrol car pulled up against the curb. Harlen and Jimmy didn't turn around. Jimmy could feel his heart racing as he tried to remain calm. Harlen just glared at the brick home in front of him. Jimmy jumped forward as he heard the voice behind him.

"What are you boys waiting for?"

Harlen turned around in the direction the voice came from. A blond man leaned out of the window of the patrol car, a stern look on his face.

Harlen forced a smile and calmly replied, "Nothing, sir. I live here. My dad is ticked off at me and I'm debating whether or not to go in and face the music."

The cop stared at Harlen, then asked, "What is your name, son?"

Jimmy twitched nervously, avoiding looking at the blond cop.

Harlen remained calm as he replied, "Harlen, Harlen Jones. You can come in with me if you think I'm lying."

Jimmy's body began twitching more than normal as he watched the blond cop staring at Harlen. Jimmy knew the cop was sizing up Harlen, wondering if he should believe him or not.

The cop finally replied, still in his stern voice, "That won't be necessary, son, but I don't want you two boys standing out on the street. Go on in the house. I'm sure your father is not going to be as harsh as you think."

Harlen smiled widely as he replied, "Yes, sir, and you are probably right. My dad has more than likely already forgot what he was mad about."

Harlen knew the cop couldn't take his eyes off the hideous scars on his face. Harlen wanted to take out his gun and blow the cop's eyes out so he wouldn't have to worry about seeing the scars. Instead, Harlen just smiled. The cop said something to his partner and pulled away from the curb. Harlen kept smiling till the patrol car disappeared down the street. He then whispered, "Assholes."

Jimmy bit down on his lip hard, his eyes darting up and down the street. His voice reached a nervous high pitch as he asked, "We are going to wait on killing him, ain't we?"

Harlen spit out his answer as he turned back toward his father's house.

"Hell, no. Why should we?"

Jimmy rolled his eyes in disbelief. Then he put his hands on Harlen's shoulder as he replied, "The cops, man, they ain't stupid. They are going to know it was us. It's not like your face is something somebody wouldn't remember."

Harlen reached out and grabbed Jimmy by the throat and squeezed hard as he sneered, "What the fuck do you mean by that?"

Jimmy's face began turning blue as he gasped for breath. His hands fell from Harlen's shoulder. Coughing, Jimmy struggled to reply.

"Sorry, man. Please, you're killing me."

Harlen let go of his grip. Jimmy began rubbing his neck as he backed away from Harlen.

"Man, you're crazy. I don't want any part of this."

Harlen smiled as he glared at his friend. There was no emotion in his voice as he said, "Then get the fuck out of here, you stinking coward. If I see your face again I'll blow it off."

Jimmy didn't respond to Harlen's threat. Jimmy turned around and began running down the sidewalk.

Harlen screamed at him as he ran away, "Run, you chickenshit! Who needs your ugly ass anyway?"

Harlen turned back toward his father's house. Hate burned inside Harlen as he reached down and patted the gun hiding inside his belt. He looked up and down the streets one more time to make sure no one was watching. He then whispered hoarsely, "Time for you to die, Daddy."

Harlen opened the gate and walked slowly toward the house. He climbed up the concrete steps and stopped at the door. Harlen took a deep breath as he reached out and grabbed hold of the doorknob. He turned it quietly; a grin creased his face. The door opened. Like always, his dad had not locked it. Harlen pushed the door farther open, fighting to stay quiet. In front of him sat his father, he sat with his back to Harlen. His father sat there holding in one hand a beer, in the other a lit cigarette. Harlen crept up behind him, keeping his hand resting on the handle of his gun. Stopping, he coldly called out to his father. "Turn around, Dad! It is your loving son."

Harlen's father's head turned quickly to the sound of his son's voice. When he saw Harlen standing behind him he leaped out of his chair shouting, "I thought I told you to keep your black ass out of my house! Get out of here before I kick the shit out of you!"

Harlen stood perfectly still, the smile still creasing on his face. His father became infuriated. He began waving his arms in the air, shouting louder.

"What are you grinning at you fucking freak? I told you to get your motherfucking ass out!" Clenching his fist, he began to walk toward Harlen but stopped in his tracks.

Harlen pulled out his gun, holding it firmly in both hands. He aimed it at his father's head. The smile left, replaced with a sneer.

"I want you to beg for your life, you lousy bastard. Come on; beg the freak to let you live!"

Harlen's father stared at his son and just stood there, showing no emotions. His defiance made Harlen feel uneasy. He screamed at his father, "Beg, damn you, and maybe I will let you live! I mean it, you bastard! I know how to use this fucking gun and I will if you don't start begging now!"

His father had a strange grin on his face. He began laughing as he spit out his words.

"Go ahead and shoot. I'd consider it a favor."

Harlen's hands began to tremble. Again he repeated his warning to his father.

"I'm not bluffing. I will shoot you. Now beg, you bastard, or die!"

Harlen's father spit at his son as he snarled out his words.

"Fuck you, freak!"

Harlen cocked back the hammer and calmly said, "Beg and I will leave. You never will have to see this freak again. I'm not bluffing. If you taught me anything, it was to truly hate."

Harlen's father took a drink of his beer. A strange softness came into his voice as he replied, "I taught you more than that, boy. I taught you how to survive in this fucked-up world. I made you lose those silly ass dreams of being a Martin Luther King. I showed you what life for people like us really is."

Harlen kept the gun pointed at his father but now was wishing he had run with Jimmy. His words came out with a mixture of tears and pain.

"I could have made a difference. Even the reverend thought I could make a difference. He told me I had a way with words."

Harlen's father began laughing as he mocked his son, "Fucking idiot, you think your words are going to feed you? I believed like you and what did it get me? Fucked right up the ass. Fuck you; fuck the reverend; fuck this whole stinking world."

The rage came back inside Harlen as he shouted, waving the gun frantically in front of him, his voice showing a hint of panic in it.

"Get on your knees and beg for your life! I'm not going to ask you again. Either beg, you bastard, or die. I'll give you a choice, something you didn't give me."

86

Harlen's father took another drink of his beer, then crushed the can and tossed it on the floor as he shouted, "Fuck you!"

Those were the last words Harlen ever heard from his father. He pulled the trigger twice. The bullets struck his father, one in the chest, the other in the head.

The vision slowly faded out of Harlen's mind. A few tears trickled down his cheek. Wiping his eyes, he looked over at the man huddling in the corner. Harlen vented his anguish at Zeke.

"I will kill you if my demands are not met. Then all those fancy dreams you spouted off about fulfilling will burn in hell along with mine."

Harlen paused to see if Zeke would reply. He didn't. Harlen glanced up at the clock on the wall. He knew there was nothing he could do now but wait and hope the visions from his past would stay buried in his mind. The silence felt soothing to his nerves. He knew he could handle death. There was no fear of dying in his mind at all. The visions of his father's bloody body lying on the floor for some strange reason scared Harlen. He didn't know if it was out of guilt or if he really had loved his dad. Whatever it may have been, all Harlen knew was that he wanted it to remain a nightmare for his sleep, not a memory while he was awake. Harlen whispered so Zeke would not hear him, "You should've begged, Dad."

10

Tina stopped her labor. She stared down at the shallow grave she had just dug in her backyard. Wiping the sweat from her forehead, she glanced around. For the first time since she had moved to Barnsville, she felt blessed for not having neighbors. The wind began to pick up quickly. Eerie darkness began forming, casting black shadows across her lawn. Looking up into the skies, Tina could see the black clouds rolling in. Lightning flashed in the distance, followed by the low rumble of thunder. Tina knew speed would be important if she was to beat the storm. Tossing the shovel aside, she hurried back into the house, running through the back door that led into the kitchen. She stopped at the kitchen sink, washing the dirt from her hands. Grabbed a towel hanging on the cupboard, she dried her hands thoroughly. Tossing the towel on the sink, she moved quickly to the dining room. Tina stopped over the body sprawled in the middle of the floor. Bending over, she grabbed Parker's feet. Struggling, she began to drag his body toward the kitchen. She grimaced in pain; her body still ached from the beating Parker had given her earlier. Determined to bury him, she fought off the pain she felt. Using every bit of strength in her body, she dragged his body toward the shallow grave waiting outside for him. Finally she reached the kitchen with Parker's body. Breathing heavily from the exertion she released her grip on Parker's legs to gather more strength. His legs fell with a thud on the floor. Tina moved around the body and headed toward the back door. She propped the door open and surveyed how much farther she would have to drag Parker's body to get to the grave. As she was staring at the grave, a depressing thought entered her mind. Turning back, she looked at Parker's body, realizing the grave she had dug might not be large enough to put him in.

"Damn it, I'll make him fit if I have to roll him in a ball."

Releasing a deep sigh, Tina moved back toward the body. She froze in her tracks, startled by the ringing of the doorbell. Tina's heart began to pound rapidly. The bell rang again. Panic rushed through her body. She ran her fingers through hair, trying to think. Fear burrowed through her mind. Her thoughts became jumbled and confused. Racing to the front door, Tina gasped. In plain sight thick red blood covered her carpet, unwanted evidence of her deed. The doorbell rang again. Glancing around the room, her eyes searched for an answer. A twinge of hope lay directly in front of her. A large gray throw rug was in front of her couch. Quickly she ran to the couch, bent over, and grabbed the rug. Clutching it. she moved to the telltale bloodstain. With care she draped the rug over it, concealing her crime. Tina then rushed to the window, peering out from behind the drapes, wanting to see who was ringing the bell. Deputy Bill Starr stood on her porch. Terror began oozing rapidly, entwining her entire body. Taking a couple of deep breaths, Tina whispered, "Relax. I've got to relax. It is only Bill. I will tell him I'm busy. I know he will leave. He is my friend. The key, though, is I must relax."

Tina halfheartedly convinced herself her plan would work. She moved toward the door and very deliberately opened it. Forcing a weak smile, Tina greeted Starr, "Bill, what a pleasant surprise. What brings you here so early in the morning?"

Starr's eyes widened as he looked at the battered face of Tina, noticeably swollen; it was obvious someone had beaten her. Quickly he asked, "My God, Tina, did Zeke do this to you?"

Through all the excitement and the planning how to get rid of Parker's body Tina had forgotten about how bad her face must appear. She shot her hand up to her face, trying to cover the bruises, stammering out her reply.

"Of c-c-course not. I f-f-fell . . . off the ladder. . . . You know h-h-how clumsy I am?"

Tina could see in Starr's eyes that he didn't believe a word she had said. She quickly added, "Bill, as you can see, I am not dressed, and I am running late. So if you could come back later I would greatly appreciate it."

Tina tried to shut the door while talking, but Starr had already made his way in, telling her as he moved past her, "Tina, I have to talk to you. I'm afraid I have some bad news."

Tina closed the door. She turned around to face Starr. He had made his way to the couch and sat down. Tina bit her lip nervously.

Her eyes darted over to the entrance leading to the kitchen. Just beyond where Starr had decided to sit lay the body of the man she had just murdered. Her trance broke as Starr called out her name.

"Tina? Those bruises aren't from falling from no ladder."

Starr's voice became angry as he questioned Tina.

"Tell me, Tina, did Zeke beat you?"

Tina's deep blue eyes danced with passion as she snapped back, "Zeke's never hit me in his life. He loves me. I told you I fell off the ladder; that's the end of it. Now please, I have a lot of errands to run. I'll talk with you later."

Starr could sense the tension in Tina's voice.

"Is there something wrong?"

Tina labored to make herself sound calm as she spoke.

"I'm sorry, Bill; my mind is in a frenzy today. Like I said, I have a full schedule today. What is this bad news you have for me?"

Tina watched as Starr began squirming uneasily in his seat. Suddenly it began to dawn on her: the bad news must involve Zeke. She immediately asked, "Has Zeke been in an accident? Is he hurt?"

Starr sensed the urgency in Tina's voice. Her smile disappeared. Concern clouded her deep blue eyes. Starr floundered for the right words to explain Zeke's predicament. For years now Starr had been there to help her through all of the pain she couldn't share with her husband. Now, when she would need him most, he couldn't find the right words to say. Carefully he tried to explain what was happening with her husband.

"Not exactly hurt . . . there has been an incident."

A look of confusion came over Tina's face as she tried to correct Starr.

"You mean accident?"

Starr shook his head no.

Tina barked out, "What are you trying to say, Bill?"

Starr motioned for Tina to sit next to him; she hesitated for a moment. Starr persisted with his hand motion insisting she sit next to him. Gruffly she walked over and took a spot next to him on the couch. Starr smiled meekly, taking both of her hands in his.

"Tina, Zeke is being held hostage at the Golden Aces."

Tina's fingers dug into Starr's palms. Her eyes widened in disbelief.

Starr quickly added, "He is not hurt and we are doing everything in our power to gain his release unharmed."

Starr, upset with himself, couldn't believe how poorly he had handled telling Tina, blurting it out like that, not working his way slowly to the problem.

Tina mumbled one word: "God."

Starr spoke softly.

"Tina, everything will work out. I promise you this."

Tina turned toward Bill, a look of defeat in her eyes as she replied, "You don't understand, Bill. There is nothing you or anyone else can do. This is God's work. I must have been crazy if I really thought I could defeat him."

Starr went to dispute Tina, but she spoke first. Her words sent a chill up and down Starr's body.

"Zeke is going to die for my sins, Bill. It is all my fault. God is angry with me, but it is my loved ones he punishes."

Starr's voice became stern as he scolded Tina, "Stop it. No one is going to die. Zeke is going to come out of this fine. I want you to stop this foolishness. We have talked about this before; now get a grip on yourself. Now is not the time to talk this silliness."

Bill rose to his feet, prying his hands away from Tina's, insisting voice, "Calm down, Tina. I will get you a glass of water. Take a deep breath and relax. I plan on staying with you till this entire ordeal is over."

Tina lowered her head, nodding it slightly, but as Starr moved toward the kitchen where he was heading dawned on her. Panic seeped into her voice as she screamed, "No, Bill, wait!"

Starr turned toward her smiling, "I will be right back, Tina. Calm down and let me get you a cold glass of water."

Tina leaped to her feet, pleading to Starr, "Please, Bill, I don't want anything."

Starr ignored her and headed for the kitchen. He abruptly stopped when he reached the kitchen entrance. Starr stood there stunned as he gazed at the bloody body sprawled on the kitchen floor.

"He deserved to die, Bill."

Starr whirled around. Anger and disbelief rang in his words.

"You did this Tina? Why?"

Tina turned away from Starr's disbelieving eyes. Speaking in a low whisper, she replied, "He tried to rape me."

Starr glanced back over his shoulder at Parker's body, his shirt completely covered with blood. Looking closer at the dead man's eyes, Starr could see the shock and terror the man must have felt. The deputy turned his attention back to Tina. His anger subsided, he calmly asked, "That is Frank Parker? Is he the one who beat you?"

Tina refused to face Starr. She only nodded her head yes. Starr moved to where she stood and put his hand on her shoulder, gently turning her to face him. He placed his hand under her chin and gently lifted it so her eyes would meet his.

"Did he rape you?"

Tears clouded Tina's eyes. She squeezed them shut as she forced out her answer: "No."

Starr took her by the arm and walked her to the couch. Setting her down, he kissed her forehead and walked to the phone.

Tina watched as he moved away from her. Fear began choking her as she watched him pick up the phone. Quickly her fears changed to demanding screams.

"Who are you calling?"

Starr looked at Tina with sympathy in his eyes as he calmly replied, "I've got to call this in, Tina, and you need medical treatment."

Tina violently shook her head no as she cried out, "Bill, please, you can't call anyone!"

Starr hung up the phone, giving Tina a long hard stare before he spoke.

"I have no choice, Tina. I am an officer of the law. It is my duty. There is no need for you to worry. You have every right to defend yourself."

Tina clasped her hands together as she pleaded, "Please, no one has to know. Help me, Bill; you are my friend. Please help me."

Starr felt trapped. The sight of her in such a battered state ripped at his heart. What kind of animal would beat a woman so badly? Despite his deep feelings toward Tina, he still could not ignore his duty.

"Tina, I have no choice. I am an officer of the law. It is my duty to report what this man did. You have nothing to worry about.

From the way he beat you, it is a clear case of self-defense. Please trust me, Tina. Like you said, I am your friend."

Tina's reply shot back quickly.

"I am pregnant, Bill. Frank believed he was the father."

"What? Why would he think that? Was there something going on between the two of you?"

Tina rose slowly to her feet.

"In a way, I guess you might say there was."

A shocked look crossed Starr's face as he blurted out, "For Christ sake, Tina, did you sleep with the man or not?"

Tina gathered all the dignity she could as she answered, "My body lay next to him, but my spirit and soul were with Zeke."

The frustration showed in Starr's voice as he snapped back, "You were sleeping with Frank Parker. Why?"

The dignity remained in Tina's voice as she calmly gave Starr his answer.

"I used him to get something that Zeke and I needed to make our lives whole."

Frustration mounted more. Anger began to build inside Starr as he shouted back, "Then Parker *is* the father?"

The dignity drained out of Tina as she quickly shouted back, "No! Zeke is the father. Frank Parker is a filthy pig. Bill, can't you see I did what I had to do to complete the dream Zeke and I have always had? That bastard lying in my kitchen tried to destroy the life that now is growing inside me. Bill, please, you must help me. You have always been there for me. Today I need you more than ever."

A sharp pain stabbed at Starr's heart. Tina was right; he always was there for her. Something about Tina made him want to be with her always, but murder! How could he possibly help her now? This strange love he had for Tina was close to destroying his marriage. He had done everything in his power to convince himself he was only a friend. A friend who was now watching a person close to him slip into madness from which she might not escape. His voice began quivering as he fought back the tears.

"Tina, I am going to call for an ambulance. You need to see a doctor."

Starr picked up the phone.

Tina reached into her robe pocket, pulling out her revolver.

"Put the phone down, Bill."

Starr lowered the phone back down onto its cradle. Not taking his eyes off Tina's gun, he quietly said, "Tina, put the gun away. I am here to help you."

Tina nodded in agreement as she replied, "You will help me, Bill, by burying that piece of trash in there."

Starr remained calm as he asked, "What about me, Tina? After I help you bury Parker, do I get the grave next to him?"

Tina's tone didn't change as she replied, "That will be up to you, Bill. I don't want to hurt you or anyone else. All I want is to have my child."

Tina paused and pointed to the swelling on her face and the black-and-blue marks on her arms, then said in a demanding voice, "Look at me, Bill. Look at the bruises on my face. Frank did this to me. He hit me with his fist and kicked me repeatedly. The bastard tried to kill me and my baby."

Starr cringed as Tina opened her robe to show the bruises on the rest of her body. Starr's voice became compassionate.

"Like I said, Tina, you did it in self-defense. No court in the land would convict you. Let me call an ambulance to check you out to make sure the baby is OK."

Tina's voice trembled as she replied, "What about Zeke? I did this for him. Do you think he would understand that? Don't you think through the entire trial they would hammer the fact that Frank and I were having an affair? Zeke and my unborn child would be scarred for eternity."

Starr moved a little closer to Tina and said in a concerned voice, "What about Zeke? Did you forget why I came here? Your husband is in trouble and he needs you now. Tina, let me help you."

Tina's eyes widened with horror; her voice trembled.

"Zeke, no, we must find a way to save Zeke."

Starr could see the pain ripping through her. Guilt began to seep through him as he quietly said, "Put the gun away, Tina. Please, don't make matters worse. I promise you everything will work out."

Tina burst into tears, lowering the gun as she did. Her words came out sobbing.

"Frank won; he managed to destroy my life from his grave."

Starr didn't rush Tina. Instead he continued to talk calmly.

"Everything is going to be fine, Tina. I won't let anything happen to you. I've always been there for you, kid. Why would I stop now? You need to trust me."

Tina looked up, her eyes glistening from the tears.

"God won, Bill; they won't let me keep my baby. Even if they do, the child will not have a father. I know God is going to take Zeke from me, too. It is over, Bill. Make your calls; it doesn't matter anymore."

Starr stared at Tina's swollen and bruised face. He then glanced over at the body of the man who had done it. Starr's voice remained compassionate.

"Zeke is not going to die, Tina. We will get him out of there unharmed."

Starr stopped and looked at Tina. He could see she didn't believe him. Why should she? Her whole life was falling apart. Starr felt a strange feeling coming over him. In his years of being a lawman he never had taken a bribe or otherwise compromised his duty. But the more he looked at his friend standing there in pain, beaten, with a hopeless feeling oozing out of her, the more Starr knew what he must do. He knew that despite all the times he had been there for her, she never would need him more than she did now.

"I will help you, Tina, but we are going to do this my way."

Tina stopped crying and looked up at the deputy. A ray of hope danced in her glistening eyes as she hoarsely asked, "You are not going to turn me in?"

Starr shook his head no, then quietly added, "I need to know everything, Tina. Please don't lie to me."

Tina's voice became excited as she could see hope after all.

"What do you need to know?"

Frank knew there was no gentle way to ask his question or time, so he just blurted it out.

"How many people knew about the affair?"

Tina's face showed her embarrassment from Starr's words, but she answered without protest.

"None. Frank was very good at hiding his personal life."

Starr let out a heavy sigh as he asked his next question.

"Why did Frank really beat you, Tina? Was it because he found out you were pregnant?"

Tina lowered her head, looking at the floor. She could still envision Frank's fist pounding down on her. Her voice became softer as she replied, "Frank came here to try and convince me not to end our affair. I refused to listen. I made it clear I did not want to see him anymore. He became enraged and tried to rape me."

Starr began to feel a disgusted hate for the man lying on Tina's kitchen floor but tried to hide his feelings as he asked, "Is that when he beat you?"

Tina shook her head no and continued to recite the incident.

"I begged him to stop, but he wouldn't . . . till I told him I was pregnant. He stopped. He became terrified at the thought of it. He tried to convince me to have an abortion. Told me how something like this could ruin his career. I refused. I told him it was Zeke's baby, not his. He would not believe me. Then I made the mistake and told him I was only using him; that is when he began to beat me."

Starr looked confused and asked inquisitively, "He found out that you were using him? Are you telling me that is why you had the affair? You wanted him to father your child?"

Tina refused to look up from the floor as she shyly nodded her head yes. Then she answered, "I used him for a surrogate father. It is practiced all over the world. I just didn't tell Frank what I needed him for."

Tina looked up at Starr. She could see the worried look in his eyes as she tried to justify her actions: "I had to do something, Bill. I know it sounds sick and perverted to you, but it worked. I am carrying a child, Zeke's child. Please try to understand why I did it, Bill."

Starr shook his head slowly as he whispered, "I'm trying, Tina, but what you are telling me sounds crazy. There are so many alternatives you could have used. Like adoption for one."

Tina's eyes widened as her voice exploded with anger.

"Never! I want to feel the life growing inside me. It is important that I feel that life, very important."

Starr walked over to Tina, holding out his hand.

"Give me the gun, Tina."

Tina paused: her hands shook. A look of doubt was in her eyes as she whispered, "Bill, this is my dad's gun. I know this may sound crazy to you, but his spirit is still inside it. Bill, I heard his voice. He told me to kill the bastard, that if I allowed him to ruin my child's life he would never forgive me. You believe me, don't you? My dad did talk to me; I swear to you."

Starr showed no emotion as he replied quietly, "I'm sure you thought you heard him, Tina. It's only natural to want someone who loves you near when you're in trouble. Please give me the gun. I'll take care of everything, Tina."

Tina hesitated, then reluctantly held the gun out. Starr took it and shoved it in his belt. He then asked, without mentioning how strange her talk about her father's spirit in the gun, sounded, "How did you plan on getting rid of the body?"

Tina pointed toward the kitchen, replying, "I dug a grave in the backyard. I figured no one would find him there."

Starr realized Tina hadn't thought her plan out very well. He put his hands on her shoulder and asked, "Is that Parker's car out front?"

Tina's eyes widened, as she had not realized that she still had his car to worry about.

"Tina, if we are going to do this, it is going to be my way. We cannot afford to make any mistakes."

Tina nodded her head yes.

"Good. First thing we must do is cover up that hole you dug in the backyard. Second, we pull Parker's car into the driveway and shove him in the trunk. Then you will drive to Harrison Point in his car. I will follow behind you. When we get there we will push the car over the cliff into the river. Your troubles will sink to the bottom of the river. No one will ever find him. Do you think you can handle that, Tina?"

Tina again nodded her head yes.

"Then we will come back here and clean up the mess, get rid of any evidence that might be left behind that would involve you with Parker's disappearance."

Tina asked timidly, "Then you will take me to the Golden Aces so I can be with Zeke?"

Starr shook his head no. His voice became stern.

"We stay here and wait. You would only be in the way."

Tina took Starr's hand off her shoulder as she protested his decision.

"Bill, we have to help Zeke. If anything happens to him, then none of this is necessary. If Zeke dies, I might as well be dead myself."

"Zeke is not going to die. Hanson is a good cop; allow him to do his job."

Tina wouldn't let up as she said in a begging voice, "Bill, you don't understand. God may want to punish Zeke because of me."

Starr grabbed both of Tina's shoulders as he snapped back at her, "You have to stop this obsession that God is against you. Tina, I am going against everything I believe in for you. Don't make me feel like I am helping someone who is losing her mind."

Tina wrestled herself free from Starr's grip. Her eyes burned with anger as she replied angrily, "We are fighting God. You may think I am crazy, but it is true. You don't know the entire story or you would understand."

Starr folded his arms and quietly said, "Then explain the story to me, Tina."

Tina shook her head violently as she snapped back, "I can't. I appreciate what you are doing for me, but we have to help Zeke."

Starr unfolded his arms and pointed toward the kitchen.

"Tina, let's take care of this problem first; then we will discuss our options on Zeke. Maybe all this madness will be over by then and we can return to our normal lives."

Starr and Tina both knew that neither of them would ever be able to return to a normal life, that this day would be a living nightmare haunting them forever.

Moving closer to Starr, Tina put her arms around the portly deputy, whispering as she did. "I'm sorry, Bill. I didn't mean to drag you into this mess. I know deep down inside everything is going to work out and I have you to thank for that. I love you, Bill; you are a true friend."

Starr gently hugged Tina, stammering as he fought back the tears.

"T-t-tina when this is all over, y-y-you must promise me y–y-you will seek some help."

Tina rested her head on Starr's chest, replying softly, "Whatever you say, Bill."

A chill swept across Starr's body. Tina's voice appeared so calm. His eyes went back to the lifeless body lying on the kitchen floor.

Starr could not hold back his tears any longer. They flowed freely from his eyes as he listened to the woman he called friend breathe gently. Tina held him tighter. Suddenly Starr remembered the words his wife had shouted at him: "I swear, Bill, this bitch is going to end up destroying both of our lives!"

Starr closed his eyes tightly, trying to close out his wife's words. He found himself holding Tina tighter as he whispered, "It will all work out, Tina."

11

Hanson paced in front of his car, his nerves totally on edge. He wanted this entire ordeal over, Zeke safe, and Overstreet out of his life. Hanson stopped pacing as he watched one of Overstreet's men walk over to him. The man held a large piece of paper in his hand. Overstreet took it from him and began to read it. Folding it neatly, he shoved it in his shirt pocket, then gave instructions to the trooper nearest him. Finishing giving his orders, he walked toward Hanson.

Hanson leaned up against the car and waited for Overstreet to reach him. The sheriff knew the note had to contain more bad news. Overstreet stopped in front of Hanson, his face grim. Hanson reluctantly asked, "What's the matter? More bad news, Captain?"

Overstreet nodded as he replied, "My men found a stolen Jeep, hidden well into the woods just north of here. We lifted plenty of prints from the steering wheel and door handle. It appears we have one dangerous man in there. He is an escaped convict, Harlen Franklin Jones. This creep has been in and out of prison since he was fifteen years old. He has been on the run for two months. Your friend in there must have surprised him; our boy in there specializes in safecracking, not armed robbery."

Hanson's face showed the emotions of both anger and confusion.

"Captain, before we go any further, I want to know what right you have to withhold information from me? If you found that Jeep, why wasn't I informed?"

Overstreet shrugged his shoulders as he replied, "You are being informed now, Sheriff. This isn't a game we are playing. I needed answers and I got them. Now *you* have them."

Hanson's anger flowed through his body. He battled to restrain his temper as he demanded, "You will not keep me in the dark on anything else that involves this case. I am in charge of this crime scene, not you. Do I make myself clear?" Hanson's voice rose at the end of his statement.

Overstreet ignored the outburst. Maintaining his cool demeanor, he asked, "Do you have anything else to say, Sheriff, or would you like to know more about what we are up against?"

Hanson realized how foolish he must have sounded. He swallowed his pride and quietly stated, " Fine. Tell me, Captain, what are we up against?"

Overstreet replied in his monotone, "Harlen Jones has a rap sheet longer than my arm. At the age of fifteen he murdered his father, but because of our screwed-up court system they didn't try him as an adult. Because of his father's continual abuse to him as a child, they gave him two years of counseling. He only spent six months in a reform school; then he was on the streets. Along the way he learned the fine art of safecracking. He escaped nearly two months ago from Jackson State Prison and eluded capture till now."

Hanson shook his head slowly as he asked, "Is there anything else I should know about Mr. Jones?"

Overstreet hesitated before replying. From the little he knew about Hanson, what he had to tell him next was really going to upset him. Overstreet stared right into Hanson's eyes and calmly answered, "He killed two guards during his escape. The one thing I can tell you for certain is that . . . this man has no intention of going back to prison alive."

Hanson felt like someone had just punched him in the pit of his stomach. His friend was being held hostage by a man who would not think twice about killing. Hanson felt helpless. How do you reason with a madman? What do you offer him for the return of a friend? Hanson had no answers and his hopes of all this ending without bloodshed were rapidly disappearing.

"OK. I need to know what are we to do next?"

Overstreet stretched his huge arms and let out a yawn, then in his monotone voice replied, "I've already called for more men, including my sharpshooters. I've summoned for a helicopter, just in case Jones does get out of the building. Till we get everything situated we will appease him in any way we can. Tell him anything he wants to hear, Sheriff. We definitely need more time."

Hanson gave Overstreet a strange look. He couldn't believe how calmly this man was acting toward everything. Hanson hoped the hell he would never get so callous when dealing in people's lives. Hanson asked in a curious tone, "What about Zeke? What do we do to assure his safe release?"

Overstreet looked away from Hanson as he replied, "We do the best we can, sheriff. There are no guarantees that someone will not get hurt."

Hanson grabbed Overstreet by the arm and forced him to face him. He snapped out his words.

"That is not an answer, Captain. We are here to serve and protect. Zeke's safety has to be our first concern."

Overstreet stared down at Hanson's hand that grasped his arm. Glaring back up at Hanson, he ordered, "Please remove your hand from me."

Hanson released his grip from Overstreet's arm, yelling as he did, "What kind of man are you? We are talking about a man's life in there. His safety should be our top priority. I can't believe you are acting so callous toward an innocent man being hurt."

Overstreet's facial expression didn't change. His voice remained cool and calm as he retorted, "Sheriff, I want nothing more than to see your friend come out of there unharmed. I will do everything I can to ensure that happening, but Harlen Jones cannot be allowed to escape. There are many more lives at stake than just your friend's. Allow your heart to dictate how we handle this situation and you can count on many lives being lost. Start acting like a professional, Sheriff, or it may be you that causes that man's death."

Hanson's rage exploded. He screamed at Overstreet, "That is what you call it? You're being a professional! I disagree with you, Captain. I call it being one inhumane bastard. I assure you that anything that happens today better involve careful thought about Zeke's safety or I swear I will escort Harlen Jones out of this town myself."

Overstreet didn't respond to Hanson's statement. Instead, he looked past Hanson at the state trooper cars pulling around the corner. They were Overstreet's reinforcements. Hanson turned to see what was going on behind him. Three more state trooper cars joined the forces in back. The cars stopped and four men scurried out of each car. They all wore full battle gear and carried high-powered rifles. They were equipped for a small war.

Hanson turned back to Overstreet and in a harsh voice snapped, "This is getting out of control, Captain. I am in charge here, not you."

Overstreet replied quietly, "Not anymore, Sheriff. Jones is my jurisdiction. If you want to help that is fine, but don't get in the way or I will have you removed from here. Now if you will excuse me, I have to instruct my men where I want them stationed. I would appreciate it if you would check on crowd control in the front of the building."

Overstreet walked away, joining his men before Hanson could lash out at him. Hanson watched as Overstreet pointed out areas in the field behind the restaurant, obviously areas where he wanted to deploy his men. Overstreet also pointed to the roof of the Golden Aces. Hanson watched as one of the troopers nodded and moved quickly to the side of the building.

Hanson turned away; he had seen enough. Walking over to his car, he opened the door and slid in, slamming the car door shut. Hanson looked up into the morning sky. The sun now completely hidden behind the black clouds hovering in the sky, Hanson knew that the storm would strike anytime. In a way, though, Hanson knew the storm would be a blessing. At least it would disperse the crowd that had formed in the front of the building. Hanson leaned over and picked up the mike and began to speak.

"You there, Larry? Damn it, this is Hanson; come in, Larry."

A voice with a thick southern accent replied from the other end, "I am here, Sheriff. Sure looks like one hell of a storm brewing, sir."

Hanson ignored his deputy's comment, asking, "How are things holding up out front? Is that crowd beginning to thin out?"

The southern accent became more intense as Larry snapped back, "Hell no, Sheriff. If anything, it's gotten larger. I wish I could sell tickets; I could retire in no time."

Hanson's voice showed his irritation with his deputy's ad lib.

"Larry, please forget the commentary and just answer my questions. Do we have the crowd under control?"

Larry, more subdued replied, "Yes, sir, everything is fine. The state boys have given us extra men here to help. We have the entire town completely bottled up, just like Captain Overstreet ordered."

Overstreet! Hanson was sick of hearing his name. The arrogant ass had taken complete charge of everything. Now he even went as

103

far as to issue orders to his, Hanson's, deputies. Combined with his feeling of frustration, a feeling of uselessness began to mount inside him. Hanson needed to lash out at someone. His deputy became the first candidate.

"Since when do you take orders from Overstreet? You work for me, mister, not him. From now on you check with me first before you do anything, do you understand?"

His deputy's voice became confused and bewildered as he replied, "Yes, sir. I just thought he was relaying your orders, sir."

Hanson's anger, now at full bloom, he screamed back at his deputy, "Well, he wasn't. Hanson out."

Hanson slammed the mike down. His anger building, he pounded his fist on the dashboard. Hanson felt as if he were drowning. Between losing control of his men, this situation, and himself, the feeling of inadequacy blended in with his anger. A tapping on his car window drew his attention away from his self-pity. Standing outside his car was Overstreet, motioning to Hanson to lower his window. Hanson frowned as he rolled the window down. Sarcasm dripped as he asked, "What's the matter, Captain? Run out of people to order around?"

Overstreet's voice showed his disgust at Hanson's attitude as he spoke. "Sheriff, I would like to go over our game plan with you. That is, if you are through feeling sorry for yourself?"

Hanson wanted to reach out and grab Overstreet by the throat and choke the life right out of him. In three short hours Hanson had grown to hate the trooper. Hanson hated the way Overstreet appeared calm no matter what happened around him. Hanson felt a type of intimidation being around the man.

"Sheriff, do you want to know what we have planned or not?"

Hanson opened the car door. Sliding out, he slammed the door shut and leaned back against the car.

Overstreet shook his head in disgust at Hanson's display of childish behavior and waited for him to say something. Hanson remained mute. Overstreet reluctantly began to describe his strategy.

"As you can see, I have men deployed in six different positions in the field out there." Overstreet pointed to the field behind the restaurant and continued, "Each one of them is an expert shot. On top of the roof I placed two more men; they also are expert shots.

104

When Jones comes out of the restaurant to get inside the car he is sure to use your friend as a shield. With the way my men are deployed we are bound to get one clear shot. Your friend might be a bit shook up, but he will be alive. What I will need from you is very important for this plan to work."

Hanson folded his arms but remained quiet.

Overstreet continued, "You will have to buy us some time. Try to lull Jones into a sense of security. Tell him we will agree to all his terms. Be convincing; make sure he believes you."

Pausing, Overstreet stared hard at Hanson. Quietly he asked, "Any questions or comments, Sheriff?"

Hanson's anger now under control he had listened intently to Overstreet's plan and heard many flaws in it.

"Just a few, Captain. One, the man in there is no fool. From what you have told me about Harlen Jones, he has had many dealings with the law. Don't you think he will expect us to try something exactly like what you described? Two, what is preventing him from pulling the trigger once he is shot and blowing Zeke's brains out at the same time?"

Overstreet raised his bushy eyebrows. Smiling, he asked, "Have you ever seen a man shot in the head with a high-powered rifle? It doesn't allow much time for him to react. As far as him knowing what we have planned, yes, I think he knows what we will do out here, but he has no choice. To get to the car he has to leave the building; all we need is one split second and it is over."

The rain began to fall lightly, only a small taste of the storm that hovered above preparing to strike. Hanson wiped the few drops of rain that dropped on his face from his hat as he asked, "Why not hide someone in the backseat? Put a blanket over him, we allow Jones to get in the car, and when he tries to leave, we arrest him."

Overstreet released a heavy sigh. "He would spot something like that in a moment. No we can't allow him to get near the car. If he does we risk somebody else getting hurt. My way he does not reach the car alive and we give your friend in there his best chance of surviving."

Hanson stood erect. His eyes darted to where Overstreet's men had deployed themselves. Two of the men lay perfectly still on the roof. The group of men scattered through the fields, rifles fixed on the back door of the Golden Aces.

"It all sounds too risky. Too many things could go wrong. Zeke could wind up dead with the slightest mistake. There must be a different way?"

Overstreet spread out his arms as he asked, "I'm listening, Sheriff; do you have a better idea?"

Hanson replied softly, "No, I don't."

Overstreet nodded as he replied, "Then I guess we do it my way. We better get ready to call him. How about the money? He might want to see it before he leaves the building. Will it be a problem getting that much?"

Hanson shook his head no, replying, "The mayor is a good friend of Zeke's. He already has raised the money. One of his assistants will bring it to us."

Overstreet slapped his large hands together as he said in his usual calm voice, "Good. After the money gets here we will call Jones. With some luck this all should be over before nightfall."

Overstreet glanced at his watched, adding, "I have to call in and see what is the holdup on my request for a helicopter. This bastard is not going to elude us again."

Overstreet turned and walked over to his patrol car. Hanson watched as the trooper strutted in the rain. Hanson looked up into the rain. The cool drops from the heaven felt good on his face. The wind began to pick up in strength. Hanson rushed back inside his car to shield himself from the storm that was about to strike. Thunder crashed through the air. The skies released their fury. The light rain quickly changed to a heavy downpour. Lightning flashed across the skies, illuminating the air above the restaurant. The two men stationed on the roof clung to the small stacks lined across the roof. Neither of the two men left the positions to which they were assigned. Hanson glanced over to where Overstreet stood. The captain had taken cover in his car. Hanson's eyes then fell upon the open field, all those troopers hiding waiting for Jones to come out, under siege from Mother Nature's awesome weapon lightning. As foolish as the troopers appeared to be to stay out in the storm, Hanson admired their loyalty to Overstreet. The rain pounded harder on Hanson's car, with him now wondering if his deputies would show the same type of loyalty toward him. Shrugging his shoulders at his own thoughts, Hanson turned and stared at the back door of the restaurant, knowing he would be contacting the killer inside shortly, telling him the lies he wanted to hear, saying anything that would assure Zeke's safety. Hanson then leaned his head back on the car seat, closing his eyes to listen to the fury of the storm outside his car. With each clap of thunder Hanson squeezed his eyes tighter. It felt as if God had begun wielding his wrath on the town of Barnsville. Louder the thunder roared, warning all that no force on earth could match the destruction of the heavens. Tears trickled slowly down Hanson's face. With each clap of thunder his mind throbbed with the echoing pain. The pain stabbed at him for what he once called paradise gradually turning into hell. All he could do now was try to end this nightmare that had unfolded in his town. For he knew Barnsville after this day would never be the same. His small town finally had grown up and joined the rest of the world. What Hanson feared the most was the sick way the crowd was drawn into all of this. He knew they were here because they were concerned about Zeke, but the sad part was that he really felt the excitement was why most of the good citizens of Barnsville now stood in front of the Golden Aces restaurant. From this day forward paradise would never be the same in Barnsville. Hanson wiped his eyes, reaching over to where the phone rested on his car seat. Picking up the receiver, he dialed the restaurant. It was time to make terms with the devil.

12

Harlen patted his shirt pocket, then glanced down at the crumpled package on the floor. Turning his attention to Zeke, who still remained huddled in the corner, Harlen made a gesture as if he had a cigarette in his hand. Zeke ignored Harlen's pantomime. With a sigh of disgust Harlen gruffly asked, "Do you have a cigarette on you?"

Zeke shook his head no, replying quietly, "Sorry, I don't smoke."

Frowning, Harlen bounced off the prep table and began to pace again. He felt the urge for a smoke. His nerves were on edge. The waiting ate at him. Harlen knew the troopers were not going to just allow him to leave. He knew he would have to rely on his wits to get out of this mess, just as he had done so many times before.

The pounding of the rain on the roof echoed a deafening sound. It made the waiting more unbearable. Harlen continued to pace, his thoughts drifting in and out on how he would get out of this mess. He knew his chances of making it out of this mess alive would be slim. The one thing he did know was that he would not go back to jail, not now, not ever. Harlen stopped his pacing as the telephone began to ring. Glancing in Zeke's direction and smiling, he said, "You better hope that your friend gives me the right answers, boy. I'd hate to see your brains splashed up against these walls."

Harlen walked over to the phone. Picking it up, he spoke harshly.

"Talk to me, Sheriff. I am starting to get irritated in this place. That is not good for your friend's health."

A tense Hanson replied coldly, "We are getting everything you asked for, Mr. Jones."

Startled by hearing his name, Harlen paused to regain his composure, then calmly replied, "So you know who I am. Good. Then you also know that I am not bluffing if I tell you that if I don't have my demands met your friend in here is dead. I'm correct, Sheriff. ''

Hanson ignored Harlen's comment. Instead he proceeded to tell Harlen what he knew the bastard wanted to hear.

"We have a car coming for you." Hanson paused, then carefully added, "We are trying to raise the money. We should have it by early evening. We are borrowing it from a bank in Marquette."

Hanson again paused, then quietly finished, "It is going to take a while to get here."

Harlen snapped back quickly, "You only have three hours left, Sheriff. After that he dies. No excuses, not a damn thing, will make me change my mind. I know you're fucking stalling for time and I'm being a good sport about it. Shit, that's half the fun, playing along with your silly games. Game time is over, Sheriff, your ass is now with the big boys. Call me when you have the money."

Harlen hung up the phone, turning his attention back to the man trembling in the corner. A thought came to him. Through all the excitement he had forgotten the reason he had found himself in this mess. Waving his gun at Zeke, Harlen barked out his order.

"Get up, asshole!"

Zeke froze; the sudden anger in Harlen's voice stunned him.

Harlen repeated himself, his voice growing louder.

"You fucking deaf or something? I said get up!"

Zeke jumped to his feet. His body shook with fear. All he wanted was this nightmare to be over and for him to be back in the arms of his wife. He tried to speak, but the words wouldn't come out.

Harlen moved toward him, grabbed his arm and, snarled, "Open the safe. I still want the money in there. Especially since it's causing me such fucking grief."

Zeke nervously nodded.

Harlen released Zeke's arm and pushed him toward the office.

Zeke stumbled slightly, regained his balance, and moved quickly toward the office. Harlen followed close behind. Zeke went directly to the safe, bent down, and began to spin the dial; the numbers came much easier this time. Despite being terrified, he was able to open it on the first try. He reached in and took out the deposit bag, turned, and held it out to Harlen, who grabbed it. He shook it, then pointed at the safe, asking, "Anything else in there?"

Zeke replied meekly, "Just the rolled coins."

Harlen waved his gun behind him as he snapped out his order: "Shut the safe and move back into the kitchen."

Zeke didn't hesitate. He closed the safe door, stood up, and walked swiftly back into the kitchen. Harlen followed close behind. When they reached the kitchen, Harlen went back to the prep table. Harlen jumped back on the table, getting himself comfortable. Zeke sat back down on the hard tile floor. Greed sparkled in Harlen's eyes as he opened the deposit bag. Pulling out the wad of bills, he began counting the money. Zeke could see the anger and frustration forming on Harlen's face. Harlen cursed and counted the money a second time. Abruptly he stopped. Holding the bills high in the air, he shouted at Zeke, throwing the money in the air. Fury rang through his voice.

"This is it? Nine hundred fucking dollars! I am going through all this shit for a stinking nine hundred dollars?"

Zeke didn't reply.

Harlen's fury raged like that of a wild man. Pounding his fist hard up against the prep table, waving his arms frantically, he shouted out obscenities.

"This is a fucking joke! There has to be more fucking money than this. Nine hundred fucking dollars for a day's receipts? No fucking way! Where's the rest of it? Tell me or I'm going to splatter your goddamn brains all over these fucking walls."

Zeke backed away from Harlen. Fear gripped him as he watched the anger dance in Harlen's eyes. Zeke cringed while forcing himself to reply in an attempt to calm Harlen down.

"I'm sorry, but we are a small town. That is a good day for us. Honest, I am not lying to you. Why would I? I have no desire to die over money."

Zeke stared at Harlen. He waited to see what the man's reaction would be. Zeke watched slowly as Harlen began to calm down. Harlen glanced at the money scattered on the floor and motioned for Zeke to pick it up. He moved quickly. He didn't want to give Harlen any reason to lose his temper again. Harlen pointed to the deposit bag next to him on the table, "Put the money back in the bag and give it to me."

As Zeke slid the money back inside the bag, he made sure he didn't leave any behind. When he was sure he had it all, he stood

110

back up and gently laid the bag next to Harlen. He stood perfectly still as he waited for Harlen's next order.

Harlen looked down at the bag, then moved it to the side. He then stared at Zeke. A strange smile appeared on Harlen's face as he asked, "You would love to kill me, wouldn't you? I bet if I gave you this gun you would just enjoy the fuck out of putting a bullet through my skull."

Zeke didn't reply, not allowing his eyes to meet Harlen's. Harlen continued to badger Zeke.

"Answer me, hero. Wouldn't you love to see my black ass dead?"

Zeke timidly shook his head no. "I don't believe in violence."

Harlen burst into laughter.

Zeke's face turned beet red. He felt like a fool, his pride being stripped from him. Trying to maintain a trace of dignity, he added, "I am sincere, sir. I would not want to see anyone die."

Harlen's laughter stopped. His voice became harsh.

"Even if it meant saving your own fucking life?"

Zeke looked into Harlen's eyes, replying in an even tone, "I don't really know, maybe. I never faced that problem before."

Harlen smiled as he snapped back, "Hey, asshole, you're facing it now."

Zeke looked away from Harlen as he whispered softly, "I trust God will help me. You will get what you want and set me free."

Harlen pointed to the door as he spoke.

"They know who I am. Shit, no way are they going let my black ass out of here. Even if they have to sacrifice your ass to get to me, they will. So don't preach about God and having trust."

Zeke began to tremble as he could see the enjoyment Harlen was getting out of talking about death. Zeke's voice became shrill, his words stumbling out as he stuttered, "S-s-so y-y-you're going to k-k-kill me?"

Harlen hopped off the table and moved toward Zeke. Stopping directly in front of Zeke, he replied coldly, "Asshole, more than likely we both will be dead within the next three hours. Does that answer your question?"

Zeke backed away from Harlen, his voice tense.

"You sound like you want it to happen that way, like you want to die."

Harlen walked over to the back door and peeked out the peephole. The rain pounded on the back lot. None of the deputies were in sight. Only patrol cars took up space in the lot now. Harlen turned around to face Zeke. A slight smile creased his face as he answered Zeke's question.

"I am not afraid of dying. I lived in some form of hell most of my life. Death cannot be much worse. Unlike you, I believe in violence. You don't live in the real world. When is the last time you went hungry? Or watched a friend get shot down right in front of you because a rival gang needed to prove a point?"

Harlen paused and waited for Zeke to reply. Zeke remained silent. Harlen raved on.

"When you went to school, the only thing you worried about was lunch money. I worried about paying protection to the local gangs. Poverty and death was a way of life to me. Hell, you ask me if I want to die?"

Harlen pounded his chest as he screamed his next sentence.

"Sometimes I feel I have already died and was cast into hell! How could I possibly die again?"

Zeke watched as Harlen went on talking. He was not even looking at Zeke now. It appeared Harlen was now talking to himself, expressing the feeling that hid deep inside him.

"You talk of God and having trust in him. When I was a child I felt the same way. I went to Sunday school, where I was taught to love all men, that we all were God's children."

Harlen's voice began to soften as he looked off into the distance while talking.

"One day I left church with my friends. While walking home, I witnessed one of God's children blown apart by stray bullets from a drive-by shooting. I was four years old. My friend who died . . . only five years old. You commented earlier that I wanted to die. If you had to deal with the pain and fear that I did, you would welcome death yourself."

Zeke didn't know the right words to choose for a reply. It was clear that Harlen grew closer to madness with every word he spoke. Slowly, carefully, Zeke tried to find the words to say.

"I am sorry. . . . It sounds like you never had a chance to be happy."

Zeke waited for Harlen to scream an obscenity at him, to blame all his grief on him. Instead, Harlen smiled, a real smile. His voice became calm as he replied to Zeke's comments, "I was happy once, a long time ago. I was only nine years old and some bleeding-heart liberals felt sorry for us black kids. They sent us to camp. It was great. Trees, water, peace . . . plenty of peace. I laid under the stars one night and stared into the skies for hours. I never felt so relaxed, so free. I actually forgot about everything bad that ever happened to me. I even forgot about the scars on my face. That lasted for an entire week."

Zeke for the first time that day saw signs that Harlen could act like a normal human being. Harlen's voice had a strange touch of gentleness to it as he spoke of the camp. Zeke pursued the subject, wanting to keep the man content.

"Did you get a chance to do any fishing?"

Harlen's voice remained calm as he talked in a gentler tone.

"No, I mainly walked through the woods. I enjoyed the seclusion."

Zeke wanted to maintain the calm atmosphere, so he tried to keep the conversation going.

"I enjoy that myself. I walk alone in the woods around here. It is a good way to relax."

Harlen's mood switched rapidly. He glared at Zeke as he snarled, "Don't patronize me! I am not a child who needs sympathy from a pathetic man like you."

Zeke found himself snapping back at his attacker, "It isn't sympathy I am offering. I happen to understand what you are saying. You act like you are the only man in the world to have bad breaks in life. Guess again, Harlen; you're not. Maybe I didn't grow up in the ghetto or hear the cries of hungry children. That doesn't mean I don't care. The preacher you heard speak as a child spoke the truth. We are all God's children. Whether you like it or not."

Zeke could not believe the rage in his own voice. He waited for Harlen to beat him or, worse kill him. Harlen just stared at him, then slowly asked, "When was the last time you drove to the city? Seen the conditions those people have to grow up in? You're like all the white bleeding-heart liberals in this country. You stand on your soapbox and preach how you care and what programs you will start to help reform our lives. Then you go back to your cozy homes and forget we even exist. Why must there be laws passed to allow us to be equal? Why do people complain about welfare? We send billions of dollars to countries across the sea to help their poor. Why did they strip my daddy of his dignity? To the point where he hated me because he didn't feel like a man? We fight wars in countries to help the oppressed, yet we ignore a race of people who for generations clearly have been oppressed right here in our own country. Don't try to impress me by telling me that you care. I stopped believing in caring years ago."

Zeke felt a surge of shame creep through him. Some of the things Harlen had said, regrettably, were true. Hesitantly Zeke asked, "Why don't you speak out for your people? What you are doing now just makes matters worse. Be a leader; tell the world of the plight of your race. Lead them from the darkness you talk about to true freedom."

Harlen burst into laughter instead of anger. Moving back to the prep table, he hopped on it and made himself comfortable. His laughter now disappeared.

"We had many great leaders in my time. Where are they now? Shot down, murdered, for their beliefs. I am not a martyr; we had enough of them."

Zeke wouldn't allow it to rest but persisted, "You don't need to be a martyr to help open the eyes of the world. You only need to care and it sounds as if you really care about the fate of your race."

Harlen's calm demeanor vanished. His voice regained the harshness that had vibrated in it before.

"Stop preaching to me. You don't understand a damn thing about me or my people. The cops out there know who I am: Harlen Jones, fugitive. I killed two guards during my escape. Do you call that a leader? One of the guards I stabbed was black. I stabbed the motherfucker ten times just to make sure he was dead. I have no prejudice when it comes to staying free. I will not be caged up like an animal again. I will die first. Taking as many people with me as I can. I don't care if they are white, black, or fucking purple. If they stand in my way they will die. Are you getting my point? I do not want to save humanity, just myself."

Zeke nodded his head yes and in a whisper apologized, "I am sorry. I did not mean to upset you. It is just that you impressed me by the way you felt. I have heard many people speak on this subject;

you struck a nerve. I felt ashamed that I wasn't doing enough to help."

Harlen screamed back at Zeke, "Shit! you're doing plenty! You're giving your fucking life up to save mine. I don't want to talk about it anymore! Sit back down and shut up. Pray that your so-called friend out there meets my demands."

Zeke moved back to the corner and sat down. He resumed staring at the tile, trying to lose himself from the reality around him. The only sounds heard now in the kitchen were the pounding of the rain on the roof and the occasional roar of thunder.

Harlen stared at his prisoner sitting on the floor. Zeke had stirred up memories Harlen wanted to forget, memories of another man who had made a similar statement to him.

The thunder exploded outside the restaurant.

Harlen tried to shake the thoughts that slowly inched their way into his mind.

Lightning flashed above the crowds standing in front of the building hoping for just a glimpse of the evil man holding their town hostage.

The images of the past began forming more clearly in Harlen's head. Like the storm raging outside, Harlen's memories raged in his mind. He squeezed his eyes tightly closed in the hope he could shut out the painful past.

13

Harlen stood over his father's body. Blood covered what was left of the man's face. Harlen began to tremble as fear began to smother him. Though he hated his father, the sight of him with his face missing began to make Harlen sick to his stomach. He couldn't fight the queasy feeling ripping at his gut as he vomited all over the floor. Wiping his mouth, trying to get the sick taste out of him, Harlen glanced down again at his father's body. The fear gripped the boy even tighter. The panic rose inside him as he ran to the door and bolted outside. Faster he ran, jumping the fence, and he headed down the sidewalk, positive that someone had called the police about the gunshots. Breathing heavily Harlen continued to run till he spotted the church standing proudly in the midst of all the poverty around him. He hurried up the stairs. The only man Harlen knew he could trust would help him. Harlen walked into the church. Standing at the pulpit was Rev. James Smith. He stood staring down at his notes for Sunday's sermon. Harlen stood there and watched for a few moments, before clearing his throat to get the reverend's attention. The reverend looked up from his notes and smiled as he saw young Harlen standing in front of him. Smith stepped down from the stage and motioned for Harlen to come over to him. Harlen hesitated at first, then slowly made his way over to where the reverend was standing. Harlen stared down at the floor, not wanting to look into the holy man's eyes. Reverend Smith spoke quietly.

"What an unexpected pleasure. How are you today, Harlen?"

Harlen remained silent as he stared at the floor.

"Is there something I can help you with, Harlen? You look as if you could use a friend right now."

Tears began rolling down Harlen's face. Still he remained mute.

Reverend Smith sat down on the stage, patting a spot next to him.

"Sit next to me, Harlen."

Harlen kept his head down as he moved to where the reverend sat.

"Come on, Harlen; sit. Tell me what is troubling you. That is why you came here, isn't it?"

Harlen looked up at the reverend. Tears ran freely now as the guilt of what he had done stabbed at his heart. His words stammered out.

"I d-d-did . . a t-t-terrible thing. G-g-god, not me, should have done it."

Reverend Smith put his hand on Harlen's shoulder as he asked, 'What should God have done? Harlen, what do you feel you could possibly do better than God?"

Harlen looked away from the reverend's stare, trying to find the courage to tell him what crime he had just committed. Glancing around the church, Harlen remained silent. He began feeling a strange warmth surrounding him. The reverend's voice shattered that as it became more forceful as the reverend spoke.

"Harlen, whatever you did, God will forgive you. He is a merciful God. I've taught you that. Let it out, child; don't keep the pain bottle up inside you."

Harlen asked nervously, "Didn't you once say to me that God punishes the evil that stalks his children?"

Reverend Smith smiled as he replied, "Yes, Harlen, I did. You know, son, one of the reasons I think you are going to be the next great leader is the way you remember quotes. I see something special in you, just as God does."

The reverend patted young Harlen on the head as he asked again, "Now tell me, son, why the tears?"

Harlen looked up at the reverend, his tears running in the cracks of his scars. A tone of anguish was in his voice as he asked, "Why are people like my father still allowed to live?"

Harlen ran his fingers over his face as he continued, "Look at my face Reverend. I am a freak."

Looking away from the reverend, Harlen stared up at the crucifix above him and as if he were talking to God himself said, "My father did this to me. You always preach that all of us are equal, that each of us is special in God's eyes. Reverend, don't you think that I am one of God's children?" Harlen lowered his eyes to meet the

117

reverend's as he asked, "Why didn't God punish my father for this pain he caused to me? Did God think what my dad did to me was right?" Harlen stared at the reverend waiting for his reply.

Reverend Smith forced a smile as he answered in a warm and comforting voice, "We cannot question God's ways. We must trust him and believe what path he has chosen for us is the right one."

Harlen looked away from the reverend again, staring back down at the floor.

Reverend Smith asked, "What is this terrible thing you did, Harlen?"

Harlen remained silent. Reverend Smith's patience began to wear thin. His voice became firmer as he spoke.

"You told me once you wanted to be like Martin Luther King. That you wanted to help all blacks around the world to claim equal rights. Yet here you sit afraid to talk to a man of God. Fear is contagious, Harlen. If you want to reach the lofty goals you have set for yourself there is no room for fear. Now I will ask you again and this time I expect an answer. What did you do that is so awful?"

Harlen slowly looked back up at the reverend. Tears flowed freely as he sobbed.

"I took vengeance on the scars that keep me from being a normal kid. Reverend Smith. . . . I just killed my father."

Reverend Smith's eyes widened. His mouth dropped open in disbelief at what Harlen had just told him. The reverend whispered softly, "Oh, my God."

Harlen grabbed the reverend's sleeve and yanked on it. His voice was pleading as he tried to explain.

"I had to, reverend. I was left no choice. You don't know how evil that man was. You understand, don't you, Reverend? I had to kill the bastard. Tell me you understand, Reverend?"

Reverend Smith removed Harlen's hand from his shirtsleeve, his voice stern as he said, "Harlen, taking the law into your own hands doesn't solve anything. It makes you just as bad as your father."

Harlen shook his head violently back and forth as he screamed, "The bastard tortured me for years! The law didn't do nothing! He forced my mother to run away with another man! He was wicked and no one did anything . . . till now."

Reverend Smith's voice grew louder as he shouted back, "Then what about God. You should have put your faith in him. How can you even think of following in the footsteps of the men you admire when you commit a vicious act like murder?''

Harlen threw his hands over his ears as he shouted, ''I came here because you're the only man I trust, but even you are turning on me.''

Reverend Smith closed his eyes to control his emotion. Quietly he whispered, ''You can trust me, Harlen. What you need to do is put more faith in God.''

Harlen chuckled through his tears as he sarcastically replied , ''I waited for God to strike him dead for what he did to me. No one punished him. Not the law, not you, and not God. I know what I did is wrong in the law's eyes, but I thought you would understand. Tell me, Reverend, do you understand why he had to die?''

Reverend Smith rose to his feet and stared down at the young boy sitting in front of him. A stinging pain hit the reverend's chest as he saw the helplessness in the young boy's eyes. The reverend wanted to hold the boy and comfort him, but all he had for him were words.

''Harlen, God is the only one who can take a life.'' The reverend bit his bottom lip as he asked, ''Are you sure he is dead, son?''

Harlen nodded as he pleaded, ''You have to help me, Reverend. I have nowhere else to go. You're the only person I know that I feel I can call family. I am scared; I don't know what to do. I need you; please, Reverend, help me.''

The reverend patted Harlen on the head. His voice regained its gentle tone. He looked around the church, his mind going a mile a minute. Even though young Harlen was looking to him for help, he couldn't help but feel the stench of fear gripping him. What if the boy lost control and decided to kill him? A sense of panic gripped the reverend, but he fought to maintain his composure as he said, ''I will help you, son, but you must do everything I tell you. Do you understand what I'm telling you, Harlen?''

Harlen nodded his head yes.

The reverend looked around again, then added, ''First I want you to kneel here and pray for forgiveness. I will be right back. Don't worry; everything will be just fine.''

Harlen smiled through his tears as he thanked the reverend.

''Bless you, sir, and someday I will make you proud of me. I will make a difference in this world. I promise.''

The reverend nodded and walked away. Harlen knelt and prayed to the statue of Jesus Christ. The fear began leaving young Harlen. He knew he had made the right decision coming here to seek Reverend Smith's help. The reverend was an intelligent man. He would know what to do. Harlen soon would be safe; everything would work out fine. Reverend Smith knew how evil Harlen's father was. He had deserved to die, and Harlen was just a weapon of God. The reverend knew this. He knew that Harlen's father's vile ways had to end. Harlen looked away from the statue as he heard Reverend Smith calling out his name.

"Harlen, please come over here!"

Harlen squinted to see where the reverend was standing. He saw the man's silhouette in the doorway. Slowly Harlen rose to his feet and walked over to where the reverend stood. Harlen stopped when he reached the reverend, who stood rigid, his arms behind his back. His voice had lost all his gentleness.

"I called the police, Harlen. They should be here any moment. Even though you feel just in what you did, it was wrong. We cannot assume God wanted a man dead through your hands. Only God has the right to take a life, no matter how evil that life may be. Do you understand what I am trying to tell you, Harlen? Murder is an act against man and God."

Harlen stared with disbelief at Reverend Smith, betrayed by the one man on this earth he had trusted. Backing away, Harlen spit out his words of anger.

"You said you would help me! You lied to me! They will lock me up like an animal. For what? Killing a evil bastard like my father? Look at my face, reverend! I look like a jigsaw puzzle. My father did that. Where was the justice then? To hell with you. I am not waiting for the police and I hope your fucking soul rots in hell!" Harlen turned to leave.

The reverend shouted at him, "You are not going anywhere, son!"

Harlen heard the hammer of a gun cock back. He turned toward the sound. The reverend stood in the doorway, a revolver aimed at Harlen. Harlen smiled as he quietly asked, "You mean you would actually shoot one of God's children?"

The reverend's voice shook with terror as he stuttered out the words.

"Only if you f-f-force me to, son. N-n-now, please s-s-sit on the floor. Leave your h-h-hands where I can s-s-see them."

Harlen went on smiling. He watched as the gun shook in the old man's hand. The reverend was scared, terrified at the thought that he might be forced to take a human life. Harlen knew that he could rush the old preacher and overpower him but didn't. He did as instructed and sat on the floor. Folding his arms across his chest, Harlen continued to smile at the preacher.

Reverend Smith began to feel even uneasier at the sudden calm of the young man. Smith began to speak, his voice filled with tension.

"I know you feel as if I betrayed you, Harlen. Believe me, when you get older you will understand, maybe even thank me for today."

Harlen didn't reply. He just smiled. The reverend released a sigh of relief as the police entered the church, lowered his gun, and pointed at Harlen. The officers walked over to where Harlen sat and grabbed him by the arms. One of the officers began reading Harlen his rights; the other patted him down and pulled out the .45 revolver hidden in his belt. The police officers forced Harlen's arms in back of him and handcuffed him. They then pushed Harlen toward the door. As they escorted Harlen out of the church, the last words Harlen heard as the church doors closed behind him were Reverend Smith's saying: "May God forgive you."

The thunder exploded louder this time. The lights flickered for a brief moment. Harlen turned toward Zeke asking, "Is there an emergency light in this building?"

Zeke pointed as he quietly replied, "We have floods in three different areas. The batteries are good; we just tested them last week."

Harlen looked at the three different areas where Zeke pointed. There would be plenty of light if the power did go off. Harlen jumped off the table and walked back to the door, glaring through the peephole again at the back lot. The rain continued to rage outside. The thunder crashed louder and more frequently. In the midst of the roaring thunder Harlen whispered, "I wonder if God will ever forgive me, Reverend?"

Harlen smiled as he continued to watch the rain pound the pavement.

121

14

Hanson stared blankly at the back door of the Golden Aces, silently praying that Harlen Jones would come out with his hands in the air, surrendering himself to the law. A tapping on Hanson's passenger side window broke his trance. He turned. Standing in the rain bent over motioning to him was Overstreet. Hanson resisted the temptation to let the trooper stand in the rain and reached over and unlocked the door. Overstreet slid inside next to Hanson, took off his hat, and wiped the rain from his face. Finishing drying his face, Overstreet put his hat back on his head, looking at his reflection in the rearview mirror to make sure the hat was perfectly placed on his head. Pleased with the way his hat fitted, he remarked, "This has to be the worst storm we have had in this area in years! It sure isn't helping our situation any." Pausing for a moment, Overstreet quietly asked, "Would you like to see who we are dealing with?"

Overstreet reached inside his coat, where he had a brown envelope protected from the rain. He handed it to Hanson as he spoke.

"This is Harlen Jones's record along with his photo from Jackson State Prison."

Hanson took the envelope and opened it. His eyes scanned the report on Harlen Jones's hellish life; then Hanson glanced at the photo. A sick feeling smothered Hanson as he stared at the picture of Jones. The jagged scars covered his entire face.

Overstreet chimed in quietly with, 'Jones's father did that to him as a kid. Do you think this guy gives a damn about anything in this world? Would you?"

Hanson didn't comment on Overstreet's question. Instead Hanson found himself feeling pity for this man. The pain this poor bastard must have felt.

Hanson's thoughts where stopped as Overstreet added, "I guess it is time to call our friend in there and try to buy a little more time. Enough time to allow this rain to let up a bit."

Hanson didn't look at Overstreet as he replied quietly, "I've already called him. He is not going to give us one minute more. At three o'clock we better have what he wants or he will kill Zeke. I know he is not bluffing."

Overstreet looked puzzled at first; then a slightly angry tone entered his voice as he asked, "Why did you contact him without informing me?" Overstreet's voice grew harsher: "I thought I made it clear that this is my jurisdiction now?"

Releasing a frustrated sigh, Overstreet asked, "What did you say to him?"

Hanson's face flushed. His tone became defensive: "I attempted to convince him we needed more time." Pausing for a moment, Hanson angrily added, "He is not stupid. He knew I was stalling for more time. Damn it, Overstreet, don't treat me like a child."

Overstreet ignored Hanson's comment and asked, "What else did you say to him?"

Irritated, Hanson snapped out his reply, throwing the envelope and all the files at Overstreet as he did.

"That was about it, except I told him we knew who he was."

Overstreet's calm demeanor vanished. Exploding with anger, he pounded his fist on the dashboard.

"Why in God's name would you tell him that? Didn't you realize information like that is to our advantage?"

Before Hanson could respond, a large black limousine pulled up next to them. Hanson recognized the car. It was Mayor Todd Martin. The driver stepped out of the limousine and walked over to Hanson's patrol car. The rain pounded down on the driver who didn't even flinch. Bending over, he motioned for Hanson to roll down his window. The sheriff complied with the driver's wishes.

In a firm but very polite voice the driver spoke: "Good afternoon, Sheriff. Mayor Martin wishes you to join him in his car, please."

The driver didn't wait for a reply. Turning, he walked back to the limousine, standing perfectly still in front of the limousine door waiting for Hanson to honor the mayor's request.

Hanson turned to Overstreet and in a sarcastic voice said, "Feel free to join me, Captain. I wouldn't want to say or do anything that you would disapprove of."

Hanson didn't wait for Overstreet to reply but he opened his car door and quickly ran to where the driver stood. Overstreet followed close behind, each man trying unsuccefully to dodge the heavy rain pouring from the skies. The driver stood rigid, opening the limousine door. Hanson slid in quickly, followed by Overstreet. The driver closed the door and remained outside the limousine in nature's onslaught, waiting for the mayor's next order.

"We are set, Hank; get out of the rain."

The driver nodded and walked around to the driver's side of the car. Sitting behind the wheel, he kept his eyes forward. Rain dripped down his long face. Nonchalantly he wiped his face with a cloth that had been on the seat next to him. Then leaning over he pushed a button that allowed a glass to rise from the seat and separate him from the occupants in the backseat.

Mayor Todd Martin stood only five-foot-seven and was extremely overweight for not only his height but also his sixty-three years of age. His hair, a snowy white, remained shortly cropped on his head. His dark-rimmed glasses did not fit his round face properly. They continually slipped down the bridge of his nose. It really seemed impossible that he held such a distinguished position, demanding not only respect but also absolute fear. Todd Martin looked anything but fearless. The one thing Hanson did learn about Martin: never be fooled by appearance. Martin, a shrewd and manipulative man, if need be could be as heartless and ruthless as any person on this planet Hanson ever met.

The mayor broke the silence as he directed his questions to Hanson, ignoring Overstreet completely.

"I decided, because of the delicate nature of our problem, to handle the money transaction myself. What I need to know at this juncture is if we have everything under control?"

Hanson replied in an uncertain tone, "It depends on what you consider under control? No one has died . . . yet. We know the man who is holding Zeke hostage. He is one dangerous man, who has killed before. Frankly, Mayor, I think the whole situation stinks."

Todd Martin's expression became grim. He thought of Zeke as the son he never had. The very thought of Zeke being in danger depressed the mayor. He reached down and lifted a black briefcase from the floor. He sat it on his lap and gently patted the top of it.

124

"This is the money you asked for. One hundred thousand dollars. I had to call in quite a few favors to get it, but if it will save Zeke's life I would bargain with the devil himself."

Overstreet spoke for the first time since being in the car. He asked in a curious tone, "You don't really plan on giving him the money do you?"

The mayor glanced over at Overstreet. "Who might you be?"

Overstreet extended his hand toward the mayor as he introduced himself, "I am Captain David Overstreet. I am with the Michigan State Police. I am now in charge here, sir. The man inside of the restaurant is a fugitive from prison."

The mayor did not allow Overstreet to continue or accepted his hand to shake it. Overstreet, feeling foolish, brought his hand back to his side as the mayor snapped at him, "Slow down a minute, son."

Martin turned to Hanson, asking in a whisper, "What the hell is going on here, Bob?"

Overstreet replied instead of Hanson.

"I told you what is going on, sir. The man in there escaped from a state prison. He killed two men during his escape. I have taken charge of the situation here, so I would appreciate it if you would direct your questions to me."

Martin shot a stern look at Overstreet. "I am talking to the sheriff, not you. Please stop interrupting me every time I talk. If I want you to answer any of my questions I will direct them at you."

Overstreet's voice remained calm: "When talking about the man inside of that restaurant, you are talking to me. As I said before, this is my jurisdiction now. We are dealing with a killer. Sheriff Hanson, even though I respect him, is not qualified to handle something of this nature."

Hanson felt as if he had become invisible. Both men acted if as he were not there. It appeared this entire conversation quickly had become a power struggle, testing the wills of both men. Hanson watched as the mayor pushed his glasses back up the bridge of his nose. A strange smirk creased Martin's face. Leaning forward, putting his face directly in front of the state trooper's, he asked, "So tell me, Captain, how do you plan on handling this crisis?"

Overstreet didn't flinch. Meeting the mayor's stare, the trooper coldly replied, "I have men deployed in specified areas in the field behind us. They all are marksmen. When Jones comes out with his hostage, one of my men should have a clear shot. He takes it, this whole ordeal is over."

Martin's voice echoed his anger as he growled, "That is it? This is what you call a plan? What about Zeke Riley? Where does he fit into the scheme of this plan? Is there any thought at all about a safety factor? You feel that your men are such amazing marksmen that they can see and hit their target in this monsoon? You are an idiot, Captain. As far as I am concerned, Sheriff Hanson is in charge of this case, not you."

Overstreet attempted to defend his plan and his authority in this situation, but Martin added rudely, "This is my town, Captain. The people who live in this town rely on my judgment—"

Overstreet interrupted Martin's statement, sternly saying, "It may be your town, Mayor, but the man inside of that restaurant is my responsibility."

Martin's voice lowered as he moved closer to Overstreet.

"I have connections in places that you couldn't begin to dream of. So please listen very close to what I am about to say. We are going to comply with the demands that are given to us. After we assure the safety of Zeke Riley, then and only then we take action against the animal inside there. Do I make myself clear?"

Hanson watched as the two men battled for control, Overstreet determined to remain calm. Both men continued to ignore Hanson sitting in the car with them.

Overstreet maintained his cold, calculated demeanor as he answered, "That is impossible, Mayor. I don't think you realize how dangerous the man inside that building is. His name is Harlen Jones. We know for a fact that he has murdered at least four people, one being his own father. This man has no regard for life; do you actually think he will allow Zeke to live once he has eluded us? Mayor, I don't care what connections you may have. Harlen Jones will be either back in my custody or dead after he steps out of that restaurant."

Hanson interceded, adding his thoughts: "Mayor, as much as I hate to admit it, I must agree with Overstreet. We cannot allow this killer to escape."

Overstreet appeared more stunned by Hanson's statement than the mayor was. The last person the trooper expected to be an ally was Sheriff Hanson. Before Overstreet could enjoy the sheriff's support, the mayor turned and quickly started a guilt trip with Hanson's mind.

"Bob, Zeke is your friend. How could you possibly agree with this man? What he proposes to do will cause the death of that friend. Look outside, Bob. You are an expert marksman with pistol and rifle. Would you be able to guarantee hitting a specified target in this downpour? Both you and the captain here have admitted to me that this man is a cold-blooded killer. A man who would not think twice about killing Zeke if he felt threatened in his situation. I cannot deal with those types of odds when a friend's life hangs in the balance. I am sorry if you feel I am wrong if I feel Zeke Riley's life is more important than some convict's. Especially since we all know that this convict will be either captured or dead in the near future anyway."

The limousine filled with an eerie silence. Only the raging storm outside shattered the silence. All three men appeared to be gathering their thoughts on what to say next. Martin finally spoke.

"Barnsville since its founding never has felt the pain of a violent crime. We have been spared the violence of the outside world; that is why people stay here. This is as close to Utopia as one can imagine. We have never suffered the pain of anyone being murdered in our town. I do not plan on Zeke becoming the first. I want to talk to this Harlen Jones. Maybe I can strike up some type of deal to end this craziness."

Overstreet responded sharply to the mayor's comments.

"I don't think you have heard a single word I said, Mayor. There is no reasoning with a man like Harlen Jones. I think it is great that your precious little town has avoided reality for all these years. Unfortunately, now it is here and you better learn to deal with it. I've already told you of this man's past; what more do you need to be convinced?"

Martin leaned back in his seat and patted his chin with his finger as he said in a mocking tone, "Captain Overstreet, I truly thank you for your deep concern for our town's fate, but as I said, this is my town."

Overstreet could feel the flush of embarrassment rush through his face. He glanced first at Hanson, to see what type of reaction he would get from him. Hanson gave him none. Overstreet then turned his attention to Martin. Trying hard to keep his temper in check, Overstreet talked slowly.

"Mayor, I'm trying to treat you with the respect your position deserves, but I swear to you if I need to I will call the governor himself on this case."

Martin smiled as he replied wickedly, "Be my guest, Captain, and please give him my regards. We have been friends for years."

Overstreet cursed softly under his breath. Martin then asked him politely, "Captain, all I want is for you to be open-minded, will you at least try that for me? You know, humor an old man?"

Overstreet bit back his anger and frustration and just nodded his head yes.

Martin turned to Hanson and asked, "Is it possible for me to talk to this Harlen Jones myself?"

Hanson shot a glance at the state trooper. Overstreet nodded his head yes. Hanson could sense the anger in the big man and could see Overstreet's anger boiling inside him.

Hanson let out a heavy sigh, then quietly replied, "We keep in contact by using the portable phone in my car."

Martin clapped his hands together. Smiling, he said, "Great. I will call him from here. I want both of you young men to watch and learn how negotiations should be handled."

Martin then picked up the phone resting in its cradle in his car. Stopping, he looked over at Hanson and asked, "Have you talked to Zeke at all?"

Hanson shook his head no. Martin shook his head as he said quietly, "Well, how do we even know Zeke is alive? Two trained lawmen and neither of you asked to talk to Zeke? Christ, before we even think about moving to the next level with this monster he is going to first allow us to talk with Zeke so we know if he is alive or dead."

Hanson and Overstreet looked at each other, both embarrassed that it had taken someone other than themselves to think about talking to the hostage. Martin looked at both of them, then told Hanson, "Please give me the number of the restaurant."

Hanson handed Martin the paper with the Golden Aces' number on it. Martin took it, reached down for his phone and proceeded to make his attempt to negotiate with the devil holding his friend.

15

Martin smiled at the two men across from him as the phone at the Golden Aces began to ring. It rang twice. A harsh voice answered from the other end.

"You're early, Sheriff. It better be with some good news."

Clearing his throat, Martin replied, "Mr. Jones, I am Mayor Todd Martin. I would like to speak to you about the situation we both appear to be in."

Harlen, stunned to hear a voice besides that of the sheriff, moved the phone away from his ear. Regaining his composure, he moved the phone back and angrily asked, "Where the hell is the sheriff?"

Martin paused before answering. Sensing the hostility in the man's voice, the mayor forced himself to sound sincere in his reply.

"He is here, Mr. Jones, but I decided it was time for me to step in and start the negotiations."

Sarcastic laughter rang in Todd Martin's ear. Pure evil echoed from that end. Martin knew from Harlen's laugh that he was about to embark in a conversation with a member of an element of society he tried to shield his town from. The laughter stopped, replaced with an icy voice.

"We have nothing to negotiate. Either you follow my demands to the letter or I kill my hostage."

A strange sense of excitement ran through Martin's body. He felt young again. Here he sat in the middle of a storm talking to a madman, bargaining for a life. This would be his greatest challenge ever. The only problem was if he lost, it would mean the death of a friend. Pushing back his glasses to fit his face, he spoke in a friendly voice.

"I realize that, Mr. Jones. I assure you we plan on meeting your demands, if possible. What I must know is if we can trust you? What will prevent you from killing Mr. Riley as soon as you feel safe? Do you see the predicament that I am in?"

Martin paused, allowing Harlen to reply if he wanted. All Martin could hear was the heavy breathing on the other end. Quickly Martin continued.

"I want to end this as quickly as possible, but how can you guarantee that Zeke will be unharmed? You can't; that leaves my hands tied. So I would like a few suggestions from you. How do you feel we can handle this exchange so both sides are satisfied?"

The other end of the phone remained silent; only heavy breathing came from that end. Martin continued.

"There is no easy solution, is there, Mr. Jones? Neither you nor I trust each other. That makes everything so difficult. Till one of us starts to trust the other I cannot see an end to our problem . . . except for the obvious one: two men dying. That would be a shame."

Harlen blurted back, "Maybe you think I am bluffing, Mayor? You fucking asshole, who in the hell do you think you're talking to? You're right about one thing, dickhead. In two hours this man will die. You know what, asshole? More than likely so will I. I'm not afraid of dying; too bad this pussy with me can't say the same. So fuck you and your negotiations."

A sly grin crossed Martin's face, as he knew he had struck a nerve in his opponent, forcing him to think of the reality of his predicament. Martin continued to speak in a friendly tone despite the hostility in Harlen's voice.

"I believe you, Mr. Jones. I really do. As I said earlier, I want to meet all of your demands but I need you to help me. I don't think I am asking for much. Consider it like we were conducting any other business deal. I must know what I am buying won't be damaged. I need you to assure me of that. The money is here; transportation will be no problem. If we find a solution to this trust dilemma. You must have an idea for an exchange that will satisfy both parties. It is up to you, Mr. Jones, and how badly you want to leave my town. I do promise you this: if you harm Zeke, you will die."

Harlen's voice showed a trace of respect as he replied, "I guess you're right, Mayor. We appear to have reached an impasse. You must have some type of plan or you would not be wasting time talking to me. What do you suggest?"

Before Martin could reply to Harlen's question, Harlen added quickly, "Please don't tell me to release my hostage first. I am beginning to like you. Don't ruin it by a stupid comment like that."

Martin found himself chuckling at Harlen's comment. Glancing over at the two law officers, both of whom glared at him like he was an old fool, Martin winked at them and answered Harlen, "I do have something in mind, Mr. Jones. A plan I feel might benefit both parties involved."

Harlen's voice became softer.

"I am listening, Mayor."

Martin smiled. Harlen's voice now sounded calm and interested. Martin continued, "I would be willing to meet you halfway. I will put a portable phone in the car we give you, allow you to leave the building unharmed. You then will go to a specific area. There you will release Zeke, then contact me on the phone. I will leave my limousine number on the front seat. I will talk to Zeke, if he is safe. I will drop the money off where you ask. Once you pick up the money you will tell me the location where you left Zeke. It is a simple plan that requires nothing but trust from both sides. As you can see, Mr. Jones, I am willing to believe you won't harm Zeke as long as you receive what you want. You must feel the same way. Is it a deal?"

The air held sounds only of the rain and crashing thunder. A flash of lightning lit up the sky. It was an eerie sight. The town of Barnsville seemed to be under attack from the gods.

Harlen replied, speaking loud enough to be heard over the sudden barrage of thunder, "I will have to think about it, Mayor. The last time I trusted somebody, I wound up in a reform school. Give me your number; I will call you back shortly with my decision."

Martin quickly asked, "Would it be OK for me to talk to Zeke?"

Harlen released a heavy sigh, then replied sharply, "Make it quick, Mayor. I am not running a answering service."

Harlen pointed to Zeke, then motioned for him to come to the phone. Zeke rose slowly to his feet. He began feeling an inkling of hope. Quickly he moved to where Harlen stood holding the phone. Harlen held up his hand and whispered, "Make it short and sweet, understand?"

Zeke nodded his head yes. Harlen handed Zeke the receiver. He took it and waited for Harlen's signal to talk. Harlen motioned to Zeke that it was all right to start. He put the receiver to his ear and cautiously spoke.

"Hello?"

Martin felt a twinge of hope hearing Zeke's voice. He tried to sound positive as he spoke to Zeke.

"How are you doing, Zeke? Is he treating you OK?"

Zeke replied meekly, "I'm fine, sir. It is good to hear your voice."

Martin could hear the fear in Zeke's voice. It sounded as if he had given up hope. Martin attempted to sound reassuring.

"You hang in there, son; this will all be over shortly. I promise."

Zeke glanced over at Harlen. He could tell that he was getting impatient.

"Could you do me a favor, sir? Would you please tell Tina not to worry? Please convince her that everything is going to be just fine."

Martin found himself nodding, as he replied, "Of course I will, Zeke."

Zeke added quickly, "One other thing, sir. Please tell her that I love her."

Martin felt a lump in the middle of his throat. Zeke sounded so fragile and lost. A sadness rang in his voice as if he knew he was going to die. Trying to sound confident, Martin replied, "I will tell her, Zeke. Though I know you will be telling her yourself very soon. Please put Mr. Jones back on the phone."

Zeke nodded his head yes. Turning toward Harlen, Zeke handed him the phone. Harlen took it, jerking his head in the direction of where Zeke had been sitting. Zeke knew what Harlen was ordering him to do without the words and moved slowly back to his corner. The glimmer of hope he had felt a few seconds ago vanished with each step. Harlen waited till Zeke sat back down.

"Satisfied? He is still alive. Now give me your number. I will contact you later with my answer."

Martin gave Harlen his number, then hung up. He stared at the two men sitting across from him. Martin's voice beamed with confidence.

"I think he will accept my offer. This entire mess should be over shortly, gentlemen."

Overstreet snapped angrily, "There is no way I am going to allow you to let this man escape. He is a cold-blooded killer. You were talking to him as if you were selling him insurance. I don't care who you are, I will not allow this travesty to happen."

Martin smiled. It was a sarcastic one and, he meant for it to irritate Overstreet. Martin shook his head slightly and turned his attention to Hanson. Tilting his head slightly, trying to look directly into Hanson's eyes, he asked in a curious voice, "Do you feel the same way, Bob? Do you think what I am doing is a travesty of justice? Should I just sit back and watch as a decent man dies? Is this Harlen Jones worth the life of Zeke Riley? Tell me how you feel about this. I really want to know."

Hanson looked over at the seething state trooper, then back at Todd Martin. He felt a gnawing guilt in the pit of his stomach. Zeke was his friend, but to let a killer go scot-free seemed morally wrong. Quietly Hanson expressed his feelings to the mayor.

"I don't want anything to happen to Zeke, he is my best friend, but there must be a different way to free him? We can't just let a convicted killer free. It would be morally wrong. Sorry, Mayor, I must agree with Overstreet on this."

Martin took off his glasses and began rubbing his eyes. Carefully he fitted them back on his face, deliberately taking his time, trying to make Hanson feel uneasy. Calmly Martin asked Hanson, "So you think I am wrong? That means you agree with the plan that Mr. Overstreet proposes? Should I tell Tina why her husband died tonight or will you?"

Overstreet interceded. He could see what Martin was attempting to do to the young sheriff's mind. From the sheriff's facial expression, it was working. Martin twisted the knife of guilt right through Hanson's heart.

"You are assuming my plan will not be successful. I feel it will, that Riley will have more than a seventy percent chance of making it out unharmed."

Martin exploded with anger.

"I guess you consider that good odds? We are talking about a human life, not some damn statistic. If Jones accepts my terms, Zeke lives and you can find your precious convict within hours. I am not suggesting you let this animal go free. All I want is Zeke to have a chance to live. What is so wrong with that?"

Overstreet and Hanson glanced at each other. Hanson then asked the trooper, "Would there be any way to plant a tracking device in the car?"

Martin leaned back in his seat. He smiled, knowing he had finally reached one of them.

Overstreet hesitated before he replied, glancing at the mayor, who now was wearing a smug look on his face. Overstreet wanted to go over and wipe it off Martin's face with his fist but resisted the temptation, instead answering, "I guess it would be possible, but we still risk the chance of him discovering it. Then where would your dear friend be?"

Hanson ignored the sarcasm and continued, "Could we trace it from the ground and the air?"

"Yes, but I still don't like it," Overstreet folded his arms and leaned back in the seat, adding, "Letting this punk out will be a mistake. We have to end it here."

Martin quipped, "That sounds real professional, Captain."

Overstreet lunged forward. His anger spewed out of him as he bellowed, "Listen, you old fool! I've been dealing with these kinds of people for over ten years. You do not reach the rank of captain in the state police without conducting yourself like a professional. So why don't you tend to your town you so proudly boast about and leave the police work to those who know what they are doing?"

Martin leaned over and looked eye to eye with the raging trooper. The mayor's voice remained calm, but his eyes revealed his fury.

"This old fool fought in two wars. I watched young men die for a cause they believed in, a purpose. I will not watch one die because your pride has been wounded. I could pick up this phone and make one call and show you what kind of power I wield in this area. I won't because you are going to calm down and think. Then you are going to make the right decision. Am I correct, Mr. Overstreet?"

Hanson watched in amazement. It was clear how Todd Martin maintained his power in this town. He made the strongest man feel like a helpless fool, and Overstreet was no exception.

Overstreet's anger subsided. Embarrassment trickled through him. He sat up straight, saying, softly, "I didn't mean to call you an old fool. I'm sorry. I just don't want this man to escape to harm someone else. Can you understand that, Mayor?"

Martin put his hand on the trooper's shoulder and with true concern in his voice replied, "Of course I understand. Believe me,

Captain, I know what you are feeling. We all feel the same way, but we must work as a team. Trust me, son; my plan will work. We also will go with the transmitter placed on the car we give Jones so we know where he is at all times. If this blasted rain lets up, we can get a helicopter in the air and cover him from the sky. So what do you say? Do we stop this senseless bickering and start to act as a team?"

Overstreet nodded his head yes.

Martin turned to Hanson and, giving him a broad smile, asked, "What do you say, Bob? Are we a team?"

Hanson couldn't help but smile back. He then nodded his head yes.

Martin took his hand off Overstreet's shoulder and clasping his hands together, let out a hardy, "Great."

Overstreet quietly said, "I plan on keeping my men in place just in case something backfires on our new plan."

Martin smiled, replying, "Captain, I agree completely."

Martin's smile quickly disappeared; his voice became subdued.

"I guess you both heard me promise Zeke that I would contact his wife?"

Hanson let out a sigh, replying, "I have a deputy with her now: Bill Starr. I figured he would be the best choice to inform her on what was going on. They are very close friends. If you want me to, I could contact Starr and have him relay Zeke's message for you, sir?"

Martin shook his head no. "Thank you, Bob, but I made Zeke a promise and I will follow through with it." Martin began rubbing the back of his neck as he quietly added, "I would like some privacy when I make this call. If you gentlemen could give me a few moments alone, we can talk strategy after I am through."

Hanson and Overstreet both nodded their heads yes. Overstreet opened the car door. Both men hurried out and sprinted back to Hanson's car.

Martin watched as the two men disappeared into Hanson's patrol car. Turning his attention back to the phone, he stared painfully at it for a moment, trying to think of the right words to say to Tina, agonizing with each sentence that slipped into his mind. No matter what words he chose they sounded wrong. Zeke and Tina had formed a special type of love, a rarity in this day and age. Martin had known both of them since they were only children. Now Zeke very possibly could be dead before the day ended. Shaking off the morbid feelings that had crept into his mind, Martin tried to think of how to tell Tina exactly what Zeke wanted him to say, that he loved her.

Martin picked up the phone and slowly punched in Tina's number. He closed his eyes as he listened to the phone ring.

16

Starr paced outside Tina's bedroom, his eyes periodically darting to the kitchen. Frank Parker's body still remained lying on the tile floor. Starr closed his eyes tightly, trying hard to convince himself he was doing the right thing, trying to block out all the principles he had ever believed in. His mind battling with his heart over what was right and wrong. The battle lines drawn, his mind cried out for justice. A violent crime became the cry of war. A man lay dead on the kitchen floor, shot through the heart, his life taken from him, brutally ended, and whether he deserved it or not, Tina had taken the law into her own hands. Logic pure and simple. Starr should listen to the voices in his mind. The heart, though, battled fiercely from another side, bringing out feelings Starr had tried to bury deep inside his soul, loyalty for someone he truly cared for, a friend in deep trouble, so fragile anything could push her over the edge. She needed Starr's help to keep her out of prison. Starr wasn't blind. Tina's body was bruised and battered. She had been beaten by the same man she had shot unmercifully. What Tina did was wrong, in the eyes of the law and God, but where do friendships stop and justice begin? Starr stopped pacing and knocked on Tina's door, asking hurriedly, "Tina, are you almost ready?"

The bedroom door opened. Tina stood in the entrance staring down at the floor. She had changed into a pink blouse and a pair of faded jeans. Her hair was combed back and tied into a small ponytail. Though her face still remained swollen and the bruises still vividly visible, Tina's beauty remained. Starr knew as she appeared before him who became victorious in the battle of his mind and heart. He had no choice but to help her.

Tina smiled and shyly said, "Sorry I took so long, Bill, but I needed to shower to feel human again."

Starr nodded his head but quickly said, "I understand, Tina, but if we are going to take care of this problem we must get started."

Tina's smile disappeared. Her eyes pleaded as she asked, "Will you please try and find out about Zeke? I must know. If anything happens to him then nothing else matters."

Before Starr could answer, the sudden blaring of the telephone startled both of them. Starr turned and stared at the phone. Tina moved next to him, both glaring at the phone, each of them with the same horrible thought . . . Zeke was dead.

"Answer it, Tina. It may be about Zeke."

Tina wearily headed toward the phone, fear mounting with each step. Horrible visions of Zeke's body lying in a pool of blood raced through her mind. Each step she took her heart pounded faster. Stopping in front of the phone, she paused for an instant, attempting to gain her composure before she answered it. Glancing back at Starr, her eyes showed the fear she felt. Starr with hand motions urged her to pick up the receiver. Slowly she reached down and lifted the phone off the hook. Her voice trembled as she spoke.

"Hello?"

A warm and gentle voice replied from the other end, "Hello, Tina. This is Mayor Martin."

Tina's fears began raging out of control when she heard Martin's voice. Zeke must be dead; why else would the mayor himself call? Tina's head pounded as she screamed into the receiver, "Zeke is dead! That is why you are calling me, Mayor, right? My Zeke is dead."

A soothing voice replied, "No, Tina. Zeke is very much alive. I am calling to relay a message from him."

Tina's heart leaped with joy. Zeke was safe. Tina could not hide her excitement as she shouted, "Zeke is free! You are telling me he is no longer a hostage? I don't know how to tha—"

Martin interrupted before Tina could finish what she was saying: "Not yet, Tina, but soon. It is all being worked out. I did talk to Zeke. He told me to tell you not to worry. He also made me promise to tell you that he loves you."

Tears began rolling down Tina's face. The mayor's words felt like a dagger stabbing at her heart.

Starr, now next to Tina, put his arms around her and whispered, "Is he all right?"

Tina nodded her head yes. She resumed talking to the mayor in a pleading voice.

138

"Mayor, I need to talk to him, hear his voice, so I can be sure he is alive. I want to tell him myself that I love him. Please help me do this, Mayor."

Martin tried to make his voice sound reassuring as he replied, "I don't think that will be possible, Tina. We are negotiating for his release right now. Everything appears to be falling into place. If the man holding Zeke hostage hears a desperate woman pleading for Zeke it may weaken our bargaining power. He might feel he has the upper hand and demand more."

Tina's fear turned to anger. Her hands trembled as she screamed, "He does have the upper hand! He is holding my husband's life in its grip! I am not asking for much. All I want is to hear Zeke's voice. To be allowed to tell him I love him. Mayor, please, just a few moments on the phone with him."

Martin's voice remained calm despite the anguish in Tina's voice. He shared the pain that Tina felt. He also knew if he allowed his emotions to dictate how he handled this situation, Harlen Jones would take full advantage of it. That was not going to happen.

"I'm sorry, Tina, I cannot do that. Please understand why and trust what I'm doing. I will have Zeke home soon. I promise."

Tina continued to protest.

"Zeke thinks of you like a father. He worships you, Mayor. Can't you search your soul and try and find some compassion?"

Starr took his arms away from Tina. He couldn't hear the entire conversation, but he knew Mayor Martin. Once that man made up his mind no one would change it. Starr hoarsely whispered to Tina, "We have to take care of this other problem. Please accept what the mayor is saying. It sounds to me as if he has it totally under control."

Tina whirled around, glaring at Starr. She didn't say a word. Her eyes showed her fury. Martin's reply from the other end didn't ease her anger any.

"Tina, I love Zeke, too. That is why I am forcing myself to ignore your pleas. Please trust me, Tina. I will call you when it is over."

The dial tone buzzed in Tina's ear. She slammed the phone down. Her anger raged as she shouted at Starr, "You seem more concerned about that piece of garbage laying in my kitchen than about Zeke! I told you without Zeke nothing matters! All that I have done was for him. Right or wrong, I did it out of love!"

Tina's raging turned to tears as she begged Starr, "I need you to help me get in touch with Zeke. I need to hear his voice. To know for my own sanity he is safe."

Starr erupted with anger as he shouted at Tina, "Tina, I am going against every principle I believe in to help you! Maybe you have forgotten that I am a deputy sheriff? I am helping to cover up a crime. If we get caught, I will be arrested as an accomplice."

Pausing, Starr's voice became calmer.

"I am doing this because we are friends. I care about you and Zeke."

Starr tried to avoid looking into Tina's deep blue eyes but couldn't help seeing the pain in her eyes.

"After we dispose of Parker's body and if Zeke is still not released I will find a way to let you talk to him."

A huge smile crossed Tina's face. "I knew you would help me, Bill."

Starr shook his head back and forth and sternly lectured Tina, "I need you to stay levelheaded. Stop flying off the handle over every little thing that is said. Tina, I am really worried about you and your state of mind. When this is over I want you to seek out professional guidance."

A sly grin creased Tina's mouth, her anger suppressed as she maintained a calm demeanor and asked, "That is the second time you mentioned professional help. Do you think I am crazy, Bill?"

A cold chill swept through Starr's body. Tina's voice sounded strange. Her eyes appeared to be glaring right into his soul. The woman standing in front of him now was only a shell of the friend he knew. He began to get the sick feeling he had made a mistake in agreeing to help her. Maybe she had already slipped into complete madness.

"Do you think I am crazy, Bill?"

Starr forced himself to shake off the negative feelings. Tina needed him and he was not going to turn his back on her now.

"No, Tina, but you are not yourself. You blame God for everything that occurs anymore. You must stop believing that you are having a private war with him. Killing Parker was in self-defense. I do believe that. The bruises on your face show how he beat you. Despite the hate and anger you feel towards Parker, you will still need to deal with the guilt. That is why I want you to seek help. You may feel that what you did was necessary. I can assure you later the guilt will push you into a madding depression. Tina, I still live with the nightmares of the people I had to shoot when on the force in Detroit. I care for you, Tina. I don't want that happening to you."

Tina appeared satisfied with Starr's explanation. She walked over and put her arms around him and in an apologetic voice said, "I'm sorry, Bill. I know you are trying to help. I am just worried about Zeke. As far as my private war with God goes, maybe it sounds crazy, to you but it is true. There are things you don't know about me. Things I am ashamed to tell anyone. God has every right to be angry with me, but he is also taking it out on Zeke. That is not right."

Tina laid her head on Starr's chest, repeating as she did, "That is not right."

Starr began brushing Tina's hair back, not saying a word, wishing there was a way to end her pain and guilt. He continued to stroke her hair gently. The two of them stood in the middle of the room, wrapped in the security of each other's arms.

Starr quietly said, "We have to take care of Parker."

Tina nodded her head in agreement. Breaking her hold on Starr, she glanced at Parker's bloody body lying motionless on the kitchen floor, his eyes showing the terror he had felt before he died. No emotion crept into Tina's voice as she asked, "Are you sure you want to go through with this, Bill? You can leave. I swear to you if I get caught I won't mention your name. I don't want another life destroyed because of me."

Starr forced a smile as he replied, "What are friends for? Go fill in that hole you dug in the backyard. We don't want anything looking suspicious when Parker is reported missing."

Tina smiled and moved toward the back door.

Starr yelled out to her, "You better put on a jacket or something! It is pouring out there."

Tina nodded and walked over to the hall closet. Opening up the door, she reached in and pulled out a bright yellow raincoat and slipped it on. Starr couldn't help smiling as he watched her. She was lovely and still had that girlish look about her. Tina felt Starr's eyes watching her. Shyly she glanced up and smiled at him, then walked quickly past him to the back door. As she was walking through the kitchen, she stopped for a brief moment and stared at Parker's body sprawled on the tile floor. She then disappeared. Starr heard the back door open and close. Turning, he walked to the front door and opened it. He stared out into the pouring rain. Thunder echoed off in the distance; flashes of lightning lit up the darkened skies. Starr's eyes then darted up and down the deserted street. He scurried out of the house and ran across the street to where Parker's car was parked. He tried to open it but realized Parker had locked the doors. Cursing quietly to himself, he turned and went back to the house. Hurrying through the front door to escape the rain, he swiftly moved to the kitchen. Kneeling by the side of Parker's body was lovely Tina, no emotions, no tears, just blankly staring, it appeared Tina had slipped back into her madness again. Starr coughed to get her attention. Tina looked up, her eyes still blank.

Starr motioned toward Parker's body and said, "I need the keys. I'm guessing they're in his pocket."

Tina glanced back down at Parker's body. Her voice, cold, filled with anger as she said, "He was an evil man. Yet God blessed him with four beautiful children. Why, Bill? Tell me the logic of it? Why should Zeke and I suffer when we have so much love to offer? A bastard like this . . . never mind. You wouldn't know the answer anyway."

Tina reached down and rummaged through Parker's pants pocket. She pulled out a set of car keys, her hands trembling she handed them to Starr. He took the keys. Sadness began to overwhelm him. He stood there and watched as Tina slipped in and out of the realm of sanity. With the transfer from one personality to the next, he didn't know which Tina he would be talking to at any moment. Even though he knew Tina was not waiting for him to reply, Starr answered her questions anyway.

"Tina, God doesn't hold vendettas against certain people. He doesn't need to. All men and women will answer to him on judgment day. Think about that, Tina. Why would God want to single you out from the rest? Whatever you feel you did wrong, God will forgive you. If you ask him to. The only person who is punishing you is yourself, Tina Riley. If you don't stop, you will wind up destroying one lovely lady." Starr didn't allow Tina to reply but turned and walked away. As he neared the front door, he heard the back screen door slam shut. Starr realized this entire mess would have to end soon or Tina might slip into the darkness of insanity forever. Starr closed his eyes as he began to search for happier times with Tina. Slowly his mind drifted back in time.

Tina sat on the porch laughing, then asked, "Dad really did that to you, Bill?"

Starr, laughing along with Tina, nodded his head yes as he added, "Your dad used to play all kinds of pranks on me. He was a good man, Tina; he was always there for me." A sadness came over Starr that Tina couldn't help but see.

Quietly she asked, "Something wrong, Bill?"

Biting down on his lower lip, Starr replied slowly, "I can't help but feel a little guilty."

Tina looked puzzled as she asked, "Why?"

Starr sat down next to Tina and endeavored to say what needed to be said without hurting Tina's feelings.

"Tina, Jane and I got into a big fight today."

Tina raised her eyebrows; her voice sounded genuinely concerned as she asked, "You and Jane? I find that hard to believe; you two seem to agree on everything."

Starr nodded but added, "Everything but me coming over here."

Tina looked hurt as she inquired, "Why would Jane get mad about that? I thought she liked me?"

Starr answered quickly, "She does, Tina. It's just that I seem to be spending a lot of time here lately, and, well she's kind of jealous."

Tina started laughing as she replied, "I'm sorry, Bill, I don't mean to laugh, but jealous of me? She must know we're only friends? Do you want me to talk to her?"

Starr shook his head no and replied instead, "Maybe I should just cool it on coming over for a while. You know, till Jane gets over her silliness."

Tina stopped laughing. Her voice became panicky as she said, "Please, Bill, don't do that. I need to hear about my dad. . . . It may seem silly, but when we talk like this it makes me feel like my dad is still . . . alive."

Starr could hear the sadness in Tina's voice. He found himself staring into her blue eyes. Starr knew he was doomed; he couldn't think of a man alive who could stare into those eyes and not do what she commanded. Reluctantly Starr agreed.

"OK, Tina. I'll try and find a way to keep my wife from bashing in my skull. We still will have our weekly talks about the good old days."

Tina smiled as she repeated Starr's words.

"I like that. The good old days. Bill, have I told you lately you're the greatest friend a person could ever have?"

Starr laughed as he replied, "Yes, but feel free to tell me again."

Both his and Tina's laughter filled the night air. Tina put her arms around Bill's neck and kissed him gently on the cheek as she whispered, "No one could ever ask for a better friend than you, Bill Starr. I don't know how I would survive some of these nights without you."

Starr felt a sudden surge of warmth flow through his body, a warmth that scared him because it wasn't friendship he was now feeling. Starr shook off the strange feeling ripping inside him and quietly replied, "Tina, I promised you before and I will say it again. I will always be there for you . . . that is, if my wife don't kill me first."

Tina released her grip and, still smiling, said gently, "Bring Jane over next week. Trust me; before the night is over we will both convince her that there is nothing to worry about."

Starr smiled as he replied, "I'll do that, Tina. Now let me tell you about the time your dad put glue in my tennis shoes."

Starr's and Tina's laughter again rang through the night air.

The laughter rang in Starr's ears as his mind returned to the present time. He shook the memories completely out of his mind and returned to the task at hand. He walked to the front door and opened it, stopping before he walked out. He surveyed the street in front of him again. Seeing it still deserted, he darted out into the rain towards Parker's car. Carefully Starr shoved the car keys in the lock and opened the car door. Sliding inside, he inserted the keys into the ignition and started up the engine. Shifting the car into reverse, he backed into the driveway, pulling in as close to the house as he could. Glancing in the rearview mirror, he inched the car just past his patrol car. He turned off the engine and got out of the car. Walking to the back of Parker's car, Starr stuck the keys inside of the trunk lock. The trunk popped open. Inside sat a large red tool-box and Parker's doctor's bag, a spare tire that was flat and of course a golf bag. Starr proceeded to remove all the articles and set them in the backseat of Parker's car. After Starr emptied the trunk, he examined it closer. Satisfied it would hold Parker's body, Starr headed back to the house. The rain began to fall harder as he walked inside the house. He took off his hat and shook the excess water from it as he called out for Tina.

"Tina, are you ready?"

Tina appeared at the kitchen entrance, rain dripping from her yellow coat. Traces of mud stuck to her fingertips.

"Did you do as I asked and cover up the hole you dug?"

Tina nodded as she replied, "Yes."

Starr began looking around the room as he asked, "Are you sure we have everything? We don't want any traces of Parker being here." He paused for a moment to see if Tina would answer. When she didn't, Starr added, "Please think. Did he wear a hat? Did he bring anything that someone might recognized as being his?"

Tina's tone was forceful as she replied, "No, nothing."

Starr took another quick survey of the living room. He noticed the throw rug in the middle of the room. It was definitely out of place. He quickly asked, "Is that where the body was originally?"

Tina glanced over at the throw rug. The vision of Parker's dying eyes staring at her burned in her memory. She glanced back to Starr and answered, "Yes."

Starr shook his head as he asked in a matter-of-fact tone in his voice, "I gather you are using the rug to hide bloodstains?"

Tina nodded her head yes.

Starr rubbed his eyes as he said in a bewildered tone, "We are going to need to find a way to get rid of the blood. You can't keep that rug there forever."

Tina looked back over at the rug, then asked, "When do you think they will suspect foul play? I mean, Frank is not one of the most dependable people in the world."

Starr shrugged his shoulders, replying, "Hard to tell. If he was in the habit of not coming home at nights, maybe a few days. I gather if he wasn't the most reliable man in town, maybe one week, maybe two."

Tina didn't comment on Starr's remark.

Starr added, "I just hope he didn't mention to anyone he was going to stop here to see you or that someone did know about the affair you two were having and kept it to themselves. This is a small town and secrets are not the easiest things to keep."

Tina forced a weak smile as she reassured the deputy, "Bill, we both were careful, especially at work."

Starr shrugged his shoulders again as he said, " I guess all we have to do is dispose of the body and it all will be over."

Guilt swept through Starr from the ease with which he made that statement. A lawman all his life and now he talked of getting rid of a body as easily as if talking of disposing of trash. Starr didn't like how easily his conscience was accepting the fact of breaking the law. Shaking the bad vibes he was feeling, he motioned to Tina to follow him. As he moved back toward the front door, Tina followed close behind him. Stopping, Starr opened the door and pointed to the open trunk as he began to speak.

"We will put Parker in the trunk of his own car. You will drive his car. I will follow in mine. Once we reach Harrison Point I will take care of the rest."

Tina watched Starr closely as he went over his plan with her. A sense of security was forming inside her. Her fears began to fade. Tina began to feel hope.

Starr asked, "Any questions?"

Tina nodded her head nervously as she asked, "Is the water going to be deep enough to keep the car hidden?"

Starr's expression didn't change as he replied to her fears, "It will be deep enough, and no one ever goes to that area anyway. The path we have to drive through to get there is going to be tough, especially with all this rain. I hope his car will make it."

Tina knew Starr was right. The only path leading to Harrison Point was an old nature trail. The only people who actually went to that area were kids who wanted to make out. Harrison Point was a huge cliff that protruded out over the water. It was about a hundred feet straight down to the water. The point itself narrowed to where only one car could go in at a time. There was no way to turn around once there. The only way out was to go in reverse. Surrounding the point on all sides were the dense woods. In a strange way, one might say that Harrison Point was a prison created by the gods to lock in nature's beauty and keep mortal man from touching it with its destructive hands. Now she and Starr would invade this place to hide their act against God.

Tina asked shyly, "What if his car doesn't make it?"

Starr turned away from Tina and moved toward the kitchen, answering as he walked away, "Then we tow it. I have a tow chain in my car. One way or another, Tina, we will bury Parker and his car in Mother Nature's Graveyard."

Tina winced at Starr's statement, remembering what "Mother Nature's Graveyard" referred to. An old Indian legend made claims of warriors who had shamed themselves in battle. They would climb to the top of Harrison Point and dive into the waters below, giving their souls to God so their spirits could reach the heavens. Hence it got its nickname Mother Nature's Graveyard. Now the two of them would be adding an evil soul to the pure waters.

Starr stopped directly over Parker's body. A stench rose from it. Starr knew the longer they delayed the worse the smell would get. Tina reached where Starr stood. He motioned for her to go to the other side of the body. She did as ordered. Starr bent over and lifted Parker by the arms. Tina reached down and gripped the dead man's legs and lifted at the same time Starr did. Carefully Starr backed out of the kitchen and headed for the front door. The only sounds were the heavy breathing from the two figures carrying the body and the ticking of the wall clock. Starr and Tina tried hard not to look at each other as they neared the door. The guilt of what they were doing began to sink into their minds. When they reached the door, Starr quietly ordered Tina to gently lower the body to the floor. Together they lowered Parker to the floor. Starr then stepped outside and once again checked the entire area. Not one sign of life anywhere, it appeared the entire world consisted of only him and Tina. Glancing up into the sky, Starr realized the rain had begun to fall with less intensity. Whispering to himself, "Good" he turned and walked back into the house.

"Ready?"

Tina nodded her head yes. Together they bent over and picked up Parker's body again. Moving quickly out the door, Starr backed up right to the open trunk. Gently he and Tina lowered Parker into the trunk. Starr motioned for Tina to release Parker's legs, then pushed the body as far back as it would go in the trunk. A sigh of relief came over Tina as Starr slammed the trunk closed. The two of them stood and stared at each other for a brief moment. Starr finally broke the silence.

"It won't be long before this entire nightmare is over. I better check in before we leave."

Tina asked quickly, her voice pleading, "Will you please see if there has been any progress with Zeke?"

Starr nodded his head yes, then added, "Go wait in Parker's car."

Tina didn't argue. She walked around to the driver's side of the car and slid into it. Parker reached into his patrol car and grabbed the mike.

"Car Twenty-three reporting in. Are you there, sheriff?"

Hanson's voice boomed back at Starr, "Hanson here. How is it going, Bill? I heard from the mayor that Tina's pretty shook up?"

Starr glanced over at Tina, who patiently sat in Parker's car waiting for Starr to finish, "I think she would be doing a lot better if you would allow her to talk to Zeke. It would ease her mind considerably."

Hanson's voice came back sullenly. "Sorry, Bill. That is impossible right now. Besides, I have a feeling this whole mess will be over very shortly. We are still waiting for the creep's answer to the mayor's proposition. If he agrees, as we all feel he will do, Zeke's release could happen within the next few hours. Hang in there, buddy; it will all be over soon."

A frown formed on Starr's face. Starr held the highest respect for the sheriff, knowing that the man was a decent and honest person. The decisions he made had always been sound and reasonable . . . till now. Starr felt the sheriff was making the wrong call on this one. Tina needed to talk to her husband. Not only for her sake, but for Zeke's, as it would give a glimmer of hope. There was no logic in Hanson refusing to allow her to speak to Zeke. Starr knew the decision wasn't Hanson's but the mayor's. Starr's voice didn't hide his disapproval as he replied, "It is not me that has to hang in there, sheriff; it is Tina. I hope you are right and Zeke is free in the next few hours. If he dies, you and the mayor can come over here and explain it to Tina, because I won't."

Hanson's voice boomed back in anger, "What do you mean by that, Bill?"

Starr ignored Hanson's question and hung up the mike and slowly walked over to Parker's car. As Starr glanced up at the sky, he saw the rain finally had stopped. The dull gray clouds still hovered above, looming, ready to open up and pour again. Starr bent down by the driver's side of the window and tapped on it gently. Tina rolled down the window. Starr calmly said, "The sheriff said it won't be long before you and Zeke will be together again. It all will be over soon, Tina."

Tina smiled weakly as she replied, "Do you believe him, Bill?" Starr nodded his head yes.

Tina's smile grew larger. Her voice grew with excitement.

"Zeke is going to be so thrilled when he finds out about the baby. I know it will help him forget this entire hellish day. If we are lucky we still will be able to make our doctor's appointment tonight. Zeke needs to hear from the doctor that I am pregnant. He will never believe me if I tell him."

Starr chuckled as he replied, "Stop being so paranoid about everything. I am sure he will believe you."

Tina didn't bother to explain why Zeke would find it hard to trust her saying she was pregnant. So many times she had built up his hopes, only to bring them crashing down. This time it would be different. Tina began to feel good again. Everything was falling into place the way she planned it. She became confident for the first time since she had heard of Zeke's abduction. Zeke once again would hold her, their lives complete, all their dreams fulfilled. Finally her war would end.

Starr leaned over and kissed Tina's forehead, whispering, "Let's get this over with so we both can go back to our lives."

Tina nodded in agreement and rolled the window back up. She then backed the car slowly out of the driveway. Starr watched as she turned and headed south toward Harrison Point. He walked over to his patrol car and slid inside, cranked up the engine, and pulled out onto the street, turning in the same direction Tina did. He stepped heavy on the gas pedal to catch up with Tina. When he caught up to Parker's car, Starr eased up on the gas, making sure to keep a car's length between him and the car Tina drove. As he drove, he kept a close eye on Tina in front of him. He smiled as she waved to him. A strange pain stabbed at him. He began to wonder why he had become so willing to help someone who had committed murder. Why did all these strange feelings begin to creep into his body? Friendship? Why did holding her, feeling her body close to his, give him such pleasure he had not felt in years? Friendship? The smell of her hair still lingered in his mind. Her eyes melted his heart. Why? Friendship? Echoes of tiny voices whispered in the caverns of his mind.

You love her.

Starr bit down on his lower lip, hoping the pain would silence the whispers that turned into screams.

You love her!

Starr knew the voices were wrong. He did everything because of friendship. Parker had beaten her. The bastard had hurt her, sweet, lovely Tina. He did deserve to die. Starr knew this, for no one should hurt someone he called friend. The voices were wrong.

You love her.

Starr did everything for her because of friendship.

You love her.

Starr knew the voices would not stop. The lies he had told himself over the years didn't stop them.

"You love her."

The pain didn't stop them.

You love her.

Maybe the truth would.

"Yes, I Bill Starr, love Tina Riley."

The voices grew dimmer. Tina pulled up the narrow path heading to Harrison Point. Starr followed close behind. The voices now stopped. The stabbing pain remained because Starr knew even though he admitted that he loved Tina, she would only feel he helped her out of friendship.

17

Mayor Martin summoned Hanson and Overstreet to once again join him in his car. Martin explained the entire conversation he had had with Tina and how poorly it had gone.

"Gentlemen, we must resolve this situation soon. I could tell by the reaction I received from Zeke's wife that she is going to cause us a problem. That is something none of us need or want."

Hanson asked curiously, "Problem, Mayor? What kind of problem?"

Martin adjusted his glasses and stared hard at Hanson as he replied, "I think she may try and call the restaurant and talk to Zeke. Can you imagine the leverage that would give Jones?"

Hanson asked in a curious voice, "Did you talk to my deputy?"

Martin shook his head no, adding, "No, and I hope he has enough sense to control her actions."

Hanson started to add something, but Martin cut him off, "Bob, this entire ordeal is going to take a toll on this town. I don't want to have to worry about Tina Riley along with Zeke. Please call your deputy and explain to him how important it is to keep her calm."

Hanson nodded his head in agreement. Martin then ordered, "Good. Now please go back to your car and begin arrangements for transportation for Harlen Jones."

Hanson went to say something but stopped, deciding to wait and do what Martin had ordered.

After Hanson left the car, Martin began questioning Overstreet.

"Tell me, Captain, now that the rain is stopping how sure are you of one of your men hitting their target?"

Overstreet appeared stunned by the mayor's question. It was the mayor who had debated against Overstreet's plan in the first place. Now he was asking if it had a chance to work?

"They are the best, Mayor. Why do you ask?"

Martin leaned over and whispered, "Because I want a backup plan. If this monster doesn't want to accept my deal, I need something to fall back on quickly."

Overstreet smiled. Was he now seeing a side of the old man that was kept hidden from the townspeople? Overstreet began to sense that Martin's earlier tantrum had been for Hanson's benefit, a show for Hanson to relay to the rest of the town how the good old mayor really cared for his voters. Overstreet asked calmly, "Why? Don't you think our friend in there is going to accept your terms?"

Todd Martin leaned back in his seat, putting his hands behind his head as he replied, "More than likely he will. The man is desperate; I showed him a glimmer of hope. I think he will grab for it. Just make sure you put that gizmo in the car we give him. I don't want that bastard to make it out of this county alive."

Overstreet glanced over at the patrol car parked next to the limousine. He could see Hanson talking on the car radio. Turning his attention back to the mayor, Overstreet gave Martin a long hard look before he spoke.

"Tell me, Mayor, why all the speeches about saving Zeke? Ranting on that you didn't care if this killer escapes or not? Why not remain neutral and allow me to run the show?"

Martin frowned as he replied, "Let us get one thing straight, son. Zeke's safety is very important to me. For God sake, his parents helped me get elected. As for my speech, well, call it a force of habit. Captain, now that the rain is stopping, I guarantee you that the entire population of Barnsville will be gathered outside the Golden Aces. Those are precious voters, son. I cannot afford to make any mistakes. It could ruin my career."

Martin paused to look at the back door of the restaurant. He then asked quietly, "This trace you and the sheriff are talking about, will it work?"

Overstreet couldn't hide his disgust in the mayor's causal reasoning of his actions: "It will work, Mayor. You won't lose face with your voters."

Before Martin could respond to the sarcasm, the limousine door opened. Hanson slid in next to Overstreet. Hanson's face showed both anger and concern. He began to inform the two men of his conversation with his deputy.

"My deputy thinks we are wrong in not allowing Tina to talk to Zeke. I gave him all the reasons, but he is not accepting any of it."

Martin laid his hand on Hanson's knee as he said in a fatherly voice, "Trust me on this, Bob: we are doing the right thing. That is why you are the sheriff and he is the deputy."

Hanson's facial expression showed his doubt in the decision that they had made. He asked quietly, "Would there really be any harm in just allowing her to talk to Zeke for a minute?"

Overstreet watched intently as Martin answered Hanson's question.

"You tell me, Bob! You know what type of man we are up against; should we allow him any kind of edge? Zeke will be freed. The two of them will be together for a lifetime. I will leave it up to you, Bob. What do you want to do? Let her talk to him and take even the slightest chance Harlen will use her against us? Is it worth the minute you want to give her?"

Overstreet hid his laughter. This was very amusing to him. The old man played the sheriff as if he were a puppet on a string. Martin proceeded to put a guilt trip on Hanson for having any opinions but the one he wanted him to have.

Hanson replied meekly, "I guess you are right, Mayor, but it seems so heartless not to let her talk to him. Sorry, I guess I am allowing my emotions to get in the way of doing what is right."

Martin took his hand off Hanson's knee and leaned back in his seat, saying sympathetically, "There is nothing wrong with caring, Bob. That is what separates us from men like Jones. Everything is going to work out. Now did you make the arrangements for his transportation?"

Hanson nodded his head as he replied, "Henderson's Car Lot is willing to lend us any type of vehicle they have on their lot. All they need is for us to give the word."

Martin smiled as he said crisply, "Good. All we need to do is wait for Jones to call."

As if Martin's words were a signal, his car phone began to ring. All three men glanced at one another. Finally Martin reached next to him and picked up the phone, answering in a friendly voice, "Mayor Martin speaking."

The voice on the other end showed his weariness and impatience: "Cut the formal greeting, Mayor, you know it is me."

153

Martin remained cool as he replied, "Yes, I figured it might be you. Have you thought over my proposition, Mr. Jones?"

Harlen's voice came back with a touch of sarcasm in it.

"I decided to trust you, Mayor. We have a deal, but one screwup and I will blow Zeke's brains out right in front of you."

Martin covered the speaker of the phone, whispering to both men, "He is taking the deal." Turning his attention back to the man on the other end of the phone, ignoring Harlen's threats, he proceeded to ask for details.

"OK, Mr. Jones, how should we proceed?"

Harlen began to run off his list of demands: "I want a Jeep. There is a lot of rough terrain in this area. I don't want to be stuck in the mud somewhere outside of town. Park it flush to the back door with the driver's side door open and the engine running. Make sure the gas tank is full; you won't know how long I will allow it to idle before I come out. Finally, I want the money on the front seat. I decided I don't want to wait for you to drop it off."

Martin's voice remained steady as he retorted, "The deal was you would receive the money once Zeke's release occurred."

Harsh laughter rang in Martin's ear. Harlen replied, still chuckling, "Mayor, I thought over what you told me. We must start trusting each other. I feel that I met you halfway in our deal. The only change is now I want to feel safe before I tell you where to pick up your friend. I give you my word that if you keep up your end of the bargain, I will allow Zeke to live. Trust, isn't that what you preached to me?"

Martin pushed his glasses back up his face. Aggravation swelled inside him. He knew that Jones was outmaneuvering him, not replying right away. Martin's mind raced furiously, trying to think of something to say to turn the tide back in his favor. He drew a blank. Jones had used the Mayor's own words against him. Martin's voice lost his calmness as he protested the change of the deal.

"Yes, I said trust is important, but it is not easy to trust a man who is holding a gun at someone's head. I took the time to read your file, Mr. Jones. You have a very violent past. All signs indicate you would shoot your hostage to ensure your own safety. The first deal is the only acceptable one."

Harlen answered in a whisper, "Then he is dead, Mayor. Nice talking to you."

"No, wait; don't hang up!" Martin's voice crackled with desperation. "OK, we have a deal."

Harlen's response was short and to the point: "One hour."

A dial tone rang in Martin's ear. The mayor slammed the phone back down on its cradle, his anger seething as he snapped at the two men across from him, "He wants the money first! Bob, call Henderson and tell him we need a Jeep within the hour. Then I want you to install that tracking device. Captain, I have a few things I want to talk to you about."

Hanson looked curiously at the mayor. Why would he want to talk to Overstreet? Was he losing confidence in him? Martin broke Hanson's trance as he growled, "Move it, Sheriff. The bastard only gave us a hour."

Hanson flushed with embarrassment. He didn't appreciate being scolded like a two-year-old, especially in front of Overstreet, but to save himself from further embarrassment Hanson left the limousine and hurried to his patrol car.

Martin turned to Overstreet. His voice was like ice as he spoke.

"He wants the Jeep parked flush up against the door. Is that going to hamper your marksmen?"

Overstreet looked out his window at the back door of the restaurant and inspected it as close as he could from the distance he sat from it. His eyes darted to where his men remained stationed. Turning his attention back to the mayor, Overstreet shrugged his shoulders, replying quietly, "Hard to tell, Mayor. Can't we park it about five feet from the building? From that angle my men would have a perfect shot."

Martin shook his head no as he snapped, "No! This bastard is no fool. If we deviate from what his demands are, I am positive he will kill Zeke. There must be a better way. We need a backup plan and we need it quick."

The clouds started to break up, and the afternoon sun peeked through them. Overstreet cursed quietly to himself. He knew if the mayor did not intervene, this crisis would be over. Whether it was for politics or just an ego trip, Mayor Martin had screwed up. Allowing Harlen out of the restaurant even with a tracer on the Jeep was foolish. Now the mayor risked not only losing face and money but also getting Zeke Riley killed. Here Martin sat now in private asking Overstreet for help to pull him out of a dilemma he had

155

thrust himself into. Overstreet without asking reached over and picked up the mayor's phone and began punching in the buttons. Martin didn't protest the trooper's actions.

"Captain Overstreet here. The weather is breaking; how long will it take for you to get that bird in the air?" Overstreet glanced over at the mayor as he waited for a reply. Turning his attention back to the phone, he received his answer. A smile creased Overstreet's face.

"Great. I want two of my best sharpshooters on board. We are putting a transmitter on the Jeep that we are giving Jones. Make sure you have the right frequency to follow him. Overstreet out."

Overstreet hung up the phone. Martin began to stir as he waited for Overstreet to tell him what was going on. With a touch of arrogance, Overstreet told the mayor his backup plan.

"We are in luck. The weather is clearing enough to get the helicopter up in the air. We will let Jones think he is getting everything he asked for. The helicopter will take off a few minutes after he departs. We will wait till he drops off the hostage, then nail him."

Martin ran his fingers through his hair. For the first time since Overstreet had met Mayor Martin the trooper detected signs of nervousness. Martin had lost his cockiness. He was unsure of himself. In a strange way this made Overstreet feel good. Mayor Martin probably was the first man the trooper could remember who actually made him feel small and inadequate. Martin looked across the lot at Hanson's patrol car and, as if Hanson might be able to hear him, whispered, "What if he doesn't let Zeke go? What if he tries to leave the area and doesn't release Zeke? Then we lose Zeke and the money and maybe even him. Christ, my career could wind up in ashes."

Overstreet shook his head slowly as he replied, "This I will promise you, Mayor. Neither the money nor Harlen Jones will leave this area. As far as your friend in there goes, I would guess his chances are fifty-fifty that he makes it out alive. I think you were convincing enough that Jones will release him. Either way, with all the campaigning you did around town and with Hanson and myself you are going to come out of this looking like a hero, a man who cares for the people of his town."

Martin could sense the sarcasm in Overstreet's tone of voice and snapped back quickly, defending his actions.

156

"You hold on just a minute, Captain. I do care about the people of this town and I truly love that young man in there. Maybe you feel what I did is unethical? That all I really care about is myself? Nothing could be further from the truth. My record in this town is unblemished. No violent crimes have ever touched even the town limits. That is why every citizen in Barnsville is gathering around to see what happened. This is a new occurrence to them. In a way, it is like a form of morbid entertainment. The only problem is they expect everything to end in a positive way, with the good guys winning. So you might say that, in a matter of speaking, I am protecting them from the reality of what is really happening here."

Overstreet wanted to laugh in Martin's face. The man in front of him was a truly pompous ass. Strangely enough, he felt as if everyone he talked to was foolish enough to buy his garbage. In the short time that Overstreet had known the mayor the trooper had realized that Martin was self-centered and focused only on what could further his own career, even if it meant the life of someone he called friend. In a way, Mayor Todd Martin was no better than Harlen Jones. Martin raped people's minds and souls. He reached out his arms spewing love and trust, but in his own sick little mind he neither trusted nor loved anyone. Overstreet didn't vocalize his thoughts.

"Don't forget, Captain, I did raise the money. I used every bit of my influence to get it. I am responsible for the prompt return of that money. Do you believe I would risk that if I didn't really care?"

Overstreet didn't reply. He stared at the mayor, listening to him make excuse after excuse for his actions, trying desperately to defend his honor and creditibility.

Overstreet's silence began to irritate Martin. He snapped at him, "You don't believe a word I am saying, do you, Captain?"

"I really don't care, Mayor, if you are telling me the truth or not. My only concern is capturing a killer and trying to save a man's life in the balance. You don't need to convince me that you care. I don't live in your town, but I will tell you this. I don't want any more interference in this case. I will do what I think is right, and if you get in my way . . . maybe then I will express how I feel you handled this whole situation."

Martin took off his glasses and rubbed his eyes. Slowly he put his glasses back on, fitting them firmly into place. Overstreet could see the rage in Martin's eyes. The mayor asked in a harsh whisper, "Are you threatening me, Captain?"

A sly grin came across Overstreet's face as he replied, "No. I am warning you, Mayor. I've had enough of your silly political games. I have a job to do and I will be damned if I will allow you to stand in the way of my completing my duty."

Martin raised his hand, making a tight fist as he spit out his reply: "Don't underestimate me, Trooper. I could crush you in the blink of an eye. I do have powerful friends."

Before Overstreet replied, Martin's driver opened the car door. Hanson slid back inside the limousine. He sat next to Overstreet. Glancing at both men, Hanson could sense the tension filling the air. Curiously he asked, "Something wrong? Did Jones make more demands?"

Martin replied, his tone regaining the friendliness he had displayed earlier, "Nothing is wrong. The captain and I were discussing a possible backup plan."

Hanson looked over at Overstreet and asked, "What type of backup plan?"

Martin answered quickly, gathering his enthusiasm back in his voice as he did, "From the air, Bob. Now that the weather is lifting the captain ordered a helicopter to assist us. Isn't that right, Captain?"

Overstreet nodded his head yes. Hanson knew more than backup plans had been discussed. The anger in both men's eyes proved that. Hanson wanted to pry deeper into what really was going on but decided it could wait. There were more important matters to talk about. Hanson leaned back in the seat as he gave them his information.

"Henderson said no problem on the Jeep. Overstreet, your men are putting the transmitter on as we speak. We do have a slight problem, though. My deputy informed me that the crowds are growing larger and stretch down entire streets of the town. Maybe the rain was a blessing; at least it kept the crowds from growing. I don't want anyone getting hurt, but I don't have the manpower to force a dispersal of the crowds. I was thinking, Mayor, maybe if you went around front and asked them to go back to their homes they would listen?"

Martin shot a quick glance at Overstreet, daring him to make a sly comment. Overstreet smiled. Martin ignored him, then turned to Hanson, warmly replying, "If you think it will help, Bob, I will talk to them. I can't make any promises, though. You know how much everyone loves Zeke in this town."

Hanson nodded his head in agreement, adding, "Especially you, Mayor. Remember, he is a friend of mine also; we will get him out of this alive."

Martin leaned over and patted Hanson on the knee as he said, "I know we will, son. You and the captain better get ready to initiate our first plan. I will go around to the front of the building and see what I can do in getting the crowds to break up. You did tell them to install a phone and put my number in the Jeep?"

Hanson nodded replying, "All taken care of, Mayor."

Hanson then opened the limousine door and slid out. Overstreet followed behind him. Martin motioned to his driver. Without hesitation the man moved swiftly around to the driver's side of the limousine and disappeared inside the car. Hanson and Overstreet watched as the black limousine drove off. Hanson said without looking at Overstreet, "This town is lucky to have a man who cares as much as him running their town. Maybe if the rest of the nation's city leaders cared as much, our nation would not be falling apart."

Overstreet smiled. He wanted to tell the naive sheriff how his precious mayor was using him and every citizen in this town and the pathetic way he was using a man's life to further his popularity. The trooper didn't. He knew the sheriff wouldn't believe him. Why should he? Overstreet was the outsider. Restraining from expressing his true feelings, he remained silent. The only thing Overstreet could relate to was the convict barricaded inside the restaurant. He became the only link to the real world, a deadly reminder of what the rest of the world was like.

A voice blaring over Hanson's radio broken the silence. Overstreet watched Hanson move quickly toward his patrol car. Picking up the mike, he answered the voice on the other side, "Hanson here, what's up, Larry?"

The voice with the southern accent replied, "Henderson has the Jeep up front. The equipment you ordered for it has been installed. I can't believe we are giving this guy his own phone."

Hanson ignored the deputy's last comment and asked, "Has the mayor talked to the crowd yet?"

Larry's reply was quick: "Yeah, I guess he did."

Hanson's frustration with his deputy showed in his tone of voice.

"What do you mean, you guess? Did he or didn't he talk to the crowd in front?"

Larry's reply was slow and uncertain.

"For a minute. He told them you had everything under control and it would be over soon. He gave the money to me to put into the Jeep. He is standing outside his car with some of the townspeople. Do you want to talk to him?"

Hanson scratched his head. His voice trailed off as he answered his deputy, "No, that won't be necessary."

Overstreet, now standing next to Hanson, listening to the conversation, could see Hanson seemed puzzled that the mayor didn't say more to the crowd. Hanson tried to conceal his puzzlement when he gave his deputy his orders.

"Bring the Jeep around back and keep that crowd under control. I don't want any innocent bystanders getting hurt. Please inform the mayor we are getting ready to give Jones the Jeep. Hanson out."

Hanson hung up the mike. Overstreet could see the concern in Hanson's eyes and felt a twinge of pity for the sheriff. Overstreet knew how confused Hanson felt by the mayor's actions. The sad reality, though, was that when it all ended, whatever story the mayor told Hanson, the young sheriff would blindly believe. Overstreet spoke quietly.

"I am going to where the helicopter is waiting. I want to make sure there are no screwups in following Jones. You follow the trace from ground level. One of my men will drive with you. He is an expert in reading a tracer. We can coordinate where Jones is going and make sure he doesn't slip past us."

The Jeep pulled around the corner. Hanson watched as it pulled next to them, saying to Overstreet as it did, "Sounds good, Captain."

Overstreet walked away, moving quickly to his own car. Stopping by one of his men, he gave instructions and pointed over to where Hanson stood. Hanson watched as the man nodded his head and headed toward him. Overstreet disappeared inside his car and drove off. The trooper Overstreet had talked to made it to where Hanson stood. A young man, in his midtwenties, he wore a hat seemed too big for his small face. He carried a large black box under his arm. Stopping in front of Hanson, the trooper spoke in a polite voice.

"I am Trooper Mike Taylor. I am to accompany you. We will allow the suspect to advance about five minutes on us. The transmitter we placed on the Jeep has a radius of twenty miles. We will not lose him, sir. I can assure you of that."

Hanson smiled. The young man's confidence was a breath of fresh air. Quietly Hanson replied, "I am sure you are right, Trooper. Please get in my car. I want to be ready to roll as soon as he leaves."

The trooper nodded and got inside Hanson's car.

Hanson walked over to where the Jeep was idling. The deputy inside rolled down his window. Hanson began to give him his instructions.

"Park it flush up against the building. Leave the engine running and the driver's side door open. Don't make any sudden moves when you get out and walk away. Is that clear?"

The deputy nodded his head yes.

Hanson continued, "Good. We don't want any mistakes. No heroes. A man's life is at stake."

Hanson glanced at his watch. They still had time before the hour elapsed. Hanson was impressed by how quickly everyone had worked to get the Jeep and transmitter installed. For a small town they had worked quickly and efficiently to get the job done. Hanson quietly said, "Stay alert. I will contact our friend in there to let him know we are ready."

The deputy nodded, not saying a word.

Hanson moved back to his car. He grabbed the portable phone sitting on the seat and punched in the number of the restaurant. Jones answered on the first ring.

"That was quick, Mayor. Is everything ready?"

Hanson's voice was cold as he replied, "This is Sheriff Hanson and yes, everything is ready."

Harlen's sadistic laughter rang from the other end as he said, "You gentlemen keep changing who is talking to me. Am I offending you in some way?"

Hanson snapped back gruffly, "Mayor Martin had other matters to tend to. He will be waiting for your call. We are ready to comply with our end of the deal."

The laughter ended and Harlen's voice became stern.

"Very good, Sheriff. Let the games begin, and please, no tricks."

Hanson did not bother to comment on Harlen's sarcasm. Keeping his tone even and unemotional, the sheriff demanded, "I want to talk to Zeke."

There was a long pause; then Harlen snapped back, "We have wasted enough time. You can talk to him after I release him." Then Harlen hung up.

Hanson's face flushed with anger. He stood there listening to the dial tone. He flung the phone on the seat.

The trooper inside the car hung it up for him and asked, "Everything OK?"

Hanson nodded his head yes. He then yelled out to his deputy in the Jeep. Once Hanson got the deputy's attention, he motioned to him to move the Jeep. Hanson opened the car door and slid inside, slamming the door shut. Both he and the trooper watched as the Jeep pulled as close to the building as possible. Hanson glanced at the roof and watched intently as Overstreet's men prepared themselves for one possible clear shot. Next to Hanson the trooper opened the black box he had tucked under his arm and turned on a switch, and a small white blip began blinking on the screen. Hanson knew that it represented the Jeep.

The trooper smiled as he said, "We are ready, sir."

Hanson nodded, then turned his attention back to the Jeep. It idled at the back door of the Golden Aces. The beeping of the box next to him rang in his ear. His heart pounded. Small beads of sweat formed on his forehead. It all would be ending soon. He prayed silently that his friend would still be alive when it did. The deputy who was inside the Jeep, got out on the passenger side. He moved swiftly away from the Jeep, not making any sudden moves that would alarm the man inside. Hanson picked up his mike and informed all the cars that remained parked in the back to move out. One by one they slowly drove away. Hanson finally started the engine of his car, saying to the trooper next to him, "I hope that device works."

The trooper answered with pride in his voice, "Don't worry, sir, it works just fine. We will know exactly where that creep decides to drive to."

Hanson smiled. He asked in a warm voice, "How old are you, son?"

The trooper looked stunned by Hanson's question but firmly spouted out his age: "Twenty-three, sir. Why?"

Hanson put the car in gear as he answered, "No reason. You just appear too young to be a state trooper."

The young man appeared offended.

Hanson quickly added, "You perform like a veteran. I am impressed."

That brought a gleam to the young man's eyes. Hanson drove away slowly, glancing briefly in his rearview mirror at the black Jeep idling at the side of the building.

18

Harlen gazed through the small peephole at the deputy parking the Jeep next to the door, watching intently as the deputy got out and moved away to a different patrol car. One by one each patrol car left the back of the restaurant's lot. Harlen watched till the last one disappeared from the back of the lot. He then turned away from the back door and smiled at Zeke, who was still sitting on the floor. Harlen moved to the counter and stared at the large windows in the front of the restaurant. He smiled as he watched the parade of patrol cars roll out to the front area. The crowds returned in masses, which he knew would work in his favor. It would prevent some trigger-happy cop from trying to take a shot at him. No one wanted to risk hitting an innocent citizen standing in the crowd. Harlen turned toward Zeke and shouted, "Do you have a map of this area?"

Zeke replied quietly, "Yes, by the register, in a stand."

Harlen walked over to the register, where a brightly colored sign read: *MAPS ONLY ONE DOLLAR.*

Harlen laughed as he grabbed one. He opened it and spread it across the counter, studying it for a brief moment. He then snapped at Zeke, "Come over here and show me where we are on this damn thing!"

Zeke rose to his feet and swiftly walked to where Harlen stood.

Harlen pointed at the paper sprawled out on the counter and asked gruffly, "Show me where we are?"

Zeke moved next to Harlen, and grabbing a pencil next to the register, he circled a tiny area on the map. "We are here."

Harlen glared at the circle, eyes moving up the map till he saw the Canadian border. It appeared to be about eighty-five miles away. Harlen studied the surrounding areas more closely, trying to figure a way to reach the border avoiding the main roads. He saw one area that seemed to be a totally mountainous region, covered by dense woods. Harlen put his finger on it and asked, "Can this terrain be traveled by Jeep?"

Zeke looked down at the place Harlen's finger pointed and shook his head no.

Harlen snapped angrily, "I want a way to reach Canada without hitting any main highways. Is it possible?"

Zeke thought for a second, then meekly replied, "Either by foot or boat, but there is no way by Jeep. There is too much rough terrain."

Zeke ran his finger along the blue path on the map and said, "This river leads right to the Canadian border. By foot it would take about four days. By canoe or some kind of boat maybe a day . . . two at the most."

Zeke didn't know exactly why he gave all the information Harlen sought. Fear? Also, Zeke knew if Harlen Jones felt safe, he might keep his word and release him. It was a chance Zeke felt he must take. He glanced up from the map and saw Harlen studying the river he had run his finger across.

Harlen asked, "Are there any resorts or cabins where a boat might be docked?"

Zeke shrugged his shoulders as he volunteered the information, "I own a boat. It's not much, but it would get you to the border."

Harlen shot a look at Zeke. Then Harlen suspiciously asked, "Why would you be willing to tell me about your boat? What type of game are you trying to play with me, asshole?"

Zeke, tired, and hungry, replied weakly, "My life, that is, if you keep your word and allow me to go free once you are safe?"

Harlen smiled; what Zeke was saying made sense to him. The quicker Harlen was free, the better chance Zeke would have to live. If Harlen chose to allow him to live. Still smiling, Harlen sternly asked, "Where is this boat docked?"

Zeke pointed at the map as he answered, "My wife and I have a small cabin here, just north of Harrison Point."

Harlen stared at where Zeke's finger rested on the map, then asked, "This boat, does it have a motor?"

Zeke nodded his head yes.

Harlen added, "How far is it from this Harrison Point?"

Zeke quickly replied, "It is about two miles past it. There is a small path I sort of made that leads right to it. It won't be easy to get to; that's a pretty dense area." Zeke ran his finger down the map, then stopped. "Here, this spot right here." His finger pointed to a small dot on the map.

Harlen studied the map closely. Laying his finger on the map, he asked, "This trail here, it looks like it will go right to your cabin—no main highway to travel on at all?"

Zeke glanced at it, then shook his head no. "That is Harrison Point. It is impossible to travel there; there are no paths through those woods. The only way to get to my cabin would be by foot and even that, like I said, may be near impossible."

Harlen glanced back at the map, then up at Zeke. A smile creased Harlen's face as he said, "Perfect. That is where we will go then. The impossible for us will be the improbable for the cops."

Zeke wanted to protest but decided against it. He knew it would be useless to argue any point with this man.

Harlen folded the map and shoved it into his back pocket. "Have you ever been to this Harrison Point?"

Memories flooded Zeke's mind as he thought back to the first time he and Tina had ventured up to the point. They had sat on the edge of the cliff and gazed at the reflection of the moon on the water below. He remembered how the winds had seemed to cry like lost souls and the eerie feelings had rushed his and Tina's bodies as they lay on the grass making love. It felt as if thousands of eyes were watching. That gave Tina and him a sense of excitement they had never felt before.

"Yes, a few times."

Harlen glanced up at the clock on the wall. It was already three o'clock. Darkness would not come for at least five hours. Harlen debated with himself whether to wait and leave at dark or take his chances now. The skies were clearing, but the gray shadows of the storm still lingered. Harlen once again looked out of the main windows up front, the crowds growing, standing on the far side of the street, watching the building that he used for shelter. A sudden hatred began smothering him. The hordes of people out there were watching and waiting for him to die. None of them knew who he was or even cared. All they knew was he was a stranger in town who had violated their sanctuary. Like an old-fashioned witch hunt, with

166

him being the witch. His head began to pound as the rage ran wildly through his mind. He felt like a caged animal in a zoo, with the eyes of the entire town glaring through the windows, hoping to catch a glimpse of the wild creature cornered in their cage. He began rubbing the scars on his face as he began feeling more and more like a freak. He screamed at the top of his lungs, a shriek that rang through the restaurant.

Zeke jumped back. Fear engulfed him with the sudden screaming of his abductor. Zeke trembled as he watched Harlen clench his fist and scream louder. His shrieks were like those of a wild animal. Slowly Harlen began to regain his composure. His eyes darted to Zeke, who was now pressing his body up against the wall, staring in terror at his abductor.

Harlen smiled wickedly as he hoarsely asked, "Do you think I've lost my mind?"

Zeke didn't answer. The state of mind Harlen was in at this moment, he might do anything if provoked.

Harlen spit out his words. Anger flowed through his body. "I asked you a question?"

Zeke forced himself to reply. His words came stammering out. "N-n-no . . . p-p-please . . . what d-d-did I d-d-do?"

The wicked smile remained as Harlen watched Zeke squirm in front of him. Harlen felt a surge of power flow through his veins. Like a god he held the fate of the puny mortal in front of him. The tormenting of this man actually felt as if it healed Harlen's scars. He fed on Zeke's terror. No longer was Harlen a freak but a god holding the power of life and death in his hands. He whirled around and glared out the front windows at the masses who stood out front. He motioned with his hand for Zeke to stand next to him. Zeke moved cautiously to where Harlen was standing. Harlen glanced over at Zeke and remained smiling as he saw the fear dancing in Zeke's eyes. Harlen pointed in front of him and snarled, "Take a good look at those so-called friends of yours out there. Do you know what they are staring at?"

Zeke weakly shook his head no.

Harlen screamed out the answer, "They are waiting to watch you die! Your friends! No compassion, no love. They are sacrificing you to preserve their own puny lives. They believe if you die, I will be dead and all of this will be over. They all then would go quietly back to their sheltered lives. Oh, they will mourn for you, but to rid themselves of me they would be willing to watch you die.''

Zeke watched as Harlen raved. His eyes seemed to be in a trance as he spoke on.

"At first I thought they were only there to look at the freak, but that can't be. For they never laid eyes on me. I don't think they realize I am black. So the only conclusion I can come to is they are here to watch us die.''

Zeke overcame his fear and broke his silence as he cried out in protest, "No! They are curious, that I will agree with you on, but they have agreed to everything you asked for. The Jeep is out front, just as you demanded. All we have to do is leave.''

Harlen smiled at his pleading prisoner. If only it were to be that easy. He knew that the troopers were not just going to let him leave. No, they had some kind of plan, some way to capture or kill him. It was no more than a game of cat and mouse. Everyone now played. Winner takes all. Loser dies. Harlen planned on being the winner, no matter what.

Zeke continued to plead, "I know these people. They will keep their promises as long as you keep yours and set me free.''

Harlen touched the jagged scars on his face. He watched as Harlen appeared to go into a trance. Zeke wanted to run, to try to escape from this madman but fear denied him the courage to try. Zeke attempted to talk to Harlen again.

"They will keep their end of the deal. I'm not saying they won't try and think of a way to stop you, but you have been through this before. I don't want to die, and I really don't think you want to, either.''

Zeke swallowed back his fear and stared at Harlen to see if anything he was saying was getting through to him. He watched intently as his captor glared at him. Slowly turning, Harlen looked out the windows again. He envisioned everyone staring at him wanting to see him die. He imagined their words shouting to the heavens, "Kill the bastard. The freak don't deserve to live!''

Harlen began laughing out loud as he swore at the imaginary enemies.

"Fuck all of you! You want to see somebody die? I'll blow Zeke's motherfucking brains out. Will that thrill you pricks?''

Zeke's heart began to pound faster as he watched Harlen losing control. Zeke tried again to calm his captor down.

"It's almost over. They don't want anyone to die; that's why they are giving you everything you want. Please trust them. You need to trust somebody in your life."

Harlen whirled around and glared at Zeke. Those words were something Harlen had sworn he would never believe again. He spit at Zeke as he yelled out his curses.

"Fuck you and fuck your friends! I don't trust any bastard alive. All trust ever did for me is fuck me up the ass."

Harlen pointed toward the window as he continued to yell, "Do you really trust those bastards out there?"

Zeke meekly nodded his head yes. He tried to answer but was too frightened to say anything.

Harlen began laughing as he answered his own question, "I feel sorry for you, boy. Trust is going to sneak up on you and bite you right in the ass, just like it did for me."

Zeke forced himself to give a reply to Harlen's statement.

"Everyone needs to trust somebody sometime in their life. That's what hope's built on."

Harlen just glared at Zeke, turning and closing his eyes. His mind drifted back. Zeke's words had triggered memories Harlen tried to bury in the caverns of his mind. He thought back to the last man he had trusted and how he had betrayed him—the suffering he endured through reform school because he had put his faith in someone other than himself.

19

Harlen stood outside the new church that now stood on his block. The church rose majestically above the downtrodden neighborhood. Harlen didn't know if it was supposed to represent a symbol of hope or a sign of greed. With the people who lived on these streets as poor as they were, this towering building was like a slap in the face. Harlen tried to imagine the old church that he used to go to. The wrecking ball that had demolished the church he knew as a child did its job well. No trace of the past lingered on the lot where the new church stood. Harlen broke his trance and glanced up and down the streets. Not a soul walked the streets this night; sadly enough, no one walked these streets on any night, unless, of course, they had some kind of death wish. Slowly he crossed the street and walked toward the church. He headed directly to the back and tried the door. Harlen smiled when he realized the door was unlocked. Quietly he opened it and sneaked inside. The light from the moon shone its rays through the stained glass ceiling onto the crucifix in the front of the church. Harlen stared at it for a moment. A strange beauty shimmered around the body of Jesus hanging from the cross. For one brief moment Harlen felt a surge of warmth shimmer through his body, but the strange sounds coming from the back of the church erased it. Harlen pulled his revolver from his coat pocket and headed toward the sound. He stopped as he reached a door. Carefully he reached out and turned the door handle. He pushed the door open and quietly moved into the room.

The reverend sat at his desk writing the sermon for Sunday's service, humming an old hymn as he wrote words of wisdom for his congregation. The reverend felt full of life and happiness. His new church was just finished not more than a month ago and already its members had doubled. God showered him with blessings, and his sermon Sunday would show his thanks for those blessings. Reverend Smith knew he had just completed the best sermon he ever wrote in his entire life. The people this Sunday would raise the rafters with "Hallelujahs," praising not only God but also the reverend for bringing them hope in the wake of all the sadness around them. Suddenly a cold chill ran up and down Reverend Smith's spine. He stopped writing and spun around quickly. He saw nothing behind him but could feel the eyes of someone staring at him. He glared into the shadows of the corners of the room. Then he saw it, a silhouette of a man standing in the corner of the room. The reverend's voice rang out like thunder as he shouted, "Who is there?"

Nothing but an eerie silence. The reverend gazed harder at the silhouette, trying to make out who it might be. Again he called out, "Don't stand in the shadows! Please show yourself!"

Still nothing but silence. The reverend began to stir in his chair. He knew someone was standing just outside his room. Why wouldn't the man show himself? Was he frightened? Worse yet, did they plan on robbing the reverend? He stared hard at the silhouette, trying to make out who it was. Once again the reverend called out, his voice filled with warmth, "Please don't be frightened, tell me, who are you?"

A harsh whisper replied, "One of God's children."

The reverend began to tremble. He could sense the evil in the man's voice. Smith's tone became weaker as he asked, "Do you belong to my church, son?"

Harlen stepped out of the shadows and stood grinning at the holy man. Harlen's voice dripped with sarcasm as he replied, "I used to, but you sent me away."

The reverend's eyes widened with terror as he saw Harlen Jones standing in front of him, older now, but Reverend Smith knew who he was from the unmistakable scars on his face. The reverend tried to rise to his feet, but Harlen snapped at him quickly, "Stay seated, Reverend. I don't want you to move a muscle."

Frozen with fear, the reverend asked, "What do you want?"

Harlen burst into laughter. He felt the terror in the holy man's voice. Harlen's laughter stopped as abruptly as it had started when he said in a wicked voice, "I came here to repay you for all of your kindness you bestowed on me five years ago."

The holy man leaped to his feet. His voice shook with fear as he cried out, "I did what I thought would be best for you! I did it because I cared for your soul."

Harlen shook his head slowly as he replied in a softer voice, "I came to you because you were the only person I felt I could trust. You used to tell me that I could've been special. I believed in you. Then you turned out like everyone else. You turned me in to the fucking law."

The reverend's voice crackled with fear as he shouted out, "I did what was best for you! You committed murder, but you paid for this sin. Harlen, you still can reach for your goals. Think about it, son: if you harm me you will never be really free."

The little softness that had been in Harlen's voice disappeared as he growled back, "Because of you I spent two years of my life in a fucking hell. I was gang-raped, beaten. Why? Because I put fucking trust in you!"

The reverend held up his hands as he said in a terrified voice, "I didn't know that, but put it in the past. Harlen, you can trust me; you're one of God's children, and I will be here to help you."

Harlen didn't reply. Slowly he raised his arm that held the revolver and aimed it at the reverend, smiling as he did.

The reverend fell to his knees as he begged Harlen, "Please, I am a man of God. Show mercy and trust in me. Son, don't kill me or your soul will burn in hell for eternity."

Harlen cocked the hammer of the revolver, whispering as he did, "You should thank me. I am sending you to meet the father of all your children." Harlen squeezed the trigger.

"Sir, the Jeep is waiting. Please trust them."

Harlen broke his trance and turned to Zeke, replying gruffly, "We will go, but not because I trust your dear friends. I need rope; do you have any rope in this dump?"

Zeke stood still for a moment, confused by Harlen's demand.

Harlen barked out his command again: "Did you hear what I said? I need some damn rope!"

Harlen glanced around the room and spotted an extension cord. He reached down and grabbed it, tugging it from the wall. Clutching it in his hand, he screamed at Zeke, "Turn the fuck around and put your hands behind your back!"

Zeke, stunned by the sudden anger in Harlen's voice, turned around and put his hands behind him. Harlen wrapped the cord firmly around them, tightening the cord with each knot he put in it. Pain shot through Zeke's entire body as Harlen yanked to check the firmness of his work.

"Stay still or you will die right here."

Zeke did what Harlen ordered him to do.

Harlen looked around and saw another cord running from the register to the wall. He reached over and unplugged it. Then, yanking as hard as he could, he ripped it from the back of the register. Grabbing it, he walked over to Zeke and wrapped it around his neck, leaving a long-enough piece dangling for him to grab on. He tugged on it and Zeke let out a pained cry. Harlen eased up on the cord and leaned toward Zeke, whispering in his ear, "Now you will need to trust your friends, because if they fuck up you will die."

Harlen pressed the barrel of his gun at the back of Zeke's neck as he snarled, "Move to the back door."

Zeke nodded and did as ordered. Slowly he walked toward the door, Harlen behind him holding onto the cord attached to his neck.

Visions of Tina's beautiful eyes danced through Zeke's mind as he moved closer to the door. Tears streamed from the corner of his eyes as he could hear Tina's voice whispering in his mind, *I love you, Zeke.*

Zeke stopped in front of the door, whispering, "I love you, Tina."

Suddenly the barrel of Harlen's gun pressed harder into Zeke's neck. He cringed in pain. Harlen growled, "Remain perfectly still. I don't want any unfortunate accidents happening to you. When I tell you to walk, you walk. When I say stop, you stop. Is that clear?"

Struggling to breathe, Zeke coughed out his reply: "Yes. Could you loosen the cord a little? It is cutting into my neck."

Harlen tugged on the end of the cord, causing Zeke to gasp in pain. Harlen then sneered. "Be thankful you are still able to feel pain. That means you are still alive."

Choking, Zeke begged Harlen, "Please, I can barely breathe."

Harlen waited for a second, then loosened the noose around Zeke's neck. Pressing his gun deeper in the back of Zeke's neck, Harlen whispered, "Open the door."

Zeke reached out and pushed the bar on the door. The door flung open.

Harlen then screamed at Zeke, "No sudden moves! Just remain still."

Zeke remained perfectly still, Focusing his eyes on the black Jeep idling in front of him. Harlen pushed his body flush against Zeke's, his eyes darting around the barren lot.

Harlen then yelled out into the apparently empty lot, "I know you're out there watching, so listen carefully! If I should stumble or fall the grip on this cord will tighten, which will regrettably, snap Zeke's neck, and if he is lucky I will also get off a shot to make him die quicker. So if there is a hero out there please think twice before taking a shot."

The only sound either men heard was the roaring of the engine of the Jeep that idled in front of them. Harlen hoarsely whispered to Zeke, "Move toward the Jeep slowly. Remember, it won't take much for me to release the hammer of this gun or yank on this damn cord."

In a trembling voice Zeke replied, "None of this is necessary. I know these people; they will honor their word."

Harlen leaned over and kissed Zeke on the cheek and sarcastically said, "I know they love you; so do I. Now move slowly to the Jeep."

The two men moved cautiously out the door, heading for the shining black Jeep in front of them. The open door was only steps away from the restaurant entrance, but it appeared miles away with each step. Both men's hearts pounded as the anxiety mounted in both of them. When they reached the open door, Harlen ordered loudly, "Slide in. Remember, I hold a cord that can squeeze the life out of you."

Trembling, Zeke cautiously squatted on the seat of the Jeep. Carefully he inched over, trying desperately not to cause the cord on his neck to tighten any more than it already was. Zeke closed his eyes as the fear smothered him.

Harlen now sat behind the steering wheel, his eyes glaring around the emptied lot. He whispered to Zeke, "I know they are out there. The rooftops, out in the fields. All of your so-called friends are out there waiting, praying to be the hero to put a bullet in my skull."

Harlen reached out and grabbed the open door and slammed it closed. He glared over at Zeke, waiting for him to comment or dispute what he had just said. Zeke remained silent, his face pressed up against the window of the passenger side of the jeep. Harlen put the Jeep in gear; the jeep bolted forward. Zeke released a painful gasp as the cords around his neck tightened from the sudden movement. Harlen eased his foot off the gas pedal and drove slowly out of the back lot of the restaurant. He drove down the narrow path that led to the main street. Zeke opened his eyes and stared out the window. Rows of people lined up on the street to watch as Harlen drove to the front of the building. He pulled out onto the town's main street. Both sides of the street lined up with townspeople staring at the Jeep as it drove past them. Zeke sensed the fear and pity in their eyes.

Harlen broke Zeke's trance as he growled, "How far to this Harrison Point?"

Zeke continued to look out as he replied wearily, "Five miles."

Zeke smiled as suddenly every face in the crowd wore the face of Tina, smiling and throwing him kisses as they drove past. Zeke closed his eyes to dive deeper into his imagination. He now could hear her soft voice whispering through the air, *I love you, Zeke.*

Zeke smiled weakly as he saw Tina's piercing blue eyes staring at him. They were filled with hope. Again he could hear whispering in his mind: *I'm with you Zeke and I love you.*

A sudden pain shot through Zeke as he remembered his fight with Tina earlier in the day, how she wanted to kiss him good-bye, but his pride wouldn't allow it. Now he craved to touch her lips, to hold her body close to his. Tears rolled down his face as he realized that his last memories of Tina before he died could be of their argument. Zeke bit down on his lower lip as his thoughts raged on.

I will not die! Tina, I will hold you again; this I swear!

Zeke's thoughts were rudely ended as he heard a strange sound next to him. He opened his eyes to look at his captor.

Harlen began humming an old hymn as he drove farther away from the Golden Aces, the same hymn that the late Reverend Smith had been humming the night he died. Finally they left the town limits. Harlen pressed harder on the gas pedal to pick up speed. The Jeep roared towards it destination.

20

Tina pulled right to the edge of the cliff, the tires still spinning on the muddy trail. She felt the anxiety as the car became harder and harder to control on the treacherous path. Finally the car stopped. Tina released a sigh of relief. She glanced in the rearview mirror and watched as Starr pulled in behind her. He appeared to be having the same problems as she had gaining traction on the muddy path. Starr finally stopped his patrol car. Tina put the car in park and took her foot off the brake. Glancing one more time in the rearview mirror, Tina turned off the engine. Releasing a heavy sigh, she leaned back in the seat. The trail leading to the point had made for a treacherous journey. The storm had turned the trail into a quagmire. The car bogged down in the mud twice. Tina feared a few times that there was absolutely no way Parker's car would finish the trip.

Starr turned off the engine of his patrol car. Cautiously he opened the door. His eyes scanned every direction of the wooded area. He moved out of his vehicle, slamming the car door shut, his eyes still nervously glancing around the entire area. Finally he felt secure and walked toward Tina's car. Moving to the driver's side, he bent over and tapped on the window to get Tina's attention.

Tina gave him a weak smile as she rolled down the window: "I didn't think I was going to make it up that trail."

Starr smiled back. Opening her car door, he replied, "The trip back will be a lot easier. It is time to get rid of the body, Tina."

Tina nodded her head in agreement. Stepping out of the car, she stood by Starr's side, asking, "Are you positive this will work, Bill?"

Starr put his arms around her, drawing her close to him. He kissed her gently on the forehead. It felt so comfortable having her close to him. Fighting the urge to whisper, "I love you," to reassure her, instead he quietly said, "Relax, my dear. It will work and it all will be over shortly."

Tina rested her head on Starr's chest. He caressed her gently. Softly Tina asked, "After we are through, you will keep your promise and take me to Zeke?"

Starr fought back the hostility he had begun feeling toward Zeke, reminding himself continually that Tina was no more than a friend. Starr moved Tina away from him. He stared into her deep blue eyes, his mind still raging a battle with his heart, forcing himself to bury his true feelings for her.

"I want you to go to my car and wait for me. I'll take care of everything. I promise this will not take long."

Tina moved her hand toward Starr's face. Brushing a lock of hair to the side, her voice warm and gentle, she whispered, "Thank you, Bill. I don't think I would have made it all these years without your friendship."

Tina kissed Starr on the cheek, whispering, "I love you."

Turning away from Starr, she moved swiftly toward his car. Starr did not take his eyes off her. Her words rang in his ears. *"I love you."* He knew she meant as a friend. Tina would never love anyone but Zeke. Bill Starr was no more than a friend, a friend who would lie for her, kill for her, and even die for her. Love Tina reserved for Zeke Riley only. Starr watched as Tina slid into his car, slamming the door shut behind her. Starr ignored the thoughts that flooded his mind and reached into the open window of Parker's car and he moved the gear shift into neutral, grabbing the steering wheel with his right hand. Bracing his left hand on the side of the car, grunting, he began to slowly push the car forward, toward the cliff's edge. Reaching the edge, he gave one final push and jumped away from the car quickly. Tumbling backward he fell into the mud-soaked trail. Lying on the ground, he watched the car with Parker's body disappear over the cliff. Starr bounced to his feet and moved quickly to the edge, staring down below into the raging waters. Parker's car sank gradually into the murky waters below. Relief entered Starr's mind; the ordeal was finally over. Parker would never harm Tina again. Starr heard the car door slam behind him. He wanted to shout out his words, express to her the true reasons for his actions. Resisting the temptation, he stood there waiting for Tina to reach him. As she drew closer to him, he could see the anxiety written on her face. Stopping in front of Starr, Tina avoided looking over the edge of the cliff. In a nervous tone she asked, "Did his car sink to the bottom?"

Starr forced a weak smile, replying quietly, "Take a look, Tina; that will be the only way you will feel completely secure." He watched as Tina struggled with the idea of looking over the edge. She remained still, not daring to move any closer to the cliff's edge. Starr reached out, taking her by the hand gently. Turning, he forced her to follow him to the cliff's edge. Tina must acknowledge the burial of her ex-lover.

Tina struggled, trying to break Starr's grip on her hand, protesting vigorously, "Bill, I don't want to look; I trust you. If you say that his car has sank to the bottom, then I believe you. Please, I want to leave."

Starr ignored her pleas. Tugging on her hand, he labored to get her next to him. Standing directly by his side, Tina refused to look down into the waters. She buried her face into Starr's chest, crying softly as she pleaded, "Bill, I can't. Please, I just want to leave."

Starr's voice was stern as he ordered Tina, "Tina, look below. I want your fears to end here. That will not happen if there is even the slightest doubt in your mind. Now please, for both our sakes, look down there."

Starr eased her away from the security of his chest. Turning her around, he held her arms tightly as he faced her toward the cliff.

Slowly Tina allowed her eyes to move downward, into the waters below. She caught only a glimpse of the taillights as they disappeared beneath raging waters. Tina drifted into a strange trance, her mind racing, thoughts flooding rapidly as she glared into the waters below. She remained staring, waiting for the car to resurface, to haunt her for eternity. Starr moved closer to Tina, wrapping his arms around her waist. He wanted Tina to feel safe and completely satisfied that Frank Parker was out of her life for good.

The winds began to pick up slightly, whipping mildly across their faces. Starr glanced up into the skies. The rain was going to start again. He whispered to Tina, "It is time to go, Tina. It's over; the bastard will never hurt you again."

Starr felt the anger build inside as with Tina he watched Parker's car finally disappear. Starr then whispered to Tina, "Time to return to our lives."

Tina replied, not taking her eyes from the water as she spoke, "I wonder how many souls sacrificed themselves to this river? Warriors, proud men, dove from this cliff as a tribute to their god. What do I offer our God? Not a warrior, definitely not a proud man. God is already angry with me. Ironically, I cast one of my sins into his sacred waters."

Tina's words brought chills to Starr's body. Again Tina appeared to be slipping into the madness of her mind. Squeezing her firmly, as if he wanted to squeeze the madness from her, he said, "Tina, please stop this foolish thinking. God is not angry with you. You must believe me: God loves you."

Tina broke Starr's grip on her and whirled around to face him, her eyes showing her sadness.

Starr felt helpless, not knowing how to make her pain fade away.

Tina quietly asked him, her voice trembling, "If he loves me, as you claim he does, why has he punished me for all these years?"

Starr grabbed Tina's arms, squeezing them firmly. His voice grew harsh as he shouted at her, "Tina, how is God punishing you? You have a husband that adores you, a lovely home, career—you are an excellent nurse. Tina, God has blessed you with everything, including a child that you and Zeke always wanted."

Tears began to run freely from Tina's eyes. The agony from her past began to smother her. She screamed at Starr, "At what cost did I achieve everything in my life?"

Starr could feel Tina's entire body trembling. He eased his grip on her arms. Tina's voice shook with anger and shame.

"I slept with a man I despise to father my child. Do you know why? God would not allow me to bear another child by Zeke."

Starr's eyes widened, his voice showing his confusion as he asked, "Another child, Tina?"

Tina's face flushed with embarrassment. She meekly nodded her head yes and explained her hidden secret to Starr.

"I was young; Zeke and I only were married for a short time, when I found out I was pregnant. I wanted so much from life, to finish school and reach my dream of becoming a nurse. I wanted to help the sick, to have a purpose in life. Having a baby at that particular time would end those dreams. I decided to have an abortion. I murdered my unborn child. That is why God is punishing me."

Starr drew Tina closer to him, staring deep into her eyes, saying in a warm and gentle voice, "Tina, I can't say what you did was right or wrong. I am in no position to make a judgment like that, but women have abortions every day. Are you saying God strikes out his vengeance on every one of them? Of course not. What you are feeling is guilt. Tina, you are finding it hard to cope with a decision that you made in your life. You want to be punished, but God is not doing it, Tina; you are."

Tina's emotions poured out, "Bill, you don't understand what has been going on in my life since that decision I made. My guilt and shame forced me to seclude myself from those I cared about. My father killed himself because of me. I went to God and asked for his help."

Tina's tears ran freely now as she buried her face in her hands and shouted, "Do you know what God's answer to me was?"

Tina's pain swelled inside her as she began to tell the guilt feelings that were buried deep inside her for years. Her entire body shook as she screamed, "My father killed himself that night! Bill, I never got the chance to tell my dad how much I loved him."

Tina looked up at Starr. Her voice grew weak as she said added through her tears, "All my dad wanted was his little girl to show him love. I didn't; I was terrified he would find out about the abortion. The pain became too much for him; the loneliness unbearable. He shot himself; he used the same gun that I killed Parker with. God is punishing me by inflicting pain on the people I love."

Starr wanted to shake the madness out of Tina and tell her that not only did God love her, but so did he. Starr snapped back gruffly, "That is ridiculous. Tina, listen to me; your father took his life because he was afraid of loneliness. He could not handle living alone. Neither you nor God had anything to do with it."

Sobbing, Tina pointed to the heavens as she cried out, "I wish I could believe you, Bill! I wish I could explain away everything that happened in my life since the abortion—not being able to have a child for fifteen years, my father's suicide, Zeke giving up his dream of being a writer, Zeke being held hostage, my best friend helping me to hide a murder I just committed. Would you just call all this bad luck, Bill? It's not; it's God's wrath being sent to those who I care about. Why can't you see it, Bill? Why don't you or anybody else believe me?"

Starr grabbed her, holding her tighter against his body. Tina was now crying uncontrollably. Starr kissed her forehead, whispering, trying to calm her down.

"Go ahead and cry, sweetheart. Let all the pain out. Release the ghosts that are haunting your soul. Free yourself, because I swear to you, no harm will ever come to you again. Tina, if God is waging a war against you, then he has declared war on me also."

Tina looked up into the deputy's face, her eyes red and watery from the tears. Her voice showed the pain as she asked, "Do you mean you believe me, Bill?"

Starr stared deep into Tina's blue eyes and said with a passion he never knew he had inside him, "If God or the devil himself tries to hurt you, Tina . . . then they will need to do it over my bloody body."

Tina squeezed Starr tightly, whispering as she did, "Zeke and I are very fortunate to have you as a friend."

Tina's words of thanks were not what Starr needed to hear. Her words pierced his heart like a dagger. Friend, that was all he ever would be to her. Starr stared into Tina's deep blue eyes. Smiling, he gently said, "Thank you, Tina. I feel the same way about Zeke and you. Both of you made me and my family feel welcome when we came to this town. You are good people and I promise you that after today everything will be back to normal for both of you."

Tina rested her head against Starr's chest. She wiped the tears from her eyes. The rain again began to fall, much lighter than earlier in the day. Starr ran his fingers through Tina's hair, quietly saying, "We better go before the rain becomes heavier. The trail is bad enough already."

Tina nodded in agreement. She moved away from Starr and stared over the edge of the cliff again, gazing into the raging river below.

Starr assured her again in a soothing voice, "Parker's car is on the bottom of the river bed. No one will ever find him."

Tina put her hands on her stomach. Still staring below, she said, "If I have a boy, I would like to name him after you, Bill. To show you how much I appreciate what you have done for me."

Starr replied quietly, "I would consider that an honor, Tina, but we got to get out of here now."

Tina turned away from the cliff. She headed toward Starr's patrol car. Starr followed her. Tina stopped at the passenger side and waited. Starr reached the car and went to open the door but opened abruptly. His eyes shot a quick glance down the trail.

Tina anxiously asked, "What is wrong, Bill?"

Waving his hand at Tina, Starr snapped back his reply: "I hear something; it sounds like another car heading up the path."

Panic seeped through Tina's voice as she cried out, "We are trapped! This was all for nothing. Whoever it is will figure out what we have done."

Starr whirled around and found himself shouting at Tina, "Calm down! It might be only kids wanting a place to neck. Get into the backseat of the car and hide. I will take care of whoever is coming."

Tina didn't hesitate. She opened the back door of the patrol car and slid in. Moving to the floor, she lay quietly. Her heart pounding, fear racing through her mind, she whispered, "You won't let it end, will you, God?"

Closing her eyes, she waited and listened to what was happening outside the patrol car.

Starr nervously leaned against the car. Reaching down, he gripped the handle of his revolver. Tina's words began to haunt him: "God is punishing me by inflicting pain on the people I love."

Starr shook off the strange feelings Tina's words gave to him. God didn't wage war on mere mortals. Starr gripped the handle of his revolver tighter, praying he would not be forced to use it.

21

Hanson sat in his car watching as the Jeep disappeared down Main Street. He turned quickly to the young state trooper, asking, "Is the tracer working?"

The trooper smiled, nodding his head yes, his eyes fixed on the small white blip on the screen. Hanson glanced at his watch. He was sure he had given enough time for the Jeep to get in front of him. Starting the engine of his patrol car, glancing over at the young man next to him, Hanson asked, "We still have him on the screen, Trooper?"

Smiling, the trooper nodded, replying as he did, "Trust me, Sheriff, I've done this many times. The bastard isn't going anywhere without us knowing it."

Hanson put the gearshift in drive. As he pulled away to follow the Jeep, he said in an excited voice to the young trooper, "Good, because I think it is time we nail this creep."

Hanson pressed the gas pedal on the patrol car harder to gain more speed and proceeded to head in the direction of the Jeep. As Hanson drove off, Overstreet's voice beckoned him over the radio.

"This is Captain Overstreet. Are you reading me, Sheriff?"

Hanson picked up his mike hooked to his radio, replying quickly, "I read you, Captain. We have a fix on the Jeep. We're now in the process of following Jones to wherever the bastard is heading."

Overstreet responded quickly, "Don't get too close; we don't want him spotting you."

Overstreet paused, then added quickly, "I already have him in sight, Sheriff. We will triangulate our positions when the Jeep stops. Overstreet out."

Hanson hung up the mike and turning to the trooper, asked, "Which direction do we go?"

The young trooper didn't take his eyes off the box that sat on his lap as he replied to Hanson's question, "Our suspect is heading south."

Hanson sped up the car, making sure that Jones didn't get too far ahead of him. There was no way this bastard, after all the pain and misery he had brought to Hanson's town in one short day, was going to get away. Hanson glanced up into the evening sky, trying to catch a glimpse of the helicopter. High above he saw the flying machine circling. He winced as he spotted it. Hanson was sure if he could see it, Jones also would detect it. Gripping the steering wheel tighter, the anxiety getting stronger, Hanson watched the helicopter off in the distance.

The trooper calmly informed Hanson, "He is still heading south, sir."

Hanson nodded, half-listening to what the trooper said. The sheriff's thoughts remained fixed on the helicopter in front of him.

Again the trooper spoke. This time his voice showed a trace of emotion: "Sir, our suspect is turning east."

Hanson shot a glance at the trooper, asking quickly, "East, are you sure?"

The trooper pointed to the box on his lap, answering, "Yes, sir, he turned east."

Overstreet's voice came crackling over Hanson's radio.

"Sheriff, Jones is turning off the main highway. He has turned onto some sort of trail. I can't see him with all of these damn trees surrounding the area."

Hanson's anger boiled. Grabbing the mike, he shouted back, "You were too damn close! Jones must have spotted you."

Overstreet's tone remained even as he replied, "You're getting paranoid, Sheriff. Jones could not possibly have spotted me. The way he is rigged to your friend would make it impossible to stare into the skies. He must have a particular destination in mind. From the maps I am looking at, he has turned into a dead end. There do not appear to be any roads to travel on."

Hanson restrained his anger, calmly asking, "What path did he turn on?"

There was a long pause; then Overstreet replied, "According to my map, the trail leads to Harrison Point."

184

Hanson snapped back quickly, "Wherever he is going, he will be on foot. That area is too dense for a vehicle of any kind. The trail he is on is a dead end. It leads right to the point."

Overstreet quickly asked, "Is there an area to land a helicopter?"

Hanson found himself shouting out his reply: "No! The path is too narrow. We are just about there. We will follow him by car."

There was a brief moment of silence. Hanson pulled his car to the side of the road. The trail leading to Harrison Point lay directly in front of him. The silence shattered as Overstreet's voice boomed over Hanson's radio, "I am ordering the pilot to land! I will go in with you."

Hanson began to protest but knew it would be futile. He heard the roar of the helicopter's engine as it started to descend to the ground. The huge machine landed ten feet away from Hanson's patrol car, it's whirling blades causing a windstorm around it. Hanson watched as Overstreet jumped out of the whirlybird. Overstreet shouted out last-minute instructions to the pilot, then turned and headed for Hanson's patrol car. The helicopter lifted off into the sky behind Overstreet. He reached Hanson's car. The deputy opened the rear door, allowing Overstreet in. Sliding into the backseat he asked, "Has the Jeep stopped yet?"

Hanson glanced at the young trooper, waiting for him to give Overstreet his answer.

The trooper answered calmly, "Not yet, sir."

Hanson added, "He can't drive very far; he will be reaching the point soon. Captain, something has just occurred to me. What if Jones is dropping Zeke off, keeping his end of the bargain? I think it might be better to wait for a while, find out if he contacts the mayor and gives a location to pick Zeke up at. He is not going anywhere. Following him in now might endanger Zeke for no reason."

Overstreet leaned back in his seat. Calmly he ordered his trooper, "Taylor, call the mayor for the sheriff. See if our suspect has given any instructions on picking up the hostage."

Taylor leaned over and picked up the receiver of the portable phone on the seat between him and Hanson after Taylor rapidly punched in the buttons, Mayor Martin's voice boomed on the other end. Taylor handed the phone to Hanson.

"Hello, Mayor."

Martin's voice replied almost in a panic as he scolded Hanson, "Bob, you shouldn't be tying up my line. You know I am waiting for a call from Jones."

Hanson ignored the sternness in the mayor's voice, saying quietly, "Mayor, I hoped he already contacted you. Jones is headed for Harrison Point. I thought he might be dropping Zeke off there."

Martin's voice beamed with excitement as he gasped, "We have him cornered, Bob. Maybe he will drop Zeke off and head back on the main highway. If he was to contact me it would be after he got back on the highway. We have the bastard now."

Hanson's tone was not as confident as the mayor's as he replied, "He is no fool, Mayor. Dropping off his hostage is not a priority with him. I believe he has some type of plan or he is preparing to kill Zeke and dump his body over the point."

Hanson knew why Overstreet had allowed him to contact the mayor. Reality now seeped into the sheriff's mind. Harlen Jones had no intention of contacting the mayor or anyone else. Jones might free Zeke, but even that was unlikely. Again Overstreet appeared to be right.

The mayor screamed back at Hanson, "You are being too negative, Bob! What does Jones gain by killing Zeke? I will bet you a week's salary that as we speak Jones is tying Zeke to a tree and preparing to drive off. Heading directly into our trap."

Hanson fought back the urge to scream. Instead his voice remained calm as he ended the conversation, "You are probably right, Mayor. I will keep you informed of any further developments. If Jones does contact you, please let me know immediately." Hanson didn't wait for the mayor to reply but hung up the portable phone. Turning toward Overstreet, Hanson asked, "What do you suggest we do next?"

A slight smirk appeared on Overstreet's face at Sheriff Hanson seeking his advice. A sense of satisfaction oozed into Overstreet's body. Finally the small-town sheriff had realized he was overmatched and needed an expert.

Before Overstreet could give his solid words of wisdom, Trooper Taylor bellowed out, "Our suspect's Jeep just stopped!"

Both Hanson and Overstreet leaned over and peered at the white blip on the trooper's panel. The blip remained stationary, blinking brightly as it stayed in one precise area. Hanson knew that Jones had finally reached Harrison Point. A dilemma etched itself in Hanson's brain: Was the mayor right? Was it possible that Jones would allow Zeke his freedom? Should they play it safe and wait a while longer to see if Jones's Jeep headed back toward the highway? A wrong decision meant a man's life.

Hanson's voice displayed his tension as he snapped at the trooper, "Any movement by the Jeep yet?"

Ignoring Hanson's outburst, the trooper confidently replied, "No, sir, the vehicle he is in has not budged."

Overstreet put his hand on Hanson's shoulder and in a pampering voice said, "Sheriff, we must go in after him. It may be the only chance to save your friend. The longer we wait, the less chance of us saving him."

Hanson's mind felt as if it would explode at any moment. His eyes kept darting over to the trooper's panel. The white blip remained steadfast. Like a warning signal, the white light remained blinking, crying out to all watching: *Danger*.

Hanson wanted to rip the box off the trooper's lap and hurl it into space, thinking if he destroyed the machine the danger would end.

Overstreet persisted, "Sheriff, we are wasting valuable time. We must go after him now. You can call in and get backups to blockade any other escape routes. Sheriff, are you listening? We must act now!"

Hanson whirled around, glaring at Overstreet. Anger glowed in the sheriff's eyes. His words spit out the frustration that had mounted inside him from this entire ordeal.

"Act on what? Getting Zeke killed? I know what you are telling me is the proper way of handling this, Captain. You are blessed with years of experience in handling these types of crises. I wish I had your mundane approach to this entire affair. My conscience won't allow that. I keep getting reminded that we are dealing with a man's life. One wrong or hasty decision, a man dies. I can't cope with that, not without looking at the other alternatives."

Overstreet retorted in a gruff voice, "You asked me what I suggest we do next. I gave you what I feel is the best action to take. If you can't handle the pressure, then wait here. My man and I will go in alone."

Hanson barked back angrily, "All I am asking is that we wait for a few minutes to see what Jones is going to do. If he is dropping off Zeke and keeping his end of the bargain, then we arrest him as he tries to escape. Five more minutes, just to make sure what we are heading into."

Overstreet slammed his fist on the side of the door as he screamed out his anger: "Five minutes! Then if that Jeep doesn't move we go in after him.' Overstreet turned his attention to the young trooper, asking harshly, "Any movement on the Jeep?"

The trooper timidly shook his head no.

Overstreet glanced at his watch, saying, "Five minutes, Sheriff, not a second longer."

Hanson let out a heavy sigh and nodded to confirm what Overstreet had said. The sheriff leaned back in his seat, closing his eyes tightly, trying to close out the reality of how this day likely would end. A surge of hate crept through him as he found himself wanting this Harlen Jones to die a painful and lingering death, making him suffer as he had made everyone who cared about Zeke suffer. Personally Hanson wanted to inflict this painful death. If Jones harmed Zeke in any way, Hanson decided, he and he alone would swing the sword of justice, inflicting a pain that Harlen Jones never knew existed.

Hanson opened his eyes, slowly looking at the white blip flashing on the panel. It still didn't move. It was time for them to act, to stop this vicious animal before he destroyed any other lives. Hanson sat straight up and gripped the steering wheel tightly. His fears became engulfed by his anger. He growled at the two men in the car as he put it in gear, "Five minutes are over. It is time to end this, and God help Harlen Jones if he has harmed Zeke in any way."

Neither of the two men in the car with Hanson replied. They knew Hanson's comments stemmed from anger and frustration. Slowly he turned down the muddy path that led to Harrison Point.

22

Starr watched as he made out the image of the vehicle approaching. It was a shining black jeep. Closer it moved toward Starr and the point.

Tina lay in the backseat of the patrol car, her heart pounding as the fear built up inside her. She knew this was going to be the final battle with God. She also knew deep down inside that she was going to lose. No mortal could ever win a war against a god.

Starr's knuckles turned white as he squeezed the handle of his gun tighter. Anxiety mounted inside him. He had choices he knew he would need to make. If the person in the Jeep moving closer to him found out what he and Tina had done would he now become a killer along with being an accomplice . . . because of friendship? What next? God, was Jane right? Was Tina really going to be the cause of his destruction? But Starr knew it was too late to turn back now. Anxiously he waited as the shining black Jeep moved closer to where Starr stood.

Harlen spotted the patrol car directly in front of him. Tugging on the cord tied around Zeke's neck, he shouted, "It is a trap! You motherfucker, you led me into a fucking trap!"

Zeke gasped for air. Forcing his words, he cried out, "How? I was with you every minute. I don't know how they knew, honest."

Harlen slammed on his brakes. The jolt of the car stopping forced the cord to tighten even more around Zeke's neck. Harlen stared forward at the patrol car in front of him. He saw a portly uniformed man leaning on the car, not moving. Harlen's eyes darted in every direction. No one else was in sight. Harlen gripped the cord tighter in his hand and drew Zeke toward him, shoving his gun under Zeke's chin and harshly whispering, "If I die, your white ass will be joining me. He then pushed Zeke away from him, releasing the cord as he did. Zeke loosened the cord from his neck and waited for Harlen's next command. Zeke rubbed his neck, trying to ease the pain away.

189

Harlen watched as the man leaning on the car stood erect and moved slowly toward him. His voice showed his confusion: "Either he is very sloppy at police procedures or the stupid son of a bitch doesn't know what is going on!"

Zeke glanced in the direction where Harlen was staring. Gasping Zeke realized the man walking carelessly to the jeep was Bill Starr. Zeke wanted to shout, to warn his friend to stop, scream to him that he was walking toward his death. Harlen raised his gun and cocked back the hammer. He began to roll down the window so he could lean out and get a clear shot at the fool walking toward him. Like an animal waiting for his prey Harlen waited for the deputy to get closer.

Zeke's eyes darted toward Starr, watching in terror as he moved closer to the Jeep. Zeke's eyes then went to Harlen, whose total attention was focused on the deputy moving closer toward the Jeep. Zeke felt the panic rip through him as Harlen raised the gun and began to lean out the window. Zeke felt a surge of courage rush through him. Zeke suddenly reached out and grabbed Harlen's arm, shouting out his warning to Starr: "Look out, Bill!"

Startled at hearing Zeke's voice, Starr hit the ground, drawing his revolver from his holster at the same time, aiming it toward the sound of Zeke's voice and the black Jeep in front of him, preparing himself for whatever might be waiting for him.

Harlen smashed his elbow into Zeke's nose. Blood gushed as Zeke's head crashed up against the window. Harlen reached over and grabbed Zeke by the hair, yanking him toward him. Starr could hear the agony in Zeke's cries. Harlen opened the door to the Jeep. He slid out, dragging his hostage behind him. Maintaining his grip on Zeke's hair, Harlen pressed his gun in the back of Zeke's skull.

Starr aimed his gun but didn't have a clear shot. He remained lying on the ground, not taking his sights off the black man in front of him.

Harlen barked out his demands.

"Get rid of the gun or I will splatter his motherfucking brains all over this fucking countryside!"

Starr looked on in horror. Zeke was bleeding profusely from the nose, Harlen's gun aimed directly at the back of Zeke's head. The man using Zeke for a shield was a stranger to Starr. Somehow the man from the Golden Aces had escaped with Zeke and in some

190

kind of weird fate wound up here at Harrison Point. A sick feeling oozed through Starr as he glared at the gunman in front of him.

Harlen shouted his demand again.

"Get rid of the goddamn gun now!"

Tina shook as she heard the voices outside the car. Fear kept her frozen, unable to look up to see whom the voices outside the car belonged to.

Starr glanced quickly over his shoulder. His fears mounted; he was worried not only about Zeke but about Tina also. Starr prayed quietly that Tina wouldn't attempt to leave the patrol car. He turned his attention back to Harlen, shouting back his reply: "Let Zeke go and you're free to leave! All I care about is Zeke's safety! Trust me when I say you're free to go!"

Tina's eyes widened as she heard Starr shout out Zeke's name. A small ray of hope seeped through her.

Harlen shoved the gun deeper into the back of Zeke's neck. A trace of sarcasm rang through Harlen's voice as he shouted back, "Yes, we all should be very concerned about Zeke's safety! If you don't get rid of the gun, you can watch me blow his fucking brains out!"

Starr's voice became harsh as he snapped back, "I won't have time, because once you pull the trigger, I promise, I will shoot you!"

Harlen glared at the deputy lying on the ground and could sense that he had more experience in this type of situation. Harlen began dragging Zeke toward the front of the Jeep, never taking his eyes off Starr. Reaching the front of the Jeep, Harlen stopped, his eyes glancing to the right of him. Whispering, he asked Zeke, "How far is it to your cabin through those woods?"

Zeke's words stumbled out of his mouth: "Two miles; just keep to the river to the left of you."

Harlen turned his attention back to Starr.

"It appears we have a stalemate, Officer! So what I propose is a compromise! I will take Zeke with me! That way he will live a while longer!"

Harlen forced Zeke to his feet. Pressing the gun into Zeke's temple, he added, "Try and follow me and you can have his body."

Starr winced. He could see Zeke's face clearer. His eyes swollen, his nose still dripped blood. A sick feeling gnawed at the pit of Starr's stomach. He knew his duty. He could not let Harlen walk away, even though it might mean the life of a friend. The sick feeling grew as Starr wondered, *Is it duty, or do I want Zeke to die?*

Tina screamed as she jumped off the floor of the patrol car, "Zeke!" Tina swung the car door open and continued to shout as she ran down from the point.

Starr shook that demented thought from his mind, but before he could give his reply he heard Tina's voice screaming behind him, "Oh, my God, it's Zeke!"

Startled by the sound of Tina's voice Starr, jumped to his feet. Turning toward Tina, throwing his arms in the air, he screamed at her, "Tina, get back in the car!"

Harlen seized the opportunity that the situation gave him. Aiming his gun, he squeezed off two shots, hitting Starr in the center of the back. The impact slammed Starr back to the ground. Tina let out an earth-shattering scream that rang through the air.

"God, no!"

Zeke looked on in horror, trying to break the grip of his attacker, but was too weak. Helplessly Zeke watched as his friend crashed to the ground. Zeke's eyes widened with shock as he saw Tina running toward the downed deputy. Zeke's weary voice screamed over his pain, "My God, Tina! Tina, run!"

Harlen yanked on the cord around Zeke's neck. Forcing him to stare right into his eyes, he aimed the gun at Tina and snapped out his warning harshly: "Unless you want to see her die, I would suggest you lead me to this cabin."

Zeke didn't hesitate; as he weakly grabbed at the cord he forced himself to extend his hand toward the woods. Pointing his finger toward the woods, he moaned, "This way."

Harlen's eyes followed where Zeke's finger pointed. Smiling wickedly, Harlen dragged Zeke back toward the Jeep. Reaching in, he grabbed the briefcase that was carrying the money. Holding it tightly, he shoved Zeke in the direction he pointed to.

Zeke stopped and struggled to look one more time at his wife, who now knelt next to Starr. She looked so fragile as she knelt next to the deputy's body. Zeke could hear her screams ringing in his ears. He wanted to break free from the bastard holding him and run to his wife and hold her to tell her he would be there for her. A sharp pain ripped through him as Harlen yanked on the cord, forcing him away from his sight of Tina.

Harlen shoved him again, sneering: "Move it, before I change my mind and kill the bitch, too."

Zeke knew that this madman meant what he said. Staggering, trying to remain on his feet, Zeke moved into the woods. Harlen holding tightly onto the cord, glancing back at Tina, followed close behind Zeke.

Tina's hands shook as she knelt down and moved Starr's face out of the mud. Blood flowed freely from Starr's back. Tina rolled him over to his back. Starr's breathing became erratic. Slowly he opened his eyes, attempting a smile as he saw Tina kneeling over him. Tina's voice trembled as she tried to talk through her tears.

"I will get you to a doctor; you're going to be fine, Bill. I'm not going to let you die. Not you, too. God is not taking anybody else away from me. Do you understand me, Bill? You're not going to die!"

Starr strained to raise his arm. Tina grabbed it. Starr made a feeble attempt at touching Tina's face. She helped him by moving his hand to her face, allowing him to run his fingers across her cheek. Coughing, Starr struggled to speak.

"Tina, don't hate God; he loves you. Almost as much as I love you."

Starr began coughing up blood but forced himself to continue talking.

"Tina . . . forgive me . . ."

Starr's hand went limp. Tina cried out as she buried her face in his chest, holding his hand firmly in hers.

"Don't die, Bill; please don't die!"

Tina tightened her grip on Starr's hand. She looked up into the skies and screamed to the heavens, "Not again, God! You coward, why not take me instead? Here I am! Strike me dead! End this fucking war now! You win! Please don't take another person I love from me. God, please, I give up. . . . I give up."

Tina closed her eyes and began weeping. Gently she laid her head on Starr's chest, sobbing silently.

Hanson slammed on the brakes of his car, stopping directly behind the black Jeep. He jumped out of his car. The two men in the car with Hanson did the same. He saw Tina kneeling next to a body in front of him. At first he thought it was Zeke till he noticed Starr's patrol car parked near the point. Hanson's heart sank as he saw Bill Starr lying in a pool of blood. Guilt began to rush through him. If he listened to Overstreet would his deputy still be alive? Trying to maintain his composure, Hanson knelt down next to Tina. He reached out and rested his hand on her shoulder. Tina jumped back as he touched her. Startled, she screamed; her eyes danced with terror. Overstreet and Taylor stood in front of her. Like a cornered animal she swung out, screaming as she did. Hanson gasped as he saw the bruises covering Tina's lovely face. Horror crept through him as he looked down at his fallen friend, wondering if he had anything to do with Tina's injuries. Gently Hanson put his arms around her and held her tightly till she stopped struggling. After waiting to see if Tina would calm down, Hanson asked softly, "Tina, what happened?"

Tina tried to speak, but words did not come. She laid her head back on Starr's chest. Her moans growing louder, Hanson lifted her away from the body and asked her again, "Tina, I must know what happened? Where is the man that drove the Jeep?"

Tina struggled to free herself from Hanson's grip. Her eyes glistening with tears, the black-and-blue marks grew brighter as the tears streamed down onto them. Tina's voice trembled with hate as she spit out her words.

"God had the devil kill him!" Clenching her fist, she began pounding on Hanson's chest as she screamed, "Why? Why? Please tell me why?"

Overstreet and Taylor watched as Hanson struggled with Tina. She became hysterical, not making any sense to the men in front of her. Hanson grabbed her fist and pulled Tina toward him, wrapping his arms around her, holding her tight. Hanson's voice became stern like a father's as he tried to calm her down.

"Tina, snap out of this. I need your help. Where did the man who shot Deputy Starr go?"

Tina glared at Hanson. Her deep blue eyes danced madly with rage as she continued to rave, "God had the devil kill him. Damn all of you, why won't you believe me?"

Overstreet grew weary of Hanson's feeble attempts to talk with Tina.

"She is not in any frame of mind to tell us anything, Sheriff. There is no way he could have passed us. I suggest we split up and search the woods."

Hanson glared up at Overstreet. The sheriff's anger flowed as he snapped, "What do you suggest we do with Mrs. Riley and my deputy? Should we leave them here?"

Overstreet first looked at the young trooper, who just stood and stared in disbelief at the pain of the woman kneeling in front of him. The young trooper then stared down at the body of the deputy. This was the first dead man Taylor had ever seen. A strange sick feeling began to swell in the pit of his stomach. Taylor felt a twinge of shame build inside him, as he felt as if he was going to vomit.

Overstreet could see the pale look coming over the young trooper. Overstreet felt the same kind of sickness; you never get used to seeing death. With his tone of voice losing its calmness he snapped back to Hanson, "Of course not; we will call for an ambulance. Taylor can stay with her till it gets here. As for your deputy, I am sorry. It is always hard when you lose a man in the line of duty."

Hanson's eyes burned with hate as he screamed back at Overstreet, "You heartless bastard! This man is also my friend!"

Hanson turned back to Tina. Calming himself down, he tried again to get information from her.

"Tina, I must know what went on here and where the man in the Jeep went? Is Zeke still with him?"

The mention of Zeke snapped her out of her daze. She looked up into Hanson's eyes, whispering, "God will kill him next. Then everyone will be dead. God needs to kill Zeke to claim complete victory over me. Then I guess I will die, too."

Hanson realized he was not going to get through to Tina. She was in too bad of a shape to give him any information. Christ, what was she doing here? Who beat her? Was it Harlen? Was that how Starr died, trying to stop Harlen? No, the bruises were at least five hours old. God, Zeke didn't do this before he left for work? Impossible. Zeke worshiped Tina. Too many damn questions, everything falling apart, his friend lying dead in front of him, Hanson felt like pounding the life back into Starr so he could ask, "Why in the hell were you here, Bill Starr?" Hanson bit hard on his lower lip as he realized nothing was making any sense. Turning to Overstreet and Taylor, Hanson shouted, "Radio in for an ambulance!"

Hanson released his grip on Tina. As soon as he did, Tina rested her head on Starr's chest. Staring aimlessly into space, she refused to leave Starr.

Hanson stood up and walked over to where Overstreet stood and glanced at Taylor, who now was in the patrol car calling for help.

Overstreet asked, "What was she doing here?"

Hanson wondered that and who had beaten her. Hanson knew Starr, there had to be a good reason for him to bring Tina here, but whatever the reason was, that question would go unanswered for a while. Tina was in no frame of mind to answer any questions. Hanson replied quietly, "I don't know, but it must have been important for Bill to risk coming here. Maybe Zeke contacted him somehow; I just don't know. Till Tina is able to return to reality I don't think we will."

Overstreet looked around the entire wooded area, then at the Jeep. Turning to Hanson, Overstreet asked, "Do you have any ideas where Jones may be heading?"

Hanson nodded his head yes, answering in a confident tone, "There is only one reason Jones decided to take this path to Harrison Point. It is the only passable trail off the highway. From here he can make his way through the woods and end up at Zeke's cabin. Zeke has a boat. I am sure Jones is going to attempt to reach Canada from there. It is the only logical reason to come up here."

Overstreet, stunned by Hanson's statement, grabbed him by the arm and turned him around to face him.

"Are you telling me that you knew where Jones was going from the start? That there is a way for him to avoid all of our roadblocks?"

Hanson took his free hand and removed Overstreet's grip on his arm. Hanson snapped back, "It didn't register till now. I forgot all about Zeke's cabin. It will take them hours to reach it in the area they are going through. We can get there in a half hour using the main road."

Overstreet shot back quickly, "You take the main road and wait for them. Me, I am following them the same way they went."

Hanson gave Overstreet a sarcastic smile as he said, "You don't know these woods, Captain. I would wind up sending a search party to find you. I will go with you; any one of my deputies can lead your men to Zeke's cabin."

Before Overstreet could respond, ambulance sirens came screaming up the trail. Two men jumped out and rushed to where Hanson and Overstreet were standing. Hanson pointed to where Tina still sat, resting her head on Starr's chest. Hanson shouted out as they went to her side, "She is in some kind of shock! Please be gentle with her!"

Both men nodded to acknowledge Hanson's order. They gently lifted Tina away from Starr's body, carefully leading her to the back of the ambulance. She continued to stare blankly into space. Hanson gazed at the body of his fallen friend and dreaded the next order he gave when the two men returned.

"I do not want anyone to talk to the deputy's family. I will tell his wife personally."

Again the men nodded. This time it was with relief that they would not be the ones to be the bearers of bad news. Taylor returned, waiting for his next order. Hanson said firmly, "Trooper, I want you to drive back to the main highway and wait for my men to come. Tell them that our suspect is heading for Riley's cabin. They will lead the way; you and your men will follow."

Taylor glanced over at Overstreet, waiting for him to confirm Hanson's orders. Overstreet nodded. The young trooper eagerly asked, "I request to go with you, sir, to pursue the suspect?"

Overstreet snapped back in a sullen tone, "Request denied. You have your orders; please follow them."

The disappointment was hard to hide, but Taylor turned and headed back to the patrol car. Hanson watched as the ambulance roared backward carrying his friend's body and Zeke's wife. Hanson began to think how he was going to break the tragic news to Starr's wife. He had left the force in Detroit because of all the violence. Starr had settled down in Barnsville to make a decent life for his wife and children. How was Hanson going to explain that the only violent death in Barnsville history had claimed her husband as its first victim? Hanson tried to shake the unpleasant task ahead of him from his mind. He cared a lot for Bill and Jane. Even though Hanson knew it would be easier for him to have one of his deputies tell the tragic news to Starr's family, he knew this was something only he should do. Hanson turned to Overstreet and said, "These woods can be tricky. You may be the expert out here, but in there you listen to everything I tell you."

Overstreet got a defensive look on his face as he snapped back, "I can handle myself in the woods, Sheriff. I have camped out in the woods many a time."

Hanson remained rigid as he snapped back, "Have you ever been in these woods, Captain?"

Overstreet shook his head no, but before he could reply verbally Hanson added, "These woods are dense and have very few trails. Go in that direction and you may not be found again for years. So swallow that stupid pride of yours and listen to everything I tell you. Am I clear on that?"

Overstreet just nodded his head. He knew that the frame of mind that Hanson was in, there would be no sense in arguing with him. Hanson glared at the blood mixing in with the mud where his friend had lain and added, "I don't want Zeke to be added to the list of those who die today. My deputy is tragic proof that you were right. This fucking animal will kill to save his own skin."

Overstreet didn't reply. Instead Overstreet spun around and entered the dense woods. Hanson frowned but followed close behind him.

23

The skies opened as the rain began to fall harder. The gods once again began to lash out their power from the heavens. The roaring of thunder clapped in the distance; the winds picked up and began forcing the trees to dance to Mother Nature's tune.

Stumbling through the brush, Zeke lost his footing and fell, plunging face-first into the muddy ground below him. Gasping for breath, he tried to rise back to his feet. Exhausted, hungry, Zeke couldn't find the strength to continue. He collapsed. Harlen halted right beside Zeke, hitting him hard with the briefcase he clutched tightly in his hand. Harlen swung the case hard and hit Zeke again as he cursed violently.

"Get your ass up and move or I will make this your fucking grave site!"

Flinching from the impact of the briefcase hitting his rib cage, Zeke begged, "Please, I need to rest, just for a few minutes."

Harlen, wiping the rain off his face, peered behind him to see if anyone was following. All he could see were the bending branches and thick brush they had just traveled through. Though no one was behind him, Harlen became uneasy. Staring harder into the dense forest behind him, he was sure he would see something. Harlen sensed the presence of something. It gave him an uneasy feeling. He turned, glaring back at Zeke lying on the ground. Harlen knew he needed this coward to get him out of this wooded maze.

"Five minutes, not a second more. Do I make myself clear?"

Weakly Zeke replied, "Yes, thank you." Zeke relaxed his entire body and sprawled out on the ground.

Harlen shoved his revolver inside his belt, deciding this would be a good time for him to rest awhile himself.

On the ground Zeke lay motionless, his eyes staring into the blackened skies. The rain pounded on his face, but Zeke ignored nature's fury as his tortured mind began reliving the nightmare he had witnessed earlier, that of his friend, Bill Starr, crashing to the ground from the impact of the bullet smashing into his back, the visions slowly unwound, dancing across his mind, Starr shouting, waving his arms to warn Tina, Tina running toward Zeke's fallen friend. Entwined with the pain were questions: Why were they there? For what possible reason would either of them trek up the treacherous path to the point?

The questions burned painfully in Zeke's mind, but he didn't receive much of a chance to dwell on them. Harlen bounced back to his feet, shouting his orders at Zeke: "Time is up! Move it! We have a lot of ground to cover!"

Straining every bone in his body, Zeke struggled to his feet. The heavy downpour of rain drained what little strength he had. Harlen shoved Zeke forward, growling as he did, "This boat of yours better be where you say it is or you will wish I killed you this morning!"

Zeke kept moving, not answering Harlen's warning. Slipping and sliding through the mud, they trudged forward. The thunder roared, announcing its return. Lightning flashed above, brightening the gloomy skies. Branches slashed Zeke's face as he carefully advanced through the thick brush. Harlen followed close behind. Beginning to feel uneasy as for the first time today, he felt awkward, not in control. A strange sense of helplessness showered him. He grabbed the gun from his belt, holding it firmly in his hand. He knew this was his power, his god. It made him invincible, above mortal man. The gun would make him feel in complete control again. Never in his life had he received respect, always the freak, the joke on everyone's lips, till he found the power of the gun; then no one ever laughed at him again.

Zeke lost his footing again, falling hard into the bushes in front of him. The thunder shook through the forest, followed by lightning. A bolt flashed right above Harlen, giving off an eerie glow across his scarred face. Zeke shuddered. Harlen Jones looked like death standing over him. The jagged scars on Harlen's face appeared to come to life, crawling up and down his face.

Harlen's voice bellowed out, "Get up! Damn you, stop stalling!"

Zeke timidly replied, "I am not stalling. I'm hungry, weak, and wet. I want this all to end, but I need to rest."

Harlen snapped back rudely, "In case you forgot, we are not on a nature hike. We don't have time to rest. I know your friends by now must have figured out where we are heading. If we don't beat them to your cabin and your boat, a lot of blood will spill today."

Harlen's words brought back the nightmarish scene of Starr's death. Looking away from Harlen, trying to avoid looking at the grisly scars on the man's face, Zeke found himself blurting out questions his mind was asking.

"Was it necessary to shoot down the deputy? The man had a family; he gave you his word. For Christ sake, why did you shoot him?"

Harlen didn't show a trace of remorse in his voice as he answered, "I will kill anyone who is a threat to put me back in a cage. Your friend was foolish enough to lower his defenses to warn that woman. He paid the price for caring for someone other than himself. Now let me ask you a question. Who was that woman with the deputy?"

Barley above a whisper, Zeke replied, "My wife."

A wicked grin crossed Harlen's face as he said, "Your wife. . . . Looks to me as if your wife and that cop were having some fun while you were away. Christ, we probably pulled up at the same time he was getting ready to bang her. No wonder he wouldn't bargain for your life. Shit, you should be thanking me; looks as if I did you a fucking favor."

Screaming, Zeke lunged toward Harlen. Fury engulfed his body.

"Pig, you fucking filthy pig!"

Harlen swung the briefcase in his hand, hitting his attacker hard in the back of the head. Zeke fell face-first into the muddy ground, crying out in agony from the blow. Harlen burst into sarcastic laughter as he commented, "So the man does show some balls?"

Zeke glared up at Harlen, his eyes burning with rage. Mud covered most of his face. His rage gave him courage that he couldn't find earlier. Hate for this vile creature penetrated Zeke's body. He coldly warned his tormentor.

"Unless you know where you are going, these woods are endless. One could easily die here and not be discovered for years."

Harlen's laughter diminished. Threat was something he wasn't accustomed to, especially from a weakling like Zeke. Cocking back the hammer of his gun and aiming it at Zeke, Harlen asked curiously, "I am not afraid to die; are you?"

Zeke didn't flinch. His words remained cold as he replied, "Yes, I am afraid of death, but I am willing to face it. You have tortured and insulted me long enough, so pull the damn trigger and end this."

Harlen smiled, easing the hammer back to a safe position. Zeke continued glaring at him, not showing a trace of fear. Harlen lowered his gun to his side, his voice calmer as he said, "There is no reason either of us must die. Get me to the boat and you will be able to return to your wife breathing. It is your choice; make it now."

The rain began falling harder. Thunder echoed through the woods. Lightning lashing out its destruction in every direction, nature resumed its war on Barnsville. Winds howled as they whipped through the dense forest. Two lone figures fought their way forward in pursuit of their prey.

Hanson shouted over his shoulder at Overstreet, "Stay on the path I make and keep aware of the falling branches!"

Overstreet nodded to confirm what Hanson had just instructed him to do. The narrow path Hanson had referred to was no more than two feet wide. Blinded by the rain, Overstreet struggled to remain on the path. Shouting to Hanson, he asked, "How much further to your friend's cabin?"

Hanson stopped, waiting for Overstreet to make his way toward him. When Overstreet reached Hanson, bending over to catch his breath, he repeated, "How much further to your friend's cabin?"

Hanson tried wiping the falling rain from his face as he replied, "It is not much farther, maybe a half-mile."

Overstreet wiped the rain from his eyes as he hollered over the thunder, "Do you think they have reached it yet?" Overstreet straightened up. Still breathing heavily, he waited for Hanson's reply.

Hanson shrugged his shoulders as he said, "I doubt it; they didn't have that much of a start on us."

Overstreet took off his hat. Shaking the water from it, putting it back firmly on his head, he said humbly, "I want to apologize for my actions earlier. I must have came off as a heartless bastard. I am truly sorry about the death of your deputy."

Hanson could sense that Overstreet was sincere. It was the first time since this nightmare began that he had shown any true emotions. It also rekindled the pain of seeing Starr lying in a pool of blood. All those years on the force in Detroit and not even a scratch, only to wind up dying in a town he had felt would be his sanctuary. The memory of Tina burned in Hanson's mind as well. She was so fragile. So much pain crossed her path, the horrifying death of her father, the painful realization that she would not be able to bear any children, her husband being held hostage, and now her best friend shot down right in front of her eyes. Her mind trapped in a hell it might never escape from. Hanson forced a smile as he quietly accepted Overstreet's apology.

"Thank you. I realize you have tremendous pressure on you. All is forgiven. Now if you are ready, I think it is time to make the man responsible for all this pay."

Overstreet nodded in agreement. Hanson turned and moved through the bushes in front of him. Overstreet followed close behind, both men now carrying the same desire: to capture or kill Harlen Jones.

Zeke painfully stood up. His anger still brewing inside him, wiping the mud off his face, he asked, "How can I trust you? I watched you shoot a man in the back. It appears to me I am a dead man no matter what I choose to do."

As Harlen replied, the irritation in his voice became hard to conceal, Zeke's newfound courage surprised him.

"I shot that man to survive. I do not kill for pleasure but out of necessity. If you cooperate I have no reason to harm you. I do own a set of codes to live by, so either trust me and lead on or die and I will find the clearing to your cabin on my own."

Zeke had a wry smile on his face. He knew the chances of Harlen finding the cabin on his own were minute, especially with the storm raging as fiercely as it was. Harlen needed him if he was going to have even a spark of hope to escape.

Harlen's voice grew angrier as he shouted over the raging sounds of the thunder, "We are wasting time! Let's go!"

Zeke's eyes glanced down at the hand that Harlen gripped his pistol with and could see the tension in his hand as he held the gun tighter. His black knuckles began turning a pale white. Zeke decided not to press his luck.

"I have your word I will be released?"

Harlen cursed softly under his breath as he watched Zeke thrash his way through the branches. Resentment for this pompous white man began building inside Harlen. He held the gun, he gave the orders, yet this man acted as if he were superior. Harlen knew why. He was out of his environment, Zeke was in his, but soon the hostage's courage would disappear, the arrogance would diminish, and fear would smother Zeke again. Then Harlen's power would return and Zeke would die for his disrespect for that power.

Hanson dropped to one knee, holding up his hand for Overstreet to halt. Staring hard through the pouring rain, Hanson made out the silhouette of a body fading into the bushes. Hanson waved to Overstreet to join him. Not taking his eyes off the shadow, he watched it blend into the landscape.

Kneeling beside Hanson, Overstreet gazed out in front of him. He saw nothing but the dense bushes and rain. Still gazing directly in front of him, he whispered, "Why are we stopping?"

Hanson, not turning his eyes away from the area where he had seen the shadow, replied, "They are just ahead of us, maybe twenty yards."

Overstreet glared at the area in front of him. He still could not see a sign of either man. Hanson rose to his feet and began moving carefully forward. Overstreet jumped up, reaching out, grabbing Hanson by the arm.

"Wait! Are you sure you see them? The way the rain is falling it may be a rabbit or a deer."

Hanson jerked his arm upward, shaking Overstreet's grip from it. Keeping his voice low, he growled, "It was them; we are wasting time. Try to be quieter; the element of surprise is in our favor."

Hanson removed his revolver from his holster and moved swiftly ahead. Overstreet hesitated for a brief moment. He watched the young sheriff jog toward the thick brush. Swearing softly, Overstreet pulled out his revolver and followed him. Sliding through the mud, trying to keep their balance, along with staying quiet, the two law officers trudged forward.

Stopping at the dense bushes, Hanson whispered, pointing to the ground all around the area, "Tracks, two sets, still think it is a deer?"

Overstreet forced a weak smile. He felt foolish but would gladly be the town fool if it meant capturing Harlen Jones. Overstreet motioned to the left of him, whispering, "I will move in from the left; you move ahead carefully."

Hanson gave a thumbs-up and inched forward. The blinding rain fell harder; thunder crashed above them. They both felt as if they were marching into hell, chasing Lucifer himself.

Hanson stopped abruptly. Barely visible behind the curtain of rain he saw his prey. Glancing over to the side of him, he watched Overstreet come to a halt. Hanson waved his hand in a circling motion. Overstreet nodded, then quickly and quietly moved to position himself in front of Jones. Hanson watched the trooper move into position. Once he saw his partner entrenched, Hanson crept closer.

Harlen shouted over the thunder, asking Zeke, "Are we nearing the clearing to your cabin?"

Zeke stopped and turned around to face Harlen. Breathing heavily, his hair sopping wet, he tried to catch his breath as he nodded and gasped out his reply: "Yes. It is just over the ridge in front of us."

Zeke weakly turned and pointed to the ridge behind him.

A smile creased Harlen's face. The smell of freedom was in the air. He looked all around, being this close to the end of his journey. He found himself appreciating the beauty surrounding him. Only once in his life had he ever had the rare feeling of happiness. It was in a setting similar to the one he stood in now. Trees, grass, things many people take for granted. Not Harlen Jones, this was paradise to him. Harlen knew the only time in his entire life he had ever felt a sense of tranquillity was in an atmosphere like this. Maybe if everything worked out he could find the tranquillity he had felt that one short week as a child. Harlen began to feel a sense of hope that after he completed his final stage of his journey and made it safely to Canada he would search for the place to be at peace with himself.

Harlen noticed that Zeke was staring at him curiously. Harlen realized he must look like a fool in his hostage's eyes. Immediately Harlen regained his scowl, barking out his orders.

"Get me to that boat! Let's go!"

Zeke's eyes were not staring at Harlen but past him. Kneeling ten yards behind his tormentor was Sheriff Hanson. Zeke's heart leaped with joy, his excitement impossible to contain.

Harlen snapped out again, "Are you deaf? I said let's go! Your sorry ass is really beginning to piss me off. I don't want to repeat myself one more fucking time!"

Harlen raised his gun and aimed it at Zeke. He cocked back the hammer as he screamed out again, "You motherfucking bastard, don't think I won't blow your fucking brains out right here. This is the last time I'm going to warn you. If your fucking ass don't start moving and keep moving I just shoot you and take my fucking chances."

The thunder roared out louder, vibrating through out the area. Lightning flashed all around the skies.

Trembling, Zeke forced himself to look away from his savior. Instead he yelled loud enough so Hanson would hear him, "I'm going! I'm just tired! I need to rest for just a few minutes! Can't we just sit here for a while?"

Harlen's rage swelled inside him as he screamed back at Zeke above the thunder, "You said we're close! You can rest as much as you fucking want when we get to the cabin!"

Zeke avoided looking at Harlen. Taking a deep breath, Zeke turned back toward the ridge. At first he walked slowly then began to move more swiftly. Harlen shoved his gun back into his belt and hurried to follow Zeke. Harlen smiled as he thought the reason Zeke began moving faster was because the idiot felt he was going to allow him to live. Harlen decide Zeke would die as soon as they reached the boat. Harlen's thoughts were rudely interrupted by a voice booming over nature's wrath. Harlen picked up his pace and cursed under his breath when Hanson's voice boomed over the thunder again.

"Lay down your weapon!"

Harlen froze in his tracks. He yanked his gun from his belt and rose it toward the sound of Hanson's voice. Harlen then quickly glanced behind him. He saw a figure kneeling, aiming a gun directly at him. Harlen whirled around, but he was too late. Zeke disappeared somewhere in the brush ahead of him. Harlen's protection had escaped.

Hanson's voice echoed through the woods again.

"This is your last warning! Lay down your weapon!"

Lightning flashed overhead. Thunder roared through the air. Harlen dived to the ground, squeezing off three shots in Hanson's direction. The gunshots became muted by the thunder. Water seeped through Harlen's clothes as he lay in the mud, staring at the figure kneeling in front of him. Still clutching the briefcase containing the money, Harlen had raised his gun to fire again when a voice calmly spoke behind him.

"Drop the gun, Jones. It's over."

Harlen remained perfectly still. He knew it was over and felt a strange sense of relief flood through his body.

The voice behind him remained calm, saying "Drop the gun; spread out your arms where I can see them, now."

Memories flooded Harlen's mind in a matter of seconds. All the hell he had lived through over the years. Faces flashed before him from the deaths he had seen or caused in his lifetime. The concrete cell he had escaped from and sworn never to return to. Compared to the paths his life had journeyed, this wooded area of Barnsville would be his only heaven or hell. The words of Reverend Smith echoed in his mind: *"We are all God's children."*

Over and over the good reverend's words continued to ring in Harlen's ears: *"We are all God's children. We are all God's children. We are all God's children."*

Harlen rolled quickly onto his back, his gun firmly gripped in his hand. Grinning, Harlen screamed as he met the eyes that belonged to the voice, Overstreet.

"Fuck off and die!"

Overstreet didn't hesitate as he pulled the trigger of his gun, hitting his target twice in the skull.

Harlen cried out. His painful cries rang through the stormy skies. The impact of the bullets exploded his skull. Blood poured over his hideous scars. His gun dropped softly to his side. His body lay limp in the mud. Overstreet stood over him, no remorse, no pity. He leaned over and picked up the briefcase that was lying next to Harlen. Overstreet's job was now complete. Harlen Jones would spread no more terror to any other innocent lives.

Hanson leaped to his feet on hearing the shots. Quickly he ran toward Overstreet. Slipping and sliding, Hanson finally reached where Overstreet was standing and glanced down at the body lying on the ground. Harlen's lifeless eyes stared back up at Hanson. Blood covered what remained of Harlen's face. To that day, Hanson had never seen a dead man; now he had witnessed two deaths. His stomach felt queasy from the sight of all the blood. Even the rain could not wash it away.

A joyous cry bellowed through the air. Hanson and Overstreet turned. Behind them, Zeke Riley ran toward them. His face beaming, he cried out, "Is the bastard dead? Tell me the fucking bastard is dead!"

Weak and exhausted, Zeke crashed to the ground. Hanson quickly ran to Zeke's side and knelt down beside him, gently rolling him over. Zeke smiled, seeing Hanson's face. Hoarsely Zeke asked, "Did you ever get your morning coffee?"

Before Hanson could reply, Zeke passed out.

Hanson shouted to Overstreet, "The clearing is just over the ridge! Your men should be there by now! Please go and get some help! Zeke is in no condition to travel!. I will wait here with him!"

Overstreet nodded his head yes, commenting as he did, "Don't worry, Sheriff; he will be all right."

Overstreet took one last look at the man he had just shot. A sense of relief came over Overstreet. He then headed for the clearing and Zeke's cabin.

Hanson slid his arms under Zeke's head, lifting him gently, and rested his head in his lap, wiping the mud from Zeke's bruised and battered face. Hanson took off his cap, resting it on Zeke's face to protect him from the falling rain. Glancing over his shoulder, he watched as Overstreet made his way over the ridge. Hanson knew it wouldn't be long before Overstreet reached the clearing. Zeke would go to the hospital; his wounds would mend. Overstreet was right when he said, "He will be all right."

Zeke's physical strength would return. He was a strong and healthy person. That did not worry Hanson; what did was Zeke's mental health. He had just come through one hell of an ordeal; the last hours must have felt like an eternity to Zeke. With the threat of death looming over him every second, at the hands of that madman, the pain that must be going through this man's mind would be incredible. Hanson wondered if Zeke and Tina would ever be able to live a normal life again, if the nightmare of this day would ever leave their memories. Zeke stirred restlessly in Hanson's arms.

Hanson whispered softly to his friend, "Relax, Zeke. You are safe; it is all over."

Zeke weakly opened his eyes as he whispered, "Tina, where's Tina?"

Before Hanson could reply, Zeke passed out again. Hanson softly answered anyway.

"Everything is going to work out fine, my friend. You will be holding Tina in no time."

The rain began to fall lighter. The lightning flashed farther off in the distance. The thunder's roar grew faint. Up on the ridge the sounds of men's voices grew near.

24

The mayor's driver hung up the car phone. He walked up to the mayor, leaned over, and whispered in his ear, "Jones is dead and they recovered all the money."

Martin pushed back his glasses as he asked, "Is Zeke safe?"

The driver nodded his head yes, adding with no emotion in his voice, "Deputy Bill Starr is the only fatality other than Jones. Jones gunned Starr down during his escape. Those were the only details I received."

Todd Martin stared curiously at his driver as he asked, "What the hell was Starr doing there? Did the sheriff set up a trap or something?"

The driver shrugged his shoulders as he replied, "Like I said, the only detail the deputy gave me was that Starr was dead."

Martin looked away from his driver and began staring at the crowd still gathered by the Golden Aces restaurant. The storm did not diminish their concern for Zeke Riley's safety. Martin whispered to his driver, "Did Hanson break the news to Starr's wife yet?"

Martin's driver shook his head no as he replied, "No, sir, not yet. Sheriff Hanson's deputy asked that nothing be said. I guess he wants to inform Mrs. Starr himself. I guess we better not say anything . . . right, sir?"

Martin adjusted his glasses on his face. He glanced at the crowd standing outside the restaurant and snapped back at his driver, "The hell with him. The good people of this town deserve to know of Starr's heroics, and I am not going to miss out on the chance to tell them."

Martin's driver nodded as he replied, "Yes, sir, I agree completely."

Martin smiled, then leaned closer to his driver and asked, "What about Parker? Did you locate him yet?"

The driver shook his head no as he replied, "No sir. I checked with his office; he hasn't been in all day. His wife doesn't know where he is, either. Quite frankly, I don't think she cares."

Martin released a sigh of disgust as he snapped back, "Pretty damn sad when we can't offer medical assistance to our own citizens."

The big man nodded in agreement.

Martin added quickly, "Find the good doctor. I am sure he is with a whore somewhere in town."

The driver again nodded in agreement. Leaving the mayor's side, Martin watched as his driver walked over to one of the deputies. The driver said something in the deputy's ear; then both men got inside the patrol car and drove off.

Martin turned his attention back to the crowd. Martin opened the door to his car and slid out. Staring into the crowd, Martin held up his hands to gather their attention. Looking to make sure that the crowd now was watching him, Martin waved his hands again as he yelled out to the townspeople, "May I please have your attention!"

Martin waited till he was sure the entire crowd had focused on him. Clearing his throat, he began to speak for all the people to hear.

"I was just informed by the Michigan State Police that Zeke Riley was rescued."

A loud cheer rang through the crowd. A party atmosphere rapidly appeared as people began to hug and dance in front of Martin. Martin held up his hands again; the crowd slowly quieted back down. Martin cleared his throat. Readjusting his glasses to fit his face, he continued with his speech.

"Today is a day Barnsville should always remember. It was the day we felt the cruel reality of the society we live in. Never in the history of our town has a major crime ever been committed. We never were subjected to watching any of our good neighbors suffer needlessly. The criminal who inflicted this pain on our peaceful town is dead, brought to justice by our own Sheriff Bob Hanson."

The crowd cheered loudly, whistling and clapping. Martin again raised his hands for quiet. The noise of the crowd lowered to slight murmurs. Martin lowered his head for a moment, staying silent. Slowly he looked up and stared with sadness in his eyes at the crowd. He forced himself to continue, his voice cracking as if he were about to break down in tears.

"Today we had to fight a war against evil. We won. As in any war, there were casualities. Deputy Bill Starr became one of those casualities. He was brutally shot down in the line of duty. He sacrificed his life to protect us from madmen like we saw today. He left behind his beloved wife, Jane, and their two sons, Rob and Tom. Our hearts and prayers go out to them."

Martin paused so the impact of his words hit firmly on the crowd in front of him. Once again Martin pushed his glasses back up on his face and continued.

"I can hear the tears and sobs among you good people. I myself want to break down and cry till the pain stops. It hurts; it causes fear. We felt safe in our little heaven. We depended on no one but one another. Reality is a horrifying experience. No longer can we hide in our shells and say, 'This can't happen to us.' We must face the facts; we need protection from animals like the one who invaded our humble town today. I want you all to go home and do three things for me. One, say a prayer for the Starr family. Two, say a prayer for Zeke and Tina Riley. Three, write this day on your calendar, because today is the reason why you, the voters, will demand a larger budget for law enforcement."

The crowd went wild clapping, shouting out cheers for Todd Martin. He walked away, moving toward his limousine. He stopped and turned and waved to the crowd, then disappeared inside his car. He smiled, pleased with the way the crowd had reacted. He leaned back in his seat and waited for his driver to return. Closing his eyes, he listened to the chants of his name.

"Martin, Martin."

Zeke opened his eyes slowly. He glanced around the room. Sitting across from him was Bob Hanson. Zeke went to say something, but Hanson spoke first.

"You're in the hospital and you are doing fine."

Zeke's words struggled to come out as he demanded, "I need to see Tina."

Hanson looked away, searching for the right words to use. He could feel Zeke's eyes staring at him. Hanson squirmed in his chair. He felt uneasy about what he must tell his friend.

Hanson's silence became unnerving. Zeke's voice found strength as he shouted out his question.

"Has something happened to Tina?"

Hanson turned toward his friend and could see the anxiety in Zeke's eyes. The sheriff reached out and put his hand on Zeke's shoulder, quietly saying, "She is here, Zeke. Tina has had a traumatic experience."

Zeke knocked Hanson's hand off his shoulder, blurting out, "What in the hell are you saying, a traumatic experience? What the hell are you trying to tell me?"

Hanson's voice became more sympathetic, answering, "I'm afraid she is not herself, Zeke. The doctors told me she has lost sight of reality." Pausing for a moment, Hanson felt uneasiness rip at him as he asked Zeke, "Zeke, did you and Tina have a fight before you went to work?"

Zeke snapped back with anger, "What if we did? What the hell does that matter?"

Hanson took a deep breath as he forced himself to ask the next question.

"Was Tina . . . all right when you left her?"

Zeke fought hard to close his mind to the sight of his wife running toward Starr and Starr turning his back to Harlen. Struggling with his words, Zeke screamed at Hanson, "What the hell are you talking about? Where is Tina? I want to see her now!"

Hanson's voice became gentle as he replied, "You are in no shape to see anyone, Zeke. I will send for the doctor; he can explain what is going on."

Zeke, filled with frustration, yelled back, "Damn it, Bob, I want to see my wife! Will you take me to her or do I tear this hospital apart till I find her?"

Hanson realized arguing with his friend was useless and if Zeke had struck his wife now was not the time to judge him on his actions. Reluctantly Hanson rose from his chair, whispering, "OK, Zeke, I will take you to her."

Hanson reached out his hand. Zeke grabbed it. Struggling, he managed to get to his feet. As he gripped Hanson's hand tighter, Zeke's words came out trembling.

"Is Bill dead?"

Hanson, fighting back his emotions, just nodded his head yes.

Tears began running down Zeke's face. Despite his efforts, he couldn't shake the sight of Starr falling to the ground. Over and over it replayed in his mind. Struggling to speak, his voice showing the pain and confusion, he asked, "Why in God's name did you allow Bill to take my wife to Harrison Point? How did he know that was where we were heading?"

Hanson shrugged his shoulders. That was a question he would like to know himself. Quietly he answered, "I had nothing to do with it, Zeke. I have no idea why they were there. Only Tina can answer that question."

Zeke, still reeling in pain, asked, "Did you ask her, Bob?"

Hanson allowed Zeke to lean on him. Quietly he replied, "Like I said, Zeke, Tina is in no shape to answer any questions, and you should just lay in bed and rest. When you get your strength back I promise I will take you to see Tina."

As Zeke wiped the tears from his eyes, his voice became angry. "I need to see her, Bob; you said you would take me to her."

Hanson nodded his head yes. He knew he had no choice. If he refused to take Zeke, he knew Zeke would find away to get there himself, even if he had to crawl to Tina's bedside. Hanson's arms wrapped around his friend. Holding firmly onto Zeke, Hanson led him out of the room. They carefully headed toward the elevator.

Their trek ended quickly as an elderly nurse behind the counter's eyes widened when she spotted the two men. Moving swiftly around her station, she ran up to both of them, firmly scolding them, "What in the world do you think you are doing? Mr. Riley, you are in no shape to be out of bed. I must insist you return to your room at once."

Hanson glanced at Zeke, then back at the nurse, and replied, "I will be totally responsible for his safety, Nurse. Mr. Riley wants to see his wife."

The elderly nurse shook her head no and wiggled her finger in Hanson's face as she scolded him, "I am afraid that is out of the question, Sheriff. Now please take Mr. Riley back to his room."

Hanson glanced back at Zeke. His friend had just spent an entire day in hell, faced death, been beaten, and Hanson was damned if he wasn't going to allow Zeke to be with his wife. Hanson's voice grew harsh as he snapped back, "I will not. Seeing his wife might help Mrs. Riley back to reality. Nurse, this man has gone through enough today. If he feels he is strong enough to move through this damn hospital, then he will. Now please, step aside."

Zeke added to Hanson's demand with a plea of his own.

"Please, nurse, I need to see her. Please try to understand how important it is to me to know she is all right."

The elderly nurse's hard face eased. She forced a smile and directed her answer to Zeke, ignoring Hanson completely.

"Very well, but at least sit in a wheelchair."

Zeke smiled back at her replying, "Thank you, nurse, a chair sounds great."

Turning, the nurse headed for the row of wheel chairs lined up next to her station.

Martin opened his eyes as he heard the car door slam. The driver turned to the mayor shrugging his shoulders.

"Sorry, Mayor, Doctor Parker is nowhere to be found. We searched every motel within a ten mile radius. It is like he vanished in thin air."

Martin frowned. He glanced out of his car window. Only the deputies stood standing in the rain. The crowd had dispersed. They went back to their homes happy. In a strange way, this day may be considered a blessing to the mayor. He gained renewed support from the townspeople. Overstreet had the money he borrowed at the State Police headquarters. Everything appeared to be turning out positive. His reign as mayor would last till he died because of today.

"Sir, one of Sheriff Hanson's deputies did tell me that he was enraged that you made it public knowledge of Deputy Starr's death before he had a chance to talk with his wife."

Martin smiled as he replied.

"I guess he thought he could beat me to the punch in gathering sympathy for Starr's death?"

The driver had a queer look on his face as he replied, "Sir, I think maybe we should have told Mrs. Starr first, before she finds out from a neighbor or the news."

Martin let out a heavy sigh as he replied, "Very well. Get Mrs. Starr on the phone for me."

Martin's driver leaned over and punched in the number to Bill Starr's home. The phone rang twice before a young voice came over the other end.

"Hello."

The driver's voice remained in an even tone as he asked, "Is your mother home?"

The driver heard the phone hit the table and a young voice call out, "Mom, telephone."

The driver ignored the rudeness of the child and handed the phone to the mayor. Martin waited for Mrs. Starr to answer the phone.

"Hello, may I help you."

Martin cleared his throat and spoke in a warm and gentle voice. "Good evening Mrs. Starr."

Jane Starr's voice had a curious sound to it as she asked, "Who is this?"

Martin took a deep breath and, keeping the warmth in his voice, replied, "This is Mayor Todd Martin, I am afraid I have some bad news for you."

There was complete silence on the other end. Martin leaned over adjusting his glasses he spoke quietly. "Mrs. Starr, are you there?"

A trembling voice replied, "Yes, I am still here. What is wrong Mayor? Has something happened to Bill?"

Martin began to regret making the call. Hell this was Hanson's job, not his.

"Mrs. Starr, your husband . . . your husband bravely gave his life in the line of duty. I'm truly sorry to have to be the one to tell you this."

A deathly shrill came from the other end. Martin felt the sorrow and pain in the screams from the other end. Regrets of making the call swelled inside Martin now. Trying to remain calm and keeping the compassion in his voice, Martin called out, "Mrs. Starr, Mrs. Starr. Please calm down. I know this his hard for you and my heart goes out to you and your family. . . ."

Jane Starr cut off Martin as she screamed back, "You're lying. This is some kind of sick joke! Bill can't be dead! Liar! Sick fucking liar!"

Martin became frantic, he knew this was the wrong way of handling this. He should have allowed Hanson to go to Starr's house and break the news to Starr's wife. Trying to gain his composure, Martin attempted to calm Starr's wife down.

"Mrs. Starr I'm truly sorry that I must be the one to give you this horrible news. All I can tell you is that your husband gave his life to save another. I hope that can help soothe the pain just a little."

Starr's wife screamed back, "Why are you tormenting me? What have I done for you to be so cruel?"

Martin tried once again to sound gentle as he replied, "Please Mrs. Starr, calm down. I'm going to send one of our deputies over to your home."

Martin waited for Starr's wife to begin screaming at him again but all he heard were sobs from the other end of the phone. Quietly Martin spoke.

"Mrs. Starr, are you okay?"

Martin waited for her to reply, but still only heard the crying. Martin asked again.

"Mrs. Starr are you okay?"

Silence. Martin waited for a few moments, then gave the phone back to the driver. Rubbing his forehead, Martin whispered to his driver, "Send one of the deputies to the Starr home, I don't think she should be alone."

The driver nodded, not showing his disapproval of the callousness the Mayor displayed in telling Mrs. Starr of the death of her husband. The driver got out of the limousine and walked over to deputy standing nearest the car. The deputy nodded his head and disappeared in his car. The driver slid back in the limousine turning to the Mayor, he said, "Deputy Franklin is going to the Starr home, sir."

Martin nodded his head in approval as he replied, "Very good, now drive to the State Police Headquarters. It is time to claim back my money."

The driver nodded his head yes, and started up the engine to the limousine. Slowly the large black limousine drove down the deserted streets of Barnsville. The painful cries of Bill Starr's wife still echoed in Mayor Martin's mind.

25

The elevator stopped on the third floor. Hanson glanced down at Zeke who remained quiet sitting in the chair. He knew his friend's mind was on Tina. The ordeal Zeke had just been through was agonizing enough but now his wife was added to the nightmare. Zeke's thoughts kept replaying the horrifying vision at Harrison Point. Zeke kept seeing Bill Starr's body crashing to the ground and the painful screams of his wife as she ran towards the fallen deputy. Over and over it kept replaying in Zeke's mind.

Hanson felt the pain his friend was feeling. He wished there was a way to ease the anguish going on inside Zeke but Hanson knew the only person who could ease Zeke's pain was the woman lying in the hospital bed, Tina.

The elevator doors opened. Hanson wheeled Zeke out into the corridor, turned left and pushed the wheel chair down the long hallway. Hanson stopped at the door marked 321. Zeke looked up at Hanson, quietly asking, "Is this her room?"

Hanson nodded his head yes. Zeke labored out of the chair. Standing straight, he turned to Hanson, requesting, "I would like to talk to her alone."

Hanson softly replied, "Sure, I will wait for you out here."

Zeke forced a smile as he replied, "Thanks, you are a good friend, Bob."

Zeke grabbed the door handle. Turning it slowly, he opened the door and walked into the room.

Tina was across the room, lying in bed staring blankly at the ceiling. Standing over her was a man in his early fifties. The man was writing on a clipboard that he held in his hand. He looked up when he heard the door shut. Gray locks of hair dangled in front of his wire rim glasses. He smiled warmly as he asked, "May I help you?"

Straining to walk across the room, Zeke replied, "Yes, I am Zeke Riley. That is my wife, Tina."

The man held out his hand to Zeke as he reached the end of the bed. "I am Dr. Norton. It appears you should be in bed yourself."

Zeke looked down at himself. He was exhausted and he could use sleep. This day had been a chapter from hell for him. He looked at the doctor and lied.

"I'm fine, doctor. What is wrong with my wife?"

Norton adjusted his glasses, pointing to the chair next to the bed. Zeke gladly sat down. His body still remained weak from his ordeal. Norton then tried to explain Tina's condition.

"Physically, she was beaten pretty badly. Someone was awful angry with her. Despite the beating, the baby is fine."

Norton's words caught Zeke off guard. His eyes widened as he blurted back, "Excuse me Doctor? My wife was beaten? The baby is fine? What in the hell are you talking about?"

Norton gave Zeke a curious look, then slowly repeated himself.

"Yes Mr. Riley, someone, to put it bluntly, beat the hell out of your wife. She had contusions on her face, ribs; it is a miracle she didn't have a miscarriage."

Norton saw the shock on Zeke's face. Norton didn't know if Zeke's look was one of surprise or horror. Norton asked quietly, "You did know your wife was pregnant?"

Zeke's reply was slow and still with disbelief.

"No, I didn't. We had a doctor's appointment. We never made it. Are you sure, Doctor, that she is really pregnant?"

Norton smiled as he replied firmly, "Yes, Mr. Riley, seven weeks, maybe eight."

Zeke didn't know whether to laugh or cry at the news. Under different circumstances he would be dancing through the halls. To have a child was the main dream of their lives. Zeke, fighting back the tears, continued to question Norton.

"Did Tina tell you who beat her? Is the bastard under arrest? Why in the hell would anyone want to hurt her?"

Norton shrugged his shoulders as he replied, "Those are questions you should be asking the sheriff, Mr. Riley, not me."

"Is she going to be all right?"

Norton walked over to Tina's bed, adjusting the tube that led to her arm. He glanced at his watch, seemingly stalling for time. Finally he answered Zeke's question.

"Your wife is in deep emotional shock. Seeing her friend shot down in cold blood snapped something deep inside her mind. I have her heavily sedated, to calm her down. She continues to rave on how God is responsible for everything going wrong. She is totally oblivious to anyone around her. We put her in restraints for her own protection."

Zeke rose from his chair and moved to the bed where his wife was lying. He knelt down, taking her hand in his. Zeke cringed as he saw Tina's lovely face covered with bruises. Anger swept through him as images of some bastard striking his wife screamed through his mind. What sick bastard would beat a woman so badly? Suddenly a painful thought ripped through Zeke. Did Starr do this? Zeke felt anger and guilt pound in the pit of his stomach as he felt hate for the man he once had called friend. Without looking at the doctor, Zeke asked, "How long before she is cured of this emotional shock?"

Norton put his hand on Zeke's shoulder. Norton's voice became quiet as he answered, "A day, a week, years. It all depends on how deeply rooted the problem is. I'm sorry, Mr. Riley; we are doing the best we can."

Fighting back the tears, Zeke looked up at Norton and in a pleading voice asked, "What about the baby? Can the child survive with her in this condition?"

Norton sounded positive as he replied, "Yes, with proper care the baby should be fine. Mr. Riley, I am not going to mislead you. Your wife is a sick woman; the state she is in is dangerous not only to herself but also to others."

Zeke ignored the doctor's warnings and asked, "May I spend a few moments alone with my wife?"

Norton hesitated, then reluctantly agreed.

"Just a few minutes, Mr. Riley., I think you both need rest."

Zeke nodded his head in agreement. He heard Norton walk away. After the door slammed closed, Zeke brushed the locks of hair out of Tina's face, then leaned over and kissed her gently on the lips. Holding her hands tight, he whispered softly, "Tina, it finally happened. Our dreams are fulfilled. I am going to be a father, a damn good one. If it is a boy, I want to name him after your dad. If it is a girl, I want her to be named Tina, because that is the name of the only woman I will ever love. Can you hear me, Tina? I love you."

Zeke buried his face in Tina's shoulder. Tears streamed from his eyes. Sobbing, he began to pray, "God, please help my wife and protect our unborn child."

Zeke stopped as Tina began moaning and stirring restlessly. Zeke moved his head away from her shoulder and watched as Tina shook violently.

Her eyes suddenly opened. Her deep blue eyes were wild with anger. She glared at Zeke, then screamed as she strained to break loose the restraints, "You pray to him? God is a murderer!" Tina closed her eyes and screamed louder, "Why won't anyone believe me? How many people need to die before anyone finally knows the same truth as me?"

Zeke, startled by Tina's sudden eruption, lurched away from her. He watched as she continued to struggle to free herself from the restraints. Saliva began dripping from the corners of her mouth. She raved on, not making any sense in what she was saying.

"I warned him, but he didn't believe me; now he is dead. Anyone who is part of my life will die!"

Zeke reached out, taking her hand. He spoke quietly to try to calm her down.

"Tina, it is me: Zeke. Please, sweetheart, calm down. I am here and no one is going to ever harm you again."

Tina's eyes were filled with rage. Her voice rose shrilly as she screamed at Zeke, "Liar! Zeke is dead! God murdered him!"

Tina's words caught Zeke off guard. Smiling, he pointed to himself as he tried to calm his wife down.

"I am not dead, Tina. I am right here, by your side. Tina, please look at me."

The door crashed open. Dr. Norton and two nurses rushed in.

Zeke whirled around, screaming at them, "Leave us alone! Please give me five minutes! That is all I ask, please!"

The two nurses stopped and glanced over at the doctor. Norton spread out his arms, speaking loudly enough to be heard above Tina's screams.

"Mr. Riley, listen to her. You can't reason with her when she is in that state of mind. I need to sedate her for her own protection."

Zeke looked past the doctor to Hanson, who stood watching everything from the doorway.

"Bob, help me. Convince them to let me try and get through to her."

Norton turned, seeing the sheriff standing behind him. Before Norton could say anything, Hanson harshly asked, "What could it hurt, Doctor? For Christ sake, what could it hurt?"

Tina's screams rang through the room, cursing God with every word. Norton jerked his head at the nurses to leave the room, then he spun around, stomping out of the room, snapping at Zeke as he left, "Five minutes, Mr.Riley; then we sedate her." Hanson winked at Zeke as he closed the door.

Zeke turned his attention back to his wife. Grabbing her arms firmly, he forced her to look at him.

"Look at me, Tina! I am not dead. Please look close; it is me: Zeke."

Tina stopped screaming. Her eyes, burning with hate, glared at the man standing over her.

Zeke lowered his voice, trying to remain calm: "Who do you see, Tina? Tell me, who do you see?"

Tina's eyes bore through him, as she did not utter a word.

Zeke asked again, his voice rising "Damn it, Tina, who do you see?"

Tina's eyes didn't flinch, glaring coldly at Zeke.

Zeke tried a different approach. He softened the tone of his voice and leaned closer to his wife, smiling as he quietly said, "The doctor told me we are going to have a baby. I always dreamed about being a father; now you made it possible."

A wicked grin formed on Tina's face. Her words sent chills down Zeke's spine.

"You will never touch my baby. You lousy bastard, I know you're not really here. This is a trick, but it won't work. I buried your evil soul in hell."

Tina's words were like a hammer hitting him in the stomach. Squeezing tighter on Tina's hands, Zeke demanded a answer.

"What are you talking about, Tina? Look at me. Please, can't you see how much I need you?"

Tina tried wrestling loose from Zeke's grip as she shouted, "I killed you! I buried your evil soul in hell! You will never take my baby from me! I won't allow you to harm me again! You bastard, I told you over and over this is my baby!"

Zeke began shaking Tina, his voice rising to a high pitch.

"Snap out of this, Tina! I am Zeke! Tina, I am alive! Damn it, I am alive!"

The door opened again. Dr. Norton entered the room followed by his nurses. Zeke released his wife's arms, moving away from her, tears flowing freely from his eyes as she ranted on. Her eyes followed him, the evil grin still painted on her face. Zeke looked away, not being able to bear looking at her. Tina's voice echoed as the nurse inserted the needle into her arm, "God punished me for the pact I made with the devil! That is you, Frank Parker; may your lousy soul burn in hell!"

Zeke jumped as a hand touched him. It was Hanson. The tears still flowed from Zeke's eyes. He tried to talk to Hanson, but the words wouldn't come out. Hanson took Zeke by the arm and gently helped him to his feet whispering quietly, "Come on, Zeke, let the doctor take care of her."

Zeke looked helplessly at Hanson. He tried to reply but couldn't as the tears choked off his words.

Hanson added, "Tina is going to be fine, Zeke."

Zeke looked down at the floor and nodded. Hanson gripped Zeke tighter and together they left the room. Tina's screams grew softer, her words crashing through Zeke's mind. Zeke felt as if he were going to vomit as he kept hearing Tina's words: *"I buried your soul in hell!"*

Zeke bit down hard on his lower lip as Hanson closed the door to Tina's room.

Hanson quietly asked, "Why don't we go back to your room?"

Zeke shook his head no. His voice vibrated with pain.

"Take me home, Bob. Please, I want to go home."

Hanson shook his head back and forth as he protested Zeke's request.

"I don't think that is a very good idea. You need medical attention."

Zeke lowered his head and in a whisper replied, "All I need is to rest. I can do that at home. Either you take me home or I will call a cab."

Hanson knew it was futile to argue with Zeke, especially in the frame of mind he was in. Letting out a heavy sigh, Hanson in a regretful tone agreed, "All right, Zeke, but I think you are acting very foolish." Hanson brought the chair over for Zeke to sit in.

Zeke waved Hanson off, saying, "I feel like walking."

Hanson began to protest but stopped.

Zeke asked in a subdued voice, "Bob, why did Starr take my wife to Harrison Point? There must be a reason."

Zeke paused, then asked in a pained voice. "Do you think they were having an affair?"

Hanson, stunned by Zeke's accusation of his deputy, snapped his reply back in anger.

"Bill was a good man. A family man who adored his wife and children. How dare you smear his name like that!"

Zeke screamed back, his voice trembling with rage, "Then tell me why they were there, Bob! What about the beating Tina had? Do you know who did it? She wasn't like that when I left her for work. Damn it, Bob, someone beat my wife, my beautiful wife." Tears fell from Zeke's eyes. Sobbing, he continued, "What possible reason would there be for Starr to take my wife in the middle of a storm to Harrison Point? Why, Bob? I need some answers now."

Hanson tried to calm his voice down but couldn't, his anger seething through his words.

"I don't know and till Tina can be questioned I won't know, but I will not allow you to drag Bill Starr's memory through the gutter! Do you understand?"

Zeke could not control his emotions any longer. His words slurred through the mournful sobs, "Listen to her, Bob. She thinks I'm the devil. My God, how am I to live if Tina's not part of my life?"

Hanson realized that his anger was heartless. Zeke didn't mean what he was saying. Calming himself down, he reached over and put his arms around Zeke. He allowed all the pain to come out as he cried uncontrollably. Tina's screams finally stopped. Now only Zeke's sobbing echoed through the halls.

Hanson stopped his patrol car in Zeke's driveway. During the long drive home neither of the men spoke. The moon peeked out from the clouds, shining an eerie glow on the wet ground. Hanson broke the long silence by asking his friend quietly, "Would you like me to go in with you, Zeke?"

Zeke shook his head no as he replied, "I'd rather be alone. I need some time to think."

Hanson labored to produce a weak smile as he added, "Tina is going to be fine, Zeke. Wait and see, she will be herself in no time. She is a fighter; you know that as well as I do."

Zeke nodded in agreement, opened the car door, sliding out, and said, "Thanks, Bob. I appreciate everything you have done for me. Please forgive me for what I said about your deputy. I will be at the funeral home tomorrow. I know Bill was a decent man."

Hanson patted Zeke on the shoulder as he replied quietly, "Forget it, Zeke. If I was in your position I would think the same way. We will find out why they were there and who was responsible for hurting Tina. I promise you that."

Zeke just nodded, closed the car door, and headed for his home.

Hanson watched as Zeke reached the front door. Letting out a heavy sigh, Hanson pulled out of the driveway and slowly drove away.

Zeke opened the front door and flipped on the switch for the lights. He glanced down at the floor. Something appeared different, something out of place. Again he glanced around the room, trying to figure out what it was that didn't fit. It finally dawned on him. He walked over to the rug in the middle of the floor. Bending over, he carefully lifted it up. A large dark stain covered his carpet. He ran his finger across it; moisture still was there. Bringing his finger to his mouth, he tasted the liquid from his finger. He cringed. The taste was a distinctive one. Rising to his feet, he moved swiftly to the bedroom. He opened the door; scattered on the floor lay the tattered red rags. He bent down and picked one piece up. Holding it close to his cheek, he knew it was from his wife's favorite red dress. A sharp pain began stabbing him in his chest as he moved to the nightstand by the bed. He opened the drawer and reached in, searching for the gun Tina's father had left her. All he found was her father's suicide note, which she refused to throw away. Stepping back, Zeke plopped down on the bed, staring blankly at the note. Finally Zeke laid the note back down on the nightstand. Questions pounded at him like a sledgehammer. Why was Tina at Harrison Point? Who would beat his wife so badly? Why were there bloodstains on his carpet? Why? God, why was her favorite red dress ripped to shreds and where was her father's gun? Tina would never allow it to leave this room. Did Tina already know she was pregnant? Questions but no answers. Zeke's thoughts went back to the hospital room and the words screamed at him, the vision of Starr falling to the ground after getting hit with the impact of Harlen's bullets. Why was she at Harrison Point? Why did she scream about Parker's death? Was Parker dead? Where was Tina's father's gun? Zeke screamed at the top of his lungs as he glared at the once-beautiful red dress, "God, what is going on here?"

Zeke fell to his knees and began picking up the tattered rags. Zeke's memories began rushing through his mind. Faster and faster the memories pounded his brain. Holding tighter on the tattered red rags, he allowed a happier time to enter his thoughts.

"Zeke, this is silly."

Zeke ignored his wife as he continued to drive up the narrow path till they reached the point. He then stopped the car and looked over at his lovely wife. Smiling, he whispered, "So you think this is silly, do you? Wasn't it you who said I haven't been very romantic lately?"

Zeke didn't wait for Tina to answer as he added, "You were right. With my workload I forgot how beautiful my wife was. Tina, I want to make love to you right here, just like we did when we were young."

Tina began giggling as she stared at her husband sitting next to her in his suit, looking so prim and proper and wanting to act like a teenager again. Tina whispered through her chuckles, "Don't you think we are a little old and maybe overdressed to be doing this?"

Smiling, Zeke stared at the astounding red dress that Tina was wearing. Trying hard to remain romantic, Zeke fought off the silliness he was beginning to feel.

"Tina, I told you when I first saw you in that red dress that you were hot! I don't know why, but seeing you in that dress tonight makes me feel young again."

Zeke suddenly began to laugh at what he was saying as he blurted out, "Woman, I want your body!"

Tina began laughing as she said, "Zeke, I didn't realize you knew how to be so charming."

Both of them began to laugh uncontrollably. Zeke then put his arm around Tina. His laughter stopped as he kissed her. Zeke then leaned over and quietly whispered in Tina's ear, "I love you, Tina."

Tina squeezed Zeke hard. Tears rolled down her face as she began crying.

Zeke moved back, breaking Tina's hold on him. He looked at her curiously and quietly asked, "Tina, why are you crying?"

Through her tears Tina forced a smile. As she stared at Zeke with her deep blue eyes, she hoarsely said, "I don't know."

Zeke put his arms around Tina again and said, "Did I screw up? This was supposed to be romantic. Instead I made you cry."

Tina shook her head as she whispered through her tears, "My God, Zeke, you didn't screw up. I did; my God, I did."

Zeke, holding Tina closer to him, asked in a confused voice, "Tina, how in the world do you think you screwed up?"

Sobbing, Tina replied, "I promised you I would never wear this dress unless you were with me. I broke that promise and wore it to that damn Christmas party!"

Zeke started laughing as he kissed Tina on the cheek. Her tears turned to anger as she snapped at Zeke, "You think it's funny that I broke a promise to you?"

Zeke tried to stop laughing. He attempted to put a serious tone in his voice as he replied, "No, you're right. Wearing that dress when I wasn't there was terrible. I think you should destroy that red dress if you ever wear it again and I'm not around. That is your punishment. That and to make mad passionate love to me now."

Tina started laughing. Hiding her guilt, she whispered, "I promise you, Zeke, I will tear this dress to shreds if anyone but you sees it and I am going to make love to you like you never knew existed."

Zeke smiled as he shouted, "Now that's romantic!"

Laughter, then passion, filled the night air at Harrison Point.

Zeke's tears burned his eyes as the memories of that night faded. His attention went back to the tattered rags he was holding in his hands. Zeke then buried his face in the rags and began sobbing. His cries grew louder. Zeke then threw the rags in the air and shouted, "God, what did she mean when she said she buried Parker's soul in hell? Tina, in God's name, what have you done?"

The tattered red rags fell gracefully on the floor. Zeke remained on his knees, the pain searing through him. The night air heard nothing but Zeke's painful cries echoing through the empty house.

26

The music played a mournful tune that filtered through the entire room, muffled cries floating in the air. A large bronze casket lay displayed at the front altar, lying inside a peaceful Bill Starr. Sheriff Bob Hanson knelt beside the casket. His thoughts were interrupted by the sound of Mayor Martin's voice behind him.

"Sheriff, you did an excellent job in rescuing Zeke."

Hanson rose to his feet, bent over, and kissed the fallen deputy gently on the cheek, whispering, "I will miss you, old friend." He then turned abruptly to face the mayor. Hanson's eyes burned with rage as he asked gruffly, "May I talk to you in private, Mayor?"

Martin shrugged his shoulders as he replied, "Of course you can."

Martin then turned to his driver and motioned for him to leave. The driver hesitated for a moment, then did as instructed.

"What can I do for you, Sheriff?"

Hanson looked around, making sure no one would be able to hear him as he snarled in a low whisper, "You heartless bastard. How dare you disregard my wishes and tell Jane Starr over the fucking phone her husband was murdered? It took my deputy hours to calm her down. What in the world were you thinking?"

Martin adjusted his glasses and calmly replied, "Bob, what can I say? I handled it poorly. I guess I wanted to make sure she heard it from one of us instead of a noisy neighbor or news reporter."

Hanson, still fuming, snapped back, "Didn't you trust me to take care of it, Mayor? My God, Bill and I worked together for years. Didn't you think I would be able to ease the pain some for her?"

Martin shrugged his shoulders as he quietly said, "Maybe, maybe not, but this is not the place to discuss it. Now unless you have something else for me, I think I will pay my respects to Mrs. Starr."

Before Hanson could reply, Martin turned and walked away from him. Hanson watched as Martin put his arms around both children. Martin then kissed Jane Starr on the cheek. Hanson shook his head in disgust. He then watched as Mary Parker walked up to the casket. Hanson walked over to her and politely asked, "Is Frank coming, Mary?"

Mary didn't look at Hanson as she replied, "Frank still hasn't come home yet. We had a fight yesterday. Bob, I don't think he is ever going to come home."

Mary turned to face Hanson. Her eyes began to water as she added, "He told me I was fat and he was tired of me being pregnant all the time. Tell me, Bob, is that only my fault?"

Hanson wished he had never asked Mary. He knew Parker was a bastard, but to leave his wife because she was pregnant again? Hanson tried to sound sympathetic as he replied, "I'm sure Frank will cool down and be home by tonight, Mary."

Mary, shaking her head slowly, said in a very quiet tone, "I could care less anymore, Bob."

Mary knelt down facing the casket, made the sign of the cross, and stood back up. She then added as she began to walk away, "Too bad it isn't him lying there instead of someone decent like Bill."

Mary walked away and, like the mayor, moved toward Jane.

Hanson felt guilty because he felt the same way Parker's wife did. Hanson smiled as he saw Overstreet enter the room. The big state trooper walked down the aisle toward the casket. He stopped and extended his hand to Hanson as he spoke.

"Sheriff, I hope you don't mind me showing up, but even though I didn't know your deputy I feel the same pain as you when a lawman is killed in the line of duty."

Hanson accepted Overstreet's hand. The two men shook hands, and Hanson replied, "Captain, I think it is a very decent gesture on your part and I agree in a sense we all are part of a special family."

Overstreet looked around the parlor, glancing at the people standing around. Not seeing Zeke, the trooper asked with concern in his voice, "How is your friend doing? Has he recovered from yesterday's ordeal?"

Hanson shrugged as he replied quietly, "I think it will be a while before he fully recovers. His wife is still in the same shape we found her in; plus, to make matters worse, Zeke found out his wife is going to have a child. That has always been their dream."

Hanson then looked over Overstreet's shoulder and appeared surprised as he saw Zeke walk into the room. The sheriff lowered his voice as he said to Overstreet, "Zeke has just arrived. Please don't ask him any questions about his wife."

Overstreet nodded in agreement.

Hanson watched as Zeke walked directly to Jane Starr.

Zeke stood in front of Jane and her children. He seemed nervous as he searched for the right words to say.

Mayor Martin spoke first: "Zeke, it is great to see you. The entire town is praying for a swift recovery for Tina."

Zeke ignored Martin and in a trembling voice spoke to Jane.

"Mrs. Starr, I hope you know how sorry I am about the death of your husband. Tina and I were very close to him; if there is anything you or the children ever need, please don't hesitate to ask. I promise you I will be there for you."

Jane's eyes stared cold and hard at Zeke. Her glare made Zeke feel uneasy. Before he could add anything to what he was saying, Jane exploded with anger.

"Why couldn't your wife leave my husband alone! If it wasn't for her and her lunacy, my husband would still be alive!"

Zeke was lost for words. Jane's anger continued.

"You should have been there for her . . . not Bill!"

Jane began crying. Zeke, despite Jane's anger, put his arms around her. His voice was filled with emotion as he tried to comfort her.

"I'm sorry, Jane. I didn't know Tina was bothering Bill with all her troubles. Christ, there seems to be a lot that I don't know, but if you need to vent on me please feel free to. I don't care."

Jane looked up at Zeke, the tears still flowing as she asked, "Just tell me one thing?" Jane didn't wait for Zeke to ask, "what?"

"Why were Bill and your wife up at Harrison Point? What in God's name would they have been doing there?"

Zeke felt helpless. How could he answer her question when it was the same one he was searching for answers for? Again Tina's words burned in his mind: *"I buried your soul in hell!"*

Zeke lowered his voice as he tried to give Jane an answer.

"I don't know, Jane, but I know Bill. There must have been a good reason. He was too good of a cop; we both know that."

Jane shook as she grabbed Zeke and hugged him.

"Zeke, please forgive my anger. Please understand that I will never be able to forgive Tina."

Zeke just held Jane, not replying at all.

Jane then whispered through her tears, "Bill thought the world of both of you, Zeke, I know, but I can't ever forgive Tina. . . . I will always blame her for Bill's death. I'm sorry, Zeke, I know what you've been through, but right now I feel no compassion for you or that bitch!"

Zeke fought back his own anger; he knew it was hurt that was bringing these words from Jane's mouth, not hate. Zeke leaned and put his arms around Jane and kissed her on the cheek, his voice hoarse as he tried to speak while hiding the pain he was feeling.

"I understand, Jane."

Zeke held Jane for a few moments more, then gently released her. He turned toward where Mary Parker was standing. He just stared at her, not knowing what to say.

Mary, forcing a smile, walked over to him. She leaned over and kissed him, saying in a sympathetic voice as she did, "God will watch over Tina. If you need to talk, call me."

Zeke felt a twinge of guilt surface in him at her words. He thought of how Tina thought he was Parker and called him the devil. Zeke knew he had to talk to Mary's husband. Lowering his head, he asked, "Mary is Frank going to be here? I need to talk to him about something."

Mary burst into tears and walked away.

Zeke, stunned, looked around at Mayor Martin and Jane for some answers, his eyes pleading for someone to tell him what he had said wrong.

Martin gave Zeke his explanation: "Frank has left her. They had a fight yesterday and no one has seen him since then. She thinks he ran away with another woman. She knows he was having an affair with someone. It's not your fault, Zeke; you didn't know."

Like a knife stabbing at his heart, Zeke felt pain rip through his body. Tina's words kept haunting him. The bloodstain on the carpet and maybe a reason for Starr and Tina being on Harrison Point. Zeke felt as if he were going to vomit as slowly pieces of the puzzle began to join together. Trying to control his emotion, he excused himself and walked over to the casket.

Hanson and Overstreet didn't say a word to Zeke as he walked past them. He knelt next to the casket and whispered, "Bill, I am sad about your death. I wish there was a way you could tell me why you were at the point. I don't know whether to be pissed at you or not. You always were a good friend to both Tina and I. Now your wife tells me you were seeing Tina a lot. God, please tell me they weren't having an affair. Bill, I hope you are hearing me from wherever you are? May God have mercy on your soul."

Zeke rose slowly to his feet. Looking down one more time at Starr in the coffin, he whispered, "May God forgive both you and Tina. . . . I don't think I can."

Zeke then turned toward Hanson and Overstreet and didn't say a word as he walked past them and left the funeral parlor.

Overstreet asked Hanson after seeing the look of pain in Zeke's eyes, "Do you think maybe you should go after him? He sure looks like he could use a friend."

Hanson shook his head no as he turned back toward Starr's casket.

"I think Zeke needs to be alone for a while and I need to spend some time with my friend who I will never see again."

Hanson knelt down next to the casket and closed his eyes to pray.

Zeke stood outside Tina's room. Norton came out and put his hand on Zeke's shoulder as he said in an apologetic voice, "Sorry, Mr. Riley, there still has been no change in your wife's condition."

Looking ragged, Zeke played on Norton's sympathy as he asked in a tired voice, "May I see her?"

Norton let out a heavy sigh as he said in a stern voice, "We still have her sedated. I don't want a repeat of yesterday's disaster."

Zeke shook his head as he replied, "I promise I won't wake her. I just need to be with her, Doctor."

Norton nodded his head "OK" and opened the door.

Zeke walked in and made his way over to Tina's bed. Grabbing a chair, he moved it next to her bed and sat in it. Norton watched Zeke for a moment, then closed the door, leaving him alone with Tina.

Zeke sat there and stared at his wife. Millions of thoughts raced wildly through his mind as he gazed at his lovely wife lying in the bed in front of him. Finally Zeke asked her, even though she lay asleep, "Tina, what happened yesterday? Who in the hell beat you so badly and why? Whose blood drenched our carpet?" Pausing, Zeke continued, "Where is your father's gun? Tina, what other secrets are you keeping from me? Damn it, Tina, I need some fucking answers."

Zeke closed his eyes, then quietly added, "Tina, please tell me the baby is mine."

Tina began to stir. Her eyes fluttered, then opened quickly. Her voice was raspy as she tried to speak.

"It is my baby."

Zeke leaned over. Glancing quickly at the door to make sure Norton was not coming back in, Zeke then whispered to his wife, "Tina, it's me, Zeke."

Tina turned her head to face her husband. For the first time in what seemed like a lifetime Tina smiled at him.

"God didn't win. You're still alive."

Zeke nodded his head yes, then asked, "Do you remember what happened, sweetheart?"

Tina remained smiling as she replied, "We have a doctor's appointment."

Zeke again glanced at the door to make sure Norton wasn't coming back in as he asked, "Is that all you remember, Tina?"

Tina's reply was filled with pride.

"We are going to have a baby. We beat God."

Zeke felt anger swelling up inside him as he blurted out his next question.

"Who beat you, Tina? Please tell me. I need to know. I need to also know why were you at Harrison Point?"

Still smiling, Tina calmly replied, "It doesn't matter who did this to me. I took care of the bastard. Then I buried his evil soul."

Tina smiled, adding in a soft whisper, "He was the devil, Zeke. I killed the devil."

Zeke's anger pounded through his body as he tried to keep his voice down.

"Tina, who is the devil?"

Tina began humming cheerfully. Giggling, she replied, "Everyone knows that Frank Parker is the devil. He beat me, tried to kill our baby. I made sure his soul will burn in hell."

Zeke felt as if he were going to vomit as he sat there and listened to his wife admit to committing murder. Trying to remain calm, he asked, "Why did Parker beat you?"

Tina's smile disappeared as she snapped back, "Frank will never harm my baby again. Zeke, I won; I beat the devil and God. Don't you see our dreams are finally falling into place?"

Zeke kept his voice down despite the anger that flowed through him.

"Tina, how did you defeat God?"

Tina smiled again and said, "Only I know. Nobody else ever will."

Zeke's voice rose slightly as he blurted out his next question.

"Tina, is the baby mine?"

Tina closed her eyes. As she kept smiling, she whispered, "Our dreams are complete."

Clenching his fist, Zeke snapped back, louder this time, "Tina, did you kill Frank Parker?"

Tina, didn't reply.

Zeke felt the frustration mount inside him. His voice became harsh and cruel as he hoarsely said, "Tina you're wrong. Our dreams are not complete."

Tina opened her eyes and looked over at Zeke. Quietly she said, "We have our baby."

Zeke screamed out his reply.

"Damn it, Tina, I need to know if it is our baby! Why was Frank Parker at our home? Is it his blood that is stained into our carpet? I need some answers."

Tina refused to reply. She closed her eyes again, smiling as she did.

Zeke's anger grew. Lowering his voice, he continued to question his wife.

"Tina, were you and Frank having an affair?"

Zeke waited for Tina to answer, but she remained silent. Frustrated, Zeke pursued his questions.

"Tina, a good man is dead. His death was caused because he tried to warn you of the danger you were heading into. Bill Starr was a good friend to the both of us. Tell me, Tina, why did he bring you to Harrison Point?"

Tina opened her eyes. Still gazing at the ceiling, she whispered, "I told you, we buried the devil. Bill helped us to save our dream. He gave his life in the war against God. Why can't you understand? Everything I did, I did for you."

Zeke's voice showed his frustration as he snapped back even louder this time, "What did you do, Tina? For God sake, tell me what did you do?"

Tina turned her head to look at Zeke. Her deep blue eyes glared through him as she coldly replied, "I completed our dreams."

Zeke swallowed back the tears that had mounted inside him. Keeping his voice calm, he asked, "Did you kill Frank Parker, Tina, or did your lover Bill Starr do it? Jane told me everything. Were you fucking both of them, Tina? Starr got jealous and that was why he killed Parker? Is that why Parker is dead?"

Tina's eyes stared right into the soul of her husband as she replied in an unemotional voice, "Parker killed himself when he tried to harm our child. Forget about Parker, and Jane is a childish bitch. Bill died because he was my friend; we weren't lovers. How dare she accuse him of that!"

Tina began breathing heavily as her anger spewed over.

"Bill died for us, Zeke; Jane just can't handle that. Fuck her! Bill died for us; we should remember him for that, not. . . ."

Tina began crying before she finished her sentence. Zeke bit his lower lip hard, trying to keep himself calm as he attempted to ask Tina calmly, "Why did Bill die for us?"

Crying, Tina looked up at Zeke. Through her tears she spit out her reply.

"Because he sided with me against God!"

Zeke lowered his head, not wanting to look into those blue eyes of his wife. His life was falling apart around him. He had never thought he would ever feel anything but love for his wife, but hate and disgust began seeping from his soul toward her. Her foolish idea of being at war with God now had affected more than just the two of them. It now had taken the lives of two others. Zeke's thoughts were broken by Tina's soft and reassuring voice.

"Why do you look so sad? You should be rejoicing. Zeke, it is over; we finally have our child."

Zeke's insides began to tremble. The woman lying in front of him was not his Tina. There was no warmth in her voice, no compassion in those lovely blue eyes. Zeke felt his world caving in around him as he watched Tina wickedly smile at him. The tears flowed from his eyes as his words stammered from his mouth.

"T-t-tina, I l-l-loved you no matter what. The p-p-pain I felt when you decided to have the abortion years ago subsided. The y-y-years of watching you change because of your f-f-father's death didn't change my love, but now you are p-p-personally responsible for the d-d-deaths of two men and all you can say is our dreams are complete. Y-y-you're insensitive and a selfish bitch; you caused the d-d-destruction of our dream."

Tina's eyes grew wider. Her expression turned to anger as she screamed back, "Bastard! You stinking bastard! You never forgave me for killing our child. You lied! Fuck you! I did all this for you!"

The door to the room opened. Norton came running into the room.

Zeke turned to him and pleaded his case, "I swear to you, Doctor, I don't know what happened. She woke up and started screaming at me for no reason."

Norton and the nurses rushed past Zeke as they headed toward Tina. Norton turned around and, trying to hide his anger, snapped at Zeke. "I told you she is not stable. Please leave the room; we need to sedate her again."

Tina's face turned bright red as she continued to scream at Zeke, "It is my baby! Please, tell me our dreams are complete! Don't let God win. Zeke! Zeke, I love you!"

Zeke watched as the nurses plunged the needle into Tina's arm. The screaming stopped, and Tina began to fall asleep. Her eyes never left where Zeke was standing. They seemed to be pleading to Zeke. He didn't move, he stood there and watched Tina as she finally fell into a deep sleep.

Norton turned to Zeke with the anger he had felt now subsided. Now he showed sympathy in his eyes and voice as he said, "I'm sorry, Mr. Riley. I shouldn't have snapped at you like that."

Zeke replied softly, "Don't worry about it, Doctor. May I ask you some questions?"

Norton nodded his head yes, then led Zeke out of the room to the hallway.

"What is it you want to ask?" Norton could sense the anxiety in Zeke.

Glancing back at the room where Tina was, then back at Norton, Zeke asked, "Is my baby in any danger with all the drugs you are putting my wife on?"

Norton smiled as he shook his head no, replying, "It is only a mild sedative, Mr. Riley. We have the baby monitored continually."

Zeke looked Norton in the eyes, his voice becoming harsher as he asked, "When will my wife be able to answer questions about what happened yesterday?"

Norton seemed disturbed by the harshness in Zeke's voice. This was a question he expected to get from Hanson or some other law enforcement person but not Zeke. Norton's voice remained even as he answered Zeke's question.

"It is hard to tell, but I would not recommend putting her through any undue stress."

Zeke just stared at Norton, thoughts raging through his mind. Zeke couldn't get past the thoughts of his wife being with another man. Anger took over for any compassion he had for his wife. Tina had destroyed not only his life but also it appeared, Bill Starr's and even the bastard Frank Parker's. She had destroyed these lives because she couldn't accept the fact that they might not be able to have a child. Zeke glanced back at his wife and realized that the baby was slowly becoming the only thing that would keep his life together. Glancing back up at Norton, Zeke whispered, "Doctor, I plan on staying close to Tina till either she is released or the baby is born. I need to be close to her and the baby. Do you understand that, Doctor? This baby is very important to me."

Norton could see the desperate look in Zeke's eyes. Norton knew that it was not healthy for Zeke to be watching his wife slip in and out of reality but didn't attempt to argue with Zeke. He knew by the tone in which Zeke made his statement that it would be useless, but he tried to make sure Zeke understood what was going on with his wife.

"I see no problem with that, Mr. Riley. Remember, though, Mrs. Riley's recovery is going to take some time."

Zeke's eyes grew hard as he stared down at his wife lying in the bed. He felt no sympathy for Tina, only resentment. Now his child had become his only concern. His child was going to survive, Zeke

238

would make sure of this. He looked back up at Norton and nodded as he replied, "I realize that, Doctor, but my main concern right now is to make sure nothing happens to my baby."

Zeke didn't wait for a reply. Instead, he sat down in a chair outside the room. A strange sense of anger toward Tina began to swell inside him. For years he had to listen to how she was at war with God. For years Zeke had to put up with the mood swings and listen to her blaming each one of them on God. Zeke felt a sharp pain stab him in his chest as he thought of Jane Starr's words to him at the funeral parlor. Zeke's emotion began to run rampant as he relived the vision of Starr falling dead to the ground at Harrison Point.

Zeke closed his eyes tighter, trying to shut out the painful events that ran over and over in his mind. No matter how hard Zeke tried to fight off the visions, they continued to play in his mind. Zeke wanted to scream for mercy from the hell his mind was putting him through, but it was in vain. Over and over the images replayed in his mind. Helplessly Zeke watched.

The tattered red dress began dancing in his mind as he pictured Frank Parker and Bill Starr holding and caressing his wife. All three pointed at Zeke, laughing, mocking his very existence. He could hear the voices screaming out what he already knew.

"You are a loser, Zeke! You always were a loser!"

Zeke closed his eyes tightly and tried to shut out the painful sounds and images he was hearing and seeing, but they continued to pound in his mind. Another figure joined in the haunting images. The scars on the face—it could only be Harlen Jones. Zeke gritted his teeth as his hell moved forward, Harlen Jones laughing at him as they stood side by side and both watched Starr and Parker make love to his Zeke's wife. Harlen's wicked laugh rose above the moans of ecstasy from Tina. Harlen taunted Zeke with stabbing words.

"Tell me again, Zeke, how much she loves you" Harlen's words were followed by more hideous laughter.

Zeke felt like screaming but swallowed his pain as the visions went on unmercifully.

Zeke pictured Tina kissing Starr passionately, as if they could sense Zeke watching them. They turned toward Zeke, and then, sneering, she raised the revolver and aimed it at Zeke. He watched in horror as the bullets plunged into his chest. Zeke watched in his mind his entire body spilling thick red blood out from his chest. He watched the picture of himself falling to the ground, his soul leaving his body as his lifeless body crashed to the ground. Standing over him was Tina; she held the tattered red rags tightly in her hands. Starr, Parker, and Jones also had pieces of the dress clutched in their hands, as they continued to laugh as they watched Zeke die.

Zeke's nightmare shattered as Norton's voice rang through his ears.

"Mr. Riley, are you OK?"

Zeke opened his eyes. Sweat poured from his forehead; his heart was pounding out of control. Seeing the concern in Norton's face, Zeke forced a smile as he quietly replied, "I'm fine, Doctor. Honestly, everything is just fine."

Norton stared at Zeke with sadness, wishing he could say the right words to help ease the pain, but he knew there were no words. Norton quietly spoke to Zeke.

"I've got some other appointments I need to get to, Mr. Riley. If you need anything just call for a nurse."

Norton glanced over at Tina and added, "She is going to be fine, Mr. Riley; you need to believe that."

Zeke just nodded. Norton released a sigh and walked out of the room. Zeke sat and just stared at Tina lying in front of him. He then moved closer as he heard her mumbling under her breath, "I love you, Zeke."

Tina's words stung him, because he didn't believe Tina loved anyone. Zeke now pictured her saying those words in mockery. Zeke Riley was nothing more than a joke to her, but he would not allow her sickness to affect his child. Tina's sickness was not going to spread to the innocence of the child he had always wanted. Zeke gripped his hands tighter around the arm of the chair as he heard Tina's words echoing in his mind.

"Zeke, I love you!"

27

The winter winds whipped through the small town of Barnsville. Snow covered the wooded area that surrounded the town. Months had passed since the nightmare of the Golden Aces restaurant happened. The memory of that day slowly eased its way out of the minds of the people who lived there. The townspeople tried not to talk about the tragedy of that day. No one wanted to admit that something like that could happen in Barnsville. Kidnapping, murder—those were events that only happened in the big city.

Mayor Martin, though, made sure he took advantage of that day by playing on the fears of the citizens of Barnsville. He added seven more deputies to the town's payroll, which increased taxes by 5 percent, without a trace of protest from the voters.

Mrs. Mary Parker and her children moved out of town, Mary shamed by her husband, who presumably had deserted her. Parker had left her only a few dollars in the bank. He had squandered all the money he had made and left his wife and family virtually penniless. Inquiries were made about her husband, but there was no trace of Frank Parker. Some felt Parker's disappearance was strange, but others imagined him on a beach somewhere, clinging to a young girl's arm, swearing his wife didn't understand him and never showed him love.

Jane Starr and her boys live quietly on the outskirts of town, in the same house that Bill had bought to escape the dangers of the city. Every Sunday Jane lit a candle in church for her deceased husband. The shock of her husband's brutal murder haunted her every night. Her tears flowed and her eyes burned as she still blamed Tina Riley for Bill's death.

Sheriff Bob Hanson was frustrated by the doctor's refusal to allow him to talk to Tina. Every time Hanson tried, Norton kept telling him that Tina was still too fragile, that Tina's mind would keep slipping in and out of our reality. Hanson found himself driving up to Harrison Point almost every day and standing on the cliff staring down at the river below hoping somehow an answer would come to him. The months that passed Hanson had spent trying to solve the puzzle of why his deputy's life had ended at Harrison Point. That was one of the main reasons Dr. Norton's refusal to allow him to talk to Tina really bothered him. Hanson knew no one but Tina Riley could ever give him the reasons the tragedy had occurred. Rumors ran rampant, including the disgusting rumor that Bill and Tina had been lovers. Hanson knew that was not true, both Tina and Bill loved their spouses too much for that ever to happen. Those rumors, though, began to take their toll on Zeke. Hanson became more concerned as he watched Zeke's personality gradually change every day. It was like he only cared about the baby and not Tina. At times Hanson would cringe as he heard Zeke talking like Tina. Zeke would calmly tell Hanson that he needed to make peace with God, that he had to convince God the war with Tina was over and that God had won. Hanson did what he could for his friend, but deep inside Hanson knew that until the questions were answered about Harrison Point Zeke Riley's life would never be the same. Hanson knew the truth would come out and everyone's life would go back to normal as soon as Tina's doctor allowed him to question her.

Dr. Norton walked into the waiting room where Zeke paced back and forth. Norton stood there for a moment staring at Zeke. The doctor felt pity for the man. His life had turned into a living hell. He coughed to get Zeke's attention.

He stopped his pacing and turned toward Norton. Zeke's eyes were sagging and drawn in his clothes wrinkled from sleeping in them. His voice became raspy as he asked, "How is she, Doctor?"

Norton shook his head slowly, his voice subdued.

"I am sorry, Mr. Riley; we did everything we could. Your wife is dead."

Zeke screamed back at Norton, "How could this happen? You knew she was sick. You should have watched her closer!"

Norton's voice became apologetic as he replied.

"Mr. Riley, I swear to you I don't know how she found a razor blade. Someone must have dropped one, and she found it. I don't know any other way it could have happened. We do not allow them on that floor. Only my orderlies and nurses use them. We are investigating the incident. There is nothing else I can tell you except I'm truly sorry."

Zeke rubbed his eyes, asking, "What about the baby? Did you allow her to see her baby?"

Norton shook his head no, quietly saying, "We had every intention to allow her to see her child. When we felt the time was right, Mr. Riley. I am completely shocked that this happened. Your wife appeared to be making such good progress. Why did she decide to take her own life now, after having her baby? We focused her entire recovery on the child. That was the only time we managed to get her near reality."

Zeke's voice remained cold as he asked, "Did she leave a note? Something to say why she took her own life?"

Norton nodded his head yes. He hesitated for a brief second before he replied.

"She scribbled the words 'God finally has forgiven me.' We could not seem to get her out of the belief that God was mad at her."

Zeke just stared at Norton for a moment, then quietly said, "Maybe she was right, Doctor. Maybe in some strange way she was right."

Norton looked shocked by Zeke's words. Norton hid his shock as he replied, "Mr. Riley I will get to the bottom of this, I promise. What you need to do now is go home and get some rest."

Zeke forced a tired smile. His voice lost its harshness as he replied, "I know you mean well, Doctor, but I'm not losing my mind. I know that my wife was a very sick woman and that you and your staff did the best you could. All I'm saying is that after all these years maybe God finally decided that my wife needed his care instead of mine. Am I crazy for thinking that way, Doctor?"

Norton shook his head no as he replied, "Mr. Riley, you have been under a great amount of stress for all these months. In one way I guess I can't blame you for thinking that way. What you need is rest. Please go home and again, I swear to you, we will find out how this terrible mistake happened."

Zeke nodded slowly as he replied, "I know you will, Doctor, and you're right, I need to get out of this hospital and start to go on with my life again."

Norton smiled, adding to what Zeke had said, "Good. I'll call you if I come up with any information about your wife."

Zeke again nodded as he asked, "Is my daughter able to travel?"

Norton nodded, but concern was in his voice as he answered Zeke's question.

"Yes, but maybe it would be better if you left her under the nurse's care for a while."

Zeke's voice became panicky as he blurted out his words.

"Why? Is she sick? Is there something you're not telling me?"

Norton raised his hand in a halt position, answering quickly, "No, your daughter is just fine. I am concerned about you. You are tired and worn out. I thought maybe you would like a day or two to catch up on some sleep?"

Shaking his head no, Zeke insisted, "I would like to take my daughter home today. I hired a nanny to take care of her while I am at work. Trust me, Doctor; we will be just fine. I would appreciate it if you could start making arrangements for me, though, to bury my wife."

Norton brushed a lock of gray hair out of his eyes.

"I would be more than happy to, Mr. Riley. I will tell the nurse to prepare your child. Please once again allow me to give you my deepest regret on your loss."

Zeke put his hand on Norton's shoulder and in a calm voice replied, "Thank you, Doctor, and I apologize for jumping down your throat. I know it wasn't your fault."

Norton became rigid as he replied, "Don't worry, Mr. Riley; we will find how she obtained a razor blade. If it was negligence on the part of anyone on my staff, he or she will be dealt with severely."

Norton glanced at his watch and added, "Drive your car around front; a nurse will bring your daughter down to you."

Norton then turned and walked out the glass door.

Zeke watched as the doctor left the room and ran his hands through his hair, letting out a heavy sigh. He looked around the small waiting room for the last time. The glass door opened again. Hanson walked in. He stood in the doorway looking down at the floor. Finally he spoke in a soft and compassionate voice.

"Zeke, I wish I could say something to make the pain go away, but I don't know of any words that could do that. I hope you know I am here for you if you need me?"

244

Zeke nodded his head yes.

Hanson then asked, "Do they know why she killed herself?"

Zeke replied in a weary voice, "Bob, Tina was a very sick woman. I guess she never overcame her obsession that God was angry with her. Even the baby couldn't change her delusions. I guess seeing a friend as close as Bill gunned down in front of her took its final toll on her."

Hanson quietly replied, "I wish we knew some of the answers of why they were out there that day. Maybe if we had a chance to deal with the truth Tina would have dealt with reality better."

Anger seeped through Zeke as he snapped back at Hanson, "For Christ sake, Bob, all you seem to be worried about is why they were there. My wife is dead; don't you give a damn? I could care less why they were there; the answers died a few minutes ago in my wife's room."

Hanson's voice remained calm as he answered his angry friend's words.

"Zeke, I am truly sorry for your loss, you are a dear friend of mine and I share your pain, but another friend of mine is dead. He died in a place he should never have been. I need to know why and I plan on finding out the answer if it takes me a lifetime."

The disgust was still in Zeke's voice as he snapped back, "Bob you do what you must. My daughter is coming home today, and I need to think now what to tell her years from now about why her mother decided to take her own life. So if you will excuse me, I must leave."

Zipping up his coat, Zeke walked past Hanson and exited from the same door the doctor did.

Hanson watched closely as his friend walked to the door that led to the hospital parking lot.

The snow began to fall lightly from the skies. The new year was only a week old. New hopes and dreams surfaced for the citizens of Barnsville. The tragic events of the old year were over. A new beginning flowed through the air. Laughter of the children sang for miles around. Forgotten were the tragic deaths of the past. Forgotten were the heroes of yesterday. It was a new year and a new beginning in Barnsville.

Zeke drove slowly down the highway, glancing every chance he had at his beautiful daughter strapped in her car seat next to him. A sense of pride swelled inside him. He was a father, despite all the tragedy that showered down on him. The snowflakes became larger, satin white flakes falling from the skies, nature revealing it's winter beauty. Zeke flipped on his windshield wipers. Peering through the snow, he slowed down his car as he reached the turn. Carefully he drove up the narrow trail, keeping both hands on the steering wheel. He stopped as he reached the point and shut off the engine of the car, leaning over to his daughter strapped in her car seat. He unbuckled the buckle to the car seat, lifting her gently, making sure her snowsuit covered her entire body, tightening her scarf firmly around her face to keep out the cold. He held her high in the air, smiling, as he warmly said, "Daddy wants you to see something. I have something you must hear. Only once, my dear, then forever to be forgotten."

Zeke opened his car door, cautiously sliding out. He held his daughter close to him as he walked to the edge of the point. The wind began to howl softly, like a ghost wanting to be heard. Stopping at the very edge of the point, Zeke turned his daughter around and held her flush against his stomach as he spoke quietly to her.

"Sweetheart, this is Harrison Point. Legend has it that brave warriors sacrificed their souls to God. They did that because God was angry with them. Your mother when she was alive told me God was angry at her. Till just a few months ago I didn't believe her. I loved your mom, more than life itself. I found out why she thought God was angry with her. Your mother . . . deceived me, first by killing our first child, then by taking the chance of losing you."

Tears began rolling down Zeke's face. The pain ripped away at his soul. He forced himself to continue.

"Your mother was seeing another man. Her deceit caused the death of Bill Starr and the death of her other lover, Frank Parker."

Zeke paused and looked down at the raging river below; his thoughts went back to the past. He pictured Tina smiling at him with those deep blue eyes piercing through his soul. Then the vision of Parker and her together shattered Zeke's last happy memory of Tina. Turning his attention back to his daughter, he continued.

"All I can really figure out is your mom and her lovers must have had a fight about you."

Pausing, Zeke held his daughter closer to him as if he needed to protect her from evil spirits that lurked from the past.

"I don't know if she planned on having another abortion or not."

Zeke began to feel chills run through him as he thought back to the day Tina had convinced him that having a abortion was the right thing to do. Zeke shook the memory from his mind and continued to talk to his daughter.

"Whatever the fight was over, Parker lost. Your mother shot him, in our home. I guess that is why she came here? Bill must have wanted to help her dispose of Parker. I assume Parker is somewhere at the bottom of the river below."

The snow began to fall harder. Zeke looked up into the skies, then back at his daughter. In a strange way he began to feel better as he spoke and heard in words the terrible things Tina had done. He knew that after today his thoughts would need to be held prisoner to his and only his memories because no pain would ever enter his daughter's life. Zeke released a heavy sigh and continued to talk to his daughter.

"I told your mother I knew everything. I told her that the only way to end all this sorrow would be to give a soul to God. I know your mom loved you because I gave her a choice. I told her that either I would give your soul or she would have to give hers. I know your mother understood. I pray that you do."

Zeke freed one of his arms from holding the baby and reached into his pocket. Bringing out a pack of double-edged-razor blades that were wrapped in tattered red rags, he stared at them for a moment, gently kissing the red cloth. He tossed them over the edge, into the icy waters below. Carefully he raised the baby over his head, shouting to the heavens, "God, Tina gave you her soul, so my daughter may live! Please accept her sacrifice and bestow happiness and health on my daughter, Tina Ann Riley!"

The winds picked up, whirling around the father and young child. The sun reflected its golden charms on the snow-ridden ground. Zeke lowered young Tina, holding her close to him, rocking her gently in his arms, keeping her warm. A smile creased his face as he heard the approval of the gods. The cries of the ghostly wind echoed through his mind. Zeke kissed his daughter gently on the forehead. He then felt a chill run through him as he stared into his daughter's deep blue eyes. They were like her mother's as they seemed to be looking deep into his soul. A slight twinge of guilt vibrated through him as he continued to look into his daughter's eyes. Tears slowly rolled down his cheek. The haunting winds cried around him. Zeke held his daughter closer to him as the haunting words echoed in his mind: *"I love you Zeke."* Zeke's tears gently fell on to his daughter as he sadly whispered, "I love you, Tina."